THE WORLD'S CLASSICS

AN OUTCAST OF THE ISLANDS

JOSEPH CONRAD was born Józef Teodor Konrad Korzeniowski in the Russian part of Poland in 1857. His parents were punished by the Russians for their Polish nationalist activities and both died while Conrad was still a child. In 1874 he left Poland for France and in 1878 began a career with the British merchant navy. He spent nearly twenty years as a sailor and did not begin writing novels until he was approaching 40. He became a British subject in 1886 and settled permanently in England after his marriage to Jessie George in 1896.

Conrad is a writer of extreme subtlety and sophistication; works such as *Heart of Darkness*, *Lord Jim*, and *Nostromo* display technical complexities which have established him as one of the first English 'Modernists'. He is also noted for the unprecedented vividness with which he communicates a pessimist's view of man's personal and social destiny in such works as *The Secret Agent*, *Under Western Eyes*, and *Victory*. Despite the immediate critical recognition that they received in his life-time Conrad's major novels did not sell, and he lived in relative poverty until the commercial success of *Chance* (1913) secured for him a wider public and an assured income. In 1923 he visited the United States, with great acclaim, and he was offered a knighthood (which he declined) shortly before his death in 1924. Since then his reputation has steadily grown, and he is now seen as a writer who revolutionized the English novel and was arguably the most important single innovator of the twentieth century.

J. H. STAPE has taught at universities in Canada, France, and the Far East. Co-editor of *The Rover* in the World's Classics series, he has published frequently on Conrad and the modern novel. He is former Reviews Editor of *The Conradian: The Journal of the Joseph Conrad Society (UK)*.

HANS VAN MARLE, in addition to working as an editor, translator, and publisher, has been a consultant to the South-East Asia programmes of Amsterdam and Cornell universities. He has published numerous studies on Conrad and is an Associate Editor of the Cambridge Edition of the Works of Joseph Conrad.

THE WORLD'S CLASSICS

JOSEPH CONRAD

An Outcast of the Islands

Edited by
J. H. STAPE and **HANS VAN MARLE**

Introduction by
J. H. STAPE

Oxford   New York
OXFORD UNIVERSITY PRESS
1992

Oxford University Press, Walton Street, Oxford OX2 6DP

Oxford New York Toronto
Delhi Bombay Calcutta Madras Karachi
Petaling Jaya Singapore Hong Kong Tokyo
Nairobi Dar es Salaam Cape Town
Melbourne Auckland

and associated companies in
Berlin Ibadan

Oxford is a trade mark of Oxford University Press

First published as a World's Classics paperback 1992

British Library Cataloguing in Publication Data
Data available

Library of Congress Cataloging in Publication Data
Conrad, Joseph.
An outcast of the islands / Joseph Conrad : edited by J. H. Stape
and Hans van Marle : introduction by J. H. Stape.
p.   cm.—(World's classics)
Includes bibliographical references.
I. Stape, J. H. (John Henry)   II. Marle, Hans van.   III. Title.
IV. Series.
PR6005.04082   1992   823'.912—dc20   92–53
ISBN 0–19–282819–3

Printed in Great Britain by
BPCC Hazells Ltd.
Aylesbury, Bucks

ACKNOWLEDGEMENTS

J. H. Stape should like to thank Professor Andrzej Busza, Dr Gail Fraser, and Messrs Raymond Gauthier, James Johnson, and James Moffat for useful suggestions.

The Introduction is dedicated to the memory of Samsu Rizal Abdullah.

CONTENTS

CONTENTS

INTRODUCTION

I

Since 1920, the year Conrad's 'Author's Note' was first published, *An Outcast of the Islands* has in some sense had a double opening. The first is set in London outside the fictional action; the second, the beginning of the novel proper, launches the reader into a remoter world, the product of the interaction between imagination, personal experience, and 'history'. On reflection, this initial and rhetorical distinction blurs, for the 'Author's Note' is a carefully crafted anecdote rather than a record of fact, and characteristically mythologizes Conrad's experience. Edward Garnett's casual suggestion of a London evening that Conrad 'write another' breaks a spell of indolence (a mood important, too, in the novel itself), and Conrad sits down to the task of writing. This version of the novel's genesis plays up a casualness that documentary evidence fails to sustain. Conrad had, in fact, begun *An Outcast*—then entitled 'Two Vagabonds', and like a number of his other novels first conceived of as a short story—not in London but in Switzerland some weeks *before* he first met Edward Garnett in October 1894.[1] But his failure to recall accurately a moment that had occurred twenty-five years previously or his deliberate fabrication and embroidering of it possesses, in any event, greater evocative power than any recitation of dates or precise reconstruction of banal circumstance. What-

[1] Letter to Marguerite Poradowska, [18? Aug. 1894], *The Collected Letters of Joseph Conrad*, ed. Frederick R. Karl and Laurence Davies (Cambridge Univ. Press, 1983), i. 168–70.

ever the elusive truth, the version Conrad provides
gives emotional colouring to a moment he thought of as
a turning-point in his life: the commitment to authorship and the taking up of a new identity.

However socially defined and circumscribed that
new role, a writer is a sort of outcast, a solitary engaged
in the attempt to link the world of inner vision to that
of outer achievement. The commitment to writing is a
task that is a 'vocation', a calling demanding discipline
and concentration. In this way, then, Conrad's decision
stands in stark contrast to the plot and action of *An
Outcast*, whose protagonist, 'that idle man' (p. 76), lacks
an ability to perceive or affirm values or responsibilities
beyond or outside those founded upon himself. Lacking this foothold in the world—the novel begins with a
significant and determining misstep 'off the straight
and narrow path' (p. 3)—Peter Willems falls, even
collapses, into the abyss of himself. And while for
Conrad the demand for activity is, as he declares in
Nostromo, merely a 'consoling illusion', he none the less
argues that it provides a social identity and imposes the
restraints essential for a coherent sense of self and for
civilized existence.

In contrast to Conrad's casting of the die in committing himself to authorship, his protagonist refuses to
ground himself, to set down roots in a cultural and
social matrix, to establish genuine ties. Although this
gives him a certain imaginative grandeur, experience
fails to sustain his exalted self-conception. His high
claims are also continually denied by those he lives
with, and in the end his dream of a self capable of
existing outside ordinary norms serves only to isolate
him. In this sense Willems is a preliminary sketch for
Kurtz or Lord Jim, characters whose self-destructive
destiny he shares and whose grandiose self-valuations
are likewise consistently challenged and constrained by

the troublesome 'facts' of the 'real world'. The logical consequences of his extreme subjectivity are alienation and exile, and Willems' ardent insistence on his individualism finds its ironic confirmation in society's ultimate rejection of him. This involuntary exile, embodied in the harsh sentence Captain Lingard, his surrogate father, pronounces upon him—'You are not a human being that may be destroyed or forgiven. You are a bitter thought, a something without a body and that must be hidden' (p. 275)—richly parodies his self-chosen banishment. Having usurped society's role in becoming a law unto himself, and having succumbed to his animal nature by 'returning' to the jungle, Willems, by the rhetoric used here, becomes disembodied pure idea, condemned to the hell of a subjectivity he had earlier eagerly embraced.

The victim of his own illusions, Willems thus becomes the ready prey of those less glorious but more pragmatic creatures who, tangentially, share the world with him. But they possess only a single illusion in their belief that machinations for power will obtain for them wealth and security. This essential division of the world into idealizing 'butterflies' and pragmatic 'beetles', to recall one of Conrad's major metaphors in *Lord Jim*, structures *An Outcast*. On the level of both the novel's political and ideological allegories, the petty ambitions that both motivate and dog Willems reflect the larger but no less absurd competition between Britain and the Netherlands for domination and trade at an insignificant outpost in a remote corner of South-East Asia. By these terms, all history is fundamentally tragicomic, a futile scramble for temporary economic or territorial advantage. Willems' illusions, like those of the Dutch and English would-be conquerors, are versions writ small of the large ones that define and circumscribe the human condition. And they are unvarying, found in

Sambir as they are in the 'jungle' of the London of 'Heart of Darkness' and *The Secret Agent*.

In a universe lacking a providential scheme, as the coda to this novel establishes, activity must find its reward in humanly constructed systems of value, in arrangements that are thus inherently fallible, insecure, and temporary. Yet Conrad's stated disavowal of pessimism—'What one feels so hopelessly barren in declared pessimism is just its arrogance'[2]—and his belief in the novel as an 'act of faith', shapes a work whose keywords—'belief', 'trust', and 'hope'—are inherited from an outworn tradition. While by late-Victorian times this tradition had already begun to lose its metaphysical grounding, the individual who would, none the less, deny these values is, in Conradian terms, condemned to mere animal existence, the eventual fate of Willems and Almayer, whose obsessive search for material gratification makes them ignoble and base.

On the other hand, the fate of the naïvely heroic Captain Tom Lingard, a prototype for the stalwart Conradian hero shaped by the exigencies of life at sea, demonstrates that subscribing to such values offers no guarantee against betrayal or failure. In this light, Lingard's sentimental treatment of Willems is only a costly self-indulgence; having failed to be faithful to an ideal of conduct, Willems is clearly incapable of committing himself to friendship, or, finally, even to his own welfare. But Lingard's idealism, his failure 'to see things as they are', resembles, in harshly ironic fashion, Willems' own egotism. An unsophisticated, unintellectual type, shaped by his fidelity to the sea and believing himself exempt from the rules that govern a universe of near-Balzacian rapacity, Lingard is inevitably forced to acknowledge the sad and simple truth that Willems'

[2] 'Books' (1905), in *Notes on Life and Letters* (1921; Dent, 1949; repr. 1970), 8.

betrayal teaches: no prestige or power long remains intact. And well before his disappearance into Europe and total insignificance, Lingard is a sadly diminished man, unaware that his time has passed, living more in his memories than in a radically altered present. Like Old Singleton's struggle with the sea in *The Nigger of the 'Narcissus'*, his confrontation with Willems and the human failure he represents brings with it an awareness of mortality.

The schemes for a glorious future of Lingard's partner, Kaspar Almayer, are a parallel illusion, built similarly on the unsteady foundations of an egotism projecting itself outward on a world less tractable in fact than in imagination. These schemes, likewise dependent upon an alliance with Lingard (whom Almayer also betrays), become a further ironic device for exploring the central themes of power and identity. Like his Malay counterparts, the symbolically one-eyed Babalatchi and the totally blind Lakamba, Almayer's dreams advance only so far as they remain in the realm of the imaginary, and his attempt to actualize them leads only to inexorable failure. This is so, not because Conrad holds that villains ought to suffer—indeed, he fully realizes they usually do not—but simply because these are the terms in which he sees the universe itself: we live, as he writes in 'The Lagoon', in 'a world of illusions'.

II

In addition to marking out a new life for Conrad, *An Outcast of the Islands*, as he observes in the 'Author's Note', confirmed his public identity as a writer of 'exotic' fiction. This exoticism, however, is largely a matter of setting: the cultures and peoples of the Malay Archipelago serve mainly as a backdrop for quintessentially Western crises of identity. Hugh Clifford's comment in *The Singapore Free Press* that Conrad had a 'complete ignorance of Malays and their habits and customs' (the vast majority of his audience, of course, knew still less) is, whatever its truth, irrelevant, for as Conrad himself indicated to one of his early publishers, his intention was not social realism: 'I never did set up as an authority on Malaysia. I looked for a medium in which to express myself.'[3] Although recent criticism has amply established that no presentation can be value-free, and that a writer's explicit or implicit intentions need not govern or limit a reader's response, Conrad's imaginative energies are evidently only glancingly directed at depicting the exterior world. His Orient—no less than his Africa or South America, or London—is a product of his imagination and only secondarily a record of observation and social detailing.

This is not to claim, however, that the novel emerges free from its historical circumstances. On the contrary, it centrally addresses post-Darwinian anxieties about meaning and identity, with Willems serving as a device for presenting and analysing the late-Romantic problem of the self, recently loosened from its traditional moorings in group identity and ready at all costs to explore its own limits. But unable to understand himself or others, and rejecting the confining morality of his social milieu—'the monotonous but safe stride of virtue' (p. 3)—Willems succeeds only in projecting his desires and dreams outward, recasting himself in idealized and wholly naïve terms as the sole controller of his destiny. His assertions of his superiority, moral or racial, are ironic and grotesque, and it is hardly incidental that his awareness of and insistence on his

---

[3] *The Singapore Free Press*, 1 Sept. 1898, cited in Norman Sherry, *Conrad's Eastern World* (Cambridge Univ. Press, 1966), 139; letter to William Blackwood, 13 Dec. 1898, *Collected Letters*, ii. 130.

whiteness, a group affiliation, quickens as his personal identity falls from his grasp and he finds his actual and psychic space increasingly restricted.

The stresses of the late-Victorian period also find their reflection in Conrad's portrayal of power politics, yet however firmly grounded in historical circumstance, imperialist ambitions are in Conrad's view only another manifestation of a fundamentally human rapaciousness, limited neither by time nor by place. Thus, the rich Arab trader Abdulla, an outsider in Sambir, owner of the pompously named *Lord of the Isles*, is as much a colonizer as Lingard. And by a characteristic irony, the political and economic revolution he and Babalatchi (another outsider) bring about to replace Lingard's paternalistic and sentimental *imperium* establishes a system of exploitation that promises only greater efficiency—and ruthlessness. In this, *An Outcast* anticipates the essential themes of the more explicitly political novels of Conrad's major phase— *Nostromo, The Secret Agent,* and *Under Western Eyes*—in which power-struggles and revolutionary activity are portrayed as essentially futile gestures, incapable of reshaping or altering basic individual or societal conduct.

In this light, Aïssa's claim that all evil comes from the outside, from 'that people that steals every land, masters every sea, that knows no mercy and no truth' (p. 153), is comically inadequate as an interpretation of the nexus of political and social forces that govern human action. Rather than a historically validated reality, her reading of the colonial situation is a characteristic splitting-off and projection of the negative upon the Other, with the outsider as a convenient scapegoat for one's own moral inadequacies and failures. Conrad takes pains to establish how this situation recurs and how claims to cultural or racial superiority lack any shred of validity. Thus, for instance, Babalatchi's song about a shipwreck and 'one brother killing another for the sake of a gourd of water', a song inspired by his observing Willems and Aïssa together—'A man and a woman' (p. 138)—reaches out towards myth. Betrayal and greed recognize no national boundaries, and just as Willems and Aïssa are here cast as Adam and Eve, the story recounted is that of Cain and Abel. Cultural and individual particulars dissolve (and re-form) before the varieties of desire. Thus, far from acting as an agent to depoliticize or dehistoricize, Conrad's allegorical gestures and symbolism in *An Outcast* repudiate colonialism, just as his deflationary treatment of Willems and Almayer distinguishes the novel from the dominant pro-imperialist fictions of the period of Rudyard Kipling and Rider Haggard.

Conrad's symbolism, in the manner of many nineteenth-century novelists, attempts to score universalizing points, and his primary symbol here—the jungle, exuberant both in its growth and decay—is used to comment on the ultimate instability and ineffectuality of all human endeavour in the face of Nature. Like the sea in his sea fiction, the jungle defies human attempts to control it, remaining fundamentally resistant to the projections imposed upon it and disallowing any single historical or metaphoric appropriation.[4] And while a number of Conrad's metaphors, again in the fashion of nineteenth-century mainstream fiction, bestow anthropomorphic attributes on 'Nature', they do so not to domesticate it or to suggest a sympathetic relationship between it and human affairs but, on the contrary, to differentiate and distance. In *An Outcast*, the world 'full of life' (p. 331) stands in its solid undeniability only to

[4] On Conrad's use of the sea as a culturally determined and politically engaged symbol, see Jacques Berthoud, 'Introduction', *The Nigger of the 'Narcissus'* (1897; World's Classics Edition, 1984), esp. xix–xxi.

remind us of our transience and to emphasize our fundamental and painful alienation from its unconscious processes. As E. M. Forster presciently observed in a letter to a friend in which he recommended reading *Lord Jim* and *Tales of Unrest*:

In Conrad the interest is not the man—a Henry Jacobean creature, interesting enough—but the leagues of forest or swamp or sea in which he is a speck and his power of comprehending that he is a speck. When I read him, the whole earth becomes alive and the function of man to realise that life and to vocalise it—which he alone can do, and which he must do not mystically from an armchair like Wordsworth nor with his eyes on the clouds like Shelley, but tangibly . . .[5]

In its programmatic deliberateness Conrad's symbolism determines the presentation of the novel's major characters at the expense of some psychological realism. In a long letter responding to Edward Garnett's criticism of the completed manuscript, Conrad, in laying out his general intentions, firmly stated his main characters' allegorical purpose: 'They both long to have a significance in the order of nature or of society. To me they are typical of mankind where every individual wishes to assert his power, woman by sentiment, man by achievement of some sort—mostly base.'[6] While demonstrating the urgency of this need for meaning outside the self, the Willems–Aïssa relationship also powerfully enacts late-Victorian fears about degeneracy and atavism, the potential for 'falling back' into the pre-conscious and pre-historic, and vivifies the split between 'culture' and 'barbarism' that so obsessed a colonial power forcing its technologies

[5] Unpublished letter to Clive Carey, [15 June 1907], © 1992 The Provost and Scholars of King's College, Cambridge. Cited by permission.

[6] [24 Sept. 1895], *Collected Letters*, i. 247.

and moralities on conquered peoples. This fear is more vividly articulated in 'Heart of Darkness', but here, too, just as the jungle eventually reclaims any space not maintained by deliberate and repeated effort, the individual falls prey to primal impulses and unsocialized emotions that menace literal and symbolic ingestion, as the veneer of civilization is threatened or peeled off. Thus, Aïssa's effect on Willems on their first encounter, while embodying his longings to escape responsibility and the confining role thrust upon him by Lingard and his society, also presages her final appeal. Insistently associated with trance, dream, and sleep, she represents at the very outset what she does at the conclusion—immobility and the loss of individuality and of consciousness—in a word, death:

Willems never remembered how and when he parted from Aïssa. He caught himself drinking the muddy water out of the hollow of his hand, while his canoe was drifting in midstream past the last houses of Sambir. With his returning wits came the fear of something unknown that had taken possession of his heart . . . (p. 72).

Once a man of defined social and economic status, Willems is transformed by her into a creature alone and adrift, and his loss of consciousness signals not only a reversion to animal existence but the reassertion of the feared Other lurking, like Robert Louis Stevenson's Mr Hyde, within the post-Darwinian self. The tensions of Victorian doubleness prove ultimately unbearable and resolve themselves only as he surrenders to Aïssa as his fate.

No doubt, however, the presentation of Aïssa suffers most from Conrad's allegorical aim: the embodiment of tropical luxuriance, she also incarnates erotic power, a force which in its elemental shape necessarily conflicts with social life and even vitiates the possibility of relationship. It is also connected with the urge to death. In manipulating Willems' erotic impulse towards her, acting the part of the temptress, she domesticates and enslaves him to ensure her own security. But unable to be and unwilling to become the stereotypical hero capable of fending off her enemies and assuring her status and influence, Willems only belatedly awakens to learn that in escaping society's conventions he has betrayed himself. And in a final complex irony, Aïssa's total misunderstanding of him, combined with her desire for his conquest, makes her relation to him yet another colonizing project pointedly resembling those that form the novel's larger historical and political backdrop. Offering 'deadly happiness' (p. 141), she symbolizes a poisoned blossom bringing perfumed death, and any sentimentalizing of their relationship—whether articulated as a meditation on the nature of love or as an attempt to see her as an alternative to male power-systems, confronting and undermining patriarchal hegemony—necessarily ends in an egregious misreading of the novel. In the basic struggle for survival as well as in the secondary struggle for 'significance', Willems loses long before Aïssa fires the bullet that ends his life. And ironically, he never clearly sees that he has merely been a means by which she hopes to achieve her self-serving ends, ends that differ not a whit from those of the 'colonizers' who figure among Conrad's main targets.

III

Widely noticed in the daily press and major weeklies, *An Outcast of the Islands* brought Conrad not only a growing reputation among readers of serious fiction but two significant friendships—that with H. G. Wells, whose anonymous review in the *Saturday Review* led to correspondence and a meeting, and that with Henry

James, to whom he sent an inscribed copy of the novel.[7] While highly praising *An Outcast* and even acclaiming Conrad as a writer of 'greatness', Wells, though no stylist himself, immediately recognized the work's signal failing: 'His sentences are not unities, they are multitudinous tandems, and he has still to learn the great half of his art, the art of leaving things unwritten.'[8] Nor is the verbosity Wells noticed the novel's only flaw. The plot is occasionally static and the frame over-large for its subject. The descriptions have, with some justice, been faulted as overripe, and the dialogue suffers (but perhaps not surprisingly, given that English was Conrad's third language) from uncertainty of idiom and an occasional stilted over-literariness.

Despite these weaknesses, the novel is nevertheless thematically and technically more ambitious than *Almayer's Folly* (1895), and foreshadows the achievements and preoccupations of Conrad's major phase. While firmly wedded to the conventions of mid- and late-nineteenth-century fiction by its reliance on symbolism to establish and frame its meanings, it also reflects key modernist preoccupations with narrative form in its handling of chronology and rendering of consciousness, and, even if not to the extent characteristic of Conrad's mid-period fiction, by problematizing narrative authority. In a word, then, Conrad self-consciously both exploits and breaks with Victorian narrative procedures, forcing the reader raised on Dickens and Thackeray into a new relationship with fiction and undermining novelistic procedures in ways that anticipate some post-modern practice.

The interest in exploring and extending narrative possibilities that matures after *An Outcast* is none the

[7] For selected contemporary reviews of the novel, see *Conrad: The Critical Heritage*, ed. Norman Sherry (Routledge & Kegan Paul, 1973), 63–81.

[8] Ibid. 75.

less embryonically and importantly present here. Baba-latchi's song, cut off 'by a fit of soft and persistent coughing' (p. 138), re-enters the reader's consciousness a number of pages later—'There was a feeble cough-ing' (p. 143)—to forge a link between Aïssa's predatory eroticism and Willems' lack of awareness of the forces at work in the outside world. Another Conradian device—the prolonged deferral of action by narrative summary—is used to distance and give perspective to Willems' flight to Aïssa. Almayer's cynical laugh pro-vides, as it were, the opening and closing punctuation linking a scene interrupted for over ten pages (pp. 59, 71). But far more radical in its break with convention is the novel's coda, which powerfully satirizes the nine-teenth-century novel's characteristic formal closure in apportioning 'just desserts'. A self-reflexive gesture about meaning and interpretation, the nature of narra-tive, and the relationship of an (uncomprehending) audience to an (increasingly incoherent) tale, the coda issues a formal and mocking challenge to established conventions. Ever more incapacitated by drink and the rage that prompts his self-justifications, Almayer's biased and self-serving telling of the history of Lingard and Sambir shifts the novel towards meta-narrative. Retailed obsessively to the drunken Roumanian natu-ralist while the 'small, and flabby insects, dissatisfied with moonlight, streamed in and perished in thousands round the smoky light of the evil-smelling lamp' (p. 361), Almayer's attempted story parodies and subverts the narrating impulse itself, that effort to impose order and coherence on the flux of events. Mirroring the naturalist's lack of interest in Almayer's narrative are the forests, 'unchanged and sombre', listening to 'the unceasing whisper of the great river' (p. 366), that is, to another tale altogether. In contradistinction, then, to fiction, indifferent Nature offers endlessly repeated

pattern without meaning. And as a further assertion of
the futility of all systematization, the novel mockingly
refuses to close as Almayer hears 'repeated in a whispering echo' his own word: '"Hope"' (p. 368).

While such narrative concerns and Conrad's sub-
versive conclusion place him in the vanguard of modernist practice, his rendering of consciousness is more
troubled, partly because at this early stage in his career
he was actively mastering his craft and partly because
the presentation of interior states had not yet wholly
emerged from the long shadow cast by the cozy mid-
Victorian narrator–character relationship to establish
its own formal conventions. Conrad's attempt is, then,
only partially successful. In the main, the interior
monologues rely too closely on techniques for dialogue
and third-person narration. This example from
Almayer's meditations about how to rid himself of
Willems will serve:

He was thinking: Where was Lingard now? Halfway down
the river probably, in Abdulla's ship. He would be back in
about three days—perhaps less. And then? Then the
schooner would have to be got out of the river, and when
that craft was gone they—he and Lingard—would remain
here . . . (p. 293).

On the other hand, the impressionistic rendering of
Willems' consciousness at the moment of his death,
extensively prepared for by access to his meditations on
his fate, uses delayed decoding[9] to achieve ironic
distance as the dying man for the last time misunder-
stands himself, the processes of the world around him,

---

[9] A term coined by Ian Watt for the combination of 'the forward
temporal progression of the mind, as it receives messages from the outside
world, with the much slower reflexive process of making out their meaning',
Conrad in the Nineteenth Century (Chatto & Windus, 1980), 175. Yves Hervouet
argues that the technique derives from Conrad's knowledge of Flaubert in
his *The French Face of Joseph Conrad* (Cambridge Univ. Press, 1990), 199–200.

and his relationship to those processes. The burden of deciphering Willems' experiences thus falls squarely on the reader: 'His mouth was full of something salt and warm. He tried to cough; spat out. . . . Who shrieks: In the name of God, he dies!—he dies!—Who dies?—Must pick up—Night!—What? . . . Night already. . . .' (p. 360). A technical *tour de force*, the moment of Willems' death also confirms Conrad's anti-Paterian stance in suggesting that consciousness is a fallible and limited mechanism for interpreting sensation.

While such devices occasionally invite (even compel) the reader to collaborate in constructing the novel's meanings, and do so in ways very different from the collaboration elicited from the 'dear reader' of the high-Victorian novel, the range of Eastern allusions and even more the handling of language act, on the other hand, to alienate and estrange, intruding upon and ultimately breaking down the illusions of complicity and common cultural identity between the mid-Victorian novelist and his audience. Neither a matter of ambience or local colour, nor simply another aspect of the novel's realism, the peppering of the text with Arabic and Malay names, with place-names of remote and 'exotic' locations, with words and phrases of Malay, and with pseudo-Oriental epithets and phraseology—'O crafty one . . . O Leader of the brave' (pp. 103–4)—(in fact, patterns of speech modelled on Arabic rather than Malay) acts to distance in recalling and highlighting the variety of existence, of self-coherent worlds radically different from but equally valid to the reader's own. While Conrad often enough immediately translates a Malay word or phrase, the reader's momentary bewilderment replicates, even if in a small way, Willems' experience with codes and grammars only partially mastered.

As much as the 'exotic' background and alien

linguistic markers, familiar literary and cultural references placed in this setting also enact a cultural disloca-
tion, for they serve to recall and then immediately to
deny the context they allude to. Thus, the casual
description of Omar as a 'piratical and son-less Æneas'
(p. 54) and of Aïssa as a kind of Medusa—'as if those
words had changed him into stone' (p. 150)—inten-
tionally bring cultural traditions into collision. And the
pseudo-Koranic 'Willems the clever, Willems the successful' (p. 31) and the description of Aïssa as 'an houri
of the seventh Heaven' (p. 105) work similarly to stake
out other imported frames of reference. In short, the
cultural confrontations and struggle for hegemony
occurring in the plot also take shape in the novel's
literary allusions and several competing discourses and
vocabularies. These simultaneously establish and rela-
tivize boundaries, so that narrative and linguistic devices ultimately force the reader to confront directly
the arbitrariness of all codes and the permeability of all
borders. Stripped of their native linguistic, moral, and
national identities, of the comforting illusions provided
by ideological heritages and traditions, the novel's
characters force an awareness of the inherent strange-
ness of mere being.

Conrad's very thoroughness in depicting and insist-
ing upon this awareness has, it might be argued, at least
in part contributed to the novel's neglect, for works
that so systematically erect barriers to identification
and sympathy rarely win large readerships. But *An
Outcast of the Islands* is and ought to be read by anyone
seeking out reasons for Conrad's 'classic' status. Whatever its imperfections in construction or characteriza-
tion, its straining towards modernism established a
strikingly new voice on the literary scene. And as an
unselfpitying threnody for a world recently passed, one
whose naïveté could allow it to pretend to coherence

and explanatory power, it offers a compendium of *fin de siècle* beliefs and attitudes, irrevocably outdated even as the novel was being written. The new universe limned here, as Conrad's plot and narrative techniques establish, no longer has a centre or pretends to one, and humankind has retreated to the backdrop, a self-aware 'speck' as Forster would have it, observing itself caught up in nature's unconscious and repetitive processes.

NOTE ON THE TEXT

The specified copy-text for the Oxford World's Classics edition of Conrad is Dent's Collected Edition published by J. M. Dent (London) between 1946 and 1955. *An Outcast of the Islands* was published in that edition in 1949 from plates Dent had previously used for its Uniform Edition (1923–8). These plates were, in fact, originally made by Doubleday, Page (New York) for its 'Sun-Dial' edition, of which the present text is thus an issue.

The complete manuscript of the novel, dated 14 September 1895, is at the Rosenbach Museum and Library, Philadelphia. The manuscript of the 'Author's Note', completed on 29 January 1919, is held at the Huntington Library, San Marino, California. Proofs for the Heinemann setting are at Hofstra University, Hempstead, New York.

The novel's publication history may be summarized as follows:

(i) Publication of the first English edition by T. Fisher Unwin (London) on 4 March 1896.

(ii) Publication of the first American edition by D. Appleton (New York) about 15 August 1896.

(iii) Publication of a foreign edition by B. Tauchnitz (Leipzig) in two volumes in 1896.

(iv) Publication of the second American edition by Doubleday, Page (New York) in its limited 'Sun-Dial' edition in 1920; first publication of the 'Author's Note'.

(v) Publication of the second English edition by William Heinemann (London) in 1921 in its limited Collected Edition; type was distributed after printing.

(vi) Publication by Doubleday throughout the

1920s in variously named collected 'editions': these are all issues of the second American edition.

(vii) Publication of the third English edition in 1929 in Ernest Benn's Essex Library (London).

(viii) Publication in Dent's Uniform (1923) and Collected (1949) Editions: these are issues of the second American edition.

(ix) Publication of the fourth English edition in 1975 in Penguin Books' Modern Classics series (Harmondsworth).

Mary Gifford Belcher's unpublished doctoral thesis, 'A Critical Edition of Joseph Conrad's *An Outcast of the Islands*' (Texas Tech University, 1981) offers a study of the novel's complex publication history and discusses the numerous variants between editions. A more readily available summary of a few of these differences is Elmer A. Ordonez's 'Notes on the Revisions in *An Outcast of the Islands*', *Notes and Queries*, NS 15: 8 (1968), 287–9.

The first American edition was censored by the publisher, with some of the more sensual descriptions and language of the first English edition edited out. Among the significant variants is the dropping out of a paragraph (also missing in the third English edition) in Part II, Chapter 6. The text of this paragraph, whose omission is signalled by an asterisk on page 155, is as follows:

Let him touch her only; speak to her while he held her in his arms, under the gaze of his eyes, close, face to face! In the tenderness of his caress he would melt her obstinacy, destroy her fears, and talking to her the only language common to them both—that speech without words, the language of the senses—he would make her understand, he would obtain her consent to any wish of his. Again he called out, and this time his voice trembled with eagerness and apprehension—

'Aïssa!'

The present volume is a 'reading' rather than a critical text of the novel. Some emendations have been made to correct errors in the copy-text and remove some inconsistencies in punctuation and spelling. These are listed below:

List of Emendations

ii	PUES EL DELITO MAYOR / DEL HOMBRE ES HABER NACIDO *for* PUES EL DELITO / MAYOR DEL HOMBRE / ES HABER NACITO
ii	Calderón *for* Calderon
3.20	patent leather *for* patent-leather
6.9	towards *for* toward
7.1	zigzagging *for* zig-zagging
11.17	towards *for* toward
15.14	towards *for* toward
27.6	You *for* you
33.5	overpowering *for* over-powering
36.21	afterwards *for* afterward
41.1	Willems' *for* Willem's
43.10	*Flash*'s *for* Flash's
43.15	Hudig's *for* Hudigs'
44.31	taffrail *for* taff-rail
46.11	Haï—ya *for* Hai—ya
47.26	Orang Putih *for* Orang-Putih
49.15	rice-clearing *for* rice clearing
52.1	Orang Laut *for* Orang-Laut
55.2	siri vessel *for* siri-vessel
64.13	Willems' *for* Willem's
69.30	Willems' *for* Willem's
73.27	tobacco smoke *for* tobacco-smoke
80.9	tree-tops *for* treetops
86.1	palm leaf *for* palm-leaf
94.12	towards *for* toward
97.30	bloodshot *for* blood-shot
99.6	asphalt *for* asphalte
102.32	Ay—wa *for* Ay wa
103.24	Ay—wa *for* Ay wa

112.20   Halfway *for* Half-way
112.35   landing-place *for* landing place
163.18   now! . . . *for* now! . .
167.35   midday *for* mid-day
169.28   flies . . . *for* flies . . . .
171.33   split-rattan *for* split rattan
178.10   Penang *for* Panang
189.1   it? *for* it.
201.10   nipa palms *for* nipa-palms
234.18   fire- *for* fire
237.21   rice-birds *for* rice birds
239.22   Lekas *for* Lakas
247.28   overpowering *for* over-powering
265.2   shan't *for* sha'n't
265.3   shan't *for* sha'n't
271.30   overturned *for* over-turned
291.29   glowed, *for* glowed
292.3   sun-rays *for* sunrays
299.11   protégé *for* *protégé*
301.14   clothes-peg *for* clothespeg
311.2   the . . . *for* the . .
312.7   heart-rending *for* heartrending
317.9   Ya—wa *for* Ya-wa
317.19   bright red *for* bright-red
319.7   shan't *for* sha'n't
324.15   yoke line *for* yoke-line
336.7   watch . . . *for* watch . .
357.19   Ya—wa *for* Ya-wa
366.18   shan't *for* sha'n't

Asterisks

An asterisk in the text indicates the availability of an explanatory note.

SELECT BIBLIOGRAPHY

Dent's Collected Edition (1946–55) contains almost all of Conrad's works except for the dramatizations and some minor items. *Congo Diary and Other Uncollected Pieces*, edited by Zdzisław Najder (1978) contains the Congo notebooks, the fragment called *The Sisters*, *The Nature of a Crime* written in collaboration with Ford Madox Hueffer (later Ford Madox Ford), and various minor writings. Cambridge University Press is currently publishing a critical edition of the canon.

A complete scholarly edition of Conrad's letters, *The Collected Letters of Joseph Conrad*, edited by Frederick R. Karl and Laurence Davies, began appearing in 1983. Other important editions are as follows: *Joseph Conrad: Life and Letters*, edited by G. Jean-Aubry (1927); *Letters from Joseph Conrad, 1895–1924*, edited by Edward Garnett (1928); *Letters of Joseph Conrad to Marguerite Poradowska*, translated and edited by John A. Gee and Paul J. Sturm (1940); *Conrad's Polish Background: Letters to and from Polish Friends*, edited by Zdzisław Najder (1964); and *Joseph Conrad's Letters to R. B. Cunninghame Graham*, edited by C. T. Watts (1969). There are further collections edited by Richard Curle (1928), G. Jean-Aubry (1929), William Blackburn (1958), René Rapin (1966), and Dale B. J. Randall (1968).

Memoirs of Conrad include those by Ford Madox Ford (1924), Jessie Conrad (1926 and 1935), Richard Curle (1928), Borys Conrad (1970), and John Conrad (1981). Documents related to Conrad's Polish experience and relations are collected in Zdzisław Najder (ed.), *Conrad Under Familial Eyes* (1983). The most reliable and scholarly treatment of Conrad's life is Zdzisław Najder's *Joseph Conrad: A Chronicle* (1983). Critical biographies have also been written by Jocelyn Baines (1960), Bernard Meyer (a 'psychoanalytic' biography, 1967), Frederick R. Karl (1979), and Jeffrey Meyers (1991).

Two biographically related studies that make substantial

use of documentary material are: Norman Sherry's *Conrad's Eastern World* (1966) and *Conrad's Western World* (1971). There are further relevant studies by Richard Curle (1914), Gustav Morf (1930 and 1976), Edward Crankshaw (1936), J. H. Retinger (1941), Jerry Allen (1965), Norman Sherry (1972), Cedric Watts (1989), and Owen Knowles (1989).

Of the numerous critical books on Conrad the following may be found useful: Douglas Hewitt, *Conrad: A Reassessment* (1952); Thomas C. Moser, *Joseph Conrad: Achievement and Decline* (1957); Albert J. Guerard, *Conrad the Novelist* (1958); Avrom Fleishman, *Conrad's Politics* (1967); David Thorburn, *Conrad's Romanticism* (1968); Jacques Berthoud, *Joseph Conrad: The Major Phase* (1978); and Ian Watt, *Conrad in the Nineteenth Century* (1979). Other studies of interest are by: Eloise Knapp Hay (1963), Paul Kirschner (1968), C. B. Cox (1974), Cedric Watts (1982), and Daphna Erdinast-Vulcan (1991). There are important essays on Conrad in: F. R. Leavis, *The Great Tradition* (1948) and '*Anna Karenina' and Other Essays* (1967); J. Hillis Miller, *Poets of Reality* (1965); Norman Sherry (ed.), *Joseph Conrad: A Commemoration* (1976); and Ted Billy (ed.), *Critical Essays on Joseph Conrad* (1987). Two scholarly journals are devoted exclusively to Conrad studies: *Conradiana* (Texas Tech University, Lubbock, Texas) and *The Conradian* (Joseph Conrad Society, UK, London).

On *An Outcast of the Islands*, in particular, the following may be of interest: J. D. Gordan, *Joseph Conrad: The Making of a Novelist* (1940); R. A. Gekoski, '*An Outcast of the Islands*: A New Reading', *Conradiana*, 2: 3 (1969–70), 47–58; Juliet McLauchlan, 'Almayer and Willems—"How Not To Be"', *Conradiana*, 11 (1979), 113–41; Peter Knox-Shaw, 'Conrad Dismantles Providence: Deserted Idylls in *An Outcast of the Islands*', in his *The Explorer in English Fiction* (1987), 113–35; Heliéna Krenn, *Conrad's Lingard Trilogy: Empire, Race, and Women in the Malay Novels* (1990).

A CHRONOLOGY OF
JOSEPH CONRAD

A detailed factual account of Conrad's life and career may be found in Owen Knowles, *A Conrad Chronology* (1989).

1857   (3 Dec.) Born Józef Teodor Konrad Korzeniowski, of Polish parents in the Ukraine.

1861   His father, poet, dramatist, translator, and political activist Apollo Korzeniowski, arrested in Warsaw by Russian authorities for patriotic conspiracy.

1862   Conrad's parents exiled to Vologda in northern Russia; their son accompanies them.

1865   Death of his mother.

1869   Death of his father in Cracow; Conrad's uncle Tadeusz Bobrowski becomes his guardian.

1874   Leaves Poland for Marseilles to become a trainee seaman in the French merchant navy.

1876   As a 'steward' in the *Saint-Antoine*, becomes acquainted with Dominique Cervoni (who appears in *The Mirror of the Sea*, *A Personal Record*, and *The Arrow of Gold*, and is a source for the protagonist in *Nostromo* and for Peyrol in *The Rover*).

1878   (Mar.) Shoots himself in the chest but is not seriously injured; Bobrowski comes from the Ukraine and clears his debts.
(Apr.) Joins his first British ship, the *Mavis*.
Later in the year serves in the *Skimmer of the Sea* and the *Duke of Sutherland*.

1886   (Aug.) Becomes a British subject; formerly, as a Russian subject and son of a convict, Conrad

had been liable for Russian military service.
(Nov.) Passes the examination for a Master's certificate.

1887   In hospital in Singapore with an injury sustained in the *Highland Forest*.

1887–8   As an officer in the *Vidar* becomes familiar with the Malay Archipelago.

1888   Master of the *Otago*, his only command.

1889   Resigns from the *Otago*; settles briefly in London and begins to write *Almayer's Folly*.

1890   Begins friendship with Marguerite Poradowska. Works in the Congo Free State for the Société pour le Commerce du Haut-Congo.

1891–3   His pleasantest experience at sea, as first officer in the *Torrens*; meets John Galsworthy, who is among the passengers and becomes a loyal friend.

1894   (Feb.) Death of Bobrowski.
(Aug.) Begins *An Outcast of the Islands*.
(Oct.) *Almayer's Folly* accepted by Unwin. Meets Edward Garnett, reader at Unwin's and an influential and lifelong literary friend.
(Nov.) Meets Jessie George.

1895   *Almayer's Folly* published.
(Sept.) Completes *An Outcast of the Islands*.

1896   (Mar.) *An Outcast of the Islands* published.
(24 Mar.) Marries Jessie George.
Begins work on *The Rescue* and initiates correspondence with Henry James. Becomes acquainted with H. G. Wells.

1897   *The Nigger of the 'Narcissus'* published. Begins friendship with R. B. Cunninghame Graham.

1898   *Tales of Unrest* ('Karain', 'The Idiots', 'An Outpost of Progress', 'The Return', 'The Lagoon') published. Collaborates with Ford Madox Ford (then surnamed Hueffer). Takes over from Ford the lease of a Kentish farmhouse, The Pent. Friendship with Stephen Crane. Borys Conrad born.

1899   'Heart of Darkness' serialized in *Blackwood's Magazine*.

1899–1900   *Lord Jim* serialized in *Blackwood's Magazine*.

1900   *Lord Jim* published as a book. Stephen Crane dies. J.B. Pinker becomes Conrad's literary agent.

1901   *The Inheritors* (collaboration with Ford) published.

1902   *Youth: A Narrative,* and *Two Other Stories* ('Youth', 'Heart of Darkness', 'The End of the Tether') published.

1903   *Typhoon, and Other Stories* ('Typhoon', 'Amy Foster', 'Falk', 'To-morrow') and *Romance* (collaboration with Ford) published.

1904   Jessie Conrad injures her knees and is partially disabled for life. *Nostromo* published.

1906   *The Mirror of the Sea* published. John Conrad born.

1907   *The Secret Agent* published. The Conrads move to Someries, Luton Hoo.

1908   *A Set of Six* ('Gaspar Ruiz', 'The Informer', 'The Brute', 'An Anarchist', 'The Duel', 'Il Conde') published.

1909   Quarrels with Ford. The Conrads move to Aldington.

1910   Completes *Under Western Eyes* and suffers a nervous breakdown. On his recovery the Conrads move to Capel House, Orlestone.

1911   *Under Western Eyes* published.

1912   *A Personal Record* and *'Twixt Land and Sea* ('A Smile of Fortune', 'The Secret Sharer', 'Freya of the Seven Isles') published.

1913   *Chance* published.

1914   *Chance* has very good sales, especially in America; the earlier works now find a larger public. The Conrads visit Poland and are trapped there for some weeks by the outbreak of war.

1915   *Within the Tides* ('The Planter of Malata', 'The Partner', 'The Inn of the Two Witches', 'Because of the Dollars') and *Victory* published.

1917   *The Shadow-Line* published.

1919   (Jan.) Completes the 'Author's Note' to *An Outcast of the Islands*.
        The Arrow of Gold published. The Conrads move to Oswalds, Bishopsbourne, near Canterbury.

1920   *The Rescue* published, twenty-four years after it was begun.

1921   *Notes on Life and Letters* published. Visits Corsica, does research for *The Rover* and *Suspense*.

1923   Visits America and is lionized. *The Rover* published.

1924   (May) Declines a knighthood.
        (3 Aug.) Dies of a heart attack at Oswalds; buried at Canterbury.
        The Nature of a Crime (collaboration with Ford) published as a book.

1925   *Tales of Hearsay* ('The Warrior's Soul', 'Prince Roman', 'The Tale', 'The Black Mate') and *Suspense* (unfinished novel) published.

1926   *Last Essays* published.

1928   *The Sisters* (fragment) published.

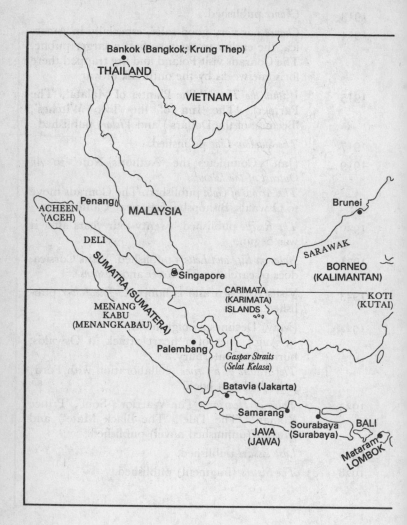

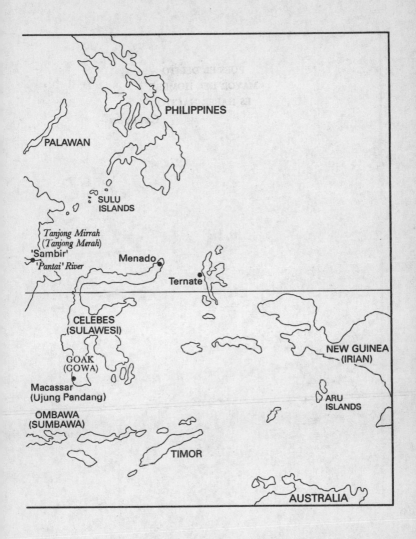

PUES EL DELITO
MAYOR DEL HOMBRE
ES HABER NACITO
*Calderón**

AN OUTCAST
OF THE ISLANDS

To
Edward Lancelot Sanderson*

AUTHOR'S NOTE

"An Outcast of the Islands" is my second novel in the absolute sense of the word; second in conception, second in execution, second as it were in its essence. There was no hesitation, half-formed plan, vague idea, or the vaguest reverie of anything else between it and *"Almayer's Folly."* The only doubt I suffered from, after the publication of *"Almayer's Folly,"* was whether I should write another line for print.* Those days, now grown so dim, had their poignant moments. Neither in my mind nor in my heart had I then given up the sea. In truth I was clinging to it desperately, all the more desperately because, against my will, I could not help feeling that there was something changed in my relation to it. *"Almayer's Folly,"* had been finished and done with. The mood itself was gone. But it had left the memory of an experience that, both in thought and emotion was unconnected with the sea, and I suppose that part of my moral being which is rooted in consistency was badly shaken. I was a victim of contrary stresses which produced a state of immobility. I gave myself up to indolence. Since it was impossible for me to face both ways I had elected to face nothing. The discovery of new values in life is a very chaotic experience; there is a tremendous amount of jostling and confusion and a momentary feeling of darkness. I let my spirit float supine over that chaos.

A phrase of Edward Garnett's*is, as a matter of fact, responsible for this book. The first of the friends I made for myself by my pen it was but natural that he should be the recipient, at that time, of my confidences. One evening when we had dined together and he had listened to the account of my perplexities (I fear he must have been growing a little tired of them) he pointed out that there was no need to determine my future absolutely. Then he added: "You have the style, you have the temperament; why not write another?" I believe that as far as one man may wish to influence another man's life Edward Garnett had a great desire that I should go on writing. At that time, and I may say, ever afterwards, he was always very patient and gentle with me. What strikes me most however in the phrase quoted above which was offered to me in a tone of detachment is not its gentleness but its effective wisdom. Had he said, "Why not go on writing," it is very probable he would have scared me away from pen and ink for ever; but there was nothing either to frighten one or arouse one's antagonism in the mere suggestion to "write another." And thus a dead point in the revolution of my affairs was insidiously got over. The word "another" did it. At about eleven o'clock of a nice London night, Edward and I walked along interminable streets talking of many things, and I remember that on getting home I sat down and wrote about half a page of *An Outcast of the Islands* before I slept.* This was committing myself definitely, I won't say to another life, but to another book. There is apparently something in my character which will not allow me to abandon for good any piece of work I have begun. I have laid aside many beginnings. I have laid them aside with sorrow, with disgust, with rage, with melancholy and even with self-contempt; but even at the worst I had an uneasy consciousness that I would have to go back to them.

"*An Outcast of the Islands*" belongs to those novels of mine that were never laid aside; and though it brought me the qualification of "exotic writer"*I don't think the charge was at all justified. For the life of me I don't see that there is the slightest exotic spirit in the conception or style of that novel. It is certainly the most *tropical* of my eastern tales. The mere scenery got a great hold on me as I went on, perhaps because (I may just as well confess that) the story itself was never very near my heart. It engaged my imagination much more than my affection. As to my feeling for Willems it was but the regard one cannot help having for one's own creation. Obviously I could not be indifferent to a man on whose head I had brought so much evil simply by imagining him such as he appears in the novel—and that, too, on a very slight foundation.

The man who suggested Willems to me was not particularly interesting in himself. My interest was aroused by his dependent position, his strange, dubious status of a mistrusted, disliked, worn-out European living on the reluctant toleration of that Settlement hidden in the heart of the forest-land, up that sombre stream which our ship was the only white men's ship to visit. With his hollow, clean-shaved cheeks, a heavy grey moustache and eyes without any expression whatever, clad always in a spotless sleeping suit much befrogged in front, which left his lean neck wholly uncovered, and with his bare feet in a pair of straw slippers, he wandered silently amongst the houses in daylight, almost as dumb as an animal and apparently much more homeless. I don't know what he did with himself at night. He must have had a place, a hut, a palm-leaf shed, some sort of hovel where he kept his razor and his change of sleeping suits. An air of futile mystery hung over him, something not exactly

dark but obviously ugly. The only definite statement I could extract from anybody was that it was he
who had "brought the Arabs into the river."* That
must have happened many years before. But how
did he bring them into the river? He could hardly
have done it in his arms like a lot of kittens. I knew
that Almayer* founded the chronology of all his misfortunes on the date of that fateful advent; and yet the
very first time we dined with Almayer there was Willems sitting at table with us in the manner of the skele-
ton at the feast, obviously shunned by everybody,
never addressed by any one, and for all recognition of
his existence getting now and then from Almayer a
venomous glance which I observed with great
surprise. In the course of the whole evening he ventured one single remark which I didn't catch because
his articulation was imperfect, as of a man who had
forgotten how to speak. I was the only person who
seemed aware of the sound. Willems subsided. Pres-
ently he retired, pointedly unnoticed—into the forest
maybe? Its immensity was there, within three hundred
yards of the verandah, ready to swallow up anything.
Almayer conversing with my captain did not stop talking
while he glared angrily at the retreating back. Didn't
that fellow bring the Arabs into the river! Nevertheless
Willems turned up next morning on Almayer's verandah.
From the bridge of the steamer I could see plainly these
two, breakfasting together, tête à tête and, I suppose, in
dead silence, one with his air of being no longer interested in this world and the other raising his eyes now
and then with intense dislike.

It was clear that in those days Willems lived on
Almayer's charity. Yet on returning two months
later to Sambir*I heard that he had gone on an expedition up the river in charge of a steam-launch belonging

to the Arabs, to make some discovery or other. On account of the strange reluctance that everyone manifested to talk about Willems it was impossible for me to get at the rights of that transaction. Moreover, I was a newcomer, the youngest of the company, and, I suspect, not judged quite fit as yet for a full confidence. I was not much concerned about that exclusion. The faint suggestion of plots and mysteries pertaining to all matters touching Almayer's affairs amused me vastly. Almayer was obviously very much affected. I believe he missed Willems immensely. He wore an air of sinister preoccupation and talked confidentially with my captain. I could catch only snatches of mumbled sentences. Then one morning as I came along the deck to take my place at the breakfast table Almayer checked himself in his low-toned discourse. My captain's face was perfectly impenetrable. There was a moment of profound silence and then as if unable to contain himself Almayer burst out in a loud vicious tone:

"One thing's certain; if he finds anything worth having up there they will poison him like a dog."

Disconnected though it was, that phrase, as food for thought, was distinctly worth hearing. We left the river three days afterwards and I never returned to Sambir; but whatever happened to the protagonist*of my Willems nobody can deny that I have recorded for him a less squalid fate.

J. C.

1919.

PART I

AN OUTCAST OF THE ISLANDS

CHAPTER ONE

WHEN he stepped off the straight and narrow path of his peculiar honesty, it was with an inward assertion of unflinching resolve to fall back again into the monotonous but safe stride of virtue as soon as his little excursion into the wayside quagmires had produced the desired effect. It was going to be a short episode —a sentence in brackets, so to speak—in the flowing tale of his life: a thing of no moment, to be done unwillingly, yet neatly, and to be quickly forgotten. He imagined that he could go on afterwards looking at the sunshine, enjoying the shade, breathing in the perfume of flowers in the small garden before his house. He fancied that nothing would be changed, that he would be able as heretofore to tyrannize good-humouredly over his half-caste wife, to notice with tender contempt his pale yellow child, to patronize loftily his dark-skinned brother-in-law, who loved pink neckties and wore patent leather boots on his little feet, and was so humble before the white husband of the lucky sister. Those were the delights of his life, and he was unable to conceive that the moral significance of any act of his could interfere with the very nature of things, could dim the light of the sun, could destroy the perfume of the flowers, the submission of his wife, the smile of his child, the awe-struck respect of Leonard da Souza and of all the Da Souza family. That family's admiration was the great luxury of his life. It rounded and completed his existence in a perpetual assurance of unquestionable superiority. He loved to breathe the coarse incense they offered before the shrine of the successful white man; the man that had done them the honour to marry their daughter, sister, cousin; the rising man sure to climb very high; the confidential clerk of Hudig* & Co. They were a numerous and an unclean crowd, living in ruined bamboo houses, surrounded by neglected compounds, on the outskirts of Macassar. He kept them at arm's length and even further off, perhaps, having no illusions as to their worth. They were a half-caste, lazy lot, and he saw them as they were—ragged, lean, unwashed, undersized men of various ages, shuffling about aimlessly in slippers; motionless old women who looked like monstrous bags of pink calico* stuffed with shapeless lumps of fat, and deposited askew upon decaying rattan chairs in shady corners of dusty verandahs; young women, slim and yellow, big-eyed, long-haired, moving languidly amongst the dirt and rubbish of their dwellings as if every step they took was going to be their very last. He heard their shrill quarrellings, the squalling of their children, the grunting of their pigs; he smelt the odours of the heaps of garbage in their courtyards: and he was greatly disgusted. But he fed and clothed that shabby multitude; those degenerate descendants of Portuguese conquerors;*he was their providence; he kept them singing his praises in the midst of their laziness, of their dirt, of their immense and hopeless squalor: and he was greatly delighted. They wanted much, but he could give them all they wanted without ruining himself. In exchange he had their silent fear, their loquacious love, their noisy veneration. It is a fine thing to be a providence, and to be told so on every day of one's life.

It gives one a feeling of enormously remote superiority, and Willems* revelled in it. He did not analyze the state of his mind, but probably his greatest delight lay in the unexpressed but intimate conviction that, should he close his hand, all those admiring human beings would starve. His munificence had demoralized them. An easy task. Since he descended amongst them and married Joanna they had lost the little aptitude and strength for work they might have had to put forth under the stress of extreme necessity. They lived now by the grace of his will. This was power. Willems loved it.

In another, and perhaps a lower plane, his days did not want for their less complex but more obvious pleasures. He liked the simple games of skill—billiards; also games not so simple, and calling for quite another kind of skill—poker. He had been the aptest pupil of a steady-eyed, sententious American, who had drifted mysteriously into Macassar from the wastes of the Pacific, and, after knocking about for a time in the eddies of town life, had drifted out enigmatically into the sunny solitudes of the Indian Ocean. The memory of the Californian stranger was perpetuated in the game of poker—which became popular in the capital of Celebes from that time—and in a powerful cocktail, the recipe for which is transmitted—in the Kwang-tung* dialect—from head boy to head boy of the Chinese servants in the Sunda Hotel*even to this day. Willems was a connoisseur in the drink and an adept at the game. Of those accomplishments he was moderately proud. Of the confidence reposed in him by Hudig—the master—he was boastfully and obtrusively proud. This arose from his great benevolence, and from an exalted sense of his duty to himself and the world at large. He experienced that irresistible impulse to impart information

which is inseparable from gross ignorance. There is
always some one thing which the ignorant man knows,
and that thing is the only thing worth knowing; it
fills the ignorant man's universe. Willems knew all
about himself. On the day when, with many misgiv-
ings, he ran away from a Dutch East-Indiaman in
Samarang roads, he had commenced that study of
himself, of his own ways, of his own abilities, of those
fate-compelling qualities of his which led him towards
that lucrative position which he now filled. Being of a
modest and diffident nature, his successes amazed,
almost frightened him, and ended—as he got over the
succeeding shocks of surprise—by making him ferociously conceited. He believed in his genius and in his
knowledge of the world. Others should know of it also;
for their own good and for his greater glory. All those
friendly men who slapped him on the back and greeted
him noisily should have the benefit of his example. For
that he must talk. He talked to them conscientiously.
In the afternoon he expounded his theory of success
over the little tables, dipping now and then his moustache in the crushed ice of the cocktails; in the evening
he would often hold forth, cue in hand, to a young listener across the billiard table. The billiard balls stood
still as if listening also, under the vivid brilliance of the
shaded oil lamps hung low over the cloth; while away
in the shadows of the big room the Chinaman marker
would lean wearily against the wall, the blank mask of
his face looking pale under the mahogany marking-
board; his eyelids dropped in the drowsy fatigue of late
hours and in the buzzing monotony of the unintelligible
stream of words poured out by the white man. In a
sudden pause of the talk the game would recommence
with a sharp click and go on for a time in the flowing
soft whirr and the subdued thuds as the balls rolled

zigzagging towards the inevitably successful cannon.
Through the big windows and the open doors the salt
dampness of the sea, the vague smell of mould and
flowers from the garden of the hotel drifted in and
mingled with the odour of lamp oil, growing heavier
as the night advanced. The players' heads dived into
the light as they bent down for the stroke, springing
back again smartly into the greenish gloom of broad
lamp-shades; the clock ticked methodically; the unmoved Chinaman* continuously repeated the score in a
lifeless voice, like a big talking doll—and Willems
would win the game. With a remark that it was getting
late, and that he was a married man, he would say a
patronizing good-night and step out into the long,
empty street. At that hour its white dust was like a
dazzling streak of moonlight where the eye sought repose
in the dimmer gleam of rare oil lamps. Willems
walked homewards, following the line of walls over-
topped by the luxuriant vegetation of the front gardens. The houses right and left were hidden behind
the black masses of flowering shrubs. Willems had
the street to himself. He would walk in the middle,
his shadow gliding obsequiously before him. He looked
down on it complacently. The shadow of a successful
man! He would be slightly dizzy with the cocktails
and with the intoxication of his own glory. As he often
told people, he came east fourteen years ago—a cabin
boy. A small boy. His shadow must have been very
small at that time; he thought with a smile that he was
not aware then he had anything—even a shadow—
which he dared call his own. And now he was looking
at the shadow of the confidential clerk of Hudig & Co.
going home. How glorious! How good was life for
those that were on the winning side! He had won the
game of life; also the game of billiards. He walked

faster, jingling his winnings, and thinking of the white
stone days that had marked the path of his existence.
He thought of the trip to Lombok for ponies*—that
first important transaction confided to him by Hudig;
then he reviewed the more important affairs: the quiet
deal in opium; the illegal traffic in gunpowder; the great
affair of smuggled firearms, the difficult business of the
Rajah of Goak. He carried that last through by sheer
pluck; he had bearded the savage old ruler in his council
room; he had bribed him with a gilt glass coach, which,
rumour said, was used as a hen-coop*now; he had over-
persuaded him; he had bested him in every way. That
was the way to get on. He disapproved of the elemen-
tary dishonesty that dips the hand in the cash-box, but
one could evade the laws and push the principles of
trade to their furthest consequences. Some call that
cheating. Those are the fools, the weak, the contemptible. The wise, the strong, the respected, have no
scruples. Where there are scruples there can be no
power. On that text he preached often to the young
men. It was his doctrine, and he, himself, was a shining
example of its truth.

Night after night he went home thus, after a day of
toil and pleasure, drunk with the sound of his own voice
celebrating his own prosperity. On his thirtieth birthday he went home thus. He had spent in good company a nice, noisy evening, and, as he walked along the
empty street, the feeling of his own greatness grew upon
him, lifted him above the white dust of the road, and
filled him with exultation and regrets. He had not
done himself justice over there in the hotel, he had not
talked enough about himself, he had not impressed his
hearers enough. Never mind. Some other time. Now
he would go home and make his wife get up and listen
to him. Why should she not get up?—and mix a cock-

tail for him—and listen patiently. Just so. She shall.
If he wanted he could make all the Da Souza family
get up. He had only to say a word and they would
all come and sit silently in their night vestments on
the hard, cold ground of his compound and listen, as
long as he wished to go on explaining to them from the
top of the stairs, how great and good he was. They
would. However, his wife would do—for to-night.

His wife! He winced inwardly. A dismal woman
with startled eyes and dolorously drooping mouth, that
would listen to him in pained wonder and mute stillness.
She was used to those night-discourses now. She had
rebelled once—at the beginning. Only once. Now,
while he sprawled in the long chair and drank and
talked, she would stand at the further end of the table,
her hands resting on the edge, her frightened eyes
watching his lips, without a sound, without a stir, hardly
breathing, till he dismissed her with a contemptuous:
"Go to bed, dummy." She would draw a long breath
then and trail out of the room, relieved but unmoved.
Nothing could startle her, make her scold or make her
cry. She did not complain, she did not rebel.* That
first difference of theirs was decisive. Too decisive,
thought Willems, discontentedly. It had frightened
the soul out of her body apparently. A dismal woman!
A damn'd business altogether! What the devil did he
want to go and saddle himself. . . . Ah! Well! he
wanted a home, and the match seemed to please Hudig,
and Hudig gave him the bungalow, that flower-bowered
house to which he was wending his way in the cool
moonlight. And he had the worship of the Da Souza
tribe. A man of his stamp could carry off anything,
do anything, aspire to anything. In another five years
those white people who attended the Sunday card-
parties of the Governor*would accept him—half-caste

wife and all! Hooray! He saw his shadow dart forward and wave a hat, as big as a rum barrel, at the
end of an arm several yards long. . . . Who
shouted hooray? . . . He smiled shamefacedly to
himself, and, pushing his hands deep into his pockets,
walked faster with a suddenly grave face.

Behind him—to the left—a cigar end glowed in the
gateway of Mr. Vinck's front yard. Leaning against
one of the brick pillars, Mr. Vinck, the cashier of Hudig
& Co., smoked the last cheroot of the evening. Amongst
the shadows of the trimmed bushes Mrs. Vinck crunched
slowly, with measured steps, the gravel of the circular
path before the house.

"There's Willems going home on foot—and drunk I
fancy," said Mr. Vinck over his shoulder. "I saw him
jump and wave his hat."

The crunching of the gravel stopped.

"Horrid man," said Mrs. Vinck, calmly. "I have
heard he beats his wife."

"Oh no, my dear, no," muttered absently Mr. Vinck,
with a vague gesture. The aspect of Willems as a wife-
beater presented to him no interest. How women do
misjudge! If Willems wanted to torture his wife he
would have recourse to less primitive methods. Mr.
Vinck knew Willems well, and believed him to be very
able, very smart—objectionably so. As he took the
last quick draws at the stump of his cheroot, Mr. Vinck
reflected that the confidence accorded by Hudig to
Willems was open, under the circumstances, to loyal
criticism from Hudig's cashier.

"He is becoming dangerous; he knows too much.
He will have to be got rid of," said Mr. Vinck aloud.
But Mrs. Vinck had gone in already, and after shaking
his head he threw away his cheroot and followed her
slowly.

Willems walked on homeward weaving the splendid web of his future. The road to greatness lay plainly before his eyes, straight and shining, without any obstacle that he could see. He had stepped off the path of honesty, as he understood it, but he would soon regain it, never to leave it any more! It was a very small matter. He would soon put it right again. Meantime his duty was not to be found out, and he trusted in his skill, in his luck, in his well-established reputation that would disarm suspicion if anybody dared to suspect. But nobody would dare! True, he was conscious of a slight deterioration. He had appropriated temporarily some of Hudig's money. A deplorable necessity. But he judged himself with the indulgence that should be extended to the weaknesses of genius. He would make reparation and all would be as before; nobody would be the loser for it, and he would go on unchecked towards the brilliant goal of his ambition.

Hudig's partner!

Before going up the steps of his house he stood for awhile, his feet well apart, chin in hand, contemplating mentally Hudig's future partner. A glorious occupation. He saw him quite safe; solid as the hills; deep—deep as an abyss; discreet as the grave.

CHAPTER TWO

THE sea, perhaps because of its saltness, roughens
the outside but keeps sweet the kernel of its servants'
soul. The old sea; the sea of many years ago, whose
servants were devoted slaves and went from youth to
age or to a sudden grave without needing to open the
book of life, because they could look at eternity reflected on the element that gave the life and dealt the
death. Like a beautiful and unscrupulous woman, the
sea of the past was glorious in its smiles, irresistible in
its anger, capricious, enticing, illogical, irresponsible;
a thing to love, a thing to fear. It cast a spell, it gave
joy, it lulled gently into boundless faith; then with
quick and causeless anger it killed. But its cruelty was
redeemed by the charm of its inscrutable mystery, by
the immensity of its promise, by the supreme witchery
of its possible favour. Strong men with childlike hearts
were faithful to it, were content to live by its grace—
to die by its will. That was the sea before the time
when the French mind set the Egyptian muscle* in
motion and produced a dismal but profitable ditch.
Then a great pall of smoke sent out by countless steam-
boats was spread over the restless mirror of the Infinite. The hand of the engineer tore down the veil
of the terrible beauty in order that greedy and faithless
landlubbers might pocket dividends. The mystery
was destroyed. Like all mysteries, it lived only in
the hearts of its worshippers. The hearts changed; the
men changed. The once loving and devoted servants
went out armed with fire and iron, and conquering

the fear of their own hearts became a calculating crowd
of cold and exacting masters. The sea of the past
was an incomparably beautiful mistress, with inscrutable face, with cruel and promising eyes. The sea of
to-day is a used-up drudge, wrinkled and defaced by the
churned-up wakes of brutal propellers, robbed of the
enslaving charm of its vastness, stripped of its beauty,
of its mystery and of its promise.

Tom Lingard* was a master, a lover, a servant of
the sea. The sea took him young, fashioned him body
and soul; gave him his fierce aspect, his loud voice, his
fearless eyes, his stupidly guileless heart. Generously
it gave him his absurd faith in himself, his universal
love of creation, his wide indulgence, his contemptuous
severity, his straightforward simplicity of motive and
honesty of aim. Having made him what he was,
womanlike, the sea served him humbly and let him
bask unharmed in the sunshine of its terribly uncertain
favour. Tom Lingard grew rich on the sea and by the
sea. He loved it with the ardent affection of a lover,
he made light of it with the assurance of perfect mastery, he feared it with the wise fear of a brave man, and
he took liberties with it as a spoiled child might do with
a paternal and good-natured ogre. He was grateful
to it, with the gratitude of an honest heart. His greatest pride lay in his profound conviction of its faithful-
ness—in the deep sense of his unerring knowledge of its
treachery.

The little brig *Flash**was the instrument of Lingard's
fortune. They came north together—both young—
out of an Australian port, and after a very few years
there was not a white man in the islands, from Palembang to Ternate, from Ombawa to Palawan, that did
not know Captain Tom and his lucky craft. He was
liked for his reckless generosity, for his unswerving

honesty, and at first was a little feared on account of his violent temper. Very soon, however, they found him out, and the word went round that Captain Tom's fury was less dangerous than many a man's smile. He prospered greatly. After his first—and successful— fight with the sea robbers, when he rescued, as rumour had it, the yacht of some big wig from home, somewhere down Carimata way,* his great popularity began. As years went on it grew apace. Always visiting out-of-the-way places of that part of the world, always in search of new markets for his cargoes—not so much for profit as for the pleasure of finding them—he soon became known to the Malays, and by his successful recklessness in several encounters with pirates, established the terror of his name. Those white men with whom he had business, and who naturally were on the look-out for his weaknesses, could easily see that it was enough to give him his Malay title to flatter him greatly. So when there was anything to be gained by it, and sometimes out of pure and unprofitable good nature, they would drop the ceremonious "Captain Lingard" and address him half seriously as Rajah Laut—the King of the Sea.*

He carried the name bravely on his broad shoulders. He had carried it many years already when the boy Willems ran barefooted on the deck of the ship *Kosmopoliet IV:* in Samarang roads, looking with innocent eyes on the strange shore and objurgating his immediate surroundings with blasphemous lips, while his childish brain worked upon the heroic idea of running away. From the poop of the *Flash* Lingard saw in the early morning the Dutch ship get lumberingly under weigh,* bound for the eastern ports. Very late in the evening of the same day he stood on the quay of the landing canal, ready to go on board of his brig. The night was starry and clear; the little custom-house building was shut up, and as the gharry that brought him down disappeared up the long avenue of dusty trees leading to the town, Lingard thought himself alone on the quay. He roused up his sleeping boat-crew and stood waiting for them to get ready, when he felt a tug at his coat and a thin voice said, very distinctly—

"English captain."

Lingard turned round quickly, and what seemed to be a very lean boy jumped back with commendable activity.

"Who are you? Where do you spring from?" asked Lingard, in startled surprise.

From a safe distance the boy pointed towards a cargo lighter moored to the quay.

"Been hiding there, have you?" said Lingard. "Well, what do you want? Speak out, confound you. You did not come here to scare me to death, for fun, did you?"

The boy tried to explain in imperfect English, but very soon Lingard interrupted him.

"I see," he exclaimed, "you ran away from the big ship that sailed this morning. Well, why don't you go to your countrymen here?"

"Ship gone only a little way—to Sourabaya.' Make me go back to the ship," explained the boy.

"Best thing for you," affirmed Lingard with conviction.

"No," retorted the boy; "me want stop here; not want go home. Get money here; home no good."

"This beats all my going a-fishing," commented the astonished Lingard. "It's money you want? Well! well! And you were not afraid to run away, you bag of bones, you!"

The boy intimated that he was frightened of nothing

but of being sent back to the ship. Lingard looked
at him in meditative silence.

"Come closer," he said at last. He took the boy
by the chin, and turning up his face gave him a searching look. "How old are you?"

"Seventeen."

"There's not much of you for seventeen. Are you
hungry?"

"A little."

"Will you come with me, in that brig there?"

The boy moved without a word towards the boat and
scrambled into the bows.

"Knows his place,"* muttered Lingard to himself as
he stepped heavily into the stern sheets and took up
the yoke lines. "Give way there."

The Malay boat crew lay back together, and the gig
sprang away from the quay heading towards the brig's
riding light.

Such was the beginning of Willems' career.

Lingard learned in half an hour all that there was
of Willems' commonplace story. Father outdoor clerk
of some ship-broker in Rotterdam; mother dead. The
boy quick in learning, but idle in school. The strait-
ened circumstances in the house filled with small
brothers and sisters, sufficiently clothed and fed but
otherwise running wild, while the disconsolate widower
tramped about all day in a shabby overcoat and imperfect boots on the muddy quays, and in the evening
piloted wearily the half-intoxicated foreign skippers
amongst the places of cheap delights, returning home
late, sick with too much smoking and drinking—for
company's sake—with these men, who expected such
attentions in the way of business. Then the offer of
the good-natured captain of *Kosmopoliet IV.*, who was
pleased to do something for the patient and obliging

fellow; young Willems' great joy, his still greater disappointment with the sea that looked so charming from afar, but proved so hard and exacting on closer acquaintance—and then this running away by a sudden impulse. The boy was hopelessly at variance with the spirit of the sea. He had an instinctive contempt for the honest simplicity of that work which led to nothing he cared for. Lingard soon found this out. He offered to send him home in an English ship, but the boy begged hard to be permitted to remain. He wrote a beautiful hand, became soon perfect in English, was quick at figures; and Lingard made him useful in that way. As he grew older his trading instincts developed themselves astonishingly, and Lingard left him often to trade in one island or another while he, himself, made an intermediate trip to some out-of-the-way place. On Willems expressing a wish to that effect, Lingard let him enter Hudig's service. He felt a little sore at that abandonment because he had attached himself, in a way, to his protégé. Still he was proud of him, and spoke up for him loyally. At first it was, "Smart boy that—never make a seaman though." Then when Willems was helping in the trading he referred to him as "that clever young fellow." Later when Willems became the confidential agent of Hudig, employed in many a delicate affair, the simple-hearted old seaman would point an admiring finger at his back and whisper to whoever stood near at the moment, "Long-headed* chap that; deuced long-headed chap. Look at him. Confidential man of old Hudig. I picked him up in a ditch, you may say, like a starved cat. Skin and bone. 'Pon my word I did. And now he knows more than I do about island trading. Fact. I am not joking. More than I do," he would repeat, seriously, with innocent pride in his honest eyes.

From the safe elevation of his commercial successes Willems patronized Lingard. He had a liking for his benefactor, not unmixed with some disdain for the crude directness of the old fellow's methods of conduct. There were, however, certain sides of Lingard's character for which Willems felt a qualified respect. The talkative seaman knew how to be silent on certain matters that to Willems were very interesting. Besides, Lingard was rich, and that in itself was enough to compel Willems' unwilling admiration. In his confidential chats with Hudig, Willems generally alluded to the benevolent Englishman as the "lucky old fool" in a very distinct tone of vexation; Hudig would grunt an unqualified assent, and then the two would look at each other in a sudden immobility of pupils fixed by a stare of unexpressed thought.

"You can't find out where he gets all that india-rubber; hey Willems?" Hudig would ask at last, turning away and bending over the papers on his desk.

"No, Mr. Hudig. Not yet. But I am trying," was Willems' invariable reply, delivered with a ring of regretful deprecation.

"Try! Always try! You may try! You think yourself clever perhaps," rumbled on Hudig, without looking up. "I have been trading with him twenty—thirty years now. The old fox. And I have tried. Bah!"

He stretched out a short, podgy leg and contemplated the bare instep and the grass slipper hanging by the toes. "You can't make him drunk?" he would add, after a pause of stertorous breathing.

"No, Mr. Hudig, I can't really," protested Willems, earnestly.

"Well, don't try. I know him. Don't try," advised the master, and, bending again over his desk, his staring bloodshot eyes close to the paper, he would go on tracing laboriously with his thick fingers the slim unsteady letters of his correspondence, while Willems waited respectfully for his further good pleasure before asking, with great deference—

"Any orders, Mr. Hudig?"

"Hm! yes. Go to Bun-Hin* yourself and see the dollars of that payment counted and packed, and have them put on board the mail-boat for Ternate.* She's due here this afternoon."

"Yes, Mr. Hudig."

"And, look here. If the boat is late, leave the case in Bun-Hin's godown till to-morrow. Seal it up. Eight seals as usual. Don't take it away till the boat is here."

"No, Mr. Hudig."

"And don't forget about these opium cases. It's for to-night. Use my own boatmen. Tranship them from the *Caroline** to the Arab barque," went on the master in his hoarse undertone. "And don't you come to me with another story of a case dropped overboard like last time," he added, with sudden ferocity, looking up at his confidential clerk.

"No, Mr. Hudig. I will take care."

"That's all. Tell that pig as you go out that if he doesn't make the punkah go a little better I will break every bone in his body," finished up Hudig, wiping his purple face with a red silk handkerchief nearly as big as a counterpane.

Noiselessly Willems went out, shutting carefully behind him the little green door through which he passed to the warehouse. Hudig, pen in hand, listened to him bullying the punkah boy with profane violence, born of unbounded zeal for the master's comfort, before he returned to his writing amid the rustling of papers fluttering in the wind sent down by the punkah that waved in wide sweeps above his head.

Willems would nod familiarly to Mr. Vinck, who had his desk close to the little door of the private office, and march down the warehouse with an important air. Mr. Vinck—extreme dislike lurking in every wrinkle of his gentlemanly countenance—would follow with his eyes the white figure flitting in the gloom amongst the piles of bales and cases till it passed out through the big archway into the glare of the street.

CHAPTER THREE

THE opportunity and the temptation were too much
for Willems, and under the pressure of sudden necessity
he abused that trust which was his pride, the perpetual
sign of his cleverness and a load too heavy for him to
carry. A run of bad luck at cards, the failure of a small
speculation undertaken on his own account, an unexpected demand for money from one or another member
of the Da Souza family—and almost before he was well
aware of it he was off the path of his peculiar honesty.
It was such a faint and ill-defined track that it took him
some time to find out how far he had strayed amongst
the brambles of the dangerous wilderness he had been
skirting for so many years, without any other guide than
his own convenience and that doctrine of success which
he had found for himself in the book of life—in those
interesting chapters that the Devil has been permitted
to write in it, to test the sharpness of men's eyesight
and the steadfastness of their hearts. For one short,
dark and solitary moment he was dismayed, but he had
that courage that will not scale heights, yet will wade
bravely through the mud—if there be no other road.
He applied himself to the task of restitution, and devoted himself to the duty of not being found out. On
his thirtieth birthday he had almost accomplished the
task—and the duty had been faithfully and cleverly
performed. He saw himself safe. Again he could look
hopefully towards the goal of his legitimate ambition.
Nobody would dare to suspect him, and in a few days
there would be nothing to suspect. He was elated.

He did not know that his prosperity had touched then its high-water mark, and that the tide was already on the turn.

Two days afterwards he knew. Mr. Vinck, hearing the rattle of the door-handle, jumped up from his desk—where he had been tremulously listening to the loud voices in the private office—and buried his face in the big safe with nervous haste. For the last time Willems passed through the little green door leading to Hudig's sanctum, which, during the past half-hour, might have been taken—from the fiendish noise within—for the cavern of some wild beast. Willems' troubled eyes took in the quick impression of men and things as he came out from the place of his humiliation. He saw the scared expression of the punkah boy; the Chinamen tellers sitting on their heels with unmovable faces turned up blankly towards him while their arrested hands hovered over the little piles of bright guilders ranged on the floor; Mr. Vinck's shoulder-blades with the fleshy rims of two red ears above. He saw the long avenue of gin cases stretching from where he stood to the arched doorway beyond which he would be able to breathe perhaps. A thin rope's end lay across his path and he saw it distinctly, yet stumbled heavily over it as if it had been a bar of iron. Then he found himself in the street at last, but could not find air enough to fill his lungs. He walked towards his home, gasping.

As the sound of Hudig's insults that lingered in his ears grew fainter by the lapse of time, the feeling of shame was replaced slowly by a passion of anger against himself and still more against the stupid concourse of circumstances that had driven him into his idiotic indiscretion. Idiotic indiscretion; that is how he defined his guilt to himself. Could there be anything worse from the point of view of his undeniable cleverness?

What a fatal aberration of an acute mind! He did not recognize himself there. He must have been mad. That's it. A sudden gust of madness. And now the work of long years was destroyed utterly. What would become of him?

Before he could answer that question he found himself in the garden before his house, Hudig's wedding gift. He looked at it with a vague surprise to find it there. His past was so utterly gone from him that the dwelling which belonged to it appeared to him incongruous standing there intact, neat, and cheerful in the sunshine of the hot afternoon. The house was a pretty little structure all doors and windows, surrounded on all sides by the deep verandah supported on slender columns clothed in the green foliage of creepers, which also fringed the overhanging eaves of the high-pitched roof. Slowly, Willems mounted the dozen steps that led to the verandah. He paused at every step. He must tell his wife. He felt frightened at the prospect, and his alarm dismayed him. Frightened to face her! Nothing could give him a better measure of the greatness of the change around him, and in him. Another man—and another life with the faith in himself gone. He could not be worth much if he was afraid to face that woman.

He dared not enter the house through the open door of the dining-room, but stood irresolute by the little work-table where trailed a white piece of calico, with a needle stuck in it, as if the work had been left hurriedly. The pink-crested cockatoo started, on his appearance, into clumsy activity and began to climb laboriously up and down his perch, calling "Joanna" with indistinct loudness and a persistent screech that prolonged the last syllable of the name as if in a peal of insane laughter. The screen in the doorway moved gently once or twice in the breeze, and each time Willems started slightly, expecting his wife, but he never lifted his eyes, although straining his ears for the sound of her footsteps. Gradually he lost himself in his thoughts, in the endless speculation as to the manner in which she would receive his news—and his orders. In this preoccupation he almost forgot the fear of her presence. No doubt she will cry, she will lament, she will be helpless and frightened and passive as ever. And he would have to drag that limp weight on and on through the darkness of a spoiled life. Horrible! Of course he could not abandon her and the child to certain misery or possible starvation. The wife and the child of Willems. Willems the successful, the smart; Willems the conf . . . . Pah! And what was Willems now? Willems the. . . . He strangled the half-born thought, and cleared his throat to stifle a groan. Ah! Won't they talk to-night in the billiard-room—his world, where he had been first—all those men to whom he had been so superciliously condescending. Won't they talk with surprise, and affected regret, and grave faces, and wise nods. Some of them owed him money, but he never pressed anybody. Not he. Willems, the prince of good fellows, they called him. And now they will rejoice, no doubt, at his downfall. A crowd of imbeciles. In his abasement he was yet aware of his superiority over those fellows, who were merely honest or simply not found out yet. A crowd of imbeciles! He shook his fist at the evoked image of his friends, and the startled parrot fluttered its wings and shrieked in desperate fright.

In a short glance upwards Willems saw his wife come round the corner of the house. He lowered his eyelids quickly, and waited silently till she came near and stood on the other side of the little table. He would not look

at her face, but he could see the red dressing-gown he
knew so well. She trailed through life in that red
dressing-gown, with its row of dirty blue bows down
the front, stained, and hooked on awry; a torn flounce
at the bottom following her like a snake as she moved
languidly about, with her hair negligently caught up,
and a tangled wisp straggling untidily down her back.
His gaze travelled upwards from bow to bow, noticing
those that hung only by a thread, but it did not go beyond her chin. He looked at her lean throat, at the
obtrusive collarbone visible in the disarray of the upper
part of her attire. He saw the thin arm and the bony
hand clasping the child she carried, and he felt an immense distaste for those encumbrances of his life. He
waited for her to say something, but as he felt her eyes
rest on him in unbroken silence he sighed and began to
speak.

It was a hard task. He spoke slowly, lingering
amongst the memories of this early life in his reluctance
to confess that this was the end of it and the beginning
of a less splendid existence. In his conviction of having
made her happiness in the full satisfaction of all material
wants he never doubted for a moment that she was
ready to keep him company on no matter how hard
and stony a road. He was not elated by this certitude.
He had married her to please Hudig, and the greatness
of his sacrifice ought to have made her happy without
any further exertion on his part. She had years of
glory as Willems' wife, and years of comfort, of loyal
care, and of such tenderness as she deserved. He had
guarded her carefully from any bodily hurt; and of any
other suffering he had no conception. The assertion of
his superiority was only another benefit conferred on
her. All this was a matter of course, but he told her all
this so as to bring vividly before her the greatness of her

loss. She was so dull of understanding that she would not grasp it else. And now it was at an end. They would have to go. Leave this house, leave this island, go far away where he was unknown. To the English Strait-Settlements*perhaps. He would find an opening there for his abilities—and juster men to deal with than old Hudig. He laughed bitterly.

"You have the money I left at home this morning, Joanna?" he asked. "We will want it all now."

As he spoke those words he thought he was a fine fellow. Nothing new that. Still, he surpassed there his own expectations. Hang it all, there are sacred things in life, after all. The marriage tie was one of them, and he was not the man to break it. The solidity of his principles caused him great satisfaction, but he did not care to look at his wife, for all that. He waited for her to speak. Then he would have to console her; tell her not to be a crying fool; to get ready to go. Go where? How? When? He shook his head. They must leave at once; that was the principal thing. He felt a sudden need to hurry up his departure.

"Well, Joanna," he said, a little impatiently— "don't stand there in a trance. Do you hear? We must. . . ."

He looked up at his wife, and whatever he was going to add remained unspoken. She was staring at him with her big, slanting eyes, that seemed to him twice their natural size. The child, its dirty little face pressed to its mother's shoulder, was sleeping peacefully. The deep silence of the house was not broken, but rather accentuated, by the low mutter of the cockatoo, now very still on its perch. As Willems was looking at Joanna her upper lip was drawn up on one side, giving to her melancholy face a vicious expression altogether new to his experience. He stepped back in his surprise.

"Oh! You great man!" she said distinctly, but in a voice that was hardly above a whisper.

Those words, and still more her tone, stunned him as if somebody had fired a gun close to his ear. He stared back at her stupidly.

"Oh! You great man!" she repeated slowly, glancing right and left as if meditating a sudden escape. "And you think that I am going to starve with you. You are nobody now. You think my mamma and Leonard would let me go away? And with you! With you," she repeated scornfully, raising her voice, which woke up the child and caused it to whimper feebly.

"Joanna!" exclaimed Willems.

"Do not speak to me. I have heard what I have waited for all these years. You are less than dirt, you that have wiped your feet on me. I have waited for this. I am not afraid now. I do not want you; do not come near me. Ah—h!" she screamed shrilly, as he held out his hand in an entreating gesture— "Ah! Keep off me! Keep off me! Keep off!"

She backed away, looking at him with eyes both angry and frightened. Willems stared motionless, in dumb amazement at the mystery of anger and revolt in the head of his wife. Why? What had he ever done to her? This was the day of injustice indeed. First Hudig —and now his wife. He felt a terror at this hate that had lived stealthily so near him for years. He tried to speak, but she shrieked again, and it was like a needle through his heart. Again he raised his hand.

"Help!" called Mrs. Willems, in a piercing voice. "Help!"

"Be quiet! You fool!" shouted Willems, trying to drown the noise of his wife and child in his own angry accents and rattling violently the little zinc table in his exasperation.

From under the house, where there were bathrooms and a tool closet, appeared Leonard, a rusty iron bar in his hand. He called threateningly from the bottom of the stairs.

"Do not hurt her, Mr. Willems. You are a savage. Not at all like we, whites."*

"You too!" said the bewildered Willems. "I haven't touched her. Is this a madhouse?" He moved towards the stairs, and Leonard dropped the bar with a clang and made for the gate of the compound. Willems turned back to his wife.

"So you expected this," he said. "It is a conspiracy. Who's that sobbing and groaning in the room? Some more of your precious family. Hey?"

She was more calm now, and putting hastily the crying child in the big chair walked towards him with sudden fearlessness.

"My mother," she said, "my mother who came to defend me from you—man from nowhere; a vagabond!"

"You did not call me a vagabond when you hung round my neck—before we were married," said Willems, contemptuously.

"You took good care that I should not hang round your neck after we were," she answered, clenching her hands, and putting her face close to his. "You boasted while I suffered and said nothing. What has become of your greatness; of our greatness—you were always speaking about? Now I am going to live on the charity of your master. Yes. That is true. He sent Leonard to tell me so. And you will go and boast somewhere else, and starve. So! Ah! I can breathe now! This house is mine."

"Enough!" said Willems, slowly, with an arresting gesture.

She leaped back, the fright again in her eyes, snatched up the child, pressed it to her breast, and, falling into a chair, drummed insanely with her heels on the resounding floor of the verandah.

"I shall go," said Willems, steadily. "I thank you. For the first time in your life you make me happy. You were a stone round my neck; you understand. I did not mean to tell you that as long as you lived, but you made me—now. Before I pass this gate you shall be gone from my mind. You made it very easy. I thank you."

He turned and went down the steps without giving her a glance, while she sat upright and quiet, with wide-open eyes, the child crying querulously in her arms. At the gate he came suddenly upon Leonard, who had been dodging about there and failed to get out of the way in time.

"Do not be brutal, Mr. Willems," said Leonard, hurriedly. "It is unbecoming between white men with all those natives looking on." Leonard's legs trembled very much, and his voice wavered between high and low tones without any attempt at control on his part. "Restrain your improper violence," he went on mumbling rapidly. "I am a respectable man of very good family, while you . . . . it is regrettable . . . they all say so . . . ."

"What?" thundered Willems. He felt a sudden impulse of mad anger, and before he knew what had happened he was looking at Leonard da Souza rolling in the dust at his feet. He stepped over his prostrate brother-in-law and tore blindly down the street, everybody making way for the frantic white man.

When he came to himself he was beyond the outskirts of the town, stumbling on the hard and cracked earth of reaped rice fields. How did he get there?

It was dark. He must get back. As he walked towards
the town slowly, his mind reviewed the events of the
day and he felt a sense of bitter loneliness. His wife
had turned him out of his own house. He had as-
saulted brutally his brother-in-law, a member of the
Da Souza family—of that band of his worshippers.
He did. Well, no! It was some other man. Another
man was coming back. A man without a past, without a future, yet full of pain and shame and anger. He
stopped and looked round. A dog or two glided across
the empty street and rushed past him with a frightened snarl. He was now in the midst of the Malay
quarter whose bamboo houses, hidden in the verdure
of their little gardens, were dark and silent. Men,
women and children slept in there. Human beings.
Would he ever sleep, and where? He felt as if he was
the outcast of all mankind, and as he looked hopelessly
round, before resuming his weary march, it seemed to
him that the world was bigger, the night more vast and
more black; but he went on doggedly with his head down
as if pushing his way through some thick brambles.
Then suddenly he felt planks under his feet and, looking up, saw the red light at the end of the jetty. He
walked quite to the end and stood leaning against the
post, under the lamp, looking at the roadstead where
two vessels at anchor swayed their slender rigging
amongst the stars. The end of the jetty; and here in
one step more the end of life; the end of everything.
Better so. What else could he do? Nothing ever comes
back. He saw it clearly. The respect and admiration
of them all, the old habits and old affections finished
abruptly in the clear perception of the cause of his disgrace. He saw all this; and for a time he came out of
himself, out of his selfishness—out of the constant
preoccupation of his interests and his desires—out of

the temple of self and the concentration of personal thought.

His thoughts now wandered home. Standing in the tepid stillness of a starry tropical night he felt the breath of the bitter east wind, he saw the high and narrow fronts of tall houses under the gloom of a clouded sky; and on muddy quays he saw the shabby, high-shouldered figure—the patient, faded face of the weary man earning bread for the children that waited for him in a dingy home. It was miserable, miserable. But it would never come back. What was there in common between those things and Willems the clever, Willems the successful. He had cut himself adrift from that home many years ago. Better for him then. Better for them now. All this was gone, never to come back again; and suddenly he shivered, seeing himself alone in the presence of unknown and terrible dangers.

For the first time in his life he felt afraid of the future, because he had lost his faith, the faith in his own success. And he had destroyed it foolishly with his own hands!

CHAPTER FOUR

His meditation which resembled slow drifting into suicide was interrupted by Lingard, who, with a loud "I've got you at last!" dropped his hand heavily on Willems' shoulder. This time it was the old seaman himself going out of his way to pick up the uninteresting waif—all that there was left of that sudden and sordid shipwreck. To Willems, the rough, friendly voice was a quick and fleeting relief followed by a sharper pang of anger and unavailing regret. That voice carried him back to the beginning of his promising career, the end of which was very visible now from the jetty where they both stood. He shook himself free from the friendly grasp, saying with ready bitterness—

"It's all your fault. Give me a push now, do, and send me over. I have been standing here waiting for help. You are the man—of all men. You helped at the beginning; you ought to have a hand in the end."

"I have better use for you than to throw you to the fishes," said Lingard, seriously, taking Willems by the arm and forcing him gently to walk up the jetty. "I have been buzzing over this town like a bluebottle fly, looking for you high and low. I have heard a lot. I will tell you what, Willems; you are no saint, that's a fact. And you have not been over-wise either. I am not throwing stones," he added, hastily, as Willems made an effort to get away, "but I am not going to mince matters. Never could! You keep quiet while I talk. Can't you?"

With a gesture of resignation and a half-stifled groan

Willems submitted to the stronger will, and the two men paced slowly up and down the resounding planks, while Lingard disclosed to Willems the exact manner of his undoing. After the first shock Willems lost the faculty of surprise in the overpowering feeling of indignation. So it was Vinck and Leonard who had served him so. They had watched him, tracked his misdeeds, reported them to Hudig. They had bribed obscure Chinamen, wormed out confidences from tipsy skippers, got at various boatmen, and had pieced out in that way the story of his irregularities. The blackness of this dark intrigue filled him with horror. He could understand Vinck. There was no love lost between them. But Leonard! Leonard!

"Why, Captain Lingard," he burst out, "the fellow licked my boots."

"Yes, yes, yes," said Lingard, testily, "we know that, and you did your best to cram your boot down his throat. No man likes that, my boy."

"I was always giving money to all that hungry lot," went on Willems, passionately. "Always my hand in my pocket. They never had to ask twice."

"Just so. Your generosity frightened them. They asked themselves where all that came from, and concluded that it was safer to throw you overboard. After all, Hudig is a much greater man than you, my friend, and they have a claim on him also."

"What do you mean, Captain Lingard?"

"What do I mean?" repeated Lingard, slowly. "Why, you are not going to make me believe you did not know your wife was Hudig's daughter. Come now!"

Willems stopped suddenly and swayed about.

"Ah! I understand," he gasped. "I never heard . . . Lately I thought there was . . . But no, I never guessed."

"Oh, you simpleton!" said Lingard, pityingly.
"'Pon my word," he muttered to himself, "I don't
believe the fellow knew. Well! well! Steady now.
Pull yourself together. What's wrong there. She is
a good wife to you."

"Excellent wife," said Willems, in a dreary voice,
looking far over the black and scintillating water.

"Very well then," went on Lingard, with increasing
friendliness. "Nothing wrong there. But did you
really think that Hudig was marrying you off and giving
you a house and I don't know what, out of love for
you?"

"I had served him well," answered Willems. "How
well, you know yourself—through thick and thin. No
matter what work and what risk, I was always there;
always ready."

How well he saw the greatness of his work and
the immensity of that injustice which was his reward.
She was that man's daughter! In the light of this
disclosure the facts of the last five years of his life
stood clearly revealed in their full meaning. He had
spoken first to Joanna at the gate of their dwelling as
he went to his work in the brilliant flush of the early
morning, when women and flowers are charming even
to the dullest eyes. A most respectable family—two
women and a young man—were his next-door neigh-
bours. Nobody ever came to their little house but the
priest, a native from the Spanish islands, now and then.
The young man Leonard he had met in town, and was
flattered by the little fellow's immense respect for the
great Willems. He let him bring chairs, call the waiters,
chalk his cues when playing billiards, express his
admiration in choice words. He even condescended
to listen patiently to Leonard's allusions to "our
beloved father," a man of official position, a govern-

ment agent in Koti, where he died of cholera, alas! a victim to duty, like a good Catholic, and a good man. It sounded very respectable, and Willems approved of those feeling references. Moreover, he prided himself upon having no colour-prejudices and no racial antipathies. He consented to drink curaçoa* one afternoon on the verandah of Mrs. da Souza's house. He remembered Joanna that day, swinging in a hammock. She was untidy even then, he remembered, and that was the only impression he carried away from that visit. He had no time for love in those glorious days, no time even for a passing fancy, but gradually he fell into the habit of calling almost every day at that little house where he was greeted by Mrs. da Souza's shrill voice screaming for Joanna to come and entertain the gentleman from Hudig & Co. And then the sudden and unexpected visit of the priest. He remembered the man's flat, yellow face, his thin legs, his propitiatory smile, his beaming black eyes, his conciliating manner, his veiled hints which he did not understand at the time. How he wondered what the man wanted, and how unceremoniously he got rid of him. And then came vividly into his recollection the morning when he met again that fellow coming out of Hudig's office, and how he was amused at the incongruous visit. And that morning with Hudig! Would he ever forget it? Would he ever forget his surprise as the master, instead of plunging at once into business, looked at him thoughtfully before turning, with a furtive smile, to the papers on the desk? He could hear him now, his nose in the paper before him, dropping astonishing words in the intervals of wheezy breathing.

"Heard said . . . called there often . . . most respectable ladies . . . knew the father very well . . . estimable . . . best thing for a

young man . . . settle down. . . . Person-
ally, very glad to hear . . . thing arranged. . .
. Suitable recognition of valuable services. . . .
Best thing—best thing to do."

And he believed! What credulity! What an ass!
Hudig knew the father! Rather. And so did everybody else probably; all except himself. How proud
he had been of Hudig's benevolent interest in his fate!
How proud he was when invited by Hudig to stay with
him at his little house in the country—where he could
meet men, men of official position—as a friend. Vinck
had been green with envy. Oh, yes! He had believed
in the best thing, and took the girl like a gift of fortune.
How he boasted to Hudig of being free from prejudices.
The old scoundrel must have been laughing in his sleeve
at his fool of a confidential clerk. He took the girl,
guessing nothing. How could he? There had been a
father of some kind to the common knowledge. Men
knew him; spoke about him. A lank man of hopelessly
mixed descent, but otherwise—apparently—unobjec-
tionable. The shady relations came out afterwards,
but—with his freedom from prejudices—he did not mind
them, because, with their humble dependence, they
completed his triumphant life. Taken in! taken in!
Hudig had found an easy way to provide for the begging
crowd. He had shifted the burden of his youthful
vagaries on to the shoulders of his confidential clerk;
and while he worked for the master, the master had
cheated him; had stolen his very self from him. He
was married. He belonged to that woman, no matter
what she might do! . . . Had sworn . . . for
all life! . . . Thrown himself away. . . . And
that man dared this very morning call him a thief!
Damnation!

"Let go, Lingard!" he shouted, trying to get away

by a sudden jerk from the watchful old seaman. "Let me go and kill that . . ."

"No you don't!" panted Lingard, hanging on manfully. "You want to kill, do you? You lunatic. Ah!—I've got you now! Be quiet, I say!"

They struggled violently, Lingard forcing Willems slowly towards the guard-rail. Under their feet the jetty sounded like a drum in the quiet night. On the shore end the native caretaker of the wharf watched the combat, squatting behind the safe shelter of some big cases. The next day he informed his friends, with calm satisfaction, that two drunken white men had fought on the jetty. It had been a great fight. They fought without arms, like wild beasts, after the manner of white men. No! nobody was killed, or there would have been trouble and a report to make. How could he know why they fought? White men have no reason when they are like that.

Just as Lingard was beginning to fear that he would be unable to restrain much longer the violence of the younger man, he felt Willems' muscles relaxing, and took advantage of this opportunity to pin him, by a last effort, to the rail. They both panted heavily, speechless, their faces very close.

"All right," muttered Willems at last. "Don't break my back over this infernal rail. I will be quiet."

"Now you are reasonable," said Lingard, much relieved. "What made you fly into that passion?" he asked, leading him back to the end of the jetty, and, still holding him prudently with one hand, he fumbled with the other for his whistle and blew a shrill and prolonged blast. Over the smooth water of the roadstead came in answer a faint cry from one of the ships at anchor.

"My boat will be here directly," said Lingard.

"Think of what you are going to do. I sail to-night."

"What is there for me to do, except one thing?" said Willems, gloomily.

"Look here," said Lingard; "I picked you up as a boy, and consider myself responsible for you in a way. You took your life into your own hands many years ago—but still . . ."

He paused, listening, till he heard the regular grind of the oars in the rowlocks of the approaching boat then went on again.

"I have made it all right with Hudig. You owe him nothing now. Go back to your wife. She is a good woman. Go back to her."

"Why, Captain Lingard," exclaimed Willems, "she . . ."

"It was most affecting," went on Lingard, without heeding him. "I went to your house to look for you and there I saw her despair. It was heart-breaking. She called for you; she entreated me to find you. She spoke wildly, poor woman, as if all this was her fault."

Willems listened amazed. The blind old idiot! How queerly he misunderstood! But if it was true, if it was even true, the very idea of seeing her filled his soul with intense loathing. He did not break his oath, but he would not go back to her. Let hers be the sin of that separation; of the sacred bond broken. He revelled in the extreme purity of his heart, and he would not go back to her. Let her come back to him. He had the comfortable conviction that he would never see her again, and that through her own fault only. In this conviction he told himself solemnly that if she would come to him he would receive her with generous forgiveness, because such was the praiseworthy solidity of his principles. But he hesitated whether he would or would not disclose to Lingard the revolting completeness of his humiliation. Turned out of his house—and by his wife; that woman who hardly dared to breathe in his presence, yesterday. He remained perplexed and silent. No. He lacked the courage to tell the ignoble story.

As the boat of the brig appeared suddenly on the black water close to the jetty, Lingard broke the painful silence.

"I always thought," he said, sadly, "I always thought you were somewhat heartless, Willems, and apt to cast adrift those that thought most of you. I appeal to what is best in you; do not abandon that woman."

"I have not abandoned her," answered Willems, quickly, with conscious truthfulness. "Why should I? As you so justly observed, she has been a good wife to me. A very good, quiet, obedient, loving wife, and I love her as much as she loves me. Every bit. But as to going back now, to that place where I . . . To walk again amongst those men who yesterday were ready to crawl before me, and then feel on my back the sting of their pitying or satisfied smiles—no! I can't. I would rather hide from them at the bottom of the sea," he went on, with resolute energy. "I don't think, Captain Lingard," he added, more quietly, "I don't think that you realize what my position was there."

In a wide sweep of his hand he took in the sleeping shore from north to south, as if wishing it a proud and threatening good-bye. For a short moment he forgot his downfall in the recollection of his brilliant triumphs. Amongst the men of his class and occupation who slept in those dark houses he had been indeed the first.

"It is hard," muttered Lingard, pensively. "But whose the fault? Whose the fault?"

"Captain Lingard!" cried Willems, under the sudden

impulse of a felicitous inspiration, "if you leave me here on this jetty—it's murder. I shall never return to that place alive, wife or no wife. You may just as well cut my throat at once."

The old seaman started.

"Don't try to frighten me, Willems," he said, with great severity, and paused.

Above the accents of Willems' brazen despair he heard, with considerable uneasiness, the whisper of his own absurd conscience. He meditated for awhile with an irresolute air.

"I could tell you to go and drown yourself, and be damned to you," he said, with an unsuccessful assumption of brutality in his manner, "but I won't. We are responsible for one another—worse luck. I am almost ashamed of myself, but I can understand your dirty pride. I can! By . . ."

He broke off with a loud sigh and walked briskly to the steps, at the bottom of which lay his boat, rising and falling gently on the slight and invisible swell.

"Below there! Got a lamp in the boat? Well, light it and bring it up, one of you. Hurry now!"

He tore out a page of his pocketbook, moistened his pencil with great energy and waited, stamping his feet impatiently.

"I will see this thing through," he muttered to himself. "And I will have it all square and ship-shape; see if I don't! Are you going to bring that lamp, you son of a crippled mud-turtle? I am waiting."

The gleam of the light on the paper placated his professional anger, and he wrote rapidly, the final dash of his signature curling the paper up in a triangular tear.

"Take that to this white Tuan's house. I will send the boat back for you in half an hour."

The coxswain raised his lamp deliberately to Willems' face.

"This Tuan? Tau! I know."

"Quick then!" said Lingard, taking the lamp from him—and the man went off at a run.

"Kassi mem! To the lady herself," called Lingard after him.

Then, when the man disappeared, he turned to Willems.

"I have written to your wife," he said. "If you do not return for good, you do not go back to that house only for another parting. You must come as you stand. I won't have that poor woman tormented. I will see to it that you are not separated for long. Trust me!"

Willems shivered, then smiled in the darkness.

"No fear of that," he muttered, enigmatically. "I trust you implicitly, Captain Lingard," he added, in a louder tone.

Lingard led the way down the steps, swinging the lamp and speaking over his shoulder.

"It is the second time, Willems, I take you in hand. Mind it is the last. The second time; and the only difference between then and now is that you were barefooted then and have boots now. In fourteen years. With all your smartness! A poor result that. A very poor result."

He stood for awhile on the lowest platform of the steps, the light of the lamp falling on the upturned face of the stroke oar, who held the gunwale of the boat close alongside, ready for the captain to step in.

"You see," he went on, argumentatively, fumbling about the top of the lamp, "you got yourself so crooked amongst those 'longshore quill-drivers that you could not run clear in any way. That's what comes of such talk as yours, and of such a life. A man sees so much falsehood that he begins to lie to himself. Pah!" he said, in disgust, "there's only one place for an honest man. The sea, my boy, the sea! But you never would; didn't think there was enough money in it; and now— look!"

He blew the light out, and, stepping into the boat, stretched quickly his hand towards Willems, with friendly care. Willems sat by him in silence, and the boat shoved off, sweeping in a wide circle towards the brig.

"Your compassion is all for my wife, Captain Lingard," said Willems, moodily. "Do you think I am so very happy?"

"No! no!" said Lingard, heartily. "Not a word more shall pass my lips. I had to speak my mind once, seeing that I knew you from a child, so to speak. And now I shall forget; but you are young yet. Life is very long,"*he went on, with unconscious sadness; "let this be a lesson to you."

He laid his hand affectionately on Willems' shoulder, and they both sat silent till the boat came alongside the ship's ladder.

When on board Lingard gave orders to his mate, and leading Willems on the poop, sat on the breech of one of the brass six-pounders with which his vessel was armed. The boat went off again to bring back the messenger. As soon as it was seen returning dark forms appeared on the brig's spars; then the sails fell in festoons with a swish of their heavy folds, and hung motionless under the yards in the dead calm of the clear and dewy night. From the forward end came the clink of the windlass, and soon afterwards the hail of the chief mate informing Lingard that the cable was hove short.

"Hold on everything," hailed back Lingard; "we

must wait for the land-breeze before we let go our hold
of the ground."

He approached Willems, who sat on the skylight,
his body bent down, his head low, and his hands hanging listlessly between his knees.

"I am going to take you to Sambir," he said.
"You've never heard of the place, have you?   Well, it's
up that river of mine about which people talk so much
and know so little.   I've found out the entrance for a ship
of *Flash*'s size.   It isn't easy.   You'll see.   I will show
you.   You have been at sea long enough to take an
interest. . . .   Pity you didn't stick to it.   Well,
I am going there.   I have my own trading post in the
place.   Almayer is my partner.   You knew him when
he was at Hudig's.   Oh, he lives there as happy as a
king.   D'ye see, I have them all in my pocket.   The
rajah is an old friend of mine.   My word is law—and I
am the only trader.   No other white man but Almayer
had ever been in that settlement.   You will live quietly
there till I come back from my next cruise to the westward.   We shall see then what can be done for you.
Never fear.   I have no doubt my secret will be safe
with you.   Keep mum about my river when you get
amongst the traders again.   There's many would give
their ears for the knowledge of it.   I'll tell you something: that's where I get all my guttah and rattans.*
Simply inexhaustible, my boy."

While Lingard spoke Willems looked up quickly,
but soon his head fell on his breast in the discouraging
certitude that the knowledge he and Hudig had wished
for so much had come to him too late.   He sat in a
listless attitude.

"You will help Almayer in his trading if you have a
heart for it," continued Lingard, "just to kill time till I
come back for you.   Only six weeks or so."

Over their heads the damp sails fluttered noisily in
the first faint puff of the breeze; then, as the airs fresh-
ened, the brig tended to the wind, and the silenced
canvas lay quietly aback. The mate spoke with low
distinctness from the shadows of the quarter-deck.

"There's the breeze. Which way do you want to
cast her, Captain Lingard?"

Lingard's eyes, that had been fixed aloft, glanced
down at the dejected figure of the man sitting on the
skylight. He seemed to hesitate for a minute.

"To the northward, to the northward," he answered,
testily, as if annoyed at his own fleeting thought, "and
bear a hand there. Every puff of wind is worth money
in these seas."

He remained motionless, listening to the rattle of
blocks and the creaking of trusses as the head-yards
were hauled round. Sail was made on the ship and
the windlass manned again while he stood still, lost in
thought. He only roused himself when a barefooted
seacannie glided past him silently on his way to the
wheel.

"Put the helm aport! Hard over!" he said, in his
harsh sea-voice, to the man whose face appeared suddenly out of the darkness in the circle of light thrown
upwards from the binnacle lamps.

The anchor was secured, the yards trimmed, and the
brig began to move out of the roadstead. The sea
woke up under the push of the sharp cutwater, and whispered softly to the gliding craft in that tender and rip-
pling murmur in which it speaks sometimes to those it
nurses and loves. Lingard stood by the taffrail listening, with a pleased smile till the *Flash* began to draw
close to the only other vessel in the anchorage.

"Here, Willems," he said, calling him to his side,
"d'ye see that barque here? That's an Arab vessel.

White men have mostly given up the game, but this
fellow drops in my wake often, and lives in hopes of
cutting me out in that settlement. Not while I live,
I trust. You see, Willems, I brought prosperity to
that place. I composed their quarrels, and saw them
grow under my eyes. There's peace and happiness
there. I am more master there than his Dutch Excellency*down in Batavia ever will be when some day a
lazy man-of-war blunders at last against the river.
I mean to keep the Arabs out of it, with their lies and
their intrigues. I shall keep the venomous breed out,
if it costs me my fortune."

The *Flash* drew quietly abreast of the barque, and
was beginning to drop it astern when a white figure
started up on the poop of the Arab vessel, and a voice
called out—

"Greeting to the Rajah Laut!"

"To you greeting!" answered Lingard, after a moment of hesitating surprise. Then he turned to Willems with a grim smile. "That's Abdulla's voice,"
he said. "Mighty civil all of a sudden, isn't he? I
wonder what it means. Just like his impudence! No
matter! His civility or his impudence are all one to
me. I know that this fellow will be under way and
after me like a shot. I don't care! I have the heels of
anything that floats in these seas," he added, while his
proud and loving glance ran over and rested fondly
amongst the brig's lofty and graceful spars.

CHAPTER FIVE

"It was the writing on his forehead," said Babalatchi,* adding a couple of small sticks to the little fire
by which he was squatting, and without looking at
Lakamba who lay down supported on his elbow on
the other side of the embers. "It was written when he
was born that he should end his life in darkness, and
now he is like a man walking in a black night—with
his eyes open, yet seeing not. I knew him well when
he had slaves, and many wives, and much merchandise,
and trading praus, and praus for fighting. Haï—ya!
He was a great fighter in the days before the breath of
the Merciful*put out the light in his eyes. He was a
pilgrim, and had many virtues: he was brave, his hand
was open, and he was a great robber. For many years
he led the men that drank blood on the sea: first in
prayer and first in fight! Have I not stood behind him
when his face was turned to the West? Have I not
watched by his side ships with high masts burning in a
straight flame on the calm water? Have I not followed him on dark nights amongst sleeping men that
woke up only to die? His sword was swifter than the
fire from Heaven, and struck before it flashed. Haï!
Tuan! Those were the days and that was a leader,
and I myself was younger; and in those days there were
not so many fireships with guns that deal fiery death
from afar. Over the hill and over the forest—O!
Tuan Lakamba! they dropped whistling fireballs into
the creek where our praus took refuge, and where they
dared not follow men who had arms in their hands."

He shook his head with mournful regret and threw another handful of fuel on the fire. The burst of clear flame lit up his broad, dark, and pock-marked face, where the big lips, stained with betel-juice, looked like a deep and bleeding gash of a fresh wound. The reflection of the firelight gleamed brightly in his solitary eye, lending it for a moment a fierce animation that died out together with the short-lived flame. With quick touches of his bare hands he raked the embers into a heap, then, wiping the warm ash on his waistcloth—his only garment—he clasped his thin legs with his entwined fingers, and rested his chin on his drawn-up knees. Lakamba stirred slightly without changing his position or taking his eyes off the glowing coals, on which they had been fixed in dreamy immobility.

"Yes," went on Babalatchi, in a low monotone, as if pursuing aloud a train of thought that had its beginning in the silent contemplation of the unstable nature of earthly greatness—"yes. He has been rich and strong, and now he lives on alms: old, feeble, blind, and without companions, but for his daughter. The Rajah Patalolo gives him rice, and the pale woman—his daughter—cooks it for him, for he has no slave."

"I saw her from afar," muttered Lakamba, disparagingly. "A she-dog with white teeth,* like a woman of the Orang Putih."

"Right, right," assented Babalatchi; "but you have not seen her near. Her mother was a woman from the west; a Baghdadi* woman with veiled face. Now she goes uncovered, like our women do, for she is poor and he is blind, and nobody ever comes near them unless to ask for a charm or a blessing and depart quickly for fear of his anger and of the Rajah's hand. You have not been on that side of the river?"

"Not for a long time. If I go . . ."

"True! true!" interrupted Babalatchi, soothingly; "but I go often alone—for your good—and look—and listen. When the time comes; when we both go together towards the Rajah's campong, it will be to enter—and to remain."

Lakamba sat up and looked at Babalatchi gloomily.

"This is good talk, once, twice; when it is heard too often it becomes foolish, like the prattle of children."

"Many, many times have I seen the cloudy sky and have heard the wind of the rainy seasons," said Babalatchi, impressively.

"And where is your wisdom? It must be with the wind and the clouds of seasons past, for I do not hear it in your talk."

"Those are the words of the ungrateful!" shouted Babalatchi, with sudden exasperation. "Verily, our only refuge is with the One, the Mighty, the Redresser of . . ."

"Peace! Peace!" growled the startled Lakamba. "It is but a friend's talk."

Babalatchi subsided into his former attitude, muttering to himself. After awhile he went on again in a louder voice—

"Since the Rajah Laut left another white man here in Sambir, the daughter of the blind Omar el Badavi has spoken to other ears than mine."

"Would a white man listen to a beggar's daughter?" said Lakamba, doubtingly.

"Haï! I have seen . . ."

"And what did you see? O one-eyed one!" exclaimed Lakamba, contemptuously.

"I have seen the strange white man walking on the narrow path before the sun could dry the drops of dew on the bushes, and I have heard the whisper of his voice when he spoke through the smoke of the morning fire to that woman with big eyes and a pale skin. Woman in body, but in heart a man! She knows no fear and no shame. I have heard her voice too."

He nodded twice at Lakamba sagaciously and gave himself up to silent musing, his solitary eye fixed immovably upon the straight wall of forest on the opposite bank. Lakamba lay silent, staring vacantly. Under them Lingard's own river rippled softly amongst the piles supporting the bamboo platform of the little watch-house before which they were lying. Behind the house the ground rose in a gentle swell of a low hill cleared of the big timber, but thickly overgrown with the grass and bushes, now withered and burnt up in the long drought of the dry season. This old rice-clearing, which had been several years lying fallow, was framed on three sides by the impenetrable and tangled growth of the untouched forest, and on the fourth came down to the muddy river bank. There was not a breath of wind on the land or river, but high above, in the transparent sky, little clouds rushed past the moon, now appearing in her diffused rays with the brilliance of silver, now obscuring her face with the blackness of ebony. Far away, in the middle of the river, a fish would leap now and then with a short splash, the very loudness of which measured the profundity of the overpowering silence that swallowed up the sharp sound suddenly.

Lakamba dozed uneasily off, but the wakeful Babalatchi sat thinking deeply, sighing from time to time, and slapping himself over his naked torso incessantly in a vain endeavour to keep off an occasional and wandering mosquito that, rising as high as the platform above the swarms of the riverside, would settle with a ping of triumph on the unexpected victim.

The moon, pursuing her silent and toilsome path, attained her highest elevation, and chasing the shadow of the roof-eaves from Lakamba's face, seemed to hang arrested over their heads. Babalatchi revived the fire and woke up his companion, who sat up yawning and shivering discontentedly.

Babalatchi spoke again in a voice which was like the murmur of a brook that runs over the stones: low, monotonous, persistent; irresistible in its power to wear out and to destroy the hardest obstacles. Lakamba listened, silent but interested. They were Malay adventurers; ambitious men of that place and time; the Bohemians of their race. In the early days of the settlement, before the ruler Patalolo had shaken off his allegiance to the Sultan of Koti, Lakamba appeared in the river with two small trading vessels. He was disappointed to find already some semblance of organization amongst the settlers of various races who recognized the unobtrusive sway of old Patalolo, and he was not politic enough to conceal his disappointment. He declared himself to be a man from the east, from those parts where no white man ruled, and to be of an oppressed race, but of a princely family. And truly enough he had all the gifts of an exiled prince. He was discontented, ungrateful, turbulent; a man full of envy and ready for intrigue, with brave words and empty promises for ever on his lips. He was obstinate, but his will was made up of short impulses that never lasted long enough to carry him to the goal of his ambition. Received coldly by the suspicious Patalolo, he persisted—permission or no permission—in clearing the ground on a good spot some fourteen miles* down the river from Sambir, and built himself a house there, which he fortified by a high palisade. As he had many followers and seemed very reckless, the old Rajah did not think it prudent at the time to interfere with him by force. Once settled, he began to intrigue. The quarrel of Patalolo with the Sultan of Koti was of his fomenting, but failed to produce the result he expected because the Sultan could not back him up effectively at such a great distance. Disappointed in that scheme, he promptly organized an outbreak of the Bugis settlers, and besieged the old Rajah in his stockade with much noisy valour and a fair chance of success; but Lingard then appeared on the scene with the armed brig, and the old seaman's hairy forefinger, shaken menacingly in his face, quelled his martial ardour. No man cared to encounter the Rajah Laut, and Lakamba, with momentary resignation, subsided into a half-cultivator, half-trader, and nursed in his fortified house his wrath and his ambition, keeping it for use on a more propitious occasion. Still faithful to his character of a prince-pretender, he would not recognize the constituted authorities, answering sulkily the Rajah's messenger, who claimed the tribute for the cultivated fields, that the Rajah had better come and take it himself. By Lingard's advice he was left alone, notwithstanding his rebellious mood; and for many days he lived undisturbed amongst his wives and retainers, cherishing that persistent and causeless hope of better times, the possession of which seems to be the universal privilege of exiled greatness.

But the passing days brought no change. The hope grew faint and the hot ambition burnt itself out, leaving only a feeble and expiring spark amongst a heap of dull and tepid ashes of indolent acquiescence with the decrees of Fate, till Babalatchi fanned it again into a bright flame. Babalatchi had blundered upon the river while in search of a safe refuge for his disreputable head. He was a vagabond of the seas, a

true Orang Laut, living by rapine and plunder of coasts
and ships in his prosperous days; earning his living by
honest and irksome toil when the days of adversity
were upon him. So, although at times leading the
Sulu rovers, he had also served as Serang of country
ships,* and in that wise had visited the distant seas,
beheld the glories of Bombay,* the might of the Mascati
Sultan;* had even struggled in a pious throng for the
privilege of touching with his lips the Sacred Stone* of
the Holy City. He gathered experience and wisdom
in many lands, and after attaching himself to Omar el
Badavi, he affected great piety (as became a pilgrim),
although unable to read the inspired words of the
Prophet. He was brave and bloodthirsty without any
affection, and he hated the white men who interfered
with the manly pursuits of throat-cutting, kidnapping,
slave-dealing, and fire-raising, that were the only possible occupation for a true man of the sea. He found
favour in the eyes of his chief, the fearless Omar el
Badavi, the leader of Brunei rovers, whom he followed
with unquestioning loyalty through the long years
of successful depredation. And when that long career
of murder, robbery and violence received its first
serious check at the hands of white men, he stood faithfully by his chief, looked steadily at the bursting shells,
was undismayed by the flames of the burning strong-
hold, by the death of his companions, by the shrieks of
their women, the wailing of their children; by the sudden ruin and destruction of all that he deemed indispensable to a happy and glorious existence. The beaten
ground between the houses was slippery with blood,
and the dark mangroves of the muddy creeks were full
of sighs of the dying men who were stricken down before
they could see their enemy. They died helplessly, for
into the tangled forest there was no escape, and their

swift praus, in which they had so often scoured the
coast and the seas, now wedged together in the narrow
creek, were burning fiercely. Babalatchi, with the
clear perception of the coming end, devoted all his
energies to saving if it was but only one of them.
He succeeded in time. When the end came in the
explosion of the stored powder-barrels, he was ready
to look for his chief. He found him half dead and
totally blinded, with nobody near him but his daughter
Aïssa:—the sons had fallen earlier in the day, as
became men of their courage. Helped by the girl
with the steadfast heart, Babalatchi carried Omar on
board the light prau and succeeded in escaping, but
with very few companions only. As they hauled their
craft into the network of dark and silent creeks, they
could hear the cheering of the crews of the man-of-
war's boats dashing to the attack of the rover's village.
Aïssa, sitting on the high after-deck, her father's
blackened and bleeding head in her lap, looked up with
fearless eyes at Babalatchi. "They shall find only
smoke, blood and dead men, and women mad with fear
there, but nothing else living," she said, mournfully.
Babalatchi, pressing with his right hand the deep gash
on his shoulder, answered sadly: "They are very strong.
When we fight with them we can only die. Yet," he
added, menacingly—"some of us still live! Some of
us still live!"

For a short time he dreamed of vengeance, but his
dream was dispelled by the cold reception of the Sultan
of Sulu, with whom they sought refuge at first and who
gave them only a contemptuous and grudging hospi-
tality. While Omar, nursed by Aïssa, was recovering
from his wounds, Babalatchi attended industriously
before the exalted Presence that had extended to them
the hand of protection. For all that, when Babalatchi

spoke into the Sultan's ear certain proposals of a great
and profitable raid, that was to sweep the islands from
Ternate to Acheen, the Sultan was very angry. "I
know you, you men from the west," he exclaimed,
angrily. "Your words are poison in a Ruler's ears.
Your talk is of fire and murder and booty—but on our
heads falls the vengeance of the blood you drink.
Begone!"

There was nothing to be done. Times were changed.
So changed that, when a Spanish frigate appeared
before the island and a demand was sent to the Sultan
to deliver Omar and his companions, Babalatchi was not
surprised to hear that they were going to be made the
victims of political expediency. But from that sane
appreciation of danger to tame submission was a very
long step. And then began Omar's second flight. It
began arms in hand, for the little band had to fight in
the night on the beach for the possession of the small
canoes in which those that survived got away at last.
The story of that escape lives in the hearts of brave
men even to this day. They talk of Babalatchi and of
the strong woman who carried her blind father through
the surf under the fire of the warship from the north.
The companions of that piratical and son-less Æneas*
are dead now, but their ghosts wander over the waters
and the islands at night—after the manner of ghosts
—and haunt the fires by which sit armed men, as is
meet for the spirits of fearless warriors who died in
battle. There they may hear the story of their own
deeds, of their own courage, suffering and death, on
the lips of living men. That story is told in many
places. On the cool mats in breezy verandahs of
Rajahs' houses it is alluded to disdainfully by impassive
statesmen, but amongst armed men that throng the
courtyards it is a tale which stills the murmur of

voices and the tinkle of anklets; arrests the passage
of the siri vessel, and fixes the eyes in absorbed gaze.
They talk of the fight, of the fearless woman, of the
wise man; of long suffering on the thirsty sea in leaky
canoes; of those who died. . . . Many died. A
few survived. The chief, the woman, and another one
who became great.

There was no hint of incipient greatness in Babalatchi's unostentatious arrival in Sambir. He came
with Omar and Aïssa in a small prau loaded with green
cocoanuts, and claimed the ownership of both vessel
and cargo. How it came to pass that Babalatchi,
fleeing for his life in a small canoe, managed to end his
hazardous journey in a vessel full of a valuable com-
modity, is one of those secrets of the sea that baffle
the most searching inquiry. In truth nobody inquired
much. There were rumours of a missing trading prau
belonging to Menado, but they were vague and remained mysterious. Babalatchi told a story which—
it must be said in justice to Patalolo's knowledge of the
world—was not believed. When the Rajah ventured
to state his doubts, Babalatchi asked him in tones of
calm remonstrance whether he could reasonably suppose
that two oldish men who had only one eye amongst
them—and a young woman were likely to gain possession of anything whatever by violence? Charity was a
virtue recommended by the Prophet. There were
charitable people, and their hand was open to the de-
serving. Patalolo wagged his aged head doubtingly,
and Babalatchi withdrew with a shocked mien and put
himself forthwith under Lakamba's protection. The
two men who completed the prau's crew followed him
into that magnate's campong. The blind Omar, with
Aïssa, remained under the care of the Rajah, and the
Rajah confiscated the cargo. The prau hauled up on

the mud-bank, at the junction of the two branches of the
Pantai,* rotted in the rain, warped in the sun, fell to
pieces and gradually vanished into the smoke of household fires of the settlement. Only a forgotten plank
and a rib or two, sticking neglected in the shiny ooze
for a long time, served to remind Babalatchi during
many months that he was a stranger in the land.*

Otherwise, he felt perfectly at home in Lakamba's
establishment, where his peculiar position and influence
were quickly recognized and soon submitted to even
by the women. He had all a true vagabond's plia-
bility to circumstances and adaptiveness to momentary
surroundings. In his readiness to learn from experience that contempt for early principles so necessary
to a true statesman, he equalled the most successful
politicians of any age; and he had enough persuasiveness
and firmness of purpose to acquire a complete mastery
over Lakamba's vacillating mind—where there was
nothing stable but an all-pervading discontent. He
kept the discontent alive, he rekindled the expiring
ambition, he moderated the poor exile's not unnatural
impatience to attain a high and lucrative position. He
—the man of violence—deprecated the use of force,
for he had a clear comprehension of the difficult situation. From the same cause, he—the hater of white
men—would to some extent admit the eventual expediency of Dutch protection. But nothing should be
done in a hurry. Whatever his master Lakamba might
think, there was no use in poisoning old Patalolo, he
maintained. It could be done, of course; but what
then? As long as Lingard's influence was paramount—
as long as Almayer, Lingard's representative, was the
only great trader of the settlement, it was not worth
Lakamba's while—even if it had been possible—to grasp
the rule of the young state. Killing Almayer and Lin-

gard was so difficult and so risky that it might be dismissed as impracticable. What was wanted was an alliance; somebody to set up against the white men's influence—and somebody who, while favourable to Lakamba, would at the same time be a person of a good standing with the Dutch authorities. A rich and considered trader was wanted. Such a person once firmly established in Sambir would help them to oust the old Rajah, to remove him from power or from life if there was no other way. Then it would be time to apply to the Orang Blanda for a flag; for a recognition of their meritorious services; for that protection which would make them safe for ever! The word of a rich and loyal trader would mean something with the Ruler down in Batavia.* The first thing to do was to find such an ally and to induce him to settle in Sambir. A white trader would not do. A white man would not fall in with their ideas—would not be trustworthy. The man they wanted should be rich, unscrupulous, have many followers, and be a well-known personality in the islands. Such a man might be found amongst the Arab traders. Lingard's jealousy, said Babalatchi, kept all the traders out of the river. Some were afraid, and some did not know how to get there; others ignored the very existence of Sambir; a good many did not think it worth their while to run the risk of Lingard's enmity for the doubtful advantage of trade with a comparatively unknown settlement. The great majority were undesirable or untrustworthy. And Babalatchi mentioned regretfully the men he had known in his young days: wealthy, resolute, courageous, reckless, ready for any enterprise! But why lament the past and speak about the dead? There is one man —living—great—not far off . . .

Such was Babalatchi's line of policy laid before his

ambitious protector. Lakamba assented, his only objection being that it was very slow work. In his extreme desire to grasp dollars and power, the unintellectual exile was ready to throw himself into the arms of any wandering cut-throat whose help could be secured, and Babalatchi experienced great difficulty in restraining him from unconsidered violence. It would not do to let it be seen that they had any hand in introducing a new element into the social and political life of Sambir. There was always a possibility of failure, and in that case Lingard's vengeance would be swift and certain. No risk should be run. They must wait.

Meantime he pervaded the settlement, squatting in the course of each day by many household fires, testing the public temper and public opinion—and always talking about his impending departure. At night he would often take Lakamba's smallest canoe and depart silently to pay mysterious visits to his old chief on the other side of the river. Omar lived in odour of sanctity under the wing of Patalolo. Between the bamboo fence, enclosing the houses of the Rajah, and the wild forest, there was a banana plantation, and on its further edge stood two little houses built on low piles under a few precious fruit trees that grew on the banks of a clear brook, which, bubbling up behind the house, ran in its short and rapid course down to the big river. Along the brook a narrow path led through the dense second growth of a neglected clearing to the banana plantation and to the houses in it which the Rajah had given for residence to Omar. The Rajah was greatly impressed by Omar's ostentatious piety, by his oracular wisdom, by his many misfortunes, by the solemn fortitude with which he bore his affliction. Often the old ruler of Sambir would visit informally the blind

Arab and listen gravely to his talk during the hot hours of an afternoon. In the night, Babalatchi would call and interrupt Omar's repose, unrebuked. Aïssa, standing silently at the door of one of the huts, could see the two old friends as they sat very still by the fire in the middle of the beaten ground between the two houses, talking in an indistinct murmur far into the night. She could not hear their words, but she watched the two formless shadows curiously. Finally Babalatchi would rise and, taking her father by the wrist, would lead him back to the house, arrange his mats for him, and go out quietly. Instead of going away, Babalatchi, unconscious of Aïssa's eyes, often sat again by the fire, in a long and deep meditation. Aïssa looked with respect on that wise and brave man—she was accustomed to see at her father's side as long as she could remember —sitting alone and thoughtful in the silent night by the dying fire, his body motionless and his mind wandering in the land of memories, or—who knows?— perhaps groping for a road in the waste spaces of the uncertain future.

Babalatchi noted the arrival of Willems with alarm at this new accession to the white men's strength. Afterwards he changed his opinion. He met Willems one night on the path leading to Omar's house, and noticed later on, with only a moderate surprise, that the blind Arab did not seem to be aware of the new white man's visits to the neighbourhood of his dwelling. Once, coming unexpectedly in the daytime, Babalatchi fancied he could see the gleam of a white jacket in the bushes on the other side of the brook. That day he watched Aïssa pensively as she moved about preparing the evening rice; but after awhile he went hurriedly away before sunset, refusing Omar's hospitable invitation, in the name of Allah, to share their meal. That same evening he startled Lakamba by announcing that the time had come at last to make the first move in their long-deferred game. Lakamba asked excitedly for explanation. Babalatchi shook his head and pointed to the flitting shadows of moving women and to the vague forms of men sitting by the evening fires in the courtyard. Not a word would he speak here, he declared. But when the whole household was reposing, Babalatchi and Lakamba passed silent amongst sleeping groups to the riverside, and, taking a canoe, paddled off stealthily on their way to the dilapidated guard-hut in the old rice-clearing. There they were safe from all eyes and ears, and could account, if need be, for their excursion by the wish to kill a deer, the spot being well known as the drinking-place of all kinds of game. In the seclusion of its quiet solitude Babalatchi explained his plan to the attentive Lakamba. His idea was to make use of Willems for the destruction of Lingard's influence.

"I know the white men, Tuan," he said, in conclusion. "In many lands have I seen them; always the slaves of their desires, always ready to give up their strength and their reason into the hands of some woman. The fate of the Believers is written by the hand of the Mighty One, but they who worship many gods are thrown into the world with smooth foreheads, for any woman's hand to mark their destruction there. Let one white man destroy another. The will of the Most High is that they should be fools. They know how to keep faith with their enemies, but towards each other they know only deception. Haï! I have seen! I have seen!"

He stretched himself full length before the fire, and closed his eye in real or simulated sleep. Lakamba,

not quite convinced, sat for a long time with his gaze
riveted on the dull embers. As the night advanced,
a slight white mist rose from the river, and the declining
moon, bowed over the tops of the forest, seemed to seek
the repose of the earth, like a wayward and wandering
lover who returns at last to lay his tired and silent head
on his beloved's breast.

CHAPTER SIX

"Lend me your gun, Almayer," said Willems, across the table on which a smoky lamp shone redly above the disorder of a finished meal. "I have a mind to go and look for a deer when the moon rises to-night."

Almayer, sitting sidewise to the table, his elbow pushed amongst the dirty plates, his chin on his breast and his legs stretched stiffly out, kept his eyes steadily on the toes of his grass slippers and laughed abruptly.

"You might say yes or no instead of making that unpleasant noise," remarked Willems, with calm irritation.

"If I believed one word of what you say, I would," answered Almayer without changing his attitude and speaking slowly, with pauses, as if dropping his words on the floor. "As it is—what's the use? You know where the gun is; you may take it or leave it. Gun. Deer. Bosh! Hunt deer! Pah! It's a . . . gazelle you are after, my honoured guest. You want gold anklets and silk sarongs for that game—my mighty hunter. And you won't get those for the asking, I promise you. All day amongst the natives. A fine help you are to me."

"You shouldn't drink so much, Almayer," said Willems, disguising his fury under an affected drawl. "You have no head. Never had, as far as I can remember, in the old days in Macassar. You drink too much."

"I drink my own," retorted Almayer, lifting his head quickly and darting an angry glance at Willems.

62

Those two specimens of the superior race glared at each other savagely for a minute, then turned away their heads at the same moment as if by previous arrangement, and both got up. Almayer kicked off his slippers and scrambled into his hammock, which hung between two wooden columns of the verandah so as to catch every rare breeze of the dry season,* and Willems, after standing irresolutely by the table for a short time, walked without a word down the steps of the house and over the courtyard towards the little wooden jetty, where several small canoes and a couple of big white whale-boats were made fast, tugging at their short painters and bumping together in the swift current of the river. He jumped into the smallest canoe, balancing himself clumsily, slipped the rattan painter, and gave an unnecessary and violent shove, which nearly sent him headlong overboard. By the time he regained his balance the canoe had drifted some fifty yards down the river. He knelt in the bottom of his little craft and fought the current with long sweeps of the paddle. Almayer sat up in his hammock, grasping his feet and peering over the river with parted lips till he made out the shadowy form of man and canoe as they struggled past the jetty again.

"I thought you would go," he shouted. "Won't you take the gun? Hey?" he yelled, straining his voice. Then he fell back in his hammock and laughed to himself feebly till he fell asleep. On the river, Willems, his eyes fixed intently ahead, swept his paddle right and left, unheeding the words that reached him faintly.

It was now three months since Lingard had landed Willems in Sambir and had departed hurriedly, leaving him in Almayer's care. The two white men did not get on well together. Almayer, remembering the time

when they both served Hudig, and when the superior
Willems treated him with offensive condescension, felt
a great dislike towards his guest.   He was also jealous of
Lingard's favour.   Almayer had married a Malay girl*
whom the old seaman had adopted in one of his accesses
of unreasoning benevolence, and as the marriage was not
a happy one from a domestic point of view, he looked to
Lingard's fortune for compensation in his matrimonial
unhappiness. The appearance of that man, who seemed
to have a claim of some sort upon Lingard, filled him
with considerable uneasiness, the more so because the
old seaman did not choose to acquaint the husband of
his adopted daughter with Willems' history, or to
confide to him his intentions as to that individual's
future fate. Suspicious from the first, Almayer discouraged Willems' attempts to help him in his trading,
and then when Willems drew back, he made, with
characteristic perverseness, a grievance of his unconcern.   From cold civility in their relations, the two men
drifted into silent hostility, then into outspoken
enmity, and both wished ardently for Lingard's return
and the end of a situation that grew more intolerable
from day to day. The time dragged slowly.   Willems
watched the succeeding sunrises wondering dismally
whether before the evening some change would occur
in the deadly dullness of his life. He missed the commercial activity of that existence which seemed to him
far off, irreparably lost, buried out of sight under the
ruins of his past success—now gone from him beyond
the possibility of redemption. He mooned disconso-
lately about Almayer's courtyard, watching from afar,
with uninterested eyes, the up-country canoes dis-
charging guttah or rattans, and loading rice or European
goods on the little wharf of Lingard & Co. Big as was
the extent of ground owned by Almayer, Willems yet felt

that there was not enough room for him inside those
neat fences. The man who, during long years, became
accustomed to think of himself as indispensable to
others, felt a bitter and savage rage at the cruel consciousness of his superfluity, of his uselessness; at the
cold hostility visible in every look of the only white man
in this barbarous corner of the world. He gnashed his
teeth when he thought of the wasted days, of the life
thrown away in the unwilling company of that peevish
and suspicious fool. He heard the reproach of his idleness in the murmurs of the river, in the unceasing whisper of the great forests. Round him everything stirred,
moved, swept by in a rush; the earth under his feet
and the heavens above his head. The very savages
around him strove, struggled, fought, worked—if only
to prolong a miserable existence; but they lived, they
lived! And it was only himself that seemed to be left
outside the scheme of creation in a hopeless immobility
filled with tormenting anger and with ever-stinging
regret.

He took to wandering about the settlement. The
afterwards flourishing Sambir was born in a swamp
and passed its youth in malodorous mud. The houses
crowded the bank, and, as if to get away from the
unhealthy shore, stepped boldly into the river, shooting over it in a close row of bamboo platforms elevated
on high piles, amongst which the current below spoke
in a soft and unceasing plaint of murmuring eddies.
There was only one path in the whole town and it ran
at the back of the houses along the succession of
blackened circular patches that marked the place of
the household fires. On the other side the virgin
forest bordered the path, coming close to it, as if to
provoke impudently any passer-by to the solution of
the gloomy problem of its depths. Nobody would

accept the deceptive challenge. There were only a
few feeble attempts at a clearing here and there, but
the ground was low and the river, retiring after its
yearly floods, left on each a gradually diminishing
mudhole, where the imported buffaloes of the Bugis
settlers wallowed happily during the heat of the day.
When Willems walked on the path, the indolent men
stretched on the shady side of the houses looked at
him with calm curiosity, the women busy round the
cooking fires would send after him wondering and timid
glances, while the children would only look once, and
then run away yelling*with fright at the horrible appearance of the man with a red and white face. These
manifestations of childish disgust and fear stung Willems with a sense of absurd humiliation; he sought in
his walks the comparative solitude of the rudimentary
clearings, but the very buffaloes snorted with alarm at
his sight, scrambled lumberingly out of the cool mud
and stared wildly in a compact herd at him as he tried
to slink unperceived along the edge of the forest. One
day, at some unguarded and sudden movement of his,
the whole herd stampeded down the path, scattered the
fires, sent the women flying with shrill cries, and left
behind a track of smashed pots, trampled rice, overturned children, and a crowd of angry men brandishing
sticks in loud-voiced pursuit. The innocent cause of
that disturbance ran shamefacedly the gauntlet of
black looks and unfriendly remarks, and hastily sought
refuge in Almayer's campong. After that he left the
settlement alone.

Later, when the enforced confinement grew irksome,
Willems took one of Almayer's many canoes and crossed
the main branch of the Pantai in search of some solitary spot where he could hide his discouragement and
his weariness. He skirted in his little craft the wall of

tangled verdure, keeping in the dead water close to the bank where the spreading nipa palms nodded their broad leaves over his head as if in contemptuous pity of the wandering outcast. Here and there he could see the beginnings of chopped-out pathways, and, with the fixed idea of getting out of sight of the busy river, he would land and follow the narrow and winding path, only to find that it led nowhere, ending abruptly in the discouragement of thorny thickets. He would go back slowly, with a bitter sense of unreasonable disappointment and sadness; oppressed by the hot smell of earth, dampness, and decay in that forest which seemed to push him mercilessly back into the glittering sunshine of the river. And he would recommence paddling with tired arms to seek another opening, to find another deception.

As he paddled up to the point where the Rajah's stockade came down to the river, the nipas were left behind rattling their leaves over the brown water, and the big trees would appear on the bank, tall, strong, indifferent in the immense solidity of their life, which endures for ages, to that short and fleeting life in the heart of the man who crept painfully amongst their shadows in search of a refuge from the unceasing reproach of his thoughts. Amongst their smooth trunks a clear brook meandered for a time in twining lacets before it made up its mind to take a leap into the hurrying river, over the edge of the steep bank. There was also a pathway there and it seemed frequented. Willems landed, and following the capricious promise of the track soon found himself in a comparatively clear space, where the confused tracery of sunlight fell through the branches and the foliage overhead, and lay on the stream that shone in an easy curve like a bright sword-blade dropped amongst the long and feathery grass.

Further on, the path continued, narrowed again in the thick undergrowth. At the end of the first turning Willems saw a flash of white and colour, a gleam of gold like a sun-ray lost in shadow, and a vision of blackness darker than the deepest shade of the forest. He stopped, surprised, and fancied he had heard light footsteps —growing lighter—ceasing. He looked around. The grass on the bank of the stream trembled and a tremulous path of its shivering, silver-grey tops ran from the water to the beginning of the thicket. And yet there was not a breath of wind. Somebody had passed there. He looked pensive while the tremor died out in a quick tremble under his eyes; and the grass stood high, unstirring, with drooping heads in the warm and motionless air.

He hurried on, driven by a suddenly awakened curiosity, and entered the narrow way between the bushes. At the next turn of the path he caught again the glimpse of coloured stuff and of a woman's black hair before him. He hastened his pace and came in full view of the object of his pursuit. The woman, who was carrying two bamboo vessels full of water,* heard his footsteps, stopped, and putting the bamboos down half turned to look back. Willems also stood still for a minute, then walked steadily on with a firm tread, while the woman moved aside to let him pass. He kept his eyes fixed straight before him, yet almost unconsciously he took in every detail of the tall and graceful figure. As he approached her the woman tossed her head slightly back, and with a free gesture of her strong, round arm, caught up the mass of loose black hair and brought it over her shoulder and across the lower part of her face. The next moment he was passing her close, walking rigidly, like a man in a trance. He heard her rapid breathing and he felt the touch of a look darted at him from half-open eyes. It touched his brain and his heart together. It seemed to him to be something loud and stirring like a shout, silent and penetrating like an inspiration. The momentum of his motion carried him past her, but an invisible force made up of surprise and curiosity and desire spun him round as soon as he had passed.

She had taken up her burden already, with the intention of pursuing her path. His sudden movement arrested her at the first step, and again she stood straight, slim, expectant, with a readiness to dart away suggested in the light immobility of her pose. High above, the branches of the trees met in a transparent shimmer of waving green mist, through which the rain of yellow rays descended upon her head, streamed in glints down her black tresses, shone with the changing glow of liquid metal on her face, and lost itself in vanishing sparks in the sombre depths of her eyes that, wide open now, with enlarged pupils, looked steadily at the man in her path. And Willems stared at her, charmed with a charm that carries with it a sense of irreparable loss, tingling with that feeling which begins like a caress and ends in a blow, in that sudden hurt of a new emotion making its way into a human heart, with the brusque stirring of sleeping sensations awakening suddenly to the rush of new hopes, new fears, new desires —and to the flight of one's old self.

She moved a step forward and again halted. A breath of wind that came through the trees, but in Willems' fancy seemed to be driven by her moving figure, rippled in a hot wave round his body and scorched his face in a burning touch. He drew it in with a long breath, the last long breath of a soldier before the rush of battle, of a lover before he takes in his arms the adored woman; the breath that gives

courage to confront the menace of death or the storm
of passion.

Who was she? Where did she come from? Wonderingly he took his eyes off her face to look round at the
serried trees of the forest that stood big and still and
straight, as if watching him and her breathlessly. He
had been baffled, repelled, almost frightened by the
intensity of that tropical life which wants the sunshine
but works in gloom; which seems to be all grace of
colour and form, all brilliance, all smiles, but is only
the blossoming of the dead; whose mystery holds the
promise of joy and beauty, yet contains nothing but
poison and decay. He had been frightened by the
vague perception of danger before, but now, as he
looked at that life again, his eyes seemed able to pierce
the fantastic veil of creepers and leaves, to look past
the solid trunks, to see through the forbidding gloom—
and the mystery was disclosed—enchanting, subduing,
beautiful. He looked at the woman. Through the
checkered light between them she appeared to him with
the impalpable distinctness of a dream. The very
spirit of that land of mysterious forests, standing before
him like an apparition behind a transparent veil—a
veil woven of sunbeams and shadows.

She had approached him still nearer. He felt a
strange impatience within him at her advance. Confused thoughts rushed through his head, disordered,
shapeless, stunning. Then he heard his own voice
asking—

"Who are you?"

"I am the daughter of the blind Omar," she answered,
in a low but steady tone. "And you," she went on, a
little louder, "you are the white trader—the great man
of this place."

"Yes," said Willems, holding her eyes with his in a

sense of extreme effort, "Yes, I am white." Then
he added, feeling as if he spoke about some other man,
"But I am the outcast of my people."

She listened to him gravely. Through the mesh of
scattered hair her face looked like the face of a golden
statue with living eyes. The heavy eyelids dropped
slightly, and from between the long eyelashes she sent
out a sidelong look: hard, keen, and narrow, like the
gleam of sharp steel. Her lips were firm and composed
in a graceful curve, but the distended nostrils, the upward poise of the half-averted head, gave to her whole
person the expression of a wild and resentful defiance.

A shadow passed over Willems' face. He put his
hand over his lips as if to keep back the words that
wanted to come out in a surge of impulsive necessity,
the outcome of dominant thought that rushes from
the heart to the brain and must be spoken in the face
of doubt, of danger, of fear, of destruction itself.

"You are beautiful," he whispered.

She looked at him again with a glance that running
in one quick flash of her eyes over his sunburnt features, his broad shoulders, his straight, tall, motionless figure, rested at last on the ground at his feet.
Then she smiled. In the sombre beauty of her face
that smile was like the first ray of light on a stormy
daybreak that darts evanescent and pale through the
gloomy clouds: the forerunner of sunrise and of thunder.

CHAPTER SEVEN

THERE are in our lives short periods which hold no place in memory but only as the recollection of a feeling. There is no remembrance of gesture, of action, of any outward manifestation of life; those are lost in the unearthly brilliance or in the unearthly gloom of such moments. We are absorbed in the contemplation of that something, within our bodies, which rejoices or suffers while the body goes on breathing, instinctively runs away or, not less instinctively, fights—perhaps dies. But death in such a moment is the privilege of the fortunate, it is a high and rare favour, a supreme grace.

Willems never remembered how and when he parted from Aïssa. He caught himself drinking the muddy water out of the hollow of his hand, while his canoe was drifting in mid-stream past the last houses of Sambir. With his returning wits came the fear of something unknown that had taken possession of his heart, of something inarticulate and masterful which could not speak and would be obeyed. His first impulse was that of revolt. He would never go back there. Never! He looked round slowly at the brilliance of things in the deadly sunshine and took up his paddle! How changed everything seemed! The river was broader, the sky was higher. How fast the canoe flew under the strokes of his paddle! Since when had he acquired the strength of two men or more? He looked up and down the reach at the forests of the bank with a confused notion that with one sweep of his hand he could tumble all these trees into the stream. His face felt burning. He drank again, and shuddered with a depraved sense of pleasure at the after-taste of slime in the water.

It was late when he reached Almayer's house, but he crossed the dark and uneven courtyard, walking lightly in the radiance of some light of his own, invisible to other eyes. His host's sulky greeting jarred him like a sudden fall down a great height. He took his place at the table opposite Almayer and tried to speak cheerfully to his gloomy companion, but when the meal was ended and they sat smoking in silence he felt an abrupt discouragement, a lassitude in all his limbs, a sense of immense sadness as after some great and irreparable loss. The darkness of the night entered his heart, bringing with it doubt and hesitation and dull anger with himself and all the world. He had an impulse to shout horrible curses, to quarrel with Almayer, to do something violent. Quite without any immediate provocation he thought he would like to assault the wretched, sulky beast. He glanced at him ferociously from under his eyebrows. The unconscious Almayer smoked thoughtfully, planning to-morrow's work probably. The man's composure seemed to Willems an unpardonable insult. Why didn't that idiot talk to-night when he wanted him to? . . . on other nights he was ready enough to chatter. And such dull nonsense too! And Willems, trying hard to repress his own senseless rage, looked fixedly through the thick tobacco smoke at the stained tablecloth.

They retired early, as usual, but in the middle of the night Willems leaped out of his hammock with a stifled execration and ran down the steps into the courtyard. The two night watchmen, who sat by a little fire talking together in a monotonous undertone, lifted their heads to look wonderingly at the discomposed features of the white man as he crossed the circle of light thrown out by their fire. He disappeared in the darkness and then came back again, passing them close, but with no sign of consciousness of their presence on his face. Backwards and forwards he paced, muttering to himself, and the two Malays, after a short consultation in whispers left the fire quietly, not thinking it safe to remain in the vicinity of a white man who behaved in such a strange manner. They retired round the corner of the godown and watched Willems curiously through the night, till the short daybreak was followed by the sudden blaze of the rising sun, and Almayer's establishment woke up to life and work.

As soon as he could get away unnoticed in the bustle of the busy riverside, Willems crossed the river on his way to the place where he had met Aïssa. He threw himself down in the grass by the side of the brook and listened for the sound of her footsteps. The brilliant light of day fell through the irregular opening in the high branches of the trees and streamed down, softened, amongst the shadows of big trunks. Here and there a narrow sunbeam touched the rugged bark of a tree with a golden splash, sparkled on the leaping water of the brook, or rested on a leaf that stood out, shimmering and distinct, on the monotonous background of sombre green tints. The clear gap of blue above his head was crossed by the quick flight of white rice-birds* whose wings flashed in the sunlight, while through it the heat poured down from the sky, clung about the steaming earth, rolled among the trees, and wrapped up Willems in the soft and odorous folds of air heavy with the faint scent of blossoms and with the acrid smell of decaying life. And in that atmosphere of Nature's workshop Willems felt soothed and lulled into forgetfulness of his past, into indifference as to his future. The recollections of his triumphs, of his wrongs and of his ambition

vanished in that warmth, which seemed to melt all
regrets, all hope, all anger, all strength out of his heart.
And he lay there, dreamily contented, in the tepid and
perfumed shelter, thinking of Aïssa's eyes; recalling the
sound of her voice, the quiver of her lips—her frowns
and her smile.

She came, of course. To her he was something new,
unknown and strange. He was bigger, stronger than
any man she had seen before, and altogether different
from all those she knew. He was of the victorious race.
With a vivid remembrance of the great catastrophe of
her life he appeared to her with all the fascination of a
great and dangerous thing; of a terror vanquished, sur-
mounted, made a plaything of. They spoke with just
such a deep voice—those victorious men; they looked
with just such hard blue eyes at their enemies. And
she made that voice speak softly to her, those eyes look
tenderly at her face! He was indeed a man. She
could not understand all he told her of his life, but the
fragments she understood she made up for herself into a
story of a man great amongst his own people, valorous
and unfortunate; an undaunted fugitive dreaming of
vengeance against his enemies. He had all the at-
tractiveness of the vague and the unknown—of the
unforeseen and of the sudden; of a being strong, dangerous, alive, and human, ready to be enslaved.

She felt that he was ready. She felt it with the
unerring intuition of a primitive woman confronted by
a simple impulse. Day after day, when they met and
she stood a little way off, listening to his words, holding
him with her look, the undefined terror of the new conquest became faint and blurred like the memory of a
dream, and the certitude grew distinct, and convincing,
and visible to the eyes like some material thing in full
sunlight. It was a deep joy, a great pride, a tangible

sweetness that seemed to leave the taste of honey on her lips. He lay stretched at her feet without moving, for he knew from experience how a slight movement of his could frighten her away in those first days of their intercourse. He lay very quiet, with all the ardour of his desire ringing in his voice and shining in his eyes, whilst his body was still, like death itself. And he looked at her, standing above him, her head lost in the shadow of broad and graceful leaves that touched her cheek; while the slender spikes of pale green orchids*streamed down from amongst the boughs and mingled with the black hair that framed her face, as if all those plants claimed her for their own—the animated and brilliant flower of all that exuberant life which, born in gloom, struggles for ever towards the sunshine.

Every day she came a little nearer. He watched her slow progress—the gradual taming of that woman by the words of his love. It was the monotonous song of praise and desire that, commencing at creation, wraps up the world like an atmosphere and shall end only in the end of all things—when there are no lips to sing and no ears to hear. He told her that she was beautiful and desirable, and he repeated it again and again; for when he told her that, he had said all there was within him—he had expressed his only thought, his only feeling. And he watched the startled look of wonder and mistrust vanish from her face with the passing days, her eyes soften, the smile dwell longer and longer on her lips; a smile as of one charmed by a delightful dream; with the slight exaltation of intoxicating triumph lurking in its dawning tenderness.

And while she was near there was nothing in the whole world—for that idle man—but her look and her smile. Nothing in the past, nothing in the future; and in the present only the luminous fact of her existence. But in the sudden darkness of her going he would be left weak and helpless, as though despoiled violently of all that was himself. He who had lived all his life with no preoccupation but that of his own career, contemptuously indifferent to all feminine influence, full of scorn for men that would submit to it, if ever so little; he, so strong, so superior even in his errors, realized at last that his very individuality was snatched from within himself by the hand of a woman. Where was the assurance and pride of his cleverness; the belief in success, the anger of failure, the wish to retrieve his fortune, the certitude of his ability to accomplish it yet? Gone. All gone. All that had been a man within him was gone, and there remained only the trouble of his heart—that heart which had become a contemptible thing; which could be fluttered by a look or a smile, tormented by a word, soothed by a promise.

When the longed-for day came at last, when she sank on the grass by his side and with a quick gesture took his hand in hers, he sat up suddenly with the movement and look of a man awakened by the crash of his own falling house. All his blood, all his sensation, all his life seemed to rush into that hand leaving him without strength, in a cold shiver, in the sudden clamminess and collapse as of a deadly gun-shot wound. He flung her hand away brutally, like something burning, and sat motionless, his head fallen forward, staring on the ground and catching his breath in painful gasps. His impulse of fear and apparent horror did not dismay her in the least. Her face was grave and her eyes looked seriously at him.* Her fingers touched the hair of his temple, ran in a light caress down his cheek, twisted gently the end of his long moustache: and while he sat in the tremor of that

contact she ran off with startling fleetness and disappeared in a peal of clear laughter, in the stir of grass,
in the nod of young twigs growing over the path; leaving behind only a vanishing trail of motion and sound.

He scrambled to his feet slowly and painfully, like
a man with a burden on his shoulders, and walked
towards the riverside. He hugged to his breast the
recollection of his fear and of his delight, but told
himself seriously over and over again that this must
be the end of that adventure. After shoving off his
canoe into the stream he lifted his eyes to the bank
and gazed at it long and steadily, as if taking his last
look at a place of charming memories. He marched
up to Almayer's house with the concentrated expression and the determined step of a man who had just
taken a momentous resolution. His face was set and
rigid, his gestures and movements were guarded and
slow. He was keeping a tight hand on himself. A
very tight hand. He had a vivid illusion—as vivid as
reality almost—of being in charge of a slippery prisoner.
He sat opposite Almayer during that dinner—which
was their last meal together—with a perfectly calm face
and within him a growing terror of escape from his own
self. Now and then he would grasp the edge of the
table and set his teeth hard in a sudden wave of acute
despair, like one who, falling down a smooth and rapid
declivity that ends in a precipice, digs his finger nails
into the yielding surface and feels himself slipping
helplessly to inevitable destruction.

Then, abruptly, came a relaxation of his muscles,
the giving way of his will. Something seemed to
snap in his head, and that wish, that idea kept back
during all those hours, darted into his brain with the
heat and noise of a conflagration. He must see her!
See her at once! Go now! To-night! He had the

raging regret of the lost hour, of every passing moment. There was no thought of resistance now. Yet with the instinctive fear of the irrevocable, with the innate falseness of the human heart, he wanted to keep open the way of retreat. He had never absented himself during the night. What did Almayer know? What would Almayer think? Better ask him for the gun. A moonlight night. . . . Look for deer. . . . A colourable pretext. He would lie to Almayer. What did it matter! He lied to himself every minute of his life. And for what? For a woman. And such. . . .

Almayer's answer showed him that deception was useless. Everything gets to be known, even in this place. Well, he did not care. Cared for nothing but for the lost seconds. What if he should suddenly die. Die before he saw her. Before he could . . .

As, with the sound of Almayer's laughter in his ears, he urged his canoe in a slanting course across the rapid current, he tried to tell himself that he could return at any moment. He would just go and look at the place where they used to meet, at the tree under which he lay when she took his hand, at the spot where she sat by his side. Just go there and then return—nothing more; but when his little skiff touched the bank he leaped out, forgetting the painter, and the canoe hung for a moment amongst the bushes and then swung out of sight before he had time to dash into the water and secure it. He was thunderstruck at first. Now he could not go back unless he called up the Rajah's people to get a boat and rowers—and the way to Pata-lolo's campong led past Aïssa's house!

He went up the path with the eager eyes and reluctant steps of a man pursuing a phantom, and when he found himself at a place where a narrow track branched off to the left towards Omar's clearing he stood still, with a look of strained attention on his face as if listening to a far-off voice—the voice of his fate. It was a sound inarticulate but full of meaning; and following it there came a rending and tearing within his breast. He twisted his fingers together, and the joints of his hands and arms cracked. On his forehead the perspiration stood out in small pearly drops. He looked round wildly. Above the shapeless darkness of the forest undergrowth rose the tree-tops with their high boughs and leaves standing out black on the pale sky—like fragments of night floating on moonbeams. Under his feet warm steam rose from the heated earth. Round him there was a great silence.

He was looking round for help. This silence, this immobility of his surroundings seemed to him a cold rebuke, a stern refusal, a cruel unconcern. There was no safety outside of himself—and in himself there was no refuge; there was only the image of that woman. He had a sudden moment of lucidity—of that cruel lucidity that comes once in life to the most benighted. He seemed to see what went on within him, and was horrified at the strange sight. He, a white man whose worst fault till then had been a little want of judgment and too much confidence in the rectitude of his kind! That woman was a complete savage, and . . . He tried to tell himself that the thing was of no consequence. It was a vain effort. The novelty of the sensations he had never experienced before in the slightest degree, yet had despised on hearsay from his safe position of a civilized man, destroyed his courage. He was disappointed with himself. He seemed to be surrendering to a wild creature the unstained purity of his life, of his race, of his civilization. He had a notion of being lost amongst shapeless things that were dangerous and ghastly. He struggled with the sense of certain defeat

—lost his footing—fell back into the darkness. With a faint cry and an upward throw of his arms he gave up as a tired swimmer gives up: because the swamped craft is gone from under his feet; because the night is dark and the shore is far—because death is better than strife.

PART II

CHAPTER ONE

THE light and heat fell upon the settlement, the clearings, and the river as if flung down by an angry hand. The land lay silent, still, and brilliant under the avalanche of burning rays that had destroyed all sound and all motion, had buried all shadows, had choked every breath. No living thing dared to affront the serenity of this cloudless sky, dared to revolt against the oppression of this glorious and cruel sunshine. Strength and resolution, body and mind alike were helpless, and tried to hide before the rush of the fire from heaven. Only the frail butterflies, the fearless children of the sun, the capricious tyrants of the flowers, fluttered audaciously in the open, and their minute shadows hovered in swarms over the drooping blossoms, ran lightly on the withering grass, or glided on the dry and cracked earth. No voice was heard in this hot noontide but the faint murmur of the river that hurried on in swirls and eddies, its sparkling wavelets chasing each other in their joyous course to the sheltering depths, to the cool refuge of the sea.

Almayer had dismissed his workmen for the midday rest, and, his little daughter on his shoulder, ran quickly across the courtyard, making for the shade of the verandah of his house. He laid the sleepy child on the seat of the big rocking-chair, on a pillow which he took out of his own hammock, and stood for a while looking down at her with tender and pensive eyes. The child, tired and hot, moved uneasily, sighed, and looked up at him with the veiled look of sleepy fatigue.

He picked up from the floor a broken palm leaf fan, and began fanning gently the flushed little face. Her eyelids fluttered and Almayer smiled. A responsive smile brightened for a second her heavy eyes, broke with a dimple the soft outline of her cheek; then the eyelids dropped suddenly, she drew a long breath through the parted lips—and was in a deep sleep before the fleeting smile could vanish from her face.

Almayer moved lightly off, took one of the wooden armchairs, and placing it close to the balustrade of the verandah sat down with a sigh of relief. He spread his elbows on the top rail and resting his chin on his clasped hands looked absently at the river, at the dance of sunlight on the flowing water. Gradually the forest of the further bank became smaller, as if sinking below the level of the river. The outlines wavered, grew thin, dissolved in the air. Before his eyes there was now only a space of undulating blue—one big, empty sky growing dark at times. . . . Where was the sunshine? . . . He felt soothed and happy, as if some gentle and invisible hand had removed from his soul the burden of his body. In another second he seemed to float out into a cool brightness where there was no such thing as memory or pain. Delicious. His eyes closed—opened—closed again.

"Almayer!"

With a sudden jerk of his whole body he sat up, grasping the front rail with both his hands, and blinked stupidly.

"What? What's that?" he muttered, looking round vaguely.

"Here! Down here, Almayer."

Half rising in his chair, Almayer looked over the rail at the foot of the verandah, and fell back with a low whistle of astonishment.

"A ghost, by heavens!" he exclaimed softly to himself.

"Will you listen to me?" went on the husky voice from the courtyard. "May I come up, Almayer?"

Almaycr stood up and leaned over the rail.

"Don't you dare," he said, in a voice subdued but distinct. "Don't you dare! The child sleeps here. And I don't want to hear you—or speak to you either."

"You must listen to me! It's something important."

"Not to me, surely."

"Yes! To you. Very important."

"You were always a humbug," said Almayer, after a short silence, in an indulgent tone. "Always! I remember the old days. Some fellows used to say there was no one like you for smartness—but you never took me in. Not quite. I never quite believed in you, Mr. Willems."

"I admit your superior intelligence," retorted Willems, with scornful impatience, from below. "Listening to me would be a further proof of it. You will be sorry if you don't."

"Oh, you funny fellow!" said Almayer, banteringly. "Well, come up. Don't make a noise, but come up. You'll catch a sunstroke down there and die on my doorstep perhaps. I don't want any tragedy here. Come on!"

Before he finished speaking Willems' head appeared above the lcvcl of the floor, then his shoulders rose gradually and he stood at last before Almayer—a masquerading spectre of the once so very confidential clerk of the richest merchant in the islands. His jacket was soiled and torn; below the waist he was clothed in a worn-out and faded sarong. He flung off his hat, uncovering his long, tangled hair that stuck in wisps on his perspiring forehead and straggled over his eyes, which glittered deep down in the sockets like the last sparks amongst the black embers of a burnt-out fire. An unclean beard grew out of the caverns of his sunburnt cheeks. The hand he put out towards Almayer was very unsteady. The once firm mouth had the tell-tale droop of mental suffering and physical exhaustion. He was barefooted. Almayer surveyed him with leisurely composure.

"Well!" he said at last, without taking the extended hand which dropped slowly along Willems' body.

"I am come," began Willems.

"So I see," interrupted Almayer. "You might have spared me this treat without making me unhappy. You have been away five weeks, if I am not mistaken. I got on very well without you—and now you are here you are not pretty to look at."

"Let me speak, will you!" exclaimed Willems.

"Don't shout like this. Do you think yourself in the forest with your . . . your friends? This is a civilized man's house. A white man's. Understand?"

"I am come," began Willems again; "I am come for your good and mine."

"You look as if you had come for a good feed," chimed in the irrepressible Almayer, while Willems waved his hand in a discouraged gesture. "Don't they give you enough to eat," went on Almayer, in a tone of easy banter, "those—what am I to call them —those new relations of yours? That old blind scoundrel must be delighted with your company. You know, he was the greatest thief and murderer of those seas. Say! do you exchange confidences? Tell me, Willems, did you kill somebody in Macassar or did you only steal something?"

"It is not true!" exclaimed Willems, hotly. "I only borrowed. . . . They all lied! I . . ."

"Sh-sh!" hissed Almayer, warningly, with a look at the sleeping child. "So you did steal," he went on, with repressed exultation. "I thought there was something of the kind. And now, here, you steal again."

For the first time Willems raised his eyes to Almayer's face.

"Oh, I don't mean from me. I haven't missed anything," said Almayer, with mocking haste. "But that girl. Hey! You stole her. You did not pay the old fellow. She is no good to him now, is she?"

"Stop that, Almayer!"

Something in Willems' tone caused Almayer to pause. He looked narrowly at the man before him, and could not help being shocked at his appearance.

"Almayer," went on Willems, "listen to me. If you are a human being you will. I suffer horribly—and for your sake."

Almayer lifted his eyebrows. "Indeed! How? But you are raving," he added, negligently.

"Ah! You don't know," whispered Willems. "She is gone. Gone," he repeated, with tears in his voice, "gone two days ago."

"No!" exclaimed the surprised Almayer. "Gone! I haven't heard that news yet." He burst into a subdued laugh. "How funny! Had enough of you already? You know it's not flattering for you, my superior countryman."

Willems—as if not hearing him—leaned against one of the columns of the roof and looked over the river. "At first," he whispered, dreamily, "my life was like a vision of heaven—or hell; I didn't know which. Since she went I know what perdition means; what darkness is. I know what it is to be torn to pieces alive. That's how I feel."

"You may come and live with me again," said Almayer, coldly. "After all, Lingard—whom I call my father and respect as such—left you under my care. You pleased yourself by going away. Very good. Now you want to come back. Be it so. I am no friend of yours. I act for Captain Lingard."

"Come back?" repeated Willems, passionately. "Come back to you and abandon her? Do you think I am mad?* Without her! Man! what are you made of? To think that she moves, lives, breathes out of my sight. I am jealous of the wind that fans her, of the air she breathes, of the earth that receives the caress of her foot, of the sun that looks at her now while I . . . I haven't seen her for two days—two days."

The intensity of Willems' feeling moved Almayer somewhat, but he affected to yawn elaborately.

"You do bore me," he muttered. "Why don't you go after her instead of coming here?"

"Why indeed?"

"Don't you know where she is? She can't be very far. No native craft has left this river for the last fortnight."

"No! not very far—and I will tell you where she is. She is in Lakamba's campong." And Willems fixed his eyes steadily on Almayer's face.

"Phew! Patalolo never sent to let me know. Strange," said Almayer, thoughtfully. "Are you afraid of that lot?" he added, after a short pause.

"I—afraid!"

"Then is it the care of your dignity which prevents you from following her there, my high-minded friend?" asked Almayer, with mock solicitude. "How noble of you!"

There was a short silence; then Willems said, quietly, "You are a fool. I should like to kick you."

"No fear," answered Almayer, carelessly; "you are too weak for that.   You look starved."

"I don't think I have eaten anything for the last two days; perhaps more—I don't remember.   It does not matter.   I am full of live embers," said Willems, gloomily.   "Look!" and he bared an arm covered with fresh scars.   "I have been biting myself to forget in that pain the fire that hurts me there!"   He struck his breast violently with his fist, reeled under his own blow, fell into a chair that stood near and closed his eyes slowly.

"Disgusting exhibition," said Almayer, loftily. "What could father ever see in you?   You are as estimable as a heap of garbage."

"You talk like that!   You, who sold your soul for a few guilders," muttered Willems, wearily, without opening his eyes.

"Not so few," said Almayer, with instinctive readiness, and stopped confused for a moment.   He recovered himself quickly, however, and went on: "But you—you have thrown yours away for nothing; flung it under the feet of a damned savage woman who has made you already the thing you are, and will kill you very soon, one way or another, with her love or with her hate.   You spoke just now about guilders.   You meant Lingard's money, I suppose.   Well, whatever I have sold, and for whatever price, I never meant you —you of all people—to spoil my bargain.   I feel pretty safe though.   Even father, even Captain Lingard, would not touch you now with a pair of tongs; not with a ten-foot pole. . . ."

He spoke excitedly, all in one breath, and, ceasing suddenly, glared at Willems and breathed hard through his nose in sulky resentment.   Willems looked at him steadily for a moment, then got up.

"Almayer," he said resolutely, "I want to become a trader in this place."

Almayer shrugged his shoulders.

"Yes. And you shall set me up. I want a house and trade goods—perhaps a little money. I ask you for it."

"Anything else you want? Perhaps this coat?" and here Almayer unbuttoned his jacket—"or my house —or my boots?"

"After all it's natural," went on Willems, without paying any attention to Almayer—"it's natural that she should expect the advantages which . . . and then I could shut up that old wretch and then . . ."

He paused, his face brightened with the soft light of dreamy enthusiasm, and he turned his eyes upwards. With his gaunt figure and dilapidated appearance he looked like some ascetic dweller in a wilderness, finding the reward of a self-denying life in a vision of dazzling glory. He went on in an impassioned murmur—

"And then I would have her all to myself away from her people—all to myself—under my own influence —to fashion—to mould—to adore—to soften—to . . . Oh! Delight! And then—then go away to some distant place where, far from all she knew, I would be all the world to her! All the world to her!"

His face changed suddenly. His eyes wandered for awhile and then became steady all at once.

"I would repay every cent, of course," he said, in a business-like tone, with something of his old assurance, of his old belief in himself, in it. "Every cent.* I need not interfere with your business. I shall cut out the small native traders. I have ideas—but never mind that now. And Captain Lingard would approve, I feel sure. After all it's a loan, and I shall be at hand. Safe thing for you."

"Ah! Captain Lingard would approve! He would

app . . ." Almayer choked. The notion of Lingard doing something for Willems enraged him. His face was purple. He spluttered insulting words. Willems looked at him coolly.

"I assure you, Almayer," he said, gently, "that I have good grounds for my demand."

"Your cursed impudence!"

"Believe me, Almayer, your position here is not so safe as you may think. An unscrupulous rival here would destroy your trade in a year. It would be ruin. Now Lingard's long absence gives courage to certain individuals. You know?—I have heard much lately. They made proposals to me . . . You are very much alone here. Even Patalolo . . ."

"Damn Patalolo! I am master in this place."

"But, Almayer, don't you see . . ."

"Yes, I see. I see a mysterious ass," interrupted Almayer, violently. "What is the meaning of your veiled threats? Don't you think I know something also? They have been intriguing for years—and nothing has happened. The Arabs have been hanging about outside this river for years—and I am still the only trader here; the master here. Do you bring me a declaration of war? Then it's from yourself only. I know all my other enemies. I ought to knock you on the head. You are not worth powder and shot though. You ought to be destroyed with a stick—like a snake."

Almayer's voice woke up the little girl, who sat up on the pillow with a sharp cry. He rushed over to the chair, caught up the child in his arms, walked back blindly, stumbled against Willems' hat which lay on the floor, and kicked it furiously down the steps.

"Clear out of this! Clear out!" he shouted.

Willems made an attempt to speak, but Almayer howled him down.

"Take yourself off! Don't you see you frighten the child—you scarecrow! No! no! dear," he went on to his little daughter, soothingly, while Willems walked down the steps slowly. "No. Don't cry. See! Bad man going away. Look! He is afraid of your papa. Nasty, bad man. Never come back again. He shall live in the woods and never come near my little girl. If he comes papa will kill him—so!" He struck his fist on the rail of the balustrade to show how he would kill Willems, and, perching the consoled child on his shoulder held her with one hand, while he pointed towards the retreating figure of his visitor.

"Look how he runs away, dearest," he said, coaxingly. "Isn't he funny. Call 'pig' after him, dearest. Call after him."

The seriousness of her face vanished into dimples. Under the long eyelashes, glistening with recent tears, her big eyes sparkled and danced with fun. She took firm hold of Almayer's hair with one hand, while she waved the other joyously and called out with all her might, in a clear note, soft and distinct like the pipe of a bird:—

"Pig! Pig! Pig!"

CHAPTER TWO

A SIGH under the flaming blue, a shiver of the sleeping
sea, a cool breath as if a door had been swung upon
the frozen spaces of the universe, and with a stir of
leaves, with the nod of boughs, with the tremble of
slender branches the sea breeze struck the coast, rushed
up the river, swept round the broad reaches, and
travelled on in a soft ripple of darkening water, in
the whisper of branches, in the rustle of leaves of the
awakened forests. It fanned in Lakamba's campong
the dull red of expiring embers into a pale brilliance;
and, under its touch, the slender, upright spirals of
smoke that rose from every glowing heap swayed,
wavered, and eddying down filled the twilight of
clustered shade trees with the aromatic scent of the
burning wood. The men who had been dozing in
the shade during the hot hours of the afternoon woke
up, and the silence of the big courtyard was broken
by the hesitating murmur of yet sleepy voices, by
coughs and yawns, with now and then a burst of laughter, a loud hail, a name or a joke sent out in a soft
drawl. Small groups squatted round the little fires,
and the monotonous undertone of talk filled the enclosure; the talk of barbarians, persistent, steady,
repeating itself in the soft syllables, in musical tones
of the never-ending discourses of those men of the
forests and the sea, who can talk most of the day and
all the night; who never exhaust a subject, never
seem able to thresh a matter out; to whom that talk
is poetry and painting and music, all art, all history;

their only accomplishment, their only superiority, their
only amusement. The talk of camp fires, which speaks
of bravery and cunning, of strange events and of far
countries, of the news of yesterday and the news of
to-morrow. The talk about the dead and the living—
about those who fought and those who loved.

Lakamba came out on the platform before his own
house and sat down—perspiring, half asleep, and sulky
—in a wooden armchair under the shade of the overhanging eaves. Through the darkness of the doorway
he could hear the soft warbling of his womenkind, busy
round the looms where they were weaving the checkered
pattern* of his gala sarongs. Right and left of him on
the flexible bamboo floor those of his followers to whom
their distinguished birth, long devotion, or faithful
service had given the privilege of using the chief's
house, were sleeping on mats or just sat up rubbing
their eyes: while the more wakeful had mustered enough
energy to draw a chessboard with red clay on a fine
mat and were now meditating silently over their moves.
Above the prostrate forms of the players, who lay face
downward supported on elbow, the soles of their feet
waving irresolutely about, in the absorbed meditation
of the game, there towered here and there the straight
figure of an attentive spectator looking down with
dispassionate but profound interest. On the edge of
the platform a row of high-heeled leather sandals stood
ranged carefully in a level line, and against the rough
wooden rail leaned the slender shafts of the spears
belonging to these gentlemen, the broad blades of
dulled steel looking very black in the reddening light
of approaching sunset.

A boy of about twelve—the personal attendant of
Lakamba—squatted at his master's feet and held up
towards him a silver siri box. Slowly Lakamba took

the box, opened it, and tearing off a piece of green leaf deposited in it a pinch of lime, a morsel of gambier, a small bit of areca nut, and wrapped up the whole with a dexterous twist. He paused, morsel in hand, seemed to miss something, turned his head from side to side, slowly, like a man with a stiff neck, and ejaculated*in an ill-humoured bass—

"Babalatchi!"

The players glanced up quickly, and looked down again directly. Those men who were standing stirred uneasily as if prodded by the sound of the chief's voice. The one nearest to Lakamba repeated the call, after a while, over the rail into the courtyard. There was a movement of upturned faces below by the fires, and the cry trailed over the enclosure in sing-song tones. The thumping of wooden pestles husking the evening rice stopped for a moment and Babalatchi's name rang afresh shrilly on women's lips in various keys. A voice far off shouted something—another, nearer, repeated it; there was a short hubbub which died out with extreme suddenness. The first crier turned to Lakamba, saying indolently—

"He is with the blind Omar."

Lakamba's lips moved inaudibly. The man who had just spoken was again deeply absorbed in the game going on at his feet; and the chief—as if he had forgotten all about it already—sat with a stolid face amongst his silent followers, leaning back squarely in his chair, his hands on the arms of his seat, his knees apart, his big bloodshot eyes blinking solemnly, as if dazzled by the noble vacuity of his thoughts.

Babalatchi had gone to see old Omar late in the afternoon. The delicate manipulation of the ancient pirate's susceptibilities, the skilful management of Aïssa's violent impulses engrossed him to the exclusion

of every other business—interfered with his regular
attendance upon his chief and protector—even disturbed his sleep for the last three nights. That day
when he left his own bamboo hut—which stood amongst
others in Lakamba's campong—his heart was heavy
with anxiety and with doubt as to the success of his
intrigue. He walked slowly, with his usual air of
detachment from his surroundings, as if unaware
that many sleepy eyes watched from all parts of the
courtyard his progress towards a small gate at its upper
end. That gate gave access to a separate enclosure
in which a rather large house, built of planks, had
been prepared by Lakamba's orders for the reception
of Omar and Aïssa. It was a superior kind of habitation which Lakamba intended for the dwelling of his
chief adviser—whose abilities were worth that honour,
he thought. But after the consultation in the deserted
clearing—when Babalatchi had disclosed his plan—
they both had agreed that the new house should be
used at first to shelter Omar and Aïssa after they had
been persuaded to leave the Rajah's place, or had been
kidnapped from there—as the case might be. Babalatchi did not mind in the least the putting off of his own
occupation of the house of honour, because it had many
advantages for the quiet working out of his plans. It
had a certain seclusion, having an enclosure of its own,
and that enclosure communicated also with Lakamba's
private courtyard at the back of his residence—a place
set apart for the female household of the chief. The
only communication with the river was through the
great front courtyard always full of armed men and
watchful eyes. Behind the whole group of buildings
there stretched the level ground of rice-clearings, which
in their turn were closed in by the wall of untouched
forests with undergrowth so thick and tangled that

nothing but a bullet—and that fired at pretty close range—could penetrate any distance there.

Babalatchi slipped quietly through the little gate and, closing it, tied up carefully the rattan fastenings. Before the house there was a square space of ground, beaten hard into the level smoothness of asphalt. A big buttressed tree, a giant left there on purpose during the process of clearing the land, roofed in the clear space with a high canopy of gnarled boughs and thick, sombre leaves. To the right—and some small distance away from the large house—a little hut of reeds, covered with mats, had been put up for the special convenience of Omar, who, being blind and infirm, had some difficulty in ascending the steep plankway that led to the more substantial dwelling, which was built on low posts and had an uncovered verandah. Close by the trunk of the tree, and facing the doorway of the hut, the household fire glowed in a small handful of embers in the midst of a large circle of white ashes. An old woman—some humble relation of one of Lakamba's wives, who had been ordered to attend on Aïssa—was squatting over the fire and lifted up her bleared eyes to gaze at Babalatchi in an uninterested manner, as he advanced rapidly across the courtyard.

Babalatchi took in the courtyard with a keen glance of his solitary eye, and without looking down at the old woman muttered a question. Silently, the woman stretched a tremulous and emaciated arm towards the hut. Babalatchi made a few steps towards the doorway, but stopped outside in the sunlight.

"O! Tuan Omar, Omar besar! It is I—Babalatchi!"

Within the hut there was a feeble groan, a fit of coughing and an indistinct murmur in the broken tones of a vague plaint. Encouraged evidently by those

signs of dismal life within, Babalatchi entered the hut,
and after some time came out leading with rigid care-
fulness the blind Omar, who followed with both his
hands on his guide's shoulders. There was a rude
seat under the tree, and there Babalatchi led his old
chief, who sat down with a sigh of relief and leaned
wearily against the rugged trunk. The rays of the
setting sun, darting under the spreading branches,
rested on the white-robed figure sitting with head
thrown back in stiff dignity, on the thin hands moving
uneasily, and on the stolid face with its eyelids dropped
over the destroyed eyeballs; a face set into the immobility of a plaster cast yellowed by age.

"Is the sun near its setting?" asked Omar, in a dull
voice.

"Very near," answered Babalatchi.

"Where am I? Why have I been taken away from
the place which I knew—where I, blind, could move
without fear? It is like black night to those who see.
And the sun is near its setting—and I have not heard
the sound of her footsteps since the morning! Twice
a strange hand has given me my food to-day. Why?
Why? Where is she?"

"She is near," said Babalatchi.

"And he?" went on Omar, with sudden eagerness,
and a drop in his voice. "Where is he? Not here.
Not here!" he repeated, turning his head from side to
side as if in deliberate attempt to see.

"No! He is not here now," said Babalatchi, soothingly. Then, after a pause, he added very low, "But
he shall soon return."

"Return! O crafty one! Will he return? I have
cursed him three times," exclaimed Omar, with weak
violence.

"He is—no doubt—accursed," assented Babalatchi,

in a conciliating manner—"and yet he will be here before very long—I know!"

"You are crafty and faithless. I have made you great. You were dirt under my feet—less than dirt," said Omar, with tremulous energy.

"I have fought by your side many times," said Babalatchi, calmly.

"Why did he come?" went on Omar. "Did you send him? Why did he come to defile the air I breathe —to mock at my fate—to poison her mind and steal her body? She has grown hard of heart to me. Hard and merciless and stealthy like rocks that tear a ship's life out under the smooth sea." He drew a long breath, struggled with his anger, then broke down suddenly. "I have been hungry," he continued, in a whimpering tone—"often I have been very hungry—and cold— and neglected—and nobody near me. She has often forgotten me—and my sons are dead, and that man is an infidel and a dog. Why did he come? Did you show him the way?"

"He found the way himself, O Leader of the brave," said Babalatchi, sadly. "I only saw a way for their destruction and our own greatness. And if I saw aright, then you shall never suffer from hunger any more. There shall be peace for us, and glory and riches."

"And I shall die to-morrow," murmured Omar, bitterly.

"Who knows? Those things have been written since the beginning of the world," whispered Babalatchi, thoughtfully.

"Do not let him come back," exclaimed Omar.

"Neither can he escape his fate," went on Babalatchi. "He shall come back, and the power of men we always hated, you and I, shall crumble into dust in our hand." Then he added with enthusiasm, "They shall fight amongst themselves and perish both."

"And you shall see all this, while, I . . ."

"True!" murmured Babalatchi, regretfully. "To you life is darkness."

"No! Flame!" exclaimed the old Arab, half rising, then falling back in his seat. "The flame of that last day! I see it yet—the last thing I saw! And I hear the noise of the rent earth—when they all died. And I live to be the plaything of a crafty one," he added, with inconsequential peevishness.

"You are my master still," said Babalatchi, humbly. "You are very wise—and in your wisdom you shall speak to Syed*Abdulla when he comes here—you shall speak to him as I advised, I, your servant, the man who fought at your right hand for many years. I have heard by a messenger that the Syed Abdulla is coming to-night, perhaps late; for those things must be done secretly, lest the white man, the trader up the river, should know of them. But he will be here. There has been a surat delivered to Lakamba. In it, Syed Abdulla says he will leave his ship, which is anchored outside the river, at the hour of noon to-day. He will be here before daylight if Allah wills."

He spoke with his eye fixed on the ground, and did not become aware of Aïssa's presence till he lifted his head when he ceased speaking. She had approached so quietly that even Omar did not hear her footsteps, and she stood now looking at them with troubled eyes and parted lips, as if she was going to speak; but at Babalatchi's entreating gesture she remained silent. Omar sat absorbed in thought.

"Ay—wa! Even so!" he said at last, in a weak voice. "I am to speak your wisdom, O Babalatchi! Tell him to trust the white man! I do not understand. I am old and blind and weak. I do not understand. I am very cold," he continued, in a lower tone, moving his shoulders uneasily. He ceased, then went on rambling in a faint whisper. "They are the sons of witches, and their father is Satan the stoned.* Sons of witches. Sons of witches." After a short silence he asked suddenly, in a firmer voice—"How many white men are there here, O crafty one?"

"There are two here. Two white men to fight one another," answered Babalatchi, with alacrity.

"And how many will be left then? How many? Tell me, you who are wise."

"The downfall of an enemy is the consolation of the unfortunate," said Babalatchi, sententiously. "They are on every sea; only the wisdom of the Most High knows their number—but you shall know that some of them suffer."

"Tell me, Babalatchi, will they die? Will they both die?" asked Omar, in sudden agitation.

Aïssa made a movement. Babalatchi held up a warning hand.

"They shall, surely, die," he said steadily, looking at the girl with unflinching eye.

"Ay—wa! But die soon! So that I can pass my hand over their faces when Allah has made them stiff."

"If such is their fate and yours," answered Babalatchi, without hesitation. "God is great!"

A violent fit of coughing doubled Omar up, and he rocked himself to and fro, wheezing and moaning in turns, while Babalatchi and the girl looked at him in silence. Then he leaned back against the tree, exhausted.

"I am alone, I am alone," he wailed feebly, groping vaguely about with his trembling hands. "Is there anybody near me? Is there anybody? I am afraid of this strange place."

"I am by your side, O Leader of the brave," said Babalatchi, touching his shoulder lightly. "Always by your side as in the days when we both were young: as in the time when we both went with arms in our hands."

"Has there been such a time, Babalatchi?" said Omar, wildly; "I have forgotten. And now when I die there will be no man, no fearless man to speak of his father's bravery. There was a woman! A woman! And she has forsaken me for an infidel dog. The hand of the Compassionate is heavy on my head! Oh, my calamity! Oh, my shame!"

He calmed down after a while, and asked quietly— "Is the sun set, Babalatchi?"

"It is now as low as the highest tree I can see from here," answered Babalatchi.

"It is the time of prayer," said Omar, attempting to get up.

Dutifully Babalatchi helped his old chief to rise, and they walked slowly towards the hut. Omar waited outside, while Babalatchi went in and came out directly, dragging after him the old Arab's praying carpet. Out of a brass vessel he poured the water of ablution on Omar's outstretched hands, and eased him carefully down into a kneeling posture, for the venerable robber was far too infirm to be able to stand. Then as Omar droned out the first words and made his first bow towards the Holy City, Babalatchi stepped noiselessly towards Aïssa, who did not move all the time.

Aïssa looked steadily at the one-eyed sage, who was approaching her slowly and with a great show of deference. For a moment they stood facing each other in silence. Babalatchi appeared embarrassed. With a sudden and quick gesture she caught hold of his arm, and with the other hand pointed towards the sinking red disc that glowed, rayless, through the floating mists of the evening.

"The third sunset! The last! And he is not here," she whispered; "what have you done, man without faith? What have you done?"

"Indeed I have kept my word," murmured Babalatchi, earnestly. "This morning Bulangi went with a canoe to look for him. He is a strange man, but our friend, and shall keep close to him and watch him without ostentation. And at the third hour of the day I have sent another canoe with four rowers. Indeed, the man you long for, O daughter of Omar! may come when he likes."

"But he is not here! I waited for him yesterday. To-day! To-morrow I shall go."

"Not alive!" muttered Babalatchi to himself. "And do you doubt your power," he went on in a louder tone—"you that to him are more beautiful than an houri of the seventh Heaven? He is your slave."

"A slave does run away sometimes," she said, gloomily, "and then the master must go and seek him out."

"And do you want to live and die a beggar?" asked Babalatchi, impatiently.

"I care not," she exclaimed, wringing her hands; and the black pupils of her wide-open eyes darted wildly here and there like petrels before the storm.

"Sh! Sh!" hissed Babalatchi, with a glance towards Omar. "Do you think, O girl! that he himself would live like a beggar, even with you?"

"He is great," she said, ardently. "He despises you all! He despises you all! He is indeed a man!"

"You know that best," muttered Babalatchi, with a fugitive smile—"but remember, woman with the strong heart, that to hold him now you must be to him like the great sea to thirsty men—a never-ceasing torment, and a madness."

He ceased and they stood in silence, both looking on the ground, and for a time nothing was heard above the crackling of the fire but the intoning of Omar glorifying the God—his God, and the Faith—his faith. Then Babalatchi cocked his head on one side and appeared to listen intently to the hum of voices in the big courtyard. The dull noise swelled into distinct shouts, then into a great tumult of voices, dying away, recommencing, growing louder, to cease again abruptly; and in those short pauses the shrill vociferations of women rushed up, as if released, towards the quiet heaven. Aïssa and Babalatchi started, but the latter gripped in his turn the girl's arm and restrained her with a strong grasp.

"Wait," he whispered.

The little door in the heavy stockade which separated Lakamba's private ground from Omar's enclosure swung back quickly, and the noble exile appeared with disturbed mien and a naked short sword in his hand. His turban was half unrolled, and the end trailed on the ground behind him. His jacket was open. He breathed thickly for a moment before he spoke.

"He came in Bulangi's boat," he said, "and walked quietly till he was in my presence, when the senseless fury of white men caused him to rush upon me. I have been in great danger," went on the ambitious nobleman in an aggrieved tone. "Do you hear that, Babalatchi? That eater of swine* aimed a blow at my face with his unclean fist. He tried to rush amongst my household. Six men are holding him now."

A fresh outburst of yells stopped Lakamba's discourse. Angry voices shouted: "Hold him. Beat him down. Strike at his head." Then the clamour ceased with sudden completeness, as if strangled by a mighty hand, and after a second of surprising silence the voice of Willems was heard alone, howling maledictions in Malay, in Dutch, and in English.

"Listen," said Lakamba, speaking with unsteady lips, "he blasphemes his God. His speech is like the raving of a mad dog. Can we hold him for ever? He must be killed!"

"Fool!" muttered Babalatchi, looking up at Aïssa, who stood with set teeth, with gleaming eyes and distended nostrils, yet obedient to the touch of his restraining hand. "It is the third day, and I have kept my promise," he said to her, speaking very low. "Remember," he added warningly—"like the sea to the thirsty! And now," he said aloud, releasing her and stepping back, "go, fearless daughter, go!"

Like an arrow, rapid and silent she flew down the enclosure, and disappeared through the gate of the courtyard. Lakamba and Babalatchi looked after her. They heard the renewed tumult, the girl's clear voice calling out, "Let him go!" Then after a pause in the din no longer than half the human breath the name of Aïssa rang in a shout loud, discordant, and piercing, which sent through them an involuntary shudder. Old Omar collapsed on his carpet and moaned feebly; Lakamba stared with gloomy contempt in the direction of the inhuman sound; but Babalatchi, forcing a smile, pushed his distinguished protector through the narrow gate in the stockade, followed him, and closed it quickly.

The old woman, who had been most of the time kneeling by the fire, now rose, glanced round fearfully and crouched hiding behind the tree. The gate of the great courtyard flew open with a great clatter before a frantic kick, and Willems darted in

carrying Aïssa in his arms. He rushed up the enclosure
like a tornado, pressing the girl to his breast, her arms
round his neck, her head hanging back over his arm,
her eyes closed and her long hair nearly touching the
ground. They appeared for a second in the glare of
the fire, then, with immense strides, he dashed up the
planks and disappeared with his burden in the doorway
of the big house.

Inside and outside the enclosure there was silence.
Omar lay supporting himself on his elbow, his terrified
face with its closed eyes giving him the appearance of
a man tormented by a nightmare.

"What is it? Help! Help me to rise!" he called
out faintly.

The old hag, still crouching in the shadow, stared
with bleared eyes at the doorway of the big house, and
took no notice of his call. He listened for a while,
then his arm gave way, and, with a deep sigh of discouragement, he let himself fall on the carpet.

The boughs of the tree nodded and trembled in the
unsteady currents of the light wind. A leaf fluttered
down slowly from some high branch and rested on the
ground, immobile, as if resting for ever, in the glow of
the fire; but soon it stirred, then soared suddenly, and
flew, spinning and turning before the breath of the
perfumed breeze, driven helplessly into the dark night
that had closed over the land.

CHAPTER THREE

For upwards of forty years Abdulla had walked in
the way of his Lord. Son of the rich Syed Selim bin
Sali, the great Mohammedan trader of the Straits, he
went forth at the age of seventeen on his first commercial expedition, as his father's representative on
board a pilgrim ship chartered by the wealthy Arab
to convey a crowd of pious Malays to the Holy Shrine.
That was in the days when steam was not in those
seas—or, at least, not so much as now. The voyage
was long, and the young man's eyes were opened to
the wonders of many lands. Allah had made it his
fate to become a pilgrim very early in life. This was
a great favour of Heaven, and it could not have been
bestowed upon a man who prized it more, or who made
himself more worthy of it by the unswerving piety of
his heart and by the religious solemnity of his demeanour. Later on it became clear that the book of his
destiny contained the programme of a wandering life.
He visited Bombay and Calcutta,* looked in at the
Persian Gulf, beheld in due course the high and barren
coasts of the Gulf of Suez, and this was the limit of his
wanderings westward. He was then twenty-seven,
and the writing on his forehead decreed that the time
had come for him to return to the Straits and take from
his dying father's hands the many threads of a business
that was spread over all the Archipelago: from Sumatra
to New Guinea, from Batavia to Palawan. Very soon
his ability, his will—strong to obstinacy—his wisdom
beyond his years, caused him to be recognized as the

head of a family whose members and connections were found in every part of those seas. An uncle here—a brother there; a father-in-law in Batavia, another in Palembang; husbands of numerous sisters; cousins innumerable scattered north, south, east, and west—in every place where there was trade: the great family lay like a network over the islands. They lent money to princes, influenced the council-rooms, faced—if need be—with peaceful intrepidity the white rulers who held the land and the sea under the edge of sharp swords; and they all paid great deference to Abdulla, listened to his advice, entered into his plans—because he was wise, pious, and fortunate.

He bore himself with the humility becoming a Believer, who never forgets, even for one moment of his waking life, that he is the servant of the Most High. He was largely charitable because the charitable man is the friend of Allah, and when he walked out of his house—built of stone, just outside the town of Penang—on his way to his godowns in the port, he had often to snatch his hand* away sharply from under the lips of men of his race and creed; and often he had to murmur deprecating words, or even to rebuke with severity those who attempted to touch his knees with their finger-tips in gratitude or supplication. He was very handsome, and carried his small head high with meek gravity. His lofty brow, straight nose, narrow, dark face with its chiselled delicacy of feature, gave him an aristocratic appearance which proclaimed his pure descent. His beard was trimmed close and to a rounded point. His large brown eyes looked out steadily with a sweetness that was belied by the expression of his thin-lipped mouth. His aspect was serene. He had a belief in his own prosperity which nothing could shake.

Restless, like all his people, he very seldom dwelt for many days together in his splendid house in Penang. Owner of ships, he was often on board one or another of them, traversing in all directions the field of his operations. In every port he had a household—his own or that of a relation—to hail his advent with demonstrative joy. In every port there were rich and influential men eager to see him, there was business to talk over, there were important letters to read: an immense correspondence, enclosed in silk envelopes—a correspondence which had nothing to do with the infidels of colonial post-offices, but came into his hands by devious, yet safe, ways. It was left for him by taciturn nakhodas of native trading craft, or was delivered with profound salaams by travel-stained and weary men who would withdraw from his presence calling upon Allah to bless the generous giver of splendid rewards. And the news was always good, and all his attempts always succeeded, and in his ears there rang always a chorus of admiration, of gratitude, of humble entreaties.

A fortunate man. And his felicity was so complete that the good genii, who ordered the stars at his birth, had not neglected—by a refinement of benevolence strange in such primitive beings—to provide him with a desire difficult to attain, and with an enemy hard to overcome. The envy of Lingard's political and commercial successes, and the wish to get the best of him in every way, became Abdulla's mania, the paramount interest of his life, the salt of his existence.

For the last few months he had been receiving mysterious messages from Sambir urging him to decisive action. He had found the river a couple of years ago, and had been anchored more than once off that estuary where the, till then, rapid Pantai, spreading slowly over the lowlands, seems to hesitate, before it

flows gently through twenty outlets; over a maze of
mudflats, sandbanks and reefs, into the expectant sea.
He had never attempted the entrance, however, because men of his race, although brave and adventurous
travellers, lack the true seamanlike instincts, and he
was afraid of getting wrecked. He could not bear the
idea of the Rajah Laut being able to boast that Abdulla
bin Selim, like other and lesser men, had also come to
grief when trying to wrest his secret from him. Meantime he returned encouraging answers to his unknown
friends in Sambir, and waited for his opportunity in the
calm certitude of ultimate triumph.

Such was the man whom Lakamba and Babalatchi
expected to see for the first time on the night of Willems' return to Aïssa. Babalatchi, who had been tormented for three days by the fear of having over-
reached himself in his little plot, now, feeling sure of
his white man, felt lighthearted and happy as he superintended the preparations in the courtyard for Abdulla's
reception. Halfway between Lakamba's house and
the river a pile of dry wood was made ready for the
torch that would set fire to it at the moment of Abdulla's
landing. Between this and the house again there was,
ranged in a semicircle, a set of low bamboo frames,
and on those were piled all the carpets and cushions of
Lakamba's household. It had been decided that the
reception was to take place in the open air, and that it
should be made impressive by the great number of
Lakamba's retainers, who, clad in clean white, with
their red sarongs gathered round their waists, chopper
at side and lance in hand, were moving about the compound or, gathering into small knots, discussed eagerly
the coming ceremony.

Two little fires burned brightly on the water's edge
on each side of the landing-place. A small heap of

damar-gum torches lay by each, and between them
Babalatchi strolled backwards and forwards, stopping
often with his face to the river and his head on one side,
listening to the sounds that came from the darkness
over the water. There was no moon and the night was
very clear overhead, but, after the afternoon breeze
had expired in fitful puffs, the vapours hung thickening
over the glancing surface of the Pantai and clung to the
shore, hiding from view the middle of the stream.

A cry in the mist—then another—and, before Babalatchi could answer, two little canoes dashed up to the
landing-place, and two of the principal citizens of
Sambir, Daoud Sahamin and Hamet Bahassoen,* who
had been confidentially invited to meet Abdulla,
landed quickly and after greeting Babalatchi walked
up the dark courtyard towards the house. The little
stir caused by their arrival soon subsided, and another
silent hour dragged its slow length* while Babalatchi
tramped up and down between the fires, his face growing more anxious with every passing moment.

At last there was heard a loud hail from down the
river. At a call from Babalatchi men ran down to
the riverside and, snatching the torches, thrust them
into the fires, then waved them above their heads till
they burst into a flame. The smoke ascended in
thick, wispy streams, and hung in a ruddy cloud above
the glare that lit up the courtyard and flashed over the
water, showing three long canoes manned by many
paddlers lying a little off; the men in them lifting
their paddles on high and dipping them down together,
in an easy stroke that kept the small flotilla motionless in the strong current, exactly abreast of the landing-
place. A man stood up in the largest craft and called
out—

"Syed Abdulla bin Selim is here!"

Babalatchi answered aloud in a formal tone—

"Allah gladdens our hearts! Come to the land!"

Abdulla landed first, steadying himself by the help of Babalatchi's extended hand. In the short moment of his passing from the boat to the shore they exchanged sharp glances and a few rapid words.

"Who are you?"

"Babalatchi. The friend of Omar. The protected of Lakamba."

"You wrote?"

"My words were written, O Giver of alms!"

And then Abdulla walked with composed face between the two lines of men holding torches, and met Lakamba in front of the big fire that was crackling itself up into a great blaze. For a moment they stood with clasped hands invoking peace upon each other's head, then Lakamba, still holding his honoured guest by the hand, led him round the fire to the prepared seats. Babalatchi followed close behind his protector. Abdulla was accompanied by two Arabs. He, like his companions, was dressed in a white robe of starched muslin, which fell in stiff folds straight from the neck. It was buttoned from the throat halfway down with a close row of very small gold buttons; round the tight sleeves there was a narrow braid of gold lace. On his shaven head he wore a small skull-cap of plaited grass. He was shod in patent leather slippers over his naked feet. A rosary of heavy wooden beads hung by a round turn from his right wrist. He sat down slowly in the place of honour, and, dropping his slippers, tucked up his legs under him decorously.

The improvised divan was arranged in a wide semi-circle, of which the point most distant from the fire —some ten yards—was also the nearest to Lakamba's dwelling. As soon as the principal personages were seated, the verandah of the house was filled silently by the muffled-up forms of Lakamba's female belongings. They crowded close to the rail and looked down, whispering faintly. Below, the formal exchange of compliments went on for some time between Lakamba and Abdulla, who sat side by side. Babalatchi squatted humbly at his protector's feet, with nothing but a thin mat between himself and the hard ground.

Then there was a pause. Abdulla glanced round in an expectant manner, and after a while Babalatchi, who had been sitting very still in a pensive attitude, seemed to rouse himself with an effort, and began to speak in gentle and persuasive tones. He described in flowing sentences the first beginnings of Sambir, the dispute of the present ruler, Patalolo, with the Sultan of Koti, the consequent troubles ending with the rising of Bugis settlers under the leadership of Lakamba. At different points of the narrative he would turn for confirmation to Sahamin and Bahassoen, who sat listening eagerly and assented together with a "Betul! Betul! Right! Right!" ejaculated in a fervent undertone.

Warming up with his subject as the narrative proceeded, Babalatchi went on to relate the facts connected with Lingard's action at the critical period of those internal dissensions. He spoke in a restrained voice still, but with a growing energy of indignation. What was he, that man of fierce aspect, to keep all the world away from them? Was he a government? Who made him ruler? He took possession of Patalolo's mind and made his heart hard; he put severe words into his mouth and caused his hand to strike right and left. That unbeliever kept the Faithful panting under the weight of his senseless oppression.

They had to trade with him—accept such goods as he would give—such credit as he would accord. And he exacted payment every year . . .

"Very true!" exclaimed Sahamin and Bahassoen together.

Babalatchi glanced at them approvingly and turned to Abdulla.

"Listen to those men, O Protector of the oppressed!" he exclaimed. "What could we do? A man must trade. There was nobody else."

Sahamin got up, staff in hand, and spoke to Abdulla with ponderous courtesy, emphasizing his words by the solemn flourishes of his right arm.

"It is so. We are weary of paying our debts to that white man here, who is the son of the Rajah Laut. That white man—may the grave of his mother be defiled!—is not content to hold us all in his hand with a cruel grasp. He seeks to cause our very death. He trades with the Dyaks of the forest, who are no better than monkeys. He buys from them guttah and rattans—while we starve. Only two days ago I went to him and said, 'Tuan Almayer'—even so; we must speak politely to that friend of Satan—'Tuan Almayer, I have such and such goods to sell. Will you buy?' And he spoke thus—because those white men have no understanding of any courtesy—he spoke to me as if I was a slave: 'Daoud, you are a lucky man'—remark, O First amongst the Believers! that by those words he could have brought misfortune on my head—'you are a lucky man to have anything in these hard times. Bring your goods quickly, and I shall receive them in payment of what you owe me from last year.' And he laughed, and struck me on the shoulder with his open hand. May Jehannum be his lot!"

"We will fight him," said young Bahassoen, crisply.

"We shall fight if there is help and a leader. Tuan Abdulla, will you come among us?"

Abdulla did not answer at once. His lips moved in an inaudible whisper and the beads passed through his fingers with a dry click. All waited in respectful silence. "I shall come if my ship can enter this river," said Abdulla at last, in a solemn tone.

"It can, Tuan," exclaimed Babalatchi. "There is a white man here who . . ."

"I want to see Omar el Badavi and that white man you wrote about," interrupted Abdulla.

Babalatchi got on his feet quickly, and there was a general move. The women on the verandah hurried indoors, and from the crowd that had kept discreetly in distant parts of the courtyard a couple of men ran with armfuls of dry fuel, which they cast upon the fire. One of them, at a sign from Babalatchi, approached and, after getting his orders, went towards the little gate and entered Omar's enclosure. While waiting for his return, Lakamba, Abdulla, and Babalatchi talked together in low tones. Sahamin sat by himself chewing betel-nut sleepily with a slight and indolent motion of his heavy jaw. Bahassoen, his hand on the hilt of his short sword, strutted backwards and forwards in the full light of the fire, looking very warlike and reckless; the envy and admiration of Lakamba's retainers, who stood in groups or flitted about noiselessly in the shadows of the courtyard.

The messenger who had been sent to Omar came back and stood at a distance, waiting till somebody noticed him. Babalatchi beckoned him close.

"What are his words?" asked Babalatchi.

"He says that Syed Abdulla is welcome now," answered the man.

Lakamba was speaking low to Abdulla, who listened
to him with deep interest.

" . . . We could have eighty men if there was
need," he was saying—"eighty men in fourteen canoes.
The only thing we want is gunpowder . . ."

"Haï! there will be no fighting," broke in Babalatchi. "The fear of your name will be enough and the
terror of your coming."

"There may be powder too," muttered Abdulla
with great nonchalance, "if only the ship enters the
river safely."

"If the heart is stout the ship will be safe," said
Babalatchi. "We will go now and see Omar el Badavi
and the white man I have here."

Lakamba's dull eyes became animated suddenly.

"Take care, Tuan Abdulla," he said, "take care.
The behaviour of that unclean white madman is furious
in the extreme. He offered to strike . . ."

"On my head, you are safe, O Giver of alms!" interrupted Babalatchi.

Abdulla looked from one to the other, and the faintest
flicker of a passing smile disturbed for a moment his
grave composure. He turned to Babalatchi, and said
with decision—

"Let us go."

"This way, O Uplifter of our hearts!" rattled on
Babalatchi, with fussy deference. "Only a very few
paces and you shall behold Omar the brave, and a
white man of great strength and cunning. This way."

He made a sign for Lakamba to remain behind,
and with respectful touches on the elbow steered Abdulla towards the gate at the upper end of the courtyard. As they walked on slowly, followed by the two
Arabs, he kept on talking in a rapid undertone to the
great man, who never looked at him once, although

appearing to listen with flattering attention. When near the gate Babalatchi moved forward and stopped, facing Abdulla, with his hand on the fastenings.

"You shall see them both," he said. "All my words about them are true. When I saw him enslaved by the one of whom I spoke, I knew he would be soft in my hand like the mud of the river. At first he answered my talk with bad words of his own language, after the manner of white men. Afterwards, when listening to the voice he loved, he hesitated. He hesitated for many days—too many. I, knowing him well, made Omar withdraw here with his . . . household. Then this red-faced man raged for three days like a black panther that is hungry. And this evening, this very evening, he came. I have him here. He is in the grasp of one with a merciless heart. I have him here," ended Babalatchi, exultingly tapping the upright of the gate with his hand.

"That is good," murmured Abdulla.

"And he shall guide your ship and lead in the fight—if fight there be," went on Babalatchi. "If there is any killing—let him be the slayer. You should give him arms—a short gun that fires many times."

"Yes, by Allah!" assented Abdulla, with slow thoughtfulness.

"And you will have to open your hand, O First amongst the generous!" continued Babalatchi. "You will have to satisfy the rapacity of a white man, and also of one who is not a man, and therefore greedy of ornaments."

"They shall be satisfied," said Abdulla; "but . . ." He hesitated, looking down on the ground and stroking his beard, while Babalatchi waited, anxious, with parted lips. After a short time he spoke again jerkily in an indistinct whisper, so that Babalatchi had

to turn his head to catch the words. "Yes. But
Omar is the son of my father's uncle . . . and all
belonging to him are of the Faith . . . while that
man is an unbeliever. It is most unseemly . . .
very unseemly. He cannot live under my shadow.
Not that dog. Penitence! I take refuge with* my
God," he mumbled rapidly. "How can he live under
my eyes with that woman, who is of the Faith? Scan-
dal! O abomination!"

He finished with a rush and drew a long breath,
then added dubiously—

"And when that man has done all we want, what
is to be done with him?"

They stood close together, meditative and silent,
their eyes roaming idly over the courtyard. The big
bonfire burned brightly, and a wavering splash of
light lay on the dark earth at their feet, while the lazy
smoke wreathed itself slowly in gleaming coils amongst
the black boughs of the trees. They could see Lakamba, who had returned to his place, sitting hunched
up spiritlessly on the cushions, and Sahamin, who had
got on his feet again and appeared to be talking to him
with dignified animation. Men in twos or threes came
out of the shadows into the light, strolling slowly, and
passed again into the shadows, their faces turned to each
other, their arms moving in restrained gestures. Bahassoen, his head proudly thrown back, his ornaments,
embroideries, and sword-hilt flashing in the light, circled
steadily round the fire like a planet round the sun. A
cool whiff of damp air came from the darkness of the
riverside; it made Abdulla and Babalatchi shiver, and
woke them up from their abstraction.

"Open the gate and go first," said Abdulla; "there
is no danger?"

"On my life, no!" answered Babalatchi, lifting the

rattan ring.   "He is all peace and content, like a thirsty man who has drunk water after many days."

He swung the gate wide, made a few paces into the gloom of the enclosure, and retraced his steps suddenly.

"He may be made useful in many ways," he whispered to Abdulla, who had stopped short, seeing him come back.

"O Sin! O Temptation!" sighed out Abdulla, faintly. "Our refuge is with the Most High. Can I feed this infidel for ever and for ever?" he added, impatiently.

"No," breathed out Babalatchi. "No! Not for ever. Only while he serves your designs, O Dispenser of Allah's gifts! When the time comes—and your order . . . ."

He sidled close to Abdulla, and brushed with a delicate touch the hand that hung down listlessly, holding the prayer-beads.

"I am your slave and your offering," he murmured, in a distinct and polite tone, into Abdulla's ear. "When your wisdom speaks, there may be found a little poison that will not lie. Who knows?"

CHAPTER FOUR

BABALATCHI saw Abdulla pass through the low and narrow entrance into the darkness of Omar's hut; heard them exchange the usual greetings and the distinguished visitor's grave voice asking: "There is no misfortune—please God—but the sight?" and then, becoming aware of the disapproving looks of the two Arabs who had accompanied Abdulla, he followed their example and fell back out of earshot. He did it unwillingly, although he did not ignore that what was going to happen in there was now absolutely beyond his control. He roamed irresolutely about for awhile, and at last wandered with careless steps towards the fire, which had been moved, from under the tree, close to the hut and a little to windward of its entrance. He squatted on his heels and began playing pensively with live embers,* as was his habit when engrossed in thought, withdrawing his hand sharply and shaking it above his head when he burnt his fingers in a fit of deeper abstraction. Sitting there he could hear the murmur of the talk inside the hut, and he could distinguish the voices but not the words. Abdulla spoke in deep tones, and now and then this flowing monotone was interrupted by a querulous exclamation, a weak moan or a plaintive quaver of the old man. Yes. It was annoying not to be able to make out what they were saying, thought Babalatchi, as he sat gazing fixedly at the unsteady glow of the fire. But it will be right. All will be right. Abdulla inspired him with confidence. He came up fully to his expectation. From the very first moment when he set his eye on him he felt sure that this man—whom he had known by reputation only—was very resolute. Perhaps too resolute. Perhaps he would want to grasp too much later on. A shadow flitted over Babalatchi's face. On the eve of the accomplishment of his desires he felt the bitter taste of that drop of doubt which is mixed with the sweetness of every success.

When, hearing footsteps on the verandah of the big house, he lifted his head, the shadow had passed away and on his face there was an expression of watchful alertness. Willems was coming down the plankway, into the courtyard. The light within trickled through the cracks of the badly joined walls of the house, and in the illuminated doorway appeared the moving form of Aïssa. She also passed into the night outside and disappeared from view. Babalatchi wondered where she had got to, and for the moment forgot the approach of Willems. The voice of the white man speaking roughly above his head made him jump to his feet as if impelled upwards by a powerful spring.

"Where's Abdulla?"

Babalatchi waved his hand towards the hut and stood listening intently. The voices within had ceased, then recommenced again. He shot an oblique glance at Willems, whose indistinct form towered above the glow of dying embers.

"Make up this fire," said Willems, abruptly. "I want to see your face."

With obliging alacrity Babalatchi put some dry brushwood on the coals from a handy pile, keeping all the time a watchful eye on Willems. When he straightened himself up his hand wandered almost involuntarily towards his left side to feel the handle of a kriss amongst the folds of his sarong, but he tried to look unconcerned under the angry stare.

"You are in good health, please God?" he murmured.

"Yes!" answered Willems, with an unexpected loudness that caused Babalatchi to start nervously. "Yes! . . . Health! . . . You . . ."

He made a long stride and dropped both his hands on the Malay's shoulders. In the powerful grip Babalatchi swayed to and fro limply, but his face was as peaceful as when he sat—a little while ago—dreaming by the fire. With a final vicious jerk Willems let go suddenly, and turning away on his heel stretched his hands over the fire. Babalatchi stumbled backwards, recovered himself, and wriggled his shoulders laboriously.

"Tse!* Tse! Tse!" he clicked, deprecatingly. After a short silence he went on with accentuated admiration: "What a man it is! What a strong man! A man like that"—he concluded, in a tone of meditative wonder—"a man like that could upset mountains—mountains!"

He gazed hopefully for a while at Willems' broad shoulders, and continued, addressing the inimical back, in a low and persuasive voice—

"But why be angry with me? With me who think only of your good? Did I not give her refuge, in my own house? Yes, Tuan! This is my own house. I will let you have it without any recompense because she must have a shelter. Therefore you and she shall live here. Who can know a woman's mind? And such a woman! If she wanted to go away from that other place, who am I—to say no! I am Omar's servant. I said: 'Gladden my heart by taking my house.' Did I say right?"

"I'll tell you something," said Willems, without changing his position; "if she takes a fancy to go away from this place it is you who shall suffer. I will wring your neck."

"When the heart is full of love there is no room in it for justice," recommenced Babalatchi, with unmoved and persistent softness. "Why slay me? You know, Tuan, what she wants. A splendid destiny is her desire —as of all women. You have been wronged and cast out by your people. She knows that. But you are brave, you are strong—you are a man; and, Tuan— I am older than you—you are in her hand. Such is the fate of strong men. And she is of noble birth and cannot live like a slave. You know her—and you are in her hand. You are like a snared bird, because of your strength. And—remember I am a man that has seen much—submit, Tuan! Submit! . . . Or else . . ."

He drawled out the last words in a hesitating manner and broke off his sentence. Still stretching his hands in turns towards the blaze and without moving his head, Willems gave a short, lugubrious laugh, and asked—

"Or else—what?"

"She may go away again. Who knows?" finished Babalatchi, in a gentle and insinuating tone.

This time Willems spun round sharply. Babalatchi stepped back.

"If she does it will be the worse for you," said Willems, in a menacing voice. "It will be your doing, and I . . ."

Babalatchi spoke, from beyond the circle of light, with calm disdain.

"Haï—ya! I have heard before. If she goes— then I die. Good! Will that bring her back do you think—Tuan? If it is my doing it shall be well done, O white man! and—who knows—you will have to live without her."

Willems gasped and started back like a confident

wayfarer who, pursuing a path he thinks safe, should see just in time a bottomless chasm under his feet. Babalatchi came into the light and approached Willems sideways, with his head thrown back and a little on one side so as to bring his only eye to bear full on the countenance of the tall white man.

"You threaten me," said Willems, indistinctly.

"I, Tuan!" exclaimed Babalatchi, with a slight suspicion of irony in the affected surprise of his tone. "I, Tuan? Who spoke of death? Was it I? No! I spoke of life only. Only of life. Of a long life for a lonely man!"

They stood with the fire between them, both silent, both aware, each in his own way, of the importance of the passing minutes. Babalatchi's fatalism gave him only an insignificant relief in his suspense, because no fatalism can kill the thought of the future, the desire of success, the pain of waiting for the disclosure of the immutable decrees of Heaven. Fatalism is born of the fear of failure, for we all believe that we carry success in our own hands, and we suspect that our hands are weak. Babalatchi looked at Willems and congratulated himself upon his ability to manage that white man. There was a pilot for Abdulla—a victim to appease Lingard's anger in case of any mishap. He would take good care to put him forward in everything. In any case let the white men fight it out amongst themselves. They were fools. He hated them—the strong fools— and knew that for his righteous wisdom was reserved the safe triumph.

Willems measured dismally the depth of his degradation. He—a white man, the admired of white men, was held by those miserable savages whose tool he was about to become. He felt for them all the hate of his race, of his morality, of his intelligence. He looked upon himself with dismay and pity. She had him. He had heard of such things. He had heard of women who . . . He would never believe such stories. . . . Yet they were true. But his own captivity seemed more complete, terrible, and final—without the hope of any redemption. He wondered at the wickedness of Providence that had made him what he was; that, worse still, permitted such a creature as Almayer to live. He had done his duty by going to him. Why did he not understand? All men were fools. He gave him his chance. The fellow did not see it. It was hard, very hard on himself—Willems. He wanted to take her from amongst her own people. That's why he had condescended to go to Almayer. He examined himself. With a sinking heart he thought that really he could not—somehow—live without her. It was terrible and sweet. He remembered the first days. Her appearance, her face, her smile, her eyes, her words. A savage woman! Yet he perceived that he could think of nothing else but of the three days of their separation, of the few hours since their reunion. Very well. If he could not take her away, then he would go to her. . . . He had, for a moment, a wicked pleasure in the thought that what he had done could not be undone. He had given himself up. He felt proud of it. He was ready to face anything, do anything. He cared for nothing, for nobody. He thought himself very fearless, but as a matter of fact he was only drunk; drunk with the poison of passionate memories.

He stretched his hands over the fire, looked round, and called out—

"Aïssa!"

She must have been near, for she appeared at once within the light of the fire. The upper part of her body was wrapped up in the thick folds of a head covering which was pulled down over her brow, and one end of it thrown across from shoulder to shoulder hid the lower part of her face. Only her eyes were visible—sombre and gleaming like a starry night.

Willems, looking at this strange, muffled figure, felt exasperated, amazed and helpless. The ex-confidential clerk of the rich Hudig would hug to his breast settled conceptions of respectable conduct. He sought refuge within his ideas of propriety from the dismal mangroves, from the darkness of the forests and of the heathen souls of the savages that were his masters. She looked like an animated package of cheap cotton goods! It made him furious. She had disguised herself so because a man of her race was near! He told her not to do it, and she did not obey. Would his ideas ever change so as to agree with her own notions of what was becoming, proper and respectable? He was really afraid they would, in time. It seemed to him awful. She would never change! This manifestation of her sense of proprieties was another sign of their hopeless diversity; something like another step downwards for him. She was too different from him. He was so civilized! It struck him suddenly that they had nothing in common—not a thought, not a feeling; he could not make clear to her the simplest motive of any act of his . . . and he could not live without her.

The courageous man who stood facing Babalatchi gasped unexpectedly with a gasp that was half a groan. This little matter of her veiling herself*against his wish acted upon him like a disclosure of some great disaster. It increased his contempt for himself as the slave of a passion he had always derided, as the man unable to assert his will. This will, all his sensations, his personality—all this seemed to be lost in the abominable desire, in the priceless promise of that woman. He was not, of course, able to discern clearly the causes of his misery; but there are none so ignorant as not to know suffering, none so simple as not to feel and suffer from the shock of warring impulses. The ignorant must feel and suffer from their complexity as well as the wisest; but to them the pain of struggle and defeat appears strange, mysterious, remediable and unjust. He stood watching her, watching himself. He tingled with rage from head to foot, as if he had been struck in the face. Suddenly he laughed; but his laugh was like a distorted echo of some insincere mirth very far away.

From the other side of the fire Babalatchi spoke hurriedly—

"Here is Tuan Abdulla."

CHAPTER FIVE

DIRECTLY on stepping outside Omar's hut Abdulla caught sight of Willems. He expected, of course, to see a white man, but not that white man, whom he knew so well. Everybody who traded in the islands, and who had any dealings with Hudig, knew Willems. For the last two years of his stay in Macassar the confidential clerk had been managing all the local trade of the house under a very slight supervision only on the part of the master. So everybody knew Willems, Abdulla amongst others—but he was ignorant of Willems' disgrace. As a matter of fact the thing had been kept very quiet—so quiet that a good many people in Macassar were expecting Willems' return there, supposing him to be absent on some confidential mission. Abdulla, in his surprise, hesitated on the threshold. He had prepared himself to see some seaman—some old officer of Lingard's; a common man—perhaps difficult to deal with, but still no match for him. Instead, he saw himself confronted by an individual whose reputation for sagacity in business was well known to him. How did he get here, and why? Abdulla, recovering from his surprise, advanced in a dignified manner towards the fire, keeping his eyes fixed steadily on Willems. When within two paces from Willems he stopped and lifted his right hand in grave salutation. Willems nodded slightly and spoke after a while.

"We know each other, Tuan Abdulla," he said, with an assumption of easy indifference.

"We have traded together," answered Abdulla, solemnly, "but it was far from here."

"And we may trade here also," said Willems.

"The place does not matter. It is the open mind and the true heart that are required in business."

"Very true. My heart is as open as my mind. I will tell you why I am here."

"What need is there? In leaving home one learns life. You travel. Travelling is victory! You shall return with much wisdom."

"I shall never return," interrupted Willems. "I have done with my people. I am a man without brothers. Injustice destroys fidelity."

Abdulla expressed his surprise by elevating his eyebrows. At the same time he made a vague gesture with his arm that could be taken as an equivalent of an approving and conciliating "just so!"

Till then the Arab had not taken any notice of Aïssa, who stood by the fire, but now she spoke in the interval of silence following Willems' declaration. In a voice that was much deadened by her wrappings she addressed Abdulla in a few words of greeting, calling him a kinsman. Abdulla glanced at her swiftly for a second, and then, with perfect good breeding, fixed his eyes on the ground. She put out towards him her hand, covered with a corner of her face-veil,* and he took it, pressed it twice, and dropping it turned towards Willems. She looked at the two men searchingly, then backed away and seemed to melt suddenly into the night.

"I know what you came for, Tuan Abdulla," said Willems; "I have been told by that man there." He nodded towards Babalatchi, then went on slowly, "It will be a difficult thing."

"Allah makes everything easy," interjected Babalatchi, piously, from a distance.

The two men turned quickly and stood looking at him thoughtfully, as if in deep consideration of the truth of that proposition. Under their sustained gaze Babalatchi experienced an unwonted feeling of shyness, and dared not approach nearer. At last Willems moved slightly, Abdulla followed readily, and they both walked down the courtyard, their voices dying away in the darkness. Soon they were heard returning, and the voices grew distinct as their forms came out of the gloom. By the fire they wheeled again, and Babalatchi caught a few words. Willems was saying—

"I have been at sea with him many years when young. I have used my knowledge to observe the way into the river when coming in, this time."

Abdulla assented in general terms.

"In the variety of knowledge there is safety," he said; and then they passed out of earshot.

Babalatchi ran to the tree and took up his position in the solid blackness under its branches, leaning against the trunk. There he was about midway between the fire and the other limit of the two men's walk. They passed him close. Abdulla slim, very straight, his head high, and his hands hanging before him and twisting mechanically the string of beads; Willems tall, broad, looking bigger and stronger in contrast to the slight white figure by the side of which he strolled carelessly, taking one step to the other's two; his big arms in constant motion as he gesticulated vehemently, bending forward to look Abdulla in the face.

They passed and repassed close to Babalatchi some half a dozen times, and, whenever they were between him and the fire, he could see them plain enough. Sometimes they would stop short, Willems speaking emphatically, Abdulla listening with rigid attention, then, when the other had ceased, bending his head slightly as if consenting to some demand, or admitting some statement. Now and then Babalatchi caught a word here and there, a fragment of a sentence, a loud exclamation. Impelled by curiosity he crept to the very edge of the black shadow under the tree. They were nearing him, and he heard Willems say—

"You will pay that money as soon as I come on board. That I must have."

He could not catch Abdulla's reply. When they went past again, Willems was saying—

"My life is in your hand anyway. The boat that brings me on board your ship shall take the money to Omar. You must have it ready in a sealed bag."

Again they were out of hearing, but instead of coming back they stopped by the fire facing each other. Willems moved his arm, shook his hand on high talking all the time, then brought it down jerkily—stamped his foot. A short period of immobility ensued. Babalatchi, gazing intently, saw Abdulla's lips move almost imperceptibly. Suddenly Willems seized the Arab's passive hand and shook it. Babalatchi drew the long breath of relieved suspense. The conference was over. All well, apparently.

He ventured now to approach the two men, who saw him and waited in silence. Willems had retired within himself already, and wore a look of grim indifference. Abdulla moved away a step or two. Babalatchi looked at him inquisitively.

"I go now," said Abdulla, "and shall wait for you outside the river, Tuan Willems, till the second sunset. You have only one word, I know."

"Only one word," repeated Willems.

Abdulla and Babalatchi walked together down the enclosure, leaving the white man alone by the fire.

The two Arabs who had come with Abdulla preceded
them and passed at once through the little gate into
the light and the murmur of voices of the principal
courtyard, but Babalatchi and Abdulla stopped on this
side of it. Abdulla said—

"It is well. We have spoken of many things. He
consents."

"When?" asked Babalatchi, eagerly.

"On the second day from this. I have promised
everything. I mean to keep much."

"Your hand is always open, O Most Generous
amongst Believers! You will not forget your servant
who called you here. Have I not spoken the truth?
She has made roast meat of his heart."

With a horizontal sweep of his arm Abdulla seemed
to push away that last statement, and said slowly,
with much meaning—

"He must be perfectly safe; do you understand?
Perfectly safe—as if he was amongst his own people—
till . . ."

"Till when?" whispered Babalatchi.

"Till I speak," said Abdulla. "As to Omar." He
hesitated for a moment, then went on very low: "He
is very old."

"Haï—ya! Old and sick," murmured Babalatchi,
with sudden melancholy.

"He wanted me to kill that white man. He begged
me to have him killed at once," said Abdulla, contemptuously, moving again towards the gate.

"He is impatient, like those who feel death near
them," exclaimed Babalatchi, apologetically.

"Omar shall dwell with me," went on Abdulla,
"when . . . But no matter. Remember! The
white man must be safe."

"He lives in your shadow," answered Babalatchi,

solemnly. "It is enough!" He touched his forehead and fell back to let Abdulla go first.

And now they are back* in the courtyard wherefrom, at their appearance, listlessness vanishes, and all the faces become alert and interested once more. Lakamba approaches his guest, but looks at Babalatchi, who reassures him by a confident nod. Lakamba clumsily attempts a smile, and looking, with natural and ineradicable sulkiness, from under his eyebrows at the man whom he wants to honour, asks whether he would condescend to visit the place of sitting down and take food. Or perhaps he would prefer to give himself up to repose? The house is his, and what is in it, and those many men that stand afar watching the interview are his. Syed Abdulla presses his host's hand to his breast, and informs him in a confidential murmur that his habits are ascetic and his temperament inclines to melancholy. No rest; no food; no use whatever for those many men who are his. Syed Abdulla is impatient to be gone. Lakamba is sorrowful but polite, in his hesitating, gloomy way. Tuan Abdulla must have fresh boatmen, and many, to shorten the dark and fatiguing road. Haï—ya! There! Boats!

By the riverside indistinct forms leap into a noisy and disorderly activity. There are cries, orders, banter, abuse. Torches blaze sending out much more smoke than light, and in their red glare Babalatchi comes up to say that the boats are ready.

Through that lurid glare Syed Abdulla, in his long white gown, seems to glide fantastically, like a dignified apparition attended by two inferior shades, and stands for a moment at the landing-place to take leave of his host and ally—whom he loves. Syed Abdulla says so distinctly before embarking, and takes his seat in the middle of the canoe under a small canopy of blue calico

stretched on four sticks. Before and behind Syed
Abdulla, the men squatting by the gunwales hold high
the blades of their paddles in readiness for a dip, all
together. Ready? Not yet. Hold on all! Syed
Abdulla speaks again, while Lakamba and Babalatchi
stand close on the bank to hear his words. His words
are encouraging. Before the sun rises for the second
time they shall meet, and Syed Abdulla's ship shall
float on the waters of this river—at last! Lakamba and
Babalatchi have no doubt—if Allah wills. They are in
the hands of the Compassionate. No doubt. And so
is Syed Abdulla, the great trader who does not know
what the word failure means; and so is the white man
—the smartest business man in the islands—who is lying
now by Omar's fire with his head on Aïssa's lap, while
Syed Abdulla flies down the muddy river with current
and paddles between the sombre walls of the sleeping
forest; on his way to the clear and open sea where the
*Lord of the Isles** (formerly of Greenock, but condemned, sold, and registered now as of Penang) waits
for its owner, and swings erratically at anchor in the
currents of the capricious tide, under the crumbling
red cliffs of Tanjong Mirrah.*

For some time Lakamba, Sahamin, and Bahassoen
looked silently into the humid darkness which had
swallowed the big canoe that carried Abdulla and his
unvarying good fortune. Then the two guests broke
into a talk expressive of their joyful anticipations.
The venerable Sahamin, as became his advanced age,
found his delight in speculation as to the activities of a
rather remote future.ˉ He would buy praus, he would
send expeditions up the river, he would enlarge his
trade, and, backed by Abdulla's capital, he would grow
rich in a very few years. Very few. Meantime it

would be a good thing to interview Almayer to-morrow and, profiting by the last day of the hated man's prosperity, obtain some goods from him on credit. Sahamin thought it could be done by skilful wheedling. After all, that son of Satan was a fool, and the thing was worth doing, because the coming revolution would wipe all debts out. Sahamin did not mind imparting that idea to his companions, with much senile chuckling, while they strolled together from the riverside towards the residence. The bull-necked Lakamba, listening with pouted lips without the sign of a smile, without a gleam in his dull, bloodshot eyes, shuffled slowly across the courtyard between his two guests. But suddenly Bahassoen broke in upon the old man's prattle with the generous enthusiasm of his youth. . . . Trading was very good. But was the change that would make them happy effected yet? The white man should be despoiled with a strong hand! . . . He grew excited, spoke very loud, and his further discourse, delivered with his hand on the hilt of his sword, dealt incoherently with the honourable topics of throat-cutting, fire-raising, and with the far-famed valour of his ancestors.

Babalatchi remained behind, alone with the greatness of his conceptions. The sagacious statesman of Sambir sent a scornful glance after his noble protector and his noble protector's friends, and then stood meditating about that future which to the others seemed so assured. Not so to Babalatchi, who paid the penalty of his wisdom by a vague sense of insecurity that kept sleep at arm's length from his tired body. When he thought at last of leaving the waterside, it was only to strike a path for himself and to creep along the fences, avoiding the middle of the courtyard where small fires glimmered and winked as though the sinister darkness there had reflected the stars of the serene heaven. He slunk past the wicket-gate of Omar's enclosure, and crept on patiently along the light bamboo palisade till he was stopped by the angle where it joined the heavy stockade of Lakamba's private ground. Standing there, he could look over the fence and see Omar's hut and the fire before its door. He could also see the shadow of two human beings sitting between him and the red glow. A man and a woman. The sight seemed to inspire the careworn sage with a frivolous desire to sing. It could hardly be called a song; it was more in the nature of a recitative without any rhythm, delivered rapidly but distinctly in a croaking and unsteady voice; and if Babalatchi considered it a song, then it was a song with a purpose and, perhaps for that reason, artistically defective. It had all the imperfections of unskilful improvisation and its subject was gruesome. It told a tale of shipwreck and of thirst, and of one brother killing another for the sake of a gourd of water. A repulsive story which might have had a purpose but possessed no moral whatever. Yet it must have pleased Babalatchi for he repeated it twice, the second time even in louder tones than at first, causing a disturbance amongst the white rice-birds and the wild fruit-pigeons which roosted on the boughs of the big tree growing in Omar's compound. There was in the thick foliage above the singer's head a confused beating of wings, sleepy remarks in bird-language, a sharp stir of leaves. The forms by the fire moved; the shadow of the woman altered its shape, and Babalatchi's song was cut short abruptly by a fit of soft and persistent coughing. He did not try to resume his efforts after that interruption, but went away stealthily, to seek—if not sleep—then, at least, repose.

CHAPTER SIX

As soon as Abdulla and his companions had left the
enclosure, Aïssa approached Willems and stood by his
side. He took no notice of her expectant attitude till
she touched him gently, when he turned furiously
upon her and, tearing off her face-veil, trampled upon
it as though it had been a mortal enemy. She looked
at him with the faint smile of patient curiosity, with
the puzzled interest of ignorance watching the running
of a complicated piece of machinery. After he had
exhausted his rage, he stood again severe and unbend-
ing looking down at the fire, but the touch of her fingers
at the nape of his neck effaced instantly the hard lines
round his mouth; his eyes wavered uneasily; his lips
trembled slightly. Starting with the unresisting rapidity of a particle of iron—which, quiescent one moment,
leaps in the next to a powerful magnet—he moved forward, caught her in his arms and pressed her violently to
his breast. He released her as suddenly, and she stumbled a little, stepped back, breathed quickly through her
parted lips, and said in a tone of pleased reproof—

"O Fool-man! And if you had killed me in your
strong arms what would you have done?"

"You want to live . . . and to run away from
me again," he said gently. "Tell me—do you?"

She moved towards him with very short steps, her
head a little on one side, hands on hips, with a slight
balancing of her body: an approach more tantalizing
than an escape. He looked on, eager—charmed. She
spoke jestingly.

"What am I to say to a man who has been away three days from me? Three!" she repeated, holding up playfully three fingers before Willems' eyes. He snatched at the hand, but she was on her guard and whisked it behind her back.

"No!" she said. "I cannot be caught. But I will come. I am coming myself because I like. Do not move. Do not touch me with your mighty hands, O child!"

As she spoke she made a step nearer, then another. Willems did not stir. Pressing against him she stood on tiptoe to look into his eyes, and her own seemed to grow bigger, glistening and tender, appealing and promising. With that look she drew the man's soul away from him through his immobile pupils, and from Willems' features the spark of reason vanished under her gaze and was replaced by an appearance of physical well-being, an ecstasy of the senses which had taken possession of his rigid body; an ecstasy that drove out regrets, hesitation and doubt, and proclaimed its terrible work by an appalling aspect of idiotic beatitude. He never stirred a limb, hardly breathed, but stood in stiff immobility, absorbing the delight of her close contact by every pore.

"Closer! Closer!" he murmured.

Slowly she raised her arms, put them over his shoulders, and clasping her hands at the back of his neck, swung off the full length of her arms. Her head fell back, the eyelids dropped slightly, and her thick hair hung straight down: a mass of ebony touched by the red gleams of the fire. He stood unyielding under the strain, as solid and motionless as one of the big trees of the surrounding forests; and his eyes looked at the modelling of her chin, at the outline of her neck, at the swelling lines of her bosom, with the famished and concentrated expression of a starving man looking at food. She drew herself up to him and rubbed her head against his cheek slowly and gently. He sighed. She, with her hands still on his shoulders, glanced up at the placid stars and said—

"The night is half gone. We shall finish it by this fire. By this fire you shall tell me all: your words and Syed Abdulla's words; and listening to you I shall forget the three days—because I am good. Tell me—am I good?"

He said "Yes" dreamily, and she ran off towards the big house.

When she came back, balancing a roll of fine mats on her head, he had replenished the fire and was ready to help her in arranging a couch on the side of it nearest to the hut. She sank down with a quick but gracefully controlled movement, and he threw himself full length with impatient haste, as if he wished to forestall somebody. She took his head on her knees, and when he felt her hands touching his face, her fingers playing with his hair, he had an expression of being taken possession of; he experienced a sense of peace, of rest, of happiness, and of soothing delight. His hands strayed upwards about her neck, and he drew her down so as to have her face above his. Then he whispered—"I wish I could die like this—now!" She looked at him with her big sombre eyes, in which there was no responsive light. His thought was so remote from her understanding that she let the words pass by unnoticed, like the breath of the wind, like the flight of a cloud. Woman though she was, she could not comprehend, in her simplicity, the tremendous compliment of that speech, that whisper of deadly happiness, so sincere, so spontaneous, coming so straight from the heart—like every corruption. It was the voice of madness, of a delirious peace, of happi-

ness that is infamous, cowardly, and so exquisite that
the debased mind refuses to contemplate its termina-
tion: for to the victims of such happiness the moment
of its ceasing is the beginning afresh of that torture
which is its price.

With her brows slightly knitted in the determined
preoccupation of her own desires, she said—

"Now tell me all. All the words spoken between
you and Syed Abdulla."

Tell what? What words? Her voice recalled back
the consciousness that had departed under her touch,
and he became aware of the passing minutes every one
of which was like a reproach; of those minutes that falling, slow, reluctant, irresistible into the past, marked
his footsteps on the way to perdition. Not that he had
any conviction about it, any notion of the possible ending on that painful road. It was an indistinct feeling,
a threat of suffering like the confused warning of coming
disease, an inarticulate monition of evil made up of fear
and pleasure, of resignation and of revolt. He was
ashamed of his state of mind. After all, what was he
afraid of? Were those scruples? Why that hesitation
to think, to speak of what he intended doing? Scruples
were for imbeciles. His clear duty was to make himself
happy. Did he ever take an oath of fidelity to Lingard? No. Well then—he would not let any interest
of that old fool stand between Willems and Willems'
happiness. Happiness? Was he not, perchance, on a
false track? Happiness meant money. Much money.
At least he had always thought so till he had experienced
those new sensations which . . .

Aïssa's question, repeated impatiently, interrupted
his musings, and looking up at her face shining above
him in the dim light of the fire he stretched his limbs
luxuriously and obedient to her desire, he spoke slowly

and hardly above his breath. She, with her head close
to his lips, listened absorbed, interested, in attentive
immobility. The many noises of the great courtyard
were hushed up gradually by the sleep that stilled all
voices and closed all eyes. Then somebody droned
out a song with a nasal drawl at the end of every verse.
He stirred. She put her hand suddenly on his lips and
sat upright. There was a feeble coughing, a rustle of
leaves, and then a complete silence took possession of
the land; a silence cold, mournful, profound; more like
death than peace; more hard to bear than the fiercest
tumult. As soon as she removed her hand he hastened
to speak, so insupportable to him was that stillness
perfect and absolute in which his thoughts seemed to
ring with the loudness of shouts.

"Who was there making that noise?" he asked.

"I do not know. He is gone now," she answered,
hastily. "Tell me, you will not return to your people;
not without me. Not with me. Do you promise?"

"I have promised already. I have no people of my
own. Have I not told you, that you are everybody to
me?"

"Ah, yes," she said, slowly, "but I like to hear you
say that again—every day, and every night, whenever
I ask; and never to be angry because I ask. I am afraid
of white women who are shameless and have fierce eyes."
She scanned his features close for a moment and added:
"Are they very beautiful? They must be."

"I do not know," he whispered, thoughtfully. "And
if I ever did know, looking at you I have forgotten."

"Forgotten! And for three days and two nights you
have forgotten me also! Why? Why were you angry
with me when I spoke at first of Tuan Abdulla, in the
days when we lived beside the brook? You remembered
somebody then. Somebody in the land whence you

come. Your tongue is false. You are white indeed, and your heart is full of deception. I know it. And yet I cannot help believing you when you talk of your love for me. But I am afraid!"

He felt flattered and annoyed by her vehemence, and said—

"Well, I am with you now. I did come back. And it was you that went away."

"When you have helped Abdulla against the Rajah Laut, who is the first of white men, I shall not be afraid any more," she whispered.

"You must believe what I say when I tell you that there never was another woman; that there is nothing for me to regret, and nothing but my enemies to remember."

"Where do you come from?" she said, impulsive and inconsequent, in a passionate whisper. "What is that land beyond the great sea from which you come? A land of lies and of evil from which nothing but misfortune ever comes to us—who are not white. Did you not at first ask me to go there with you? That is why I went away."

"I shall never ask you again."

"And there is no woman waiting for you there?"

"No!" said Willems, firmly.

She bent over him. Her lips hovered above his face and her long hair brushed his cheeks.

"You taught me the love of your people which is of the Devil," she murmured, and bending still lower, she said faintly, "Like this?"

"Yes, like this!" he answered very low, in a voice that trembled slightly with eagerness; and she pressed suddenly her lips to his while he closed his eyes in an ecstasy of delight.

There was a long interval of silence. She stroked

his head with gentle touches, and he lay dreamily, perfectly happy but for the annoyance of an indistinct vision of a well-known figure; a man going away from him and diminishing in a long perspective of fantastic trees, whose every leaf was an eye looking after that man, who walked away growing smaller, but never getting out of sight for all his steady progress. He felt a desire to see him vanish, a hurried impatience of his disappearance, and he watched for it with a careful and irksome effort. There was something familiar about that figure. Why! Himself! He gave a sudden start and opened his eyes, quivering with the emotion of that quick return from so far, of finding himself back by the fire with the rapidity of a flash of lightning. It had been half a dream; he had slumbered in her arms for a few seconds. Only the beginning of a dream— nothing more. But it was some time before he recovered from the shock of seeing himself go away so deliberately, so definitely, so unguardedly; and going away—where? Now, if he had not woke*up in time he would never have come back again from there; from whatever place he was going to. He felt indignant. It was like an evasion, like a prisoner breaking his parole—that thing slinking off stealthily while he slept. He was very indignant, and was also astonished at the absurdity of his own emotions.

She felt him tremble, and murmuring tender words, pressed his head to her breast. Again he felt very peaceful with a peace that was as complete as the silence round them. He muttered—

"You are tired, Aïssa."

She answered so low that it was like a sigh shaped into faint words.

"I shall watch your sleep, O child!"

He lay very quiet, and listened to the beating of her

heart. That sound, light, rapid, persistent, and steady;
her very life beating against his cheek, gave him a clear
perception of secure ownership, strengthened his belief
in his possession of that human being, was like an assurance of the vague felicity of the future. There were
no regrets, no doubts, no hesitation now. Had there
ever been? All that seemed far away, ages ago—as
unreal and pale as the fading memory of some delirium.
All the anguish, suffering, strife of the past days; the
humiliation and anger of his downfall; all that was an
infamous nightmare, a thing born in sleep to be forgotten and leave no trace—and true life was this: this
dreamy immobility with his head against her heart
that beat so steadily.

He was broad awake now, with that tingling wake-
fulness of the tired body which succeeds to the few
refreshing seconds of irresistible sleep, and his wide-
open eyes looked absently at the doorway of Omar's
hut. The reed walls glistened in the light of the fire,
the smoke of which, thin and blue, drifted slanting in
a succession of rings and spirals across the doorway,
whose empty blackness seemed to him impenetrable
and enigmatical like a curtain hiding vast spaces full
of unexpected surprises. This was only his fancy,
but it was absorbing enough to make him accept the
sudden appearance of a head, coming out of the gloom,
as part of his idle fantasy or as the beginning of another
short dream, of another vagary of his overtired brain.
A face with drooping eyelids, old, thin, and yellow,
above the scattered white of a long beard that touched
the earth. A head without a body, only a foot above
the ground, turning slightly from side to side on the
edge of the circle of light as if to catch the radiating
heat of the fire on either cheek in succession. He
watched it in passive amazement, growing distinct, as

if coming nearer to him, and the confused outlines of a body crawling on all fours* came out, creeping inch by inch towards the fire, with a silent and all but imperceptible movement. He was astounded at the appearance of that blind head dragging that crippled body behind, without a sound, without a change in the composure of the sightless face, which was plain one second, blurred the next in the play of the light that drew it to itself steadily. A mute face with a kriss between its lips. This was no dream. Omar's face. But why? What was he after?

He was too indolent in the happy languor of the moment to answer the question. It darted through his brain and passed out, leaving him free to listen again to the beating of her heart; to that precious and delicate sound which filled the quiet immensity of the night. Glancing upwards he saw the motionless head of the woman looking down at him in a tender gleam of liquid white between the long eyelashes, whose shadow rested on the soft curve of her cheek; and under the caress of that look, the uneasy wonder and the obscure fear of that apparition, crouching and creeping in turns towards the fire that was its guide, were lost—were drowned in the quietude of all his senses, as pain is drowned in the flood of drowsy serenity that follows upon a dose of opium.

He altered the position of his head by ever so little, and now could see easily that apparition which he had seen a minute before and had nearly forgotten already. It had moved closer, gliding and noiseless like the shadow of some nightmare, and now it was there, very near, motionless and still as if listening; one hand and one knee advanced; the neck stretched out and the head turned full towards the fire. He could see the emaciated face, the skin shiny over the prominent bones, the black shadows of the hollow temples and sunken cheeks, and the two patches of blackness over the eyes, over those eyes that were dead and could not see. What was the impulse which drove out this blind cripple into the night to creep and crawl towards that fire? He looked at him, fascinated, but the face, with its shifting lights and shadows, let out nothing, closed and impenetrable like a walled door.

Omar raised himself to a kneeling posture and sank on his heels, with his hands hanging down before him. Willems, looking out of his dreamy numbness, could see plainly the kriss between the thin lips, a bar across the face; the handle on one side where the polished wood caught a red gleam from the fire and the thin line of the blade running to a dull black point on the other. He felt an inward shock, which left his body passive in Aïssa's embrace, but filled his breast with a tumult of powerless fear; and he perceived suddenly that it was his own death that was groping towards him; that it was the hate of himself and the hate of her love for him which drove this helpless wreck of a once brilliant and resolute pirate, to attempt a desperate deed that would be the glorious and supreme consolation of an unhappy old age. And while he looked, paralyzed with dread, at the father who had resumed his cautious advance—blind like fate, persistent like destiny—he listened with greedy eagerness to the heart of the daughter beating light, rapid, and steady against his head.

He was in the grip of horrible fear; of a fear whose cold hand robs its victim of all will and of all power; of all wish to escape, to resist, or to move; which destroys hope and despair alike, and holds the empty and useless carcass as if in a vise under the coming stroke. It was not the fear of death—he had faced danger before—it was not even the fear of that particular form of death. It was not the fear of the end, for he knew that the end would not come then. A movement, a leap, a shout would save him from the feeble hand of the blind old man, from that hand that even now was, with cautious sweeps along the ground, feeling for his body in the darkness. It was the unreasoning fear of this glimpse into the unknown things, into those motives, impulses, desires he had ignored, but that had lived in the breasts of despised men, close by his side, and were revealed to him for a second, to be hidden again behind the black mists of doubt and deception. It was not death that frightened him: it was the horror of bewildered life where he could understand nothing and nobody round him; where he could guide, control, comprehend nothing and no one—not even himself.

He felt a touch on his side. That contact, lighter than the caress of a mother's hand on the cheek of a sleeping child, had for him the force of a crushing blow. Omar had crept close, and now, kneeling above him, held the kriss in one hand while the other skimmed over his jacket up towards his breast in gentle touches; but the blind face, still turned to the heat of the fire, was set and immovable in its aspect of stony indifference to things it could not hope to see. With an effort Willems took his eyes off the deathlike mask and turned them up to Aïssa's head. She sat motionless as if she had been part of the sleeping earth, then suddenly he saw her big sombre eyes open out wide in a piercing stare and felt the convulsive pressure of her hands pinning his arms along his body. A second dragged itself out, slow and bitter, like a day of mourning; a second full of regret and grief for that faith in her which took its flight from the shattered ruins of his

trust. She was holding him! She too! He felt her
heart give a great leap, his head slipped down on her
knees, he closed his eyes and there was nothing. Nothing! It was as if she had died; as though her heart had
leaped out into the night, abandoning him, defenceless
and alone, in an empty world.

His head struck the ground heavily as she flung him
aside in her sudden rush. He lay as if stunned, face
up and, daring not move, did not see the struggle,
but heard the piercing shriek of mad fear, her low
angry words; another shriek dying out in a moan.
When he got up at last he looked at Aïssa kneeling
over her father, he saw her bent back in the effort of
holding him down, Omar's contorted limbs, a hand
thrown up above her head and her quick movement
grasping the wrist. He made an impulsive step forward, but she turned a wild face to him and called
out over her shoulder—

"Keep back! Do not come near! Do not. . . ."
And he stopped short, his arms hanging lifelessly
by his side, as if those words had changed him into
stone.* She was afraid of his possible violence, but in
the unsettling of all his convictions he was struck
with the frightful thought that she preferred to kill
her father all by herself; and the last stage of their
struggle, at which he looked as though a red fog had
filled his eyes, loomed up with an unnatural ferocity,
with a sinister meaning; like something monstrous
and depraved, forcing its complicity upon him under
the cover of that awful night. He was horrified and
grateful; drawn irresistibly to her—and ready to run
away. He could not move at first—then he did not
want to stir. He wanted to see what would happen.
He saw her lift, with a tremendous effort, the apparently lifeless body into the hut, and remained stand-

ing, after they disappeared, with the vivid image in his eyes of that head swaying on her shoulder, the lower jaw hanging down, collapsed, passive, meaningless, like the head of a corpse.

Then after a while he heard her voice speaking inside, harshly, with an agitated abruptness of tone; and in answer there were groans and broken murmurs of exhaustion. She spoke louder. He heard her saying violently—"No! No! Never!"

And again a plaintive murmur of entreaty as of some one begging for a supreme favour, with a last breath. Then she said—

"Never! I would sooner strike it into my own heart."

She came out, stood panting for a short moment in the doorway, and then stepped into the firelight. Behind her, through the darkness came the sound of words calling the vengeance of heaven on her head, rising higher, shrill, strained, repeating the curse over and over again—till the voice cracked in a passionate shriek that died out into hoarse muttering ending with a deep and prolonged sigh. She stood facing Willems, one hand behind her back, the other raised in a gesture compelling attention, and she listened in that attitude till all was still inside the hut. Then she made another step forward and her hand dropped slowly.

"Nothing but misfortune," she whispered, absently, to herself. "Nothing but misfortune to us who are not white." The anger and excitement died out of her face, and she looked straight at Willems with an intense and mournful gaze.

He recovered his senses and his power of speech with a sudden start.

"Aïssa," he exclaimed, and the words broke out through his lips with hurried nervousness. "Aïssa!

How can I live here? Trust me. Believe in me. Let us go away from here. Go very far away! Very far; you and I!"

He did not stop to ask himself whether he could escape, and how, and where. He was carried away by the flood of hate, disgust, and contempt of a white man for that blood which is not his blood, for that race which is not his race; for the brown skins; for the hearts false like the sea, blacker than night. This feeling of repulsion overmastered his reason in a clear conviction of the impossibility for him to live with her people. He urged her passionately to fly with him because out of all that abhorred crowd he wanted this one woman, but wanted her away from them, away from that race of slaves and cut-throats from which she sprang. He wanted her for himself—far from everybody, in some safe and dumb solitude. And as he spoke his anger and contempt rose, his hate became almost fear; and his desire of her grew immense, burning, illogical and merciless; crying to him through all his senses; louder than his hate, stronger than his fear, deeper than his contempt—irresistible and certain like death itself.

Standing at a little distance, just within the light—but on the threshold of that darkness from which she had come—she listened, one hand still behind her back, the other arm stretched out with the hand half open as if to catch the fleeting words that rang around her, passionate, menacing, imploring, but all tinged with the anguish of his suffering, all hurried by the impatience that gnawed his breast. And while she listened she felt a slowing down of her heart-beats as the meaning of his appeal grew clearer before her indignant eyes, as she saw with rage and pain the edifice of her love, her own work, crumble slowly to pieces, destroyed by that man's fears, by that man's falseness. Her memory recalled the days by the brook when she had listened to other words—to other thoughts—to promises and to pleadings for other things, which came from that man's lips at the bidding of her look or her smile, at the nod of her head, at the whisper of her lips. Was there then in his heart something else than her image, other desires than the desires of her love, other fears than the fear of losing her? How could that be? Had she grown ugly or old in a moment? She was appalled, surprised and angry with the anger of unexpected humiliation; and her eyes looked fixedly, sombre and steady, at that man born in the land of violence and of evil wherefrom nothing but misfortune comes to those who are not white. Instead of thinking of her caresses, instead of forgetting all the world in her embrace, he was thinking yet of his people; of that people that steals every land, masters every sea, that knows no mercy and no truth—knows nothing but its own strength. O man of strong arm and of false heart! Go with him to a far country, be lost in the throng of cold eyes and false hearts—lose him there! Never! He was mad—mad with fear; but he should not escape her! She would keep him here a slave and a master; here where he was alone with her; where he must live for her—or die. She had a right to his love which was of her making, to the love that was in him now, while he spoke those words without sense. She must put between him and other white men a barrier of hate. He must not only stay, but he must also keep his promise to Abdulla, the fulfilment of which would make her safe. . . .

"Aïssa, let us go! With you by my side I would attack them with my naked hands. Or no! Tomorrow we shall be outside, on board Abdulla's ship.

You shall come with me and then I could . . .   If
the ship went ashore by some chance, then we could
steal a canoe and escape in the confusion. . . .
You are not afraid of the sea . . .   of the sea that
would give me freedom . . ."

He was approaching her gradually with extended
arms, while he pleaded ardently in incoherent words
that ran over and tripped each other in the extreme
eagerness of his speech. She stepped back, keeping
her distance, her eyes on his face, watching on it the
play of his doubts and of his hopes with a piercing
gaze, that seemed to search out the innermost recesses
of his thought; and it was as if she had drawn slowly
the darkness round her, wrapping herself in its undulating folds that made her indistinct and vague.
He followed her step by step till at last they both
stopped, facing each other under the big tree of the
enclosure. The solitary exile of the forests, great,
motionless and solemn in his abandonment, left alone
by the life of ages that had been pushed away from
him by those pigmies that crept at his foot, towered
high and straight above their heads. He seemed to
look on, dispassionate and imposing, in his lonely
greatness, spreading his branches wide in a gesture
of lofty protection, as if to hide them in the sombre
shelter of innumerable leaves; as if moved by the
disdainful compassion of the strong, by the scornful
pity of an aged giant, to screen this struggle of two
human hearts* from the cold scrutiny of glittering
stars.

The last cry of his appeal to her mercy rose loud,
vibrated under the sombre canopy, darted among the
boughs startling the white birds that slept wing to
wing—and died without an echo, strangled in the
dense mass of unstirring leaves. He could not see

her face, but he heard her sighs and the distracted murmur of indistinct words. Then, as he listened holding his breath, she exclaimed suddenly—

"Have you heard him? He has cursed me because I love you. You brought me suffering and strife—and his curse. And now you want to take me far away where I would lose you, lose my life; because your love is my life now. What else is there? Do not move," she cried violently, as he stirred a little—"do not speak! Take this! Sleep in peace!"

He saw a shadowy movement of her arm. Something whizzed past and struck the ground behind him, close to the fire. Instinctively he turned round to look at it. A kriss without its sheath lay by the embers; a sinuous dark object, looking like something that had been alive and was now crushed, dead and very inoffensive; a black wavy outline very distinct and still in the dull red glow. Without thinking he moved to pick it up, stooping with the sad and humble movement of a beggar gathering the alms flung into the dust of the roadside. Was this the answer to his pleading, to the hot and living words that came from his heart? Was this the answer thrown at him like an insult, that thing made of wood and iron, insignificant and venomous, fragile and deadly? He held it by the blade and looked at the handle stupidly for a moment before he let it fall again at his feet; and when he turned round he faced only the night:—the night immense, profound and quiet; a sea of darkness in which she had disappeared without leaving a trace.

He moved forward with uncertain steps, putting out both his hands before him with the anguish of a man blinded suddenly.

"Aïssa!" he cried—"come to me at once."

He peered and listened, but saw nothing, heard

nothing. After a while the solid blackness seemed to wave before his eyes like a curtain disclosing movements but hiding forms, and he heard light and hurried footsteps, then the short clatter of the gate leading to Lakamba's private enclosure. He sprang forward and brought up against the rough timber in time to hear the words, "Quick! Quick!" and the sound of the wooden bar dropped on the other side, securing the gate. With his arms thrown up, the palms against the paling, he slid down in a heap on the ground.

"Aïssa," he said, pleadingly, pressing his lips to a chink between the stakes. "Aïssa, do you hear me? Come back! I will do what you want, give you all you desire—if I have to set the whole Sambir on fire and put that fire out with blood. Only come back. Now! At once! Are you there? Do you hear me? Aïssa!"

On the other side there were startled whispers of feminine voices; a frightened little laugh suddenly interrupted; some woman's admiring murmur—"This is brave talk!" Then after a short silence Aïssa cried—

"Sleep in peace—for the time of your going is near. Now I am afraid of you. Afraid of your fear. When you return with Tuan Abdulla you shall be great. You will find me here. And there will be nothing but love. Nothing else!—Always!—Till we die!"

He listened to the shuffle of footsteps going away, and staggered to his feet, mute with the excess of his passionate anger against that being so savage and so charming; loathing her, himself, everybody he had ever known; the earth, the sky, the very air he drew into his oppressed chest; loathing it because it made him live, loathing her because she made him suffer. But he could not leave that gate through which she had passed. He wandered a little way off, then swerved round, came back and fell down again by the stockade only to rise suddenly in another attempt to break away from the spell that held him, that brought him back there, dumb, obedient and furious.   And under the immobilized gesture of lofty protection in the branches outspread wide above his head, under the high branches where white birds slept wing to wing in the shelter of countless leaves, he tossed like a grain of dust in a whirlwind—sinking and rising—round and round—always near that gate.   All through the languid stillness of that night he fought with the impalpable; he fought with the shadows, with the darkness, with the silence. He fought without a sound, striking futile blows, dashing from side to side; obstinate, hopeless, and always beaten back; like a man bewitched within the invisible sweep of a magic circle.

PART III

CHAPTER ONE

"Yes! Cat, dog, anything that can scratch or bite;
as long as it is harmful enough and mangy enough.
A sick tiger would make you happy—of all things.
A half-dead tiger that you could weep over and palm
upon some poor devil in your power, to tend and
nurse for you. Never mind the consequences—to the
poor devil. Let him be mangled or eaten up, of course!
You haven't any pity to spare for the victims of your
infernal charity. Not you! Your tender heart bleeds
only for what is poisonous and deadly. I curse the
day when you set your benevolent eyes on him. I
curse it . . . ."

"Now then! Now then!" growled Lingard in his
moustache. Almayer, who had talked himself up to
the choking point, drew a long breath and went on—

"Yes! It has been always so. Always. As far
back as I can remember. Don't you recollect? What
about that half-starved dog you brought on board in
Bankok in your arms. In your arms by . . . !
It went mad next day and bit the serang. You don't
mean to say you have forgotten? The best serang
you ever had! You said so yourself while you were
helping us to lash him down to the chain-cable, just
before he died in his fits. Now, didn't you? Two
wives and ever so many children the man left. That
was your doing. . . . And when you went out of
your way and risked your ship to rescue some Chinamen from a water-logged junk in Formosa Straits,*
that was also a clever piece of business. Wasn't it?

Those damned Chinamen rose on you before forty-eight hours. They were cut-throats, those poor fishermen. You knew they were cut-throats before you made up your mind to run down on a lee shore in a gale of wind to save them. A mad trick! If they hadn't been scoundrels—hopeless scoundrels—you would not have put your ship in jeopardy for them, I know. You would not have risked the lives of your crew—that crew you loved so—and your own life. Wasn't that foolish! And, besides, you were not honest. Suppose you had been drowned? I would have been in a pretty mess then, left alone here with that adopted daughter of yours. Your duty was to myself first. I married that girl because you promised to make my fortune. You know you did! And then three months afterwards you go and do that mad trick—for a lot of Chinamen too. Chinamen! You have no morality. I might have been ruined for the sake of those murderous scoundrels that, after all, had to be driven overboard after killing ever so many of your crew—of your beloved crew! Do you call that honest?"

"Well, well!" muttered Lingard, chewing nervously the stump of his cheroot that had gone out and looking at Almayer—who stamped wildly about the verandah —much as a shepherd might look at a pet sheep in his obedient flock turning unexpectedly upon him in enraged revolt. He seemed disconcerted, contemptuously angry yet somewhat amused; and also a little hurt as if at some bitter jest at his own expense. Almayer stopped suddenly, and crossing his arms on his breast, bent his body forward and went on speaking.

"I might have been left then in an awkward hole— all on account of your absurd disregard for your safety —yet I bore no grudge. I knew your weaknesses.

But now—when I think of it! Now we are ruined.
Ruined! Ruined! My poor little Nina. Ruined!"

He slapped his thighs smartly, walked with small
steps this way and that, seized a chair, planted it with
a bang before Lingard, and sat down staring at the
old seaman with haggard eyes. Lingard, returning
his stare steadily, dived slowly into various pockets,
fished out at last a box of matches and proceeded to
light his cheroot carefully, rolling it round and round
between his lips, without taking his gaze for a moment
off the distressed Almayer. Then from behind a cloud
of tobacco smoke he said calmly—

"If you had been in trouble as often as I have, my
boy, you wouldn't carry on so. I have been ruined
more than once. Well, here I am."

"Yes, here you are," interrupted Almayer. "Much
good it is to me. Had you been here a mon'h ago it
would have been of some use. But now! . . . You
might as well be a thousand miles off."

"You scold like a drunken fish-wife," said Lingard,
serenely. He got up and moved slowly to the front
rail of the verandah. The floor shook and the whole
house vibrated under his heavy step. For a moment
he stood with his back to Almayer, looking out on the
river and forest of the east bank, then turned round
and gazed mildly down upon him.

"It's very lonely this morning here. Hey?" he said.

Almayer lifted up his head.

"Ah! you notice it—don't you? I should think
it is lonely! Yes, Captain Lingard, your day is over
in Sambir. Only a month ago this verandah would
have been full of people coming to greet you. Fellows
would be coming up those steps grinning and salaaming—to you and to me. But our day is over. And
not by my fault either. You can't say that. It's all

the doing of that pet rascal of yours. Ah! He is a beauty! You should have seen him leading that hellish crowd. You would have been proud of your old favourite."

"Smart fellow that," muttered Lingard, thoughtfully. Almayer jumped up with a shriek.

"And that's all you have to say! Smart fellow! O Lord!"

"Don't make a show of yourself. Sit down. Let's talk quietly. I want to know all about it. So he led?"

"He was the soul of the whole thing. He piloted Abdulla's ship in. He ordered everything and everybody," said Almayer, who sat down again, with a resigned air.

"When did it happen—exactly?"

"On the sixteenth I heard the first rumours of Abdulla's ship being in the river; a thing I refused to believe at first. Next day I could not doubt any more. There was a great council held openly in Lakamba's place where almost everybody in Sambir attended. On the eighteenth the *Lord of the Isles* was anchored in Sambir reach, abreast of my house. Let's see. Six weeks to-day, exactly."

"And all that happened like this? All of a sudden. You never heard anything—no warning. Nothing. Never had an idea that something was up? Come, Almayer!"

"Heard! Yes, I used to hear something every day. Mostly lies. Is there anything else in Sambir?"

"You might not have believed them," observed Lingard. "In fact you ought not to have believed everything that was told to you, as if you had been a green hand on his first voyage."

Almayer moved in his chair uneasily.

"That scoundrel came here one day," he said. "He

had been away from the house for a couple of months living with that woman. I only heard about him now and then from Patalolo's people when they came over. Well one day, about noon, he appeared in this courtyard, as if he had been jerked up from hell—where he belongs."

Lingard took his cheroot out, and, with his mouth full of white smoke that oozed out through his parted lips, listened, attentive. After a short pause Almayer went on, looking at the floor moodily—

"I must say he looked awful. Had a bad bout of the ague probably. The left shore is very unhealthy. Strange that only the breadth of the river . . ."

He dropped off into deep thoughtfulness as if he had forgotten his grievances in a bitter meditation upon the unsanitary condition of the virgin forests on the left bank. Lingard took this opportunity to expel the smoke in a mighty expiration and threw the stump of his cheroot over his shoulder.

"Go on," he said, after a while. "He came to see you . . ."

"But it wasn't unhealthy enough to finish him, worse luck!" went on Almayer, rousing himself, "and, as I said, he turned up here with his brazen impudence. He bullied me, he threatened vaguely. He wanted to scare me, to blackmail me. Me! And, by heaven—he said you would approve. You! Can you conceive such impudence? I couldn't exactly make out what he was driving at. Had I known, I would have approved him. Yes! With a bang on the head. But how could I guess that he knew enough to pilot a ship through the entrance you always said was so difficult. And, after all, that was the only danger. I could deal with anybody here—but when Abdulla came. . . . That barque of his is armed. He carries twelve brass six-

pounders,* and about thirty men. Desperate beggars.
Sumatra men, from Deli and Acheen. Fight all day
and ask for more in the evening. That kind."

"I know, I know," said Lingard, impatiently.

"Of course, then, they were cheeky as much as you
please after he anchored abreast of our jetty. Willems
brought her up himself in the best berth. I could see
him from this verandah standing forward, together with
the half-caste master. And that woman was there too.
Close to him. I heard they took her on board off Lakamba's place. Willems said he would not go higher
without her. Stormed and raged. Frightened them,
I believe. Abdulla had to interfere. She came off
alone in a canoe, and no sooner on deck than she fell
at his feet before all hands, embraced his knees, wept,
raved, begged his pardon. Why? I wonder. Everybody in Sambir is talking of it. They never heard tell
or saw anything like it. I have all this from Ali, who
goes about in the settlement and brings me the news.
I had better know what is going on—hadn't I? From
what I can make out, they—he and that woman—are
looked upon as something mysterious—beyond comprehension. Some think them mad. They live alone
with an old woman in a house outside Lakamba's campong and are greatly respected—or feared, I should say
rather. At least, he is. He is very violent. She knows
nobody, sees nobody, will speak to nobody but him.
Never leaves him for a moment. It's the talk of the
place. There are other rumours. From what I hear I
suspect that Lakamba and Abdulla are tired of him.
There's also talk of him going away in the *Lord of the
Isles*—when she leaves here for the southward—as a
kind of Abdulla's agent. At any rate, he must take the
ship out. The half-caste is not equal to it as yet."

Lingard, who had listened absorbed till then, began

now to walk with measured steps. Almayer ceased talking and followed him with his eyes as he paced up and down with a quarter-deck swing, tormenting and twisting his long white beard, his face perplexed and thoughtful.

"So he came to you first of all, did he?" asked Lingard, without stopping.

"Yes. I told you so. He did come. Came to extort money, goods—I don't know what else. Wanted to set up as a trader—the swine! I kicked his hat into the courtyard, and he went after it, and that was the last of him till he showed up with Abdulla. How could I know that he could do harm in that way? Or in any way at that! Any local rising I could put down easy with my own men and with Patalolo's help."

"Oh! yes. Patalolo. No good. Eh? Did you try him at all?"

"Didn't I!" exclaimed Almayer. "I went to see him myself on the twelfth. That was four days before Abdulla entered the river. In fact, same day Willems tried to get at me. I did feel a little uneasy then. Patalolo assured me that there was no human being that did not love me in Sambir. Looked as wise as an owl. Told me not to listen to the lies of wicked people from down the river. He was alluding to that man Bulangi, who lives up the sea reach, and who had sent me word that a strange ship was anchored outside—which, of course, I repeated to Patalolo. He would not believe. Kept on mumbling 'No! No! No!' like an old parrot, his head all of a tremble, all beslobbered with betel-nut juice. I thought there was something queer about him. Seemed so restless, and as if in a hurry to get rid of me. Well. Next day that one-eyed malefactor who lives with Lakamba— what's his name—Babalatchi, put in an appearance here. Came about midday, casually

like, and stood there on this verandah chatting about
one thing and another. Asking when I expected you,
and so on. Then, incidentally, he mentioned that they
—his master and himself—were very much bothered
by a ferocious white man—my friend—who was hanging about that woman—Omar's daughter. Asked my
advice. Very deferential and proper. I told him the
white man was not my friend, and that they had better
kick him out. Whereupon he went away salaaming,
and protesting his friendship and his master's goodwill.
Of course I know now the infernal nigger*came to spy
and to talk over some of my men. Anyway, eight were
missing at the evening muster. Then I took alarm.
Did not dare to leave my house unguarded. You know
what my wife is, don't you? And I did not care to take
the child with me—it being late—so I sent a message to
Patalolo to say that we ought to consult; that there
were rumours and uneasiness in the settlement. Do
you know what answer I got?"

Lingard stopped short in his walk before Almayer,
who went on, after an impressive pause, with growing
animation.

"Ali brought it: 'The Rajah sends a friend's greeting,
and does not understand the message.' That was all.
Not a word more could Ali get out of him. I could see
that Ali was pretty well scared. He hung about, arranging my hammock—one thing and another. Then
just before going away he mentioned that the water-
gate of the Rajah's place was heavily barred, but that
he could see only very few men about the courtyard.
Finally he said, 'There is darkness in our Rajah's house,
but no sleep. Only darkness and fear and the wailing
of women.' Cheerful, wasn't it? It made me feel
cold down my back somehow. After Ali slipped away I
stood here—by this table, and listened to the shouting

and drumming in the settlement. Racket enough for
twenty weddings. It was a little past midnight then."

Again Almayer stopped in his narrative with an
abrupt shutting of lips, as if he had said all that there
was to tell, and Lingard stood staring at him, pensive
and silent. A big bluebottle fly flew in recklessly
into the cool verandah, and darted with loud buzzing
between the two men. Lingard struck at it with his
hat. The fly swerved, and Almayer dodged his head
out of the way. Then Lingard aimed another inef-
fectual blow; Almayer jumped up and waved his arms
about. The fly buzzed desperately, and the vibration
of minute wings sounded in the peace of the early morning like a far-off string orchestra accompanying the
hollow, determined stamping of the two men, who, with
heads thrown back and arms gyrating on high, or again
bending low with infuriated lunges, were intent upon
killing the intruder. But suddenly the buzz died out in
a thin thrill away in the open space of the courtyard,
leaving Lingard and Almayer standing face to face in the
fresh silence of the young day, looking very puzzled and
idle, their arms hanging uselessly by their sides—like
men disheartened by some portentous failure.

"Look at that!" muttered Lingard. "Got away
after all."

"Nuisance," said Almayer in the same tone. "Riverside is overrun with them. This house is badly placed
. . . mosquitos . . . and these big flies . . .
last week stung Nina . . . been ill four days
. . . poor child. . . . I wonder what such
damned things are made for!"

CHAPTER TWO

AFTER a long silence, during which Almayer had moved towards the table and sat down, his head between his hands, staring straight before him, Lingard, who had recommenced walking, cleared his throat and said—

"What was it you were saying?"

"Ah! Yes! You should have seen this settlement that night. I don't think anybody went to bed. I walked down to the point, and could see them. They had a big bonfire in the palm grove, and the talk went on there till the morning. When I came back here and sat in the dark verandah in this quiet house I felt so frightfully lonely that I stole in and took the child out of her cot and brought her here into my hammock. If it hadn't been for her I am sure I would have gone mad; I felt so utterly alone and helpless. Remember, I hadn't heard from you for four months. Didn't know whether you were alive or dead. Patalolo would have nothing to do with me. My own men were deserting me like rats do a sinking hulk. That was a black night for me, Captain Lingard. A black night as I sat here not knowing what would happen next. They were so excited and rowdy that I really feared they would come and burn the house over my head. I went and brought my revolver. Laid it loaded on the table. There were such awful yells now and then. Luckily the child slept through it, and seeing her so pretty and peaceful steadied me somehow. Couldn't believe there was any violence in this world, looking at her

lying so quiet and so unconscious of what went on.
But it was very hard. Everything was at an end.
You must understand that on that night there was no
government in Sambir. Nothing to restrain those
fellows. Patalolo had collapsed. I was abandoned by
my own people, and all that lot could vent their spite
on me if they wanted. They know no gratitude.
How many times haven't I saved this settlement from
starvation? Absolute starvation. Only three months
ago I distributed again a lot of rice on credit. There
was nothing to eat in this infernal place. They came
begging on their knees. There isn't a man in Sambir,
big or little, who is not in debt to Lingard & Co. Not
one. You ought to be satisfied. You always said that
was the right policy for us. Well, I carried it out. Ah!
Captain Lingard, a policy like that should be backed by
loaded rifles . . ."

"You had them!" exclaimed Lingard in the midst
of his promenade, that went on more rapid as Almayer
talked: the headlong tramp of a man hurrying on to do
something violent. The verandah was full of dust,
oppressive and choking, which rose under the old seaman's feet, and made Almayer cough again and
again.

"Yes, I had! Twenty. And not a finger to pull a
trigger. It's easy to talk," he spluttered, his face very
red.

Lingard dropped into a chair, and leaned back with
one hand stretched out at length upon the table, the
other thrown over the back of his seat. The dust
settled, and the sun surging above the forest flooded
the verandah with a clear light. Almayer got up and
busied himself in lowering the split-rattan screens that
hung between the columns of the verandah.

"Phew!" said Lingard, "it will be a hot day. That's

right, my boy. Keep the sun out. We don't want to
be roasted alive here."

Almayer came back, sat down, and spoke very
calmly—

"In the morning I went across to see Patalolo. I
took the child with me, of course. I found the water-
gate barred, and had to walk round through the bushes.
Patalolo received me lying on the floor, in the dark,
all the shutters closed. I could get nothing out of
him but lamentations and groans. He said you must
be dead. That Lakamba was coming now with Abdulla's guns to kill everybody. Said he did not mind
being killed, as he was an old man, but that the wish of
his heart was to make a pilgrimage. He was tired of
men's ingratitude—he had no heirs—he wanted to go
to Mecca and die there. He would ask Abdulla to let
him go. Then he abused Lakamba—between sobs—
and you, a little. You prevented him from asking for a
flag that would have been respected—he was right there
—and now when his enemies were strong he was weak,
and you were not there to help him. When I tried to
put some heart into him, telling him he had four big guns
—you know the brass six-pounders you left here last
year—and that I would get powder, and that, perhaps,
together we could make head against Lakamba, he
simply howled at me. No matter which way he turned
—he shrieked—the white men would be the death of
him, while he wanted only to be a pilgrim and be at
peace. My belief is," added Almayer, after a short
pause, and fixing a dull stare upon Lingard, "that the
old fool saw this thing coming for a long time, and was
not only too frightened to do anything himself, but
actually too scared to let you or me know of his sus-
picions. Another of your particular pets! Well! You
have a lucky hand, I must say!"

Lingard struck a sudden blow on the table with his clenched hand. There was a sharp crack of splitting wood. Almayer started up violently, then fell back in his chair and looked at the table.

"There!" he said, moodily, "you don't know your own strength. This table is completely ruined. The only table I had been able to save from my wife. By and by I will have to eat squatting on the floor like a native."

Lingard laughed heartily. "Well then, don't nag at me like a woman at a drunken husband!" He became very serious after awhile, and added, "If it hadn't been for the loss of the *Flash* I would have been here three months ago, and all would have been well. No use crying over that. Don't you be uneasy, Kaspar. We will have everything ship-shape here in a very short time."

"What? You don't mean to expel Abdulla out of here by force! I tell you, you can't."

"Not I!" exclaimed Lingard. "That's all over, I am afraid. Great pity. They will suffer for it. He will squeeze them. Great pity. Damn it! I feel so sorry for them if I had the *Flash* here I would try force. Eh! Why not? However, the poor *Flash* is gone, and there is an end of it. Poor old hooker. Hey, Almayer? You made a voyage or two with me. Wasn't she a sweet craft? Could make her do anything but talk. She was better than a wife to me. Never scolded. Hey? . . . And to think that it should come to this. That I should leave her poor old bones sticking on a reef as though I had been a damned fool of a southern-going man who must have half a mile of water under his keel to be safe! Well! well! It's only those who do nothing that make no mistakes, I suppose. But it's hard. Hard."

He nodded sadly, with his eyes on the ground. Almayer looked at him with growing indignation.

"Upon my word, you are heartless," he burst out; "perfectly heartless—and selfish. It does not seem to strike you—in all that—that in losing your ship—by your recklessness, I am sure—you ruin me—us, and my little Nina. What's going to become of me and of her? That's what I want to know. You brought me here, made me your partner, and now, when everything is gone to the devil—through your fault, mind you—you talk about your ship . . . ship! You can get another. But here. This trade. That's gone now, thanks to Willems. . . . Your dear Willems!"

"Never you mind about Willems. I will look after him," said Lingard, severely. "And as to the trade . . . I will make your fortune yet, my boy. Never fear. Have you got any cargo for the schooner that brought me here?"

"The shed is full of rattans," answered Almayer, "and I have about eighty tons of guttah in the well.* The last lot I ever will have, no doubt," he added, bitterly.

"So, after all, there was no robbery. You've lost nothing actually. Well, then, you must . . . Hallo! What's the matter! . . . Here! . . ."

"Robbery! No!" screamed Almayer, throwing up his hands.

He fell back in the chair and his face became purple. A little white foam appeared on his lips and trickled down his chin, while he lay back, showing the whites of his upturned eyes. When he came to himself he saw Lingard standing over him, with an empty waterchatty in his hand.

"You had a fit of some kind," said the old seaman

with much concern. "What is it? You did give me a fright. So very sudden."

Almayer, his hair all wet and stuck to his head, as if he had been diving, sat up and gasped.

"Outrage! A fiendish outrage. I . . ."

Lingard put the chatty on the table and looked at him in attentive silence. Almayer passed his hand over his forehead and went on in an unsteady tone:

"When I remember that, I lose all control," he said. "I told you he anchored Abdulla's ship abreast our jetty, but over to the other shore, near the Rajah's place. The ship was surrounded with boats. From here it looked as if she had been landed on a raft. Every dugout in Sambir was there. Through my glass I could distinguish the faces of people on the poop—Abdulla, Willems, Lakamba—everybody. That old cringing scoundrel Sahamin was there. I could see quite plain. There seemed to be much talk and discussion. Finally I saw a ship's boat lowered. Some Arab got into her, and the boat went towards Patalolo's landing-place. It seems they had been refused admittance—so they say. I think myself that the water-gate was not unbarred quick enough to please the exalted messenger. At any rate I saw the boat come back almost directly. I was looking on, rather interested, when I saw Willems and some more go forward—very busy about something there. That woman was also amongst them. Ah, that woman . . ."

Almayer choked, and seemed on the point of having a relapse, but by a violent effort regained a comparative composure.

"All of a sudden," he continued—"bang! They fired a shot into Patalolo's gate, and before I had time to catch my breath—I was startled, you may believe —they sent another and burst the gate open. Where-

upon, I suppose, they thought they had done enough
for a while, and probably felt hungry, for a feast began
aft. Abdulla sat amongst them like an idol, cross-
legged, his hands on his lap. He's too great altogether
to eat when others do, but he presided, you see. Willems kept on dodging about forward, aloof from the
crowd, and looking at my house through the ship's
long glass. I could not resist it. I shook my fist at
him."

"Just so," said Lingard, gravely. "That was the
thing to do, of course. If you can't fight a man the
best thing is to exasperate him."

Almayer waved his hand in a superior manner, and
continued, unmoved:

"You may say what you like. You can't realize
my feelings. He saw me, and, with his eye still at
the small end of the glass, lifted his arm as if answering a hail. I thought my turn to be shot at would
come next after Patalolo, so I ran up the Union Jack
to the flagstaff in the yard. I had no other protection.
There were only three men besides Ali that stuck to me
—three cripples, for that matter, too sick to get away.
I would have fought singlehanded, I think, I was that
angry, but there was the child. What to do with her?
Couldn't send her up the river with the mother. You
know I can't trust my wife. I decided to keep very
quiet, but to let nobody land on our shore. Private
property, that; under a deed from Patalolo. I was
within my right—wasn't I? The morning was very
quiet. After they had a feed on board the barque with
Abdulla most of them went home; only the big people
remained. Towards three o'clock Sahamin crossed
alone in a small canoe. I went down on our wharf with
my gun to speak to him, but didn't let him land. The
old hypocrite said Abdulla sent greetings and wished to

talk with me on business; would I come on board?
I said no; I would not. Told him that Abdulla may
write and I would answer, but no interview, neither
on board his ship nor on shore. I also said that if
anybody attempted to land within my fences I would
shoot—no matter whom. On that he lifted his hands
to heaven, scandalized, and then paddled away pretty
smartly—to report, I suppose. An hour or so afterwards I saw Willems land a boat party at the Rajah's.
It was very quiet. Not a shot was fired, and there
was hardly any shouting. They tumbled those brass
guns you presented to Patalolo last year down the
bank into the river. It's deep there close to. The
channel runs that way, you know. About five, Willems went back on board, and I saw him join Abdulla
by the wheel aft. He talked a lot, swinging his arms
about—seemed to explain things—pointed at my house,
then down the reach. Finally, just before sunset, they
hove upon the cable and dredged the ship down nearly
half a mile to the junction of the two branches of the
river—where she is now, as you might have seen."

Lingard nodded.

"That evening, after dark—I was informed—
Abdulla landed for the first time in Sambir. He
was entertained in Sahamin's house. I sent Ali to
the settlement for news. He returned about nine,
and reported that Patalolo was sitting on Abdulla's
left hand before Sahamin's fire. There was a great
council. Ali seemed to think that Patalolo was a
prisoner, but he was wrong there. They did the
trick very neatly. Before midnight everything was
arranged as I can make out. Patalolo went back to
his demolished stockade, escorted by a dozen boats
with torches. It appears he begged Abdulla to let
him have a passage in the *Lord of the Isles* to Penang.

From there he would go to Mecca. The firing business was alluded to as a mistake. No doubt it was in a sense. Patalolo never meant resisting. So he is going as soon as the ship is ready for sea. He went on board next day with three women and half a dozen fellows as old as himself. By Abdulla's orders he was received with a salute of seven guns, and he has been living on board ever since—five weeks. I doubt whether he will leave the river alive. At any rate he won't live to reach Penang. Lakamba took over all his goods, and gave him a draft on Abdulla's house payable in Penang. He is bound to die before he gets there. Don't you see?"

He sat silent for awhile in dejected meditation, then went on:

"Of course there were several rows during the night. Various fellows took the opportunity of the unsettled state of affairs to pay off old scores and settle old grudges. I passed the night in that chair there, dozing uneasily. Now and then there would be a great tumult and yelling which would make me sit up, revolver in hand. However, nobody was killed. A few broken heads—that's all. Early in the morning Willems caused them to make a fresh move which I must say surprised me not a little. As soon as there was daylight they busied themselves in setting up a flag-pole on the space at the other end of the settlement, where Abdulla is having his houses built now. Shortly after sunrise there was a great gathering at the flag-pole. All went there. Willems was standing leaning against the mast, one arm over that woman's shoulders. They had brought an armchair for Patalolo, and Lakamba stood on the right hand of the old man, who made a speech. Everybody in Sambir was there: women, slaves, children —everybody! Then Patalolo spoke. He said that by the mercy of the Most High he was going on a pilgrimage. The dearest wish of his heart was to be accomplished. Then, turning to Lakamba, he begged him to rule justly during his—Patalolo's—absence. There was a bit of play-acting there. Lakamba said he was unworthy of the honourable burden, and Patalolo insisted. Poor old fool! It must have been bitter to him. They made him actually entreat that scoundrel. Fancy a man compelled to beg of a robber to despoil him! But the old Rajah was so frightened. Anyway, he did it, and Lakamba accepted at last. Then Willems made a speech to the crowd. Said that on his way to the west the Rajah—he meant Patalolo—would see the Great White Ruler in Batavia* and obtain his protection for Sambir. Meantime, he went on, I, an Orang Blanda and your friend, hoist the flag under the shadow of which there is safety. With that he ran up a Dutch flag* to the mast-head. It was made hurriedly, during the night, of cotton stuffs, and, being heavy, hung down the mast, while the crowd stared. Ali told me there was a great sigh of surprise, but not a word was spoken till Lakamba advanced and proclaimed in a loud voice that during all that day every one passing by the flagstaff must uncover his head and salaam before the emblem."

"But, hang it all!" exclaimed Lingard—"Abdulla is British!"

"Abdulla wasn't there at all—did not go on shore that day. Yet Ali, who has his wits about him, noticed that the space where the crowd stood was under the guns of the *Lord of the Isles*. They had put a coir warp ashore, and gave the barque a cant in the current, so as to bring the broadside to bear on the flagstaff. Clever! Eh? But nobody dreamt of resistance. When they recovered from the surprise there was a little quiet

jeering, and Bahassoen abused Làkamba violently till
one of Lakamba's men hit him on the head with a staff.
Frightful crack, I am told. Then they left off jeering.
Meantime Patalolo went away, and Lakamba sat in the
chair at the foot of the flagstaff, while the crowd surged
around, as if they could not make up their minds to go.
Suddenly there was a great noise behind Lakamba's
chair. It was that woman, who went for Willems. Ali
says she was like a wild beast, but he twisted her wrist
and made her grovel in the dust. Nobody knows
exactly what it was about. Some say it was about that
flag. He carried her off, flung her into a canoe, and
went on board Abdulla's ship. After that Sahamin
was the first to salaam to the flag. Others followed
suit. Before noon everything was quiet in the settlement, and Ali came back and told me all this."

Almayer drew a long breath. Lingard stretched out
his legs.

"Go on!" he said.

Almayer seemed to struggle with himself. At last
he spluttered out:

"The hardest is to tell yet. The most unheard-of
thing! An outrage! A fiendish outrage!"

CHAPTER THREE

"WELL! Let's know all about it. I can't imagine
. . ." began Lingard, after waiting for some time
in silence.

"Can't imagine! I should think you couldn't,"
interrupted Almayer. "Why! . . . You just listen. When Ali came back I felt a little easier in my
mind. There was then some semblance of order in
Sambir. I had the Jack up since the morning and
began to feel safer. Some of my men turned up in the
afternoon. I did not ask any questions; set them to
work as if nothing had happened. Towards the evening—it might have been five or half-past—I was on our
jetty with the child when I heard shouts at the far-off
end of the settlement. At first I didn't take much
notice. By and by Ali came to me and says, 'Master,
give me the child, there is much trouble in the settlement.' So I gave him Nina and went in, took my revolver, and passed through the house into the back
courtyard. As I came down the steps I saw all the
serving girls clear out from the cooking shed, and I
heard a big crowd howling on the other side of the dry
ditch which is the limit of our ground. Could not see
them on account of the fringe of bushes along the ditch,
but I knew that crowd was angry and after somebody.
As I stood wondering, that Jim-Eng*—you know the
Chinaman who settled here a couple of years ago?"

"He was my passenger; I brought him here," exclaimed Lingard. "A first-class Chinaman that."

"Did you? I had forgotten. Well, that Jim-Eng,

181

he burst through the bush and fell into my arms, so to
speak. He told me, panting, that they were after him
because he wouldn't take off his hat to the flag. He was
not so much scared, but he was very angry and indignant. Of course he had to run for it; there were some
fifty men after him—Lakamba's friends—but he was
full of fight. Said he was an Englishman,* and would
not take off his hat to any flag but English. I tried to
soothe him while the crowd was shouting on the other
side of the ditch. I told him he must take one of my
canoes and cross the river. Stop on the other side for a
couple of days. He wouldn't. Not he. He was
English, and he would fight the whole lot. Says he:
'They are only black fellows. We white men,' meaning
me and himself, 'can fight everybody in Sambir.' He
was mad with passion. The crowd quieted a little, and
I thought I could shelter Jim-Eng without much risk,
when all of a sudden I heard Willems' voice. He
shouted to me in English: 'Let four men enter your
compound to get that Chinaman!' I said nothing.
Told Jim-Eng to keep quiet too. Then after a while
Willems shouts again: 'Don't resist, Almayer. I give
you good advice. I am keeping this crowd back.
Don't resist them!' That beggar's voice enraged me;
I could not help it. I cried to him: 'You are a liar!'
and just then Jim-Eng, who had flung off his jacket and
had tucked up his trousers ready for a fight; just then
that fellow he snatches the revolver out of my hand and
lets fly at them through the bush. There was a sharp
cry—he must have hit somebody—and a great yell,
and before I could wink twice they were over the ditch
and through the bush and on top of us! Simply rolled
over us! There wasn't the slightest chance to resist.
I was trampled under foot, Jim-Eng got a dozen gashes
about his body, and we were carried halfway up the

yard in the first rush. My eyes and mouth were full of dust; I was on my back with three or four fellows sitting on me. I could hear Jim-Eng trying to shout not very far from me. Now and then they would throttle him and he would gurgle. I could hardly breathe myself with two heavy fellows on my chest. Willems came up running and ordered them to raise me up, but to keep good hold. They led me into the verandah. I looked round, but did not see either Ali or the child. Felt easier. Struggled a little. . . . Oh, my God!"

Almayer's face was distorted with a passing spasm of rage. Lingard moved in his chair slightly. Almayer went on after a short pause:

"They held me, shouting threats in my face. Willems took down my hammock and threw it to them. He pulled out the drawer of this table, and found there a palm and needle and some sail-twine. We were making awnings for your brig, as you had asked me last voyage before you left. He knew, of course, where to look for what he wanted. By his orders they laid me out on the floor, wrapped me in my hammock, and he started to stitch me in, as if I had been a corpse, beginning at the feet. While he worked he laughed wickedly. I called him all the names I could think of. He told them to put their dirty paws over my mouth and nose. I was nearly choked. Whenever I moved they punched me in the ribs. He went on taking fresh needlefuls as he wanted them, and working steadily. Sewed me up to my throat. Then he rose, saying, 'That will do; let go.' That woman had been standing by; they must have been reconciled. She clapped her hands. I lay on the floor like a bale of goods while he stared at me, and the woman shrieked with delight. Like a bale of goods! There was a grin on every face, and the verandah was full of them. I wished myself dead—'pon my word, Captain Lingard, I did! I do now whenever I think of it!"

Lingard's face expressed sympathetic indignation. Almayer dropped his head upon his arms on the table, and spoke in that position in an indistinct and muffled voice, without looking up.

"Finally, by his directions, they flung me into the big rocking-chair. I was sewed in so tight that I was stiff like a piece of wood. He was giving orders in a very loud voice, and that man Babalatchi saw that they were executed. They obeyed him implicitly. Meantime I lay there in the chair like a log, and that woman capered before me and made faces; snapped her fingers before my nose. Women are bad!—ain't they? I never saw her before, as far as I know. Never done anything to her. Yet she was perfectly fiendish. Can you understand it? Now and then she would leave me alone to hang round his neck for awhile, and then she would return before my chair and begin her exercises again. He looked on, indulgent. The perspiration ran down my face, got into my eyes—my arms were sewn in. I was blinded half the time; at times I could see better. She drags him before my chair. 'I am like white women,' she says, her arms round his neck. You should have seen the faces of the fellows in the verandah! They were scandalized and ashamed of themselves to see her behaviour. Suddenly she asks him, alluding to me: 'When are you going to kill him?' Imagine how I felt. I must have swooned; I don't remember exactly. I fancy there was a row; he was angry. When I got my wits again he was sitting close to me, and she was gone. I understood he sent her to my wife, who was hiding in the back room and never came out during this affair. Willems says

to me—I fancy I can hear his voice, hoarse and dull—
he says to me: 'Not a hair of your head shall be touched.'
I made no sound.   Then he goes on: 'Please remark that
the flag you have hoisted—which, by the by, is not yours
—has been respected.   Tell Captain Lingard so when
you do see him.   But,' he says, 'you first fired at the
crowd.'   'You are a liar, you blackguard!' I shouted.
He winced, I am sure.   It hurt him to see I was not
frightened.   'Anyways,' he says, 'a shot had been fired
out of your compound and a man was hit.   Still, all
your property shall be respected on account of the
Union Jack.   Moreover, I have no quarrel with Captain Lingard, who is the senior partner in this business.
As to you,' he continued, 'you will not forget this day—
not if you live to be a hundred years old—or I don't
know your nature.   You will keep the bitter taste of
this humiliation to the last day of your life, and so your
kindness to me shall be repaid.   I shall remove all the
powder you have.   This coast is under the protection
of the Netherlands,* and you have no right to have any
powder.   There are the Governor's Orders in Council
to that effect, and you know it.   Tell me where the key
of the small storehouse is?'   I said not a word, and he
waited a little, then rose, saying: 'It's your own fault
if there is any damage done.'   He ordered Babalatchi
to have the lock of the office-room forced, and went in—
rummaged amongst my drawers—could not find the
key.   Then that woman Aïssa asked my wife, and she
gave them the key.   After awhile they tumbled every
barrel into the river.   Eighty-three hundredweight!*
He superintended himself, and saw every barrel roll
into the water.   There were mutterings.   Babalatchi
was angry and tried to expostulate, but he gave him a
good shaking.   I must say he was perfectly fearless
with those fellows.   Then he came back to the veran-

dah, sat down by me again, and says: 'We found your man Ali with your little daughter hiding in the bushes up the river. We brought them in. They are perfectly safe, of course. Let me congratulate you, Almayer, upon the cleverness of your child. She recognized me at once, and cried "pig" as naturally as you would yourself. Circumstances alter feelings. You should have seen how frightened your man Ali was. Clapped his hands over her mouth. I think you spoil her, Almayer. But I am not angry. Really, you look so ridiculous in this chair that I can't feel angry.' I made a frantic effort to burst out of my hammock to get at that scoundrel's throat, but I only fell off and upset the chair over myself. He laughed and said only: 'I leave you half of your revolver cartridges and take half myself; they will fit mine. We are both white men, and should back each other up. I may want them.' I shouted at him from under the chair: 'You are a thief,' but he never looked, and went away, one hand round that woman's waist, the other on Babalatchi's shoulder, to whom he was talking—laying down the law about something or other. In less than five minutes there was nobody inside our fences. After awhile Ali came to look for me and cut me free. I haven't seen Willems since— nor anybody else for that matter. I have been left alone. I offered sixty dollars to the man who had been wounded, which were accepted. They released Jim-Eng the next day, when the flag had been hauled down. He sent six cases of opium* to me for safe keeping but has not left his house. I think he is safe enough now. Everything is very quiet."

Towards the end of his narrative Almayer lifted his head off the table, and now sat back in his chair and stared at the bamboo rafters of the roof above him. Lingard lolled in his seat with his legs stretched out.

In the peaceful gloom of the verandah, with its lowered screens, they heard faint noises from the world outside in the blazing sunshine: a hail on the river, the answer from the shore, the creak of a pulley; sounds short, interrupted, as if lost suddenly in the brilliance of noonday. Lingard got up slowly, walked to the front rail, and holding one of the screens aside, looked out in silence. Over the water and the empty courtyard came a distinct voice from a small schooner anchored abreast of the Lingard jetty.

"Serang! Take a pull at the main peak halyards. This gaff is down on the boom."

There was a shrill pipe dying in long-drawn cadence, the song of the men swinging on the rope. The voice said sharply: "That will do!" Another voice—the serang's probably—shouted: "Ikat!" and as Lingard dropped the blind and turned away all was silent again, as if there had been nothing on the other side of the swaying screen; nothing but the light, brilliant, crude, heavy, lying on a dead land like a pall of fire. Lingard sat down again, facing Almayer, his elbow on the table, in a thoughtful attitude.

"Nice little schooner," muttered Almayer, wearily. "Did you buy her?"

"No," answered Lingard. "After I lost the *Flash* we got to Palembang in our boats. I chartered her there, for six months. From young Ford,* you know. Belongs to him. He wanted a spell ashore, so I took charge myself. Of course all Ford's people on board. Strangers to me. I had to go to Singapore about the insurance; then I went to Macassar, of course. Had long passages. No wind. It was like a curse on me. I had lots of trouble with old Hudig. That delayed me much."

"Ah! Hudig! Why with Hudig?" asked Almayer, in a perfunctory manner.

"Oh! about a . . . a woman," mumbled Lingard.

Almayer looked at him with languid surprise. The old seaman had twisted his white beard into a point, and now was busy giving his moustaches a fierce curl. His little red eyes—those eyes that had smarted under the salt sprays of every sea, that had looked unwinking to windward in the gales of all latitudes—now glared at Almayer from behind the lowered eyebrows like a pair of frightened wild beasts crouching in a bush.

"Extraordinary! So like you! What can you have to do with Hudig's women? The old sinner!" said Almayer, negligently.

"What are you talking about! Wife of a friend of . . . I mean of a man I know . . ."

"Still, I don't see . . ." interjected Almayer carelessly.

"Of a man you know too. Well. Very well."

"I knew so many men before you made me bury myself in this hole!" growled Almayer, unamiably. "If she had anything to do with Hudig—that wife—then she can't be up to much. I would be sorry for the man," added Almayer, brightening up with the recollection of the scandalous tittle-tattle of the past, when he was a young man in the second capital* of the Islands—and so well informed, so well informed. He laughed. Lingard's frown deepened.

"Don't talk foolish! It's Willems' wife."

Almayer grasped the sides of his seat, his eyes and mouth opened wide.

"What? Why!" he exclaimed, bewildered.

"Willems'—wife," repeated Lingard distinctly. "You ain't deaf, are you? The wife of Willems. Just so. As to why! There was a promise. And I did not know what had happened here."

"What is it? You've been giving her money, I bet," cried Almayer.

"Well, no!" said Lingard, deliberately. "Although I suppose I shall have to . . ."

Almayer groaned.

"The fact is," went on Lingard, speaking slowly and steadily, "the fact is that I have . . . I have brought her here. Here. To Sambir."

"In heaven's name! why?" shouted Almayer, jumping up. The chair tilted and fell slowly over. He raised his clasped hands above his head and brought them down jerkily, separating his fingers with an effort, as if tearing them apart. Lingard nodded, quickly, several times.

"I have. Awkward. Hey?" he said, with a puzzled look upwards.

"Upon my word," said Almayer, tearfully. "I can't understand you at all. What will you do next! Willems' wife!"

"Wife and child. Small boy, you know. They are on board the schooner."

Almayer looked at Lingard with sudden suspicion, then turning away busied himself in picking up the chair, sat down in it turning his back upon the old sea-man, and tried to whistle, but gave it up directly. Lingard went on—

"Fact is, the fellow got into trouble with Hudig. Worked upon my feelings. I promised to arrange matters. I did. With much trouble. Hudig was angry with her for wishing to join her husband. Un-principled old fellow. You know she is his daughter. Well, I said I would see her through it all right; help Willems to a fresh start and so on. I spoke to Craig in Palembang.* He is getting on in years, and wanted a manager or partner. I promised to guarantee Willems'

good behaviour. We settled all that. Craig is an old
crony of mine. Been shipmates in the forties. He's
waiting for him now. A pretty mess! What do you
think?"

Almayer shrugged his shoulders.

"That woman broke with Hudig on my assurance
that all would be well," went on Lingard, with grow-
ing dismay. "She did. Proper thing, of course.
Wife, husband . . . together . . . as it should be
. . . Smart fellow . . . Impossible scoundrel
. . . Jolly old go! Oh! damn!"

Almayer laughed spitefully.

"How delighted he will be," he said, softly. "You
will make two people happy. Two at least!" He
laughed again, while Lingard looked at his shaking
shoulders in consternation.

"I am jammed on a lee shore this time, if ever I
was," muttered Lingard.

"Send her back quick," suggested Almayer, stifling
another laugh.

"What are you sniggering at?" growled Lingard,
angrily. "I'll work it out all clear yet. Meantime
you must receive her into this house."

"My house!" cried Almayer, turning round.

"It's mine too—a little—isn't it?" said Lingard.
"Don't argue," he shouted, as Almayer opened his
mouth. "Obey orders and hold your tongue!"

"Oh! If you take it in that tone!" mumbled Almayer, sulkily, with a gesture of assent.

"You are so aggravating too, my boy," said the old
seaman, with unexpected placidity. "You must give
me time to turn round. I can't keep her on board all
the time. I must tell her something. Say, for instance,
that he is gone up the river. Expected back every
day. That's it. D'ye hear? You must put her on

that tack and dodge her along easy, while I take the kinks out of the situation. By God!" he exclaimed, mournfully, after a short pause, "life is foul! Foul like a lee forebrace on a dirty night. And yet. And yet. One must see it clear for running before going below— for good. Now you attend to what I said," he added, sharply, "if you don't want to quarrel with me, my boy."

"I don't want to quarrel with you," murmured Almayer with unwilling deference. "Only I wish I could understand you. I know you are my best friend, Captain Lingard; only, upon my word, I can't make you out sometimes! I wish I could . . ."

Lingard burst into a loud laugh which ended shortly in a deep sigh. He closed his eyes, tilting his head over the back of his armchair; and on his face, baked by the unclouded suns of many hard years, there appeared for a moment a weariness and a look of age which startled Almayer, like an unexpected disclosure of evil.

"I am done up," said Lingard, gently. "Perfectly done up. All night on deck getting that schooner up the river. Then talking with you. Seems to me I could go to sleep on a clothes-line.* I should like to eat something though. Just see about that, Kaspar."

Almayer clapped his hands, and receiving no response was going to call, when in the central passage of the house, behind the red curtain* of the doorway opening upon the verandah, they heard a child's imperious voice speaking shrilly.

"Take me up at once. I want to be carried into the verandah. I shall be very angry. Take me up."

A man's voice answered, subdued, in humble remonstrance. The faces of Almayer and Lingard brightened at once. The old seaman called out—

"Bring the child. Lekas!"

"You will see how she has grown," exclaimed Almayer, in a jubilant tone.

Through the curtained doorway Ali appeared with little Nina Almayer in his arms. The child had one arm round his neck, and with the other she hugged a ripe pumelo nearly as big as her own head. Her little pink, sleeveless robe*had half slipped off her shoulders, but the long black hair, that framed her olive face, in which the big black eyes looked out in childish solemnity, fell in luxuriant profusion over her shoulders, all round her and over Ali's arms, like a close-meshed and delicate net of silken threads. Lingard got up to meet Ali, and as soon as she caught sight of the old seaman she dropped the fruit and put out both her hands with a cry of delight. He took her from the Malay, and she laid hold of his moustaches with an affectionate goodwill that brought unaccustomed tears into his little red eyes.

"Not so hard, little one, not so hard," he murmured, pressing with an enormous hand, that covered it entirely, the child's head to his face.

"Pick up my pumelo, O Rajah of the sea!" she said, speaking in a high-pitched, clear voice with great volubility. "There, under the table. I want it quick! Quick! You have been away fighting with many men. Ali says so. You are a mighty fighter. Ali says so. On the great sea far away, away, away."

She waved her hand, staring with dreamy vacancy, while Lingard looked at her, and squatting down groped under the table after the pumelo.

"Where does she get those notions?" said Lingard, getting up cautiously, to Almayer, who had been giving orders to Ali.

"She is always with the men. Many a time I've found her with her fingers in their rice dish, of an

evening. She does not care for her mother though—
I am glad to say. How pretty she is—and so sharp.
My very image!"

Lingard had put the child on the table, and both men
stood looking at her with radiant faces.

"A perfect little woman," whispered Lingard. "Yes,
my dear boy, we shall make her somebody. You'll
see!"

"Very little chance of that now," remarked Almayer,
sadly.

"You do not know!" exclaimed Lingard, taking up
the child again, and beginning to walk up and down the
verandah. "I have my plans. I have—listen."

And he began to explain to the interested Almayer
his plans for the future. He would interview Abdulla
and Lakamba. There must be some understanding
with those fellows now they had the upper hand.
Here he interrupted himself to swear freely, while the
child, who had been diligently fumbling about his neck,
had found his whistle and blew a loud blast now and
then close to his ear—which made him wince and
laugh as he put her hands down, scolding her lovingly.
Yes—that would be easily settled. He was a man to
be reckoned with yet. Nobody knew that better than
Almayer. Very well. Then he must patiently try and
keep some little trade together. It would be all right.
But the great thing—and here Lingard spoke lower,
bringing himself to a sudden standstill before the entranced Almayer—the great thing would be the gold
hunt up the river. He—Lingard—would devote himself to it. He had been in the interior before. There
were immense deposits of alluvial gold there. Fabulous.
He felt sure. Had seen places. Dangerous work? Of
course! But what a reward! He would explore—and
find. Not a shadow of doubt. Hang the danger!

They would first get as much as they could for themselves. Keep the thing quiet. Then after a time form
a Company.* In Batavia or in England. Yes, in
England. Much better. Splendid! Why, of course.
And that baby would be the richest woman in the
world. He—Lingard—would not, perhaps, see it—
although he felt good for many years yet—but Almayer
would. Here was something to live for yet! Hey?

But the richest woman in the world had been for the
last five minutes shouting shrilly—"Rajah Laut!
Rajah Laut! Haï! Give ear!" while the old
seaman had been speaking louder, unconsciously, to
make his deep bass heard above the impatient clamour.
He stopped now and said tenderly—

"What is it, little woman?"

"I am not a little woman. I am a white child.
Anak Putih. A white child; and the white men are
my brothers. Father says so. And Ali says so too.
Ali knows as much as father. Everything."

Almayer almost danced with paternal delight.

"I taught her. I taught her," he repeated, laughing
with tears in his eyes. "Isn't she sharp?"

"I am the slave of the white child," said Lingard,
with playful solemnity. "What is the order?"

"I want a house," she warbled, with great eagerness. "I want a house, and another house on the
roof, and another on the roof—high. High! Like
the places where they dwell—my brothers—in the
land where the sun sleeps."

"To the westward," explained Almayer, under his
breath. "She remembers everything. She wants you
to build a house of cards. You did, last time you were
here."

Lingard sat down with the child on his knees, and
Almayer pulled out violently one drawer after another,

looking for the cards, as if the fate of the world depended upon his haste. He produced a dirty double pack which was only used during Lingard's visit to Sambir, when he would sometimes play—of an evening —with Almayer, a game which he called Chinese bezique. It bored Almayer, but the old seaman delighted in it, considering it a remarkable product of Chinese genius—a race for which he had an unaccountable liking and admiration.

"Now we will get on, my little pearl," he said, putting together with extreme precaution two cards that looked absurdly flimsy between his big fingers. Little Nina watched him with intense seriousness as he went on erecting the ground floor, while he continued to speak to Almayer with his head over his shoulder so as not to endanger the structure with his breath.

"I know what I am talking about. . . . Been in California in forty-nine. . . . Not that I made much . . . then in Victoria* in the early days. . . . I know all about it. Trust me. Moreover a blind man could . . . Be quiet, little sister, or you will knock this affair down. . . . My hand pretty steady yet! Hey, Kaspar? . . . Now, delight of my heart, we shall put a third house on the top of these two . . . keep very quiet. . . . As I was saying, you got only to stoop and gather handfuls of gold . . . dust . . . there. Now here we are. Three houses on top of one another. Grand!"

He leaned back in his chair, one hand on the child's head, which he smoothed mechanically, and gesticulated with the other, speaking to Almayer.

"Once on the spot, there would be only the trouble to pick up the stuff. Then we shall all go to Europe. The child must be educated. We shall be rich. Rich

is no name for it. Down in Devonshire where I
belong, there was a fellow who built a house near
Teignmouth which had as many windows as a three-
decker has ports. Made all his money somewhere out
here in the good old days. People around said he had
been a pirate. We boys—I was a boy in a Brixham
trawler then—certainly believed that. He went
about in a bath-chair* in his grounds. Had a glass
eye . . ."

"Higher! Higher!" called out Nina, pulling the
old seaman's beard.

"You do worry me—don't you?" said Lingard,
gently, giving her a tender kiss. "What? One
more house on top of all these? Well! I will try."

The child watched him breathlessly. When the
difficult feat was accomplished she clapped her hands,
looked on steadily, and after a while gave a great sigh
of content.

"Oh! Look out!" shouted Almayer.

The structure collapsed suddenly before the child's
light breath. Lingard looked discomposed for a
moment. Almayer laughed, but the little girl began
to cry.

"Take her," said the old seaman, abruptly. Then,
after Almayer went away with the crying child, he
remained sitting by the table, looking gloomily at the
heap of cards.

"Damn this Willems," he muttered to himself.
"But I will do it yet!"

He got up, and with an angry push of his hand swept
the cards off the table. Then he fell back in his chair.

"Tired as a dog," he sighed out, closing his eyes.

CHAPTER FOUR

CONSCIOUSLY or unconsciously, men are proud of their firmness, steadfastness of purpose, directness of aim. They go straight towards their desire, to the accomplishment of virtue—sometimes of crime—in an uplifting persuasion of their firmness. They walk the road of life, the road fenced in by their tastes, prejudices, disdains or enthusiasms, generally honest, invariably stupid, and are proud of never losing their way. If they do stop, it is to look for a moment over the hedges that make them safe, to look at the misty valleys, at the distant peaks, at cliffs and morasses, at the dark forests and the hazy plains where other human beings grope their days painfully away, stumbling over the bones of the wise, over the unburied remains of their predecessors who died alone, in gloom or in sunshine, halfway from anywhere. The man of purpose does not understand, and goes on, full of contempt. He never loses his way. He knows where he is going and what he wants. Travelling on, he achieves great length without any breadth, and battered, besmirched, and weary, he touches the goal at last; he grasps the reward of his perseverance, of his virtue, of his healthy optimism: an untruthful tombstone over a dark and soon forgotten grave.*

Lingard had never hesitated in his life. Why should he? He had been a most successful trader, and a man lucky in his fights, skilful in navigation, undeniably first in seamanship in those seas. He knew it. Had he not heard the voice of common consent? The voice of the world that respected him so much; the whole world to him—for to us the limits of the universe are strictly defined by those we know. There is nothing for us outside the babble of praise and blame on familiar lips, and beyond our last acquaintance there lies only a vast chaos; a chaos of laughter and tears which concerns us not; laughter and tears unpleasant, wicked, morbid, contemptible—because heard imperfectly by ears rebellious to strange sounds. To Lingard—simple himself—all things were simple. He seldom read. Books were not much in his way, and he had to work hard navigating, trading, and also, in obedience to his benevolent instincts, shaping stray lives he found here and there under his busy hand. He remembered the Sunday-school teachings of his native village and the discourses of the black-coated gentleman connected with the Mission to Fishermen and Seamen, whose yawl-rigged boat darting through rain-squalls amongst the coasters wind-bound in Falmouth Bay,* was part of those precious pictures of his youthful days that lingered in his memory. "As clever a sky-pilot as you could wish to see," he would say with conviction, "and the best man to handle a boat in any weather I ever did meet!" Such were the agencies that had roughly shaped his young soul before he went away to see the world in a southern-going ship—before he went, ignorant and happy, heavy of hand, pure in heart, profane in speech, to give himself up to the great sea that took his life and gave him his fortune. When thinking of his rise in the world—commander of ships, then shipowner, then a man of much capital, respected wherever he went, Lingard in a word, the Rajah Laut—he was amazed and awed by his fate, that seemed to his ill-informed mind the most wondrous known in the annals of men. His experience appeared to him immense and conclusive, teaching him the lesson of the simplicity of life. In life—as in seamanship—there were only two ways of doing a thing: the right way and the wrong way. Common sense and experience taught a man the way that was right. The other was for lubbers and fools, and led, in seamanship, to loss of spars and sails or shipwreck; in life, to loss of money and consideration, or to an unlucky knock on the head. He did not consider it his duty to be angry with rascals. He was only angry with things he could not understand, but for the weaknesses of humanity he could find a contemptuous tolerance. It being manifest that he was wise and lucky—otherwise how could he have been as successful in life as he had been?—he had an inclination to set right the lives of other people, just as he could hardly refrain—in defiance of nautical etiquette—from interfering with his chief officer when the crew was sending up a new topmast, or generally when busy about, what he called, "a heavy job." He was meddlesome with perfect modesty; if he knew a thing or two there was no merit in it. "Hard knocks taught me wisdom, my boy," he used to say, "and you had better take the advice of a man who has been a fool in his time. Have another." And "my boy" as a rule took the cool drink, the advice, and the consequent help which Lingard felt himself bound in honour to give, so as to back up his opinion like an honest man. Captain Tom went sailing from island to island, appearing unexpectedly in various localities, beaming, noisy, anecdotal, commendatory or comminatory, but always welcome.

It was only since his return to Sambir that the old seaman had for the first time known doubt and unhappiness. The loss of the *Flash*—planted firmly

and for ever on a ledge of rock at the north end of
Gaspar Straits in the uncertain light of a cloudy morning—shook him considerably; and the amazing news
which he heard on his arrival in Sambir were not made
to soothe his feelings. A good many years ago—
prompted by his love of adventure—he, with infinite
trouble, had found out and surveyed—for his own
benefit only—the entrances to that river,* where,
he had heard through native report, a new settlement
of Malays was forming. No doubt he thought at the
time mostly of personal gain; but, received with hearty
friendliness by Patalolo, he soon came to like the ruler
and the people, offered his counsel and his help, and—
knowing nothing of Arcadia*—he dreamed of Arcadian
happiness for that little corner of the world which he
loved to think all his own. His deep-seated and
immovable conviction that only he—he, Lingard—
knew what was good for them was characteristic of him,
and, after all, not so very far wrong. He would make
them happy whether or no, he said, and he meant it.
His trade brought prosperity to the young state, and
the fear of his heavy hand secured its internal peace for
many years.

He looked proudly upon his work. With every
passing year he loved more the land, the people, the
muddy river that, if he could help it, would carry no
other craft but the *Flash* on its unclean and friendly
surface. As he slowly warped his vessel up-stream he
would scan with knowing looks the riverside clearings,
and pronounce solemn judgment upon the prospects of
the season's rice-crop. He knew every settler on the
banks between the sea and Sambir; he knew their
wives, their children; he knew every individual of
the multi-coloured groups that, standing on the flimsy
platforms of tiny reed dwellings built over the water,

waved their hands and shouted shrilly: "O! Kapal
layer! Haï!" while the *Flash* swept slowly through
the populated reach, to enter the lonely stretches of
sparkling brown water bordered by the dense and
silent forest, whose big trees nodded their outspread
boughs gently in the faint, warm breeze—as if in sign
of tender but melancholy welcome. He loved it all:
the landscape of brown golds and brilliant emeralds
under the dome of hot sapphire; the whispering big
trees; the loquacious nipa palms that rattled their
leaves volubly in the night breeze, as if in haste to
tell him all the secrets of the great forest behind them.
He loved the heavy scents of blossoms and black earth,
that breath of life and of death which lingered over
his brig in the damp air of tepid and peaceful nights.
He loved the narrow and sombre creeks, strangers to
sunshine: black, smooth, tortuous—like byways of
despair. He liked even the troops of sorrowful-faced
monkeys that profaned the quiet spots with capricious
gambols* and insane gestures of inhuman madness.
He loved everything there, animated or inanimated;
the very mud of the riverside; the very alligators,
enormous and stolid, basking on it with impertinent
unconcern. Their size was a source of pride to him.
"Immense fellows! Make two of them Palembang
reptiles! I tell you, old man!" he would shout, poking
some crony of his playfully in the ribs: "I tell you,
big as you are, they could swallow you in one gulp,
hat, boots and all! Magnificent beggars! Wouldn't
you like to see them? Wouldn't you! Ha! ha!
ha!"   His thunderous laughter filled the verandah,
rolled over the hotel garden, overflowed into the
street, paralyzing for a short moment the noiseless traffic
of bare brown feet; and its loud reverberations would
even startle the landlord's tame bird—a shame-

less mynah—into a momentary propriety of behaviour
under the nearest chair. In the big billiard-room
perspiring men in thin cotton singlets would stop the
game, listen, cue in hand, for a while through the
open windows, then nod their moist faces at each
other sagaciously and whisper: "The old fellow is
talking about his river."

His river! The whispers of curious men, the mystery
of the thing, were to Lingard a source of never-ending
delight. The common talk of ignorance exaggerated
the profits of his queer monopoly, and, although
strictly truthful in general, he liked, on that matter, to
mislead speculation still further by boasts full of cold
raillery. His river! By it he was not only rich—he
was interesting. This secret of his which made him
different to the other traders of those seas gave intimate satisfaction to that desire for singularity which
he shared with the rest of mankind, without being
aware of its presence within his breast. It was the
greater part of his happiness, but he only knew it
after its loss, so unforeseen, so sudden and so cruel.

After his conversation with Almayer he went on
board the schooner, sent Joanna on shore, and shut
himself up in his cabin, feeling very unwell. He
made the most of his indisposition to Almayer, who
came to visit him twice a day. It was an excuse for
doing nothing just yet. He wanted to think. He
was very angry. Angry with himself, with Willems.
Angry at what Willems had done—and also angry at
what he had left undone. The scoundrel was not
complete. The conception was perfect, but the execution, unaccountably, fell short. Why? He ought to
have cut Almayer's throat and burnt the place to
ashes—then cleared out. Got out of his way; of him,
Lingard! Yet he didn't. Was it impudence, con-

tempt—or what? He felt hurt at the implied dis-
respect of his power, and the incomplete rascality
of the proceeding disturbed him exceedingly. There
was something short, something wanting, something
that would have given him a free hand in the work of
retribution. The obvious, the right thing to do, was
to shoot Willems. Yet how could he? Had the
fellow resisted, showed fight, or ran away; had he
shown any consciousness of harm done, it would have
been more possible, more natural. But no! The
fellow actually had sent him a message. Wanted to
see him. What for? The thing could not be
explained. An unexampled, cold-blooded treachery,
awful, incomprehensible. Why did he do it? Why?
Why? The old seaman in the stuffy solitude of his
little cabin on board the schooner groaned out many
times that question, striking with an open palm his
perplexed forehead.

During his four days of seclusion he had received
two messages from the outer world; from that world
of Sambir which had, so suddenly and so finally,
slipped from his grasp. One, a few words from Willems
written on a torn-out page of a small notebook; the
other, a communication from Abdulla caligraphed
carefully on a large sheet of flimsy paper and delivered
to him in a green silk wrapper.* The first he could not
understand. It said: "Come and see me. I am not
afraid. Are you? W." He tore it up angrily, but
before the small bits of dirty paper had the time to
flutter down and settle on the floor, the anger was gone
and was replaced by a sentiment that induced him to
go on his knees, pick up the fragments of the torn
message, piece it together on the top of his chronometer
box, and contemplate it long and thoughtfully, as if he
had hoped to read the answer of the horrible riddle in

the very form of the letters that went to make up that
fresh insult. Abdulla's letter he read carefully and
rammed it into his pocket, also with anger, but with
anger that ended in a half-resigned, half-amused smile.
He would never give in as long as there was a chance.
"It's generally the safest way to stick to the ship as
long as she will swim," was one of his favourite sayings:
"The safest and the right way. To abandon a craft
because it leaks is easy—but poor work. Poor work!"
Yet he was intelligent enough to know when he was
beaten, and to accept the situation like a man, without
repining. When Almayer came on board that afternoon he handed him the letter without comment.

Almayer read it, returned it in silence, and leaning
over the taffrail (the two men were on deck) looked
down for some time at the play of the eddies round
the schooner's rudder. At last he said without looking
up—

"That's a decent enough letter. Abdulla gives him
up to you. I told you they were getting sick of him.
What are you going to do?"

Lingard cleared his throat, shuffled his feet, opened
his mouth with great determination, but said nothing
for a while. At last he murmured—

"I'll be hanged if I know—just yet."

"I wish you would do something soon . . . ."

"What's the hurry?" interrupted Lingard. "He
can't get away. As it stands he is at my mercy, as far
as I can see."

"Yes," said Almayer, reflectively—"and very little
mercy he deserves too. Abdulla's meaning—as I can
make it out amongst all those compliments—is: 'Get
rid for me of that white man—and we shall live in peace
and share the trade.'"

"You believe that?" asked Lingard, contemptuously.

"Not altogether," answered Almayer. "No doubt we will share the trade for a time—till he can grab the lot. Well, what are you going to do?"

He looked up as he spoke and was surprised to see Lingard's discomposed face.

"You ain't well. Pain anywhere?" he asked, with real solicitude.

"I have been queer—you know—these last few days, but no pain." He struck his broad chest several times, cleared his throat with a powerful "Hem!" and repeated: "No. No pain. Good for a few years yet. But I am bothered with all this, I can tell you!"

"You must take care of yourself," said Almayer. Then after a pause he added: "You will see Abdulla. Won't you?"

"I don't know. Not yet. There's plenty of time," said Lingard, impatiently.

"I wish you would do something," urged Almayer, moodily. "You know, that woman is a perfect nuisance to me. She and her brat! Yelps all day. And the children don't get on together. Yesterday the little devil wanted to fight with my Nina. Scratched her face, too. A perfect savage! Like his honourable papa. Yes, really. She worries about her husband, and whimpers from morning to night. When she isn't weeping she is furious with me. Yesterday she tormented me to tell her when he would be back and cried because he was engaged in such dangerous work. I said something about it being all right—no necessity to make a fool of herself, when she turned upon me like a wild cat. Called me a brute, selfish, heartless; raved about her beloved Peter risking his life for my benefit, while I did not care. Said I took advantage of his generous good-nature to get him to do dangerous

work—my work. That he was worth twenty of
the likes of me. That she would tell you—open
your eyes as to the kind of man I was, and so on.
That's what I've got to put up with for your sake.
You really might consider me a little. I haven't
robbed anybody," went on Almayer, with an attempt
at bitter irony—"or sold my best friend, but still
you ought to have some pity on me. It's like living
in a hot fever. She is out of her wits. You make
my house a refuge for scoundrels and lunatics. It
isn't fair. 'Pon my word it isn't! When she is
in her tantrums she is ridiculously ugly and screeches
so—it sets my teeth on edge. Thank God! my
wife got a fit of the sulks and cleared out of the house.
Lives in a riverside hut since that affair—you know.
But this Willems' wife by herself is almost more than I
can bear. And I ask myself why should I? You
are exacting and no mistake. This morning I thought
she was going to claw me. Only think! She wanted
to go prancing about the settlement. She might have
heard something there, so I told her she mustn't. It
wasn't safe outside our fences, I said. Thereupon she
rushes at me with her ten nails up to my eyes. 'You
miserable man,' she yells, 'even this place is not safe,
and you've sent him up this awful river where he may
lose his head. If he dies before forgiving me, Heaven
will punish you for your crime . . .' My crime! I
ask myself sometimes whether I am dreaming! It will
make me ill, all this. I've lost my appetite already."

He flung his hat on deck and laid hold of his hair
despairingly. Lingard looked at him with concern.

"What did she mean by it?" he muttered, thoughtfully.

"Mean! She is crazy, I tell you—and I will be, very
soon, if this lasts!"

"Just a little patience, Kaspar," pleaded Lingard. "A day or so more."

Relieved or tired by his violent outburst, Almayer calmed down, picked up his hat and, leaning against the bulwark, commenced to fan himself with it.

"Days do pass," he said, resignedly—"but that kind of thing makes a man old before his time. What is there to think about?—I can't imagine! Abdulla says plainly that if you undertake to pilot his ship out and instruct the half-caste, he will drop Willems like a hot potato and be your friend ever after. I believe him perfectly, as to Willems. It's so natural. As to being your friend it's a lie of course, but we need not bother about that just yet. You just say yes to Abdulla, and then whatever happens to Willems will be nobody's business."

He interrupted himself and remained silent for a while, glaring about with set teeth and dilated nostrils.

"You leave it to me. I'll see to it that something happens to him," he said at last, with calm ferocity. Lingard smiled faintly.

"The fellow isn't worth a shot. Not the trouble of it," he whispered, as if to himself. Almayer fired up suddenly.

"That's what you think," he cried. "You haven't been sewn up in your hammock to be made a laughing-stock of before a parcel of savages. Why! I daren't look anybody here in the face while that scoundrel is alive. I will . . . I will settle him."

"I don't think you will," growled Lingard.

"Do you think I am afraid of him?"

"Bless you! no!" said Lingard with alacrity. "Afraid! Not you. I know you. I don't doubt your courage. It's your head, my boy, your head that I . . ."

"That's it," said the aggrieved Almayer. "Go on. Why don't you call me a fool at once?"

"Because I don't want to," burst out Lingard, with nervous irritability. "If I wanted to call you a fool, I would do so without asking your leave." He began to walk athwart the narrow quarter-deck, kicking ropes' ends out of his way and growling to himself: "Delicate gentleman . . . what next? . . . I've done man's work before you could toddle. Understand . . . say what I like."

"Well! well!" said Almayer, with affected resignation. "There's no talking to you these last few days." He put on his hat, strolled to the gangway and stopped, one foot on the little inside ladder, as if hesitating, came back and planted himself in Lingard's way, compelling him to stand still and listen.

"Of course you will do what you like. You never take advice—I know that; but let me tell you that it wouldn't be honest to let that fellow get away from here. If you do nothing, that scoundrel will leave in Abdulla's ship for sure. Abdulla will make use of him to hurt you and others elsewhere. Willems knows too much about your affairs. He will cause you lots of trouble. You mark my words. Lots of trouble. To you—and to others perhaps. Think of that, Captain Lingard. That's all I've got to say. Now I must go back on shore. There's lots of work. We will begin loading this schooner to-morrow morning, first thing. All the bundles are ready. If you should want me for anything, hoist some kind of flag on the mainmast. At night two shots will fetch me." Then he added, in a friendly tone, "Won't you come and dine in the house to-night? It can't be good for you to stew on board like that, day after day."

Lingard did not answer. The image evoked by

Almayer; the picture of Willems ranging over the islands and disturbing the harmony of the universe by robbery, treachery, and violence, held him silent, entranced—painfully spellbound. Almayer, after waiting for a little while, moved reluctantly towards the gangway, lingered there, then sighed and got over the side, going down step by step. His head disappeared slowly below the rail. Lingard, who had been staring at him absently, started suddenly, ran to the side, and looking over, called out—

"Hey! Kaspar! Hold on a bit!"

Almayer signed to his boatmen to cease paddling, and turned his head towards the schooner. The boat drifted back slowly abreast of Lingard, nearly alongside.

"Look here," said Lingard, looking down—"I want a good canoe with four men to-day."

"Do you want it now?" asked Almayer.

"No! Catch this rope. Oh, you clumsy devil! . . . No, Kaspar," went on Lingard, after the bowman had got hold of the end of the brace he had thrown down into the canoe—"No, Kaspar. The sun is too much for me. And it would be better to keep my affairs quiet, too. Send the canoe—four good paddlers, mind, and your canvas chair for me to sit in. Send it about sunset. D'ye hear?"

"All right, father," said Almayer, cheerfully—"I will send Ali for a steersman, and the best men I've got. Anything else?"

"No, my lad. Only don't let them be late."

"I suppose it's no use asking you where you are going," said Almayer, tentatively. "Because if it is to see Abdulla, I . . ."

"I am not going to see Abdulla. Not to-day. Now be off with you."

He watched the canoe dart away shorewards, waved his hand in response to Almayer's nod, and walked to the taffrail smoothing out Abdulla's letter, which he had pulled out of his pocket. He read it over carefully, crumpled it up slowly, smiling the while and closing his fingers firmly over the crackling paper as though he had hold there of Abdulla's throat. Half-way to his pocket he changed his mind, and flinging the ball overboard looked at it thoughtfully as it spun round in the eddies for a moment, before the current bore it away down-stream, towards the sea.

PART IV

PART IV

CHAPTER ONE

THE night was very dark. For the first time in many months the East Coast slept unseen by the stars under a veil of motionless cloud that, driven before the first breath of the rainy monsoon, had drifted slowly from the eastward all the afternoon; pursuing the declining sun with its masses of black and grey that seemed to chase the light with wicked intent, and with an ominous and gloomy steadiness, as though conscious of the message of violence and turmoil they carried. At the sun's disappearance below the western horizon, the immense cloud, in quickened motion, grappled with the glow of retreating light, and rolling down to the clear and jagged outline of the distant mountains, hung arrested above the steaming forests; hanging low, silent and menacing over the unstirring tree-tops; withholding the blessing of rain, nursing the wrath of its thunder; undecided—as if brooding over its own power for good or for evil.

Babalatchi, coming out of the red and smoky light of his little bamboo house, glanced upwards, drew in a long breath of the warm and stagnant air, and stood for a moment with his good eye closed tightly, as if intimidated by the unwonted and deep silence of Lakamba's courtyard. When he opened his eye he had recovered his sight so far, that he could distinguish the various degrees of formless blackness which marked the places of trees, of abandoned houses, of riverside bushes, on the dark background of the night. The careworn sage walked cautiously down the deserted courtyard to the waterside, and stood on the bank listening to the voice of the invisible river that flowed at his feet; listening to the soft whispers, to the deep murmurs, to the sudden gurgles and the short hisses of the swift current racing along the bank through the hot darkness.

He stood with his face turned to the river, and it seemed to him that he could breathe easier with the knowledge of the clear vast space before him; then, after a while he leaned heavily forward on his staff, his chin fell on his breast, and a deep sigh was his answer to the selfish discourse of the river that hurried on unceasing and fast, regardless of joy or sorrow, of suffering and of strife, of failures and triumphs that lived on its banks. The brown water was there, ready to carry friends or enemies, to nurse love or hate on its submissive and heartless bosom, to help or to hinder, to save life or give death; the great and rapid river: a deliverance, a prison, a refuge or a grave.

Perchance such thoughts as these caused Babalatchi to send another mournful sigh into the trailing mists of the unconcerned Pantai. The barbarous politician had forgotten the recent success of his plottings in the melancholy contemplation of a sorrow that made the night blacker, the clammy heat more oppressive, the still air more heavy, the dumb solitude more signifi-cant of torment than of peace. He had spent the night before by the side of the dying Omar, and now, after twenty-four hours, his memory persisted in returning to that low and sombre reed hut from which the fierce spirit of the incomparably accomplished pirate took its flight, to learn too late, in a worse world, the error of its earthly ways. The mind of the savage statesman, chastened by bereavement, felt for a moment the weight of his loneliness with keen perception worthy even of a sensibility exasperated by all the refinements of tender sentiment that a glorious civilization brings in its train, among other blessings and virtues, into this excellent world. For the space of about thirty seconds, a half-naked, betel-chewing pessimist stood upon the bank of the tropical river, on the edge of the still and immense forests; a man angry, powerless, empty-handed, with a cry of bitter discontent ready on his lips; a cry that, had it come out, would have rung through the virgin solitudes of the woods, as true, as great, as profound, as any philosophical shriek that ever came from the depths of an easy-chair to disturb the impure wilderness of chimneys and roofs.

For half a minute and no more did Babalatchi face the gods in the sublime privilege of his revolt, and then the one-eyed puller of wires became himself again, full of care and wisdom and far-reaching plans, and a victim to the tormenting superstitions of his race. The night, no matter how quiet, is never perfectly silent to attentive ears, and now Babalatchi fancied he could detect in it other noises than those caused by the ripples and eddies of the river. He turned his head sharply to the right and to the left in succession, and then spun round quickly in a startled and watchful manner, as if he had expected to see the blind ghost of his departed leader wandering in the obscurity of the empty courtyard behind his back. Nothing there. Yet he had heard a noise; a strange noise! No doubt a ghostly voice of a complaining and angry spirit. He listened. Not a sound. Reassured, Babalatchi made a few paces towards his house, when a very human noise, that of hoarse coughing, reached him from the river. He stopped, listened attentively, but now without any sign of emotion, and moving briskly back to the waterside stood expectant with parted lips, trying to pierce with his eye the wavering curtain of mist that hung low over the water. He could see nothing, yet some people in a canoe must have been very near, for he heard words spoken in an ordinary tone.

"Do you think this is the place, Ali? I can see nothing."

"It must be near here, Tuan," answered another voice. "Shall we try the bank?"

"No! . . . Let drift a little. If you go poking into the bank in the dark you might stove the canoe on some log. We must be careful. . . . Let drift! Let drift! . . . This does seem to be a clearing of some sort. We may see a light by and by from some house or other. In Lakamba's campong there are many houses? Hey?"

"A great number, Tuan . . . I do not see any light."

"Nor I," grumbled the first voice again, this time nearly abreast of the silent Babalatchi who looked uneasily towards his own house, the doorway of which glowed with the dim light of a torch burning within. The house stood end on to the river, and its doorway faced down-stream, so Babalatchi reasoned rapidly that the strangers on the river could not see the light from the position their boat was in at the moment. He could not make up his mind to call out to them, and while he hesitated he heard the voices again, but now some way below the landing-place where he stood.

"Nothing. This cannot be it. Let them give way, Ali! Dayong there!"

That order was followed by the splash of paddles, then a sudden cry—

"I see a light. I see it! Now I know where to land, Tuan."

There was more splashing as the canoe was paddled sharply round and came back up-stream close to the bank.

"Call out," said very near a deep voice, which Babalatchi felt sure must belong to a white man. "Call out—and somebody may come with a torch. I can't see anything."

The loud hail that succeeded these words was emitted nearly under the silent listener's nose. Babalatchi, to preserve appearances, ran with long but noiseless strides halfway up the courtyard, and only then shouted in answer and kept on shouting as he walked slowly back again towards the river bank. He saw there an indistinct shape of a boat, not quite alongside the landing-place.

"Who speaks on the river?" asked Babalatchi, throwing a tone of surprise into his question.

"A white man," answered Lingard from the canoe. "Is there not one torch in rich Lakamba's campong to light a guest on his landing?"

"There are no torches and no men. I am alone here," said Babalatchi, with some hesitation.

"Alone!" exclaimed Lingard. "Who are you?"

"Only a servant of Lakamba. But land, Tuan Putih, and see my face. Here is my hand. No! Here! . . . By your mercy. . . . Ada! . . . Now you are safe."

"And you are alone here?" said Lingard, moving with precaution a few steps into the courtyard. "How dark it is," he muttered to himself—"one would think the world had been painted black."

"Yes. Alone. What more did you say, Tuan? I did not understand your talk."

"It is nothing. I expected to find here . . . But where are they all?"

"What matters where they are?" said Babalatchi, gloomily. "Have you come to see my people? The last departed on a long journey—and I am alone. To-morrow I go too."

"I came to see a white man," said Lingard, walking on slowly. "He is not gone, is he?"

"No!" answered Babalatchi, at his elbow. "A man with a red skin and hard eyes," he went on, musingly, "whose hand is strong, and whose heart is foolish and weak. A white man indeed . . . But still a man."

They were now at the foot of the short ladder which led to the split-bamboo platform surrounding Babalatchi's habitation. The faint light from the doorway fell down upon the two men's faces as they stood looking at each other curiously.

"Is he there?" asked Lingard, in a low voice, with a wave of his hand upwards.

Babalatchi, staring hard at his long-expected visitor, did not answer at once.

"No, not there," he said at last, placing his foot on the lowest rung and looking back. "Not there, Tuan—yet not very far. Will you sit down in my dwelling? There may be rice and fish and clear water—not from the river, but from a spring . . ."

"I am not hungry,"* interrupted Lingard, curtly, "and I did not come here to sit in your dwelling. Lead me to the white man who expects me. I have no time to lose."

"The night is long, Tuan," went on Babalatchi, softly, "and there are other nights and other days. Long. Very long . . . How much time it takes for a man to die! O Rajah Laut!"

Lingard started.

"You know me!" he exclaimed.

"Ay—wa! I have seen your face and felt your hand before—many years ago," said Babalatchi, holding on halfway up the ladder, and bending down from above to peer into Lingard's upturned face. "You do not remember—but I have not forgotten. There are many men like me: there is only one Rajah Laut."

He climbed with sudden agility the last few steps, and stood on the platform waving his hand invitingly to Lingard, who followed after a short moment of indecision.

The elastic bamboo floor of the hut bent under the heavy weight of the old seaman, who, standing within the threshold, tried to look into the smoky gloom of the low dwelling. Under the torch, thrust into the cleft of a stick, fastened at a right angle to the middle stay of the ridge pole, lay a red patch of light, showing a few shabby mats and a corner of a big wooden chest the rest of which was lost in shadow. In the obscurity of the more remote parts of the house a lance-head, a brass tray hung on the wall, the long barrel of a gun leaning against the chest, caught the stray rays of the smoky illumination in trembling gleams that wavered, disappeared, reappeared, went out, came back—as if engaged in a doubtful struggle with the darkness that, lying in wait in distant corners, seemed to dart out viciously towards its feeble enemy. The vast space under the high pitch of the roof was filled with a thick cloud of smoke, whose under-side—level like a ceiling—reflected the light of the swaying dull flame, while at the top it oozed out through the imperfect thatch of dried palm leaves. An indescribable and complicated smell, made up of the exhalation of damp earth below, of the taint of dried fish and of the effluvia of rotting vegetable matter, pervaded the place and caused Lin-

gard to sniff strongly as he strode over, sat on the
chest, and, leaning his elbows on his knees, took his
head between his hands and stared at the doorway
thoughtfully.

Babalatchi moved about in the shadows, whispering
to an indistinct form or two that flitted about at the
far end of the hut. Without stirring Lingard glanced
sideways, and caught sight of muffled-up human shapes
that hovered for a moment near the edge of light and
retreated suddenly back into the darkness. Babalatchi
approached, and sat at Lingard's feet on a rolled-up
bundle of mats.

"Will you eat rice and drink sagueir?" he said. "I
have waked up my household."

"My friend," said Lingard, without looking at him,
"when I come to see Lakamba, or any of Lakamba's
servants, I am never hungry and never thirsty. Tau!
Savee! Never! Do you think I am devoid of reason?
That there is nothing there?"

He sat up, and, fixing abruptly his eyes on Babalatchi, tapped his own forehead significantly.

"Tse! Tse! Tse! How can you talk like that,
Tuan!" exclaimed Babalatchi, in a horrified tone.

"I talk as I think. I have lived many years,"
said Lingard, stretching his arm negligently to take
up the gun, which he began to examine knowingly,
cocking it, and easing down the hammer several times.
"This is good. Mataram make.* Old, too," he went on.

"Haï!" broke in Babalatchi, eagerly. "I got it
when I was young. He was an Aru trader, a man
with a big stomach and a loud voice, and brave—very
brave. When we came up with his prau in the grey
morning, he stood aft shouting to his men and fired
this gun at us once. Only once!" . . . He
paused, laughed softly, and went on in a low, dreamy

voice. "In the grey morning we came up: forty silent men in a swift Sulu prau; and when the sun was so high"—here he held up his hands about three feet apart—"when the sun was only so high, Tuan, our work was done—and there was a feast ready for the fishes of the sea."

"Aye! aye!" muttered Lingard, nodding his head slowly. "I see. You should not let it get rusty like this," he added.

He let the gun fall between his knees, and moving back on his seat, leaned his head against the wall of the hut, crossing his arms on his breast.

"A good gun," went on Babalatchi. "Carry far and true. Better than this—there."

With the tips of his fingers he touched gently the butt of a revolver peeping out of the right pocket of Lingard's white jacket.

"Take your hand off that," said Lingard sharply, but in a good-humoured tone and without making the slightest movement.

Babalatchi smiled and hitched his seat a little further off.

For some time they sat in silence. Lingard, with his head tilted back, looked downwards with lowered eyelids at Babalatchi, who was tracing invisible lines with his finger on the mat between his feet. Outside, they could hear Ali and the other boatmen chattering and laughing round the fire they had lighted in the big and deserted courtyard.

"Well, what about that white man?" said Lingard, quietly.

It seemed as if Babalatchi had not heard the question. He went on tracing elaborate patterns on the floor for a good while. Lingard waited motionless. At last the Malay lifted his head.

"Haï! The white man. I know!" he murmured absently. "This white man or another. . . . Tuan," he said aloud with unexpected animation, "you are a man of the sea?"

"You know me. Why ask?" said Lingard, in a low tone.

"Yes. A man of the sea—even as we are. A true Orang Laut," went on Babalatchi, thoughtfully, "not like the rest of the white men."

"I am like other whites, and do not wish to speak many words when the truth is short. I came here to see the white man that helped Lakamba against Patalolo, who is my friend. Show me where that white man lives; I want him to hear my talk."

"Talk only? Tuan! Why hurry? The night is long and death is swift—as you ought to know; you who have dealt it to so many of my people. Many years ago I have faced you, arms in hand. Do you not remember? It was in Carimata—far from here."

"I cannot remember every vagabond that came in my way," protested Lingard, seriously.

"Haï! Haï!" continued Babalatchi, unmoved and dreamy. "Many years ago. Then all this"—and looking up suddenly at Lingard's beard, he flourished his fingers below his own beardless chin—"then all this was like gold in sunlight, now it is like the foam of an angry sea."

"Maybe, maybe," said Lingard, patiently, paying the involuntary tribute of a faint sigh to the memories of the past evoked by Babalatchi's words.

He had been living with Malays so long and so close that the extreme deliberation and deviousness of their mental proceedings had ceased to irritate him much. To-night, perhaps, he was less prone to impatience than ever. He was disposed, if not to listen

to Babalatchi, then to let him talk. It was evident
to him that the man had something to say, and he
hoped that from the talk a ray of light would shoot
through the thick blackness of inexplicable treachery,
to show him clearly—if only for a second—the man
upon whom he would have to execute the verdict* of
justice. Justice only! Nothing was further from his
thoughts than such an useless thing as revenge. Justice only. It was his duty that justice should be done
—and by his own hand. He did not like to think how.
To him, as to Babalatchi, it seemed that the night would
be long enough for the work he had to do. But he
did not define to himself the nature of the work, and he
sat very still, and willingly dilatory, under the fearsome
oppression of his call. What was the good to think
about it? It was inevitable, and its time was near.
Yet he could not command his memories that came
crowding round him in that evil-smelling hut, while
Babalatchi talked on in a flowing monotone, nothing of
him moving but the lips, in the artificially inanimated
face. Lingard, like an anchored ship that had broken
her sheer, darted about here and there on the rapid tide
of his recollections. The subdued sound of soft words
rang around him, but his thoughts were lost, now in the
contemplation of the past sweetness and strife of Carimata days, now in the uneasy wonder at the failure
of his judgment; at the fatal blindness of accident that
had caused him, many years ago, to rescue a half-
starved runaway from a Dutch ship in Samarang roads.
How he had liked the man: his assurance, his push,
his desire to get on, his conceited good-humour and
his selfish eloquence. He had liked his very faults—
those faults that had so many, to him, sympathetic
sides. And he had always dealt fairly by him from the
very beginning; and he would deal fairly by him now

—to the very end. This last thought darkened Lingard's features with a responsive and menacing frown. The doer of justice sat with compressed lips and a heavy heart, while in the calm darkness outside the silent world seemed to be waiting breathlessly for that justice he held in his hand—in his strong hand:—ready to strike—reluctant to move.

CHAPTER TWO

BABALATCHI ceased speaking. Lingard shifted his feet a little, uncrossed his arms, and shook his head slowly. The narrative of the events in Sambir, related from the point of view of the astute statesman, the sense of which had been caught here and there by his inattentive ears, had been yet like a thread to guide him out of the sombre labyrinth of his thoughts; and now he had come to the end of it, out of the tangled past into the pressing necessities of the present. With the palms of his hands on his knees, his elbows squared out, he looked down on Babalatchi who sat in a stiff attitude, inexpressive and mute as a talking doll the mechanism of which had at length run down.

"You people did all this," said Lingard at last, "and you will be sorry for it before the dry wind begins to blow again. Abdulla's voice will bring the Dutch rule here."

Babalatchi waved his hand towards the dark doorway.

"There are forests there. Lakamba rules the land now. Tell me, Tuan, do you think the big trees know the name of the ruler? No. They are born, they grow, they live and they die—yet know not, feel not.* It is their land."

"Even a big tree may be killed by a small axe," said Lingard, drily. "And, remember, my one-eyed friend, that axes are made by white hands. You will soon find that out, since you have hoisted the flag of the Dutch."

"Ay—wa!" said Babalatchi, slowly. "It is written that the earth belongs to those who have fair skins and hard but foolish hearts. The farther away is the master, the easier it is for the slave, Tuan! You were too near. Your voice rang in our ears always. Now it is not going to be so. The great Rajah in Batavia is strong, but he may be deceived. He must speak very loud to be heard here. But if we have need to shout, then he must hear the many voices that call for protection. He is but a white man."

"If I ever spoke to Patalolo, like an elder brother, it was for your good—for the good of all," said Lingard with great earnestness.

"This is a white man's talk," exclaimed Babalatchi, with bitter exultation. "I know you. That is how you all talk while you load your guns and sharpen your swords; and when you are ready, then to those who are weak you say: 'Obey me and be happy, or die!' You are strange, you white men. You think it is only your wisdom and your virtue and your happiness that are true. You are stronger than the wild beasts, but not so wise. A black tiger* knows when he is not hungry—you do not. He knows the difference between himself and those that can speak; you do not understand the difference between yourselves and us—who are men. You are wise and great —and you shall always be fools."

He threw up both his hands, stirring the sleeping cloud of smoke that hung above his head, and brought the open palms on the flimsy floor on each side of his outstretched legs. The whole hut shook. Lingard looked at the excited statesman curiously.

"Apa! Apa! What's the matter?" he murmured, soothingly. "Whom did I kill here? Where are my guns? What have I done? What have I eaten up?"

Babalatchi calmed down, and spoke with studied courtesy.

"You, Tuan, are of the sea, and more like what we are. Therefore I speak to you all the words that are in my heart. . . . Only once has the sea been stronger than the Rajah of the sea."

"You know it; do you?" said Lingard, with pained sharpness.

"Haï! We have heard about your ship—and some rejoiced. Not I. Amongst the whites, who are devils, you are a man."

"Trima kassi! I give you thanks," said Lingard, gravely.

Babalatchi looked down with a bashful smile, but his face became saddened directly, and when he spoke again it was in a mournful tone.

"Had you come a day sooner, Tuan, you would have seen an enemy die. You would have seen him die poor, blind, unhappy—with no son to dig his grave and speak of his wisdom and courage. Yes; you would have seen the man that fought you in Carimata many years ago, die alone—but for one friend. A great sight to you."

"Not to me," answered Lingard. "I did not even remember him till you spoke his name just now. You do not understand us. We fight, we vanquish—and we forget."

"True, true," said Babalatchi, with polite irony; "you whites are so great that you disdain to remember your enemies. No! No!" he went on, in the same tone, "you have so much mercy for us, that there is no room for any remembrance. Oh, you are great and good! But it is in my mind that amongst yourselves you know how to remember. Is it not so, Tuan?"

Lingard said nothing. His shoulders moved imperceptibly. He laid his gun across his knees and stared at the flint lock absently.

"Yes," went on Babalatchi, falling again into a mournful mood, "yes, he died in darkness. I sat by his side and held his hand, but he could not see the face of him who watched the faint breath on his lips. She, whom he had cursed because of the white man, was there too, and wept with covered face. The white man walked about the courtyard making many noises. Now and then he would come to the doorway and glare at us who mourned. He stared with wicked eyes, and then I was glad that he who was dying was blind. This is true talk. I was glad; for a white man's eyes are not good to see when the devil that lives within is looking out through them."

"Devil! Hey?" said Lingard, half aloud to himself, as if struck with the obviousness of some novel idea. Babalatchi went on:

"At the first hour of the morning he sat up—he so weak—and said plainly some words that were not meant for human ears. I held his hand tightly, but it was time for the leader of brave men to go amongst the Faithful who are happy. They of my household brought a white sheet,* and I began to dig a grave in the hut in which he died. She mourned aloud. The white man came to the doorway and shouted. He was angry. Angry with her because she beat her breast, and tore her hair, and mourned with shrill cries as a woman should. Do you understand what I say, Tuan? That white man came inside the hut with great fury, and took her by the shoulder, and dragged her out. Yes, Tuan. I saw Omar dead, and I saw her at the feet of that white dog who has deceived me. I saw his face grey, like the cold mist of the morning; I saw his pale eyes looking down at Omar's daughter beating her head on the ground at his feet. At the feet of him who is Abdulla's slave. Yes, he lives by Abdulla's will. That is why I held my hand while I saw all this. I held my hand because we are now under the flag of the Orang Blanda, and Abdulla can speak into the ears of the great. We must not have any trouble with white men. Abdulla has spoken—and I must obey."

"That's it, is it?" growled Lingard in his moustache. Then in Malay, "It seems that you are angry, O Babalatchi!"

"No; I am not angry, Tuan," answered Babalatchi, descending from the insecure heights of his indignation into the insincere depths of safe humility. "I am not angry. What am I to be angry? I am only an Orang Laut, and I have fled before your people many times. Servant of this one—protected of another; I have given my counsel here and there for a handful of rice. What am I, to be angry with a white man? What is anger without the power to strike? But you whites have taken all: the land, the sea, and the power to strike! And there is nothing left for us in the islands but your white men's justice; your great justice that knows not anger."

He got up and stood for a moment in the doorway, sniffing the hot air of the courtyard, then turned back and leaned against the stay of the ridge pole, facing Lingard who kept his seat on the chest. The torch, consumed nearly to the end, burned noisily. Small explosions took place in the heart of the flame, driving through its smoky blaze strings of hard, round puffs of white smoke, no bigger than peas, which rolled out of doors in the faint draught that came from invisible cracks of the bamboo walls. The pungent taint of unclean things below and about the hut grew heavier, weighing down Lingard's resolution and his thoughts in an irresistible numbness of the brain. He thought drowsily of himself and of that man who wanted to see him—who waited to see him. Who waited! Night and day. Waited. . . . A spiteful but vaporous idea floated through his brain that such waiting could not be very pleasant to the fellow. Well, let him wait. He would see him soon enough. And for how long? Five seconds—five minutes—say nothing—say something. What? No! Just give him time to take one good look, and then . . .

Suddenly Babalatchi began to speak in a soft voice. Lingard blinked, cleared his throat—sat up straight.

"You know all now, Tuan. Lakamba dwells in the stockaded house of Patalolo; Abdulla has begun to build godowns of plank and stone; and now that Omar is dead, I myself shall depart from this place and live with Lakamba and speak in his ear. I have served many. The best of them all sleeps in the ground in a white sheet, with nothing to mark his grave but the ashes of the hut in which he died. Yes, Tuan! the white man destroyed it himself. With a blazing brand in his hand he strode around, shouting to me to come out—shouting to me, who was throwing earth on the body of a great leader. Yes; swearing to me by the name of your God and ours that he would burn me and her in there if we did not make haste. . . . Haï! The white men are very masterful and wise. I dragged her out quickly!"

"Oh, damn it!" exclaimed Lingard—then went on in Malay, speaking earnestly. "Listen. That man is not like other white men. You know he is not. He is not a man at all. He is . . . I don't know."

Babalatchi lifted his hand deprecatingly. His eye twinkled, and his red-stained big lips, parted by an expressionless grin, uncovered a stumpy row of black teeth filed evenly to the gums.

"Haï! Haï! Not like you. Not like you," he said, increasing the softness of his tones as he neared the object uppermost in his mind during that much-desired interview. "Not like you, Tuan, who are like ourselves, only wiser and stronger. Yet he, also, is full of great cunning, and speaks of you without any respect, after the manner of white men when they talk of one another."

Lingard leaped in his seat as if he had been prodded. "He speaks! What does he say?" he shouted.

"Nay, Tuan," protested the composed Babalatchi; "what matters his talk if he is not a man? I am nothing before you—why should I repeat words of one white man about another? He did boast to Abdulla of having learned much from your wisdom in years past. Other words I have forgotten. Indeed, Tuan, I have . . ."

Lingard cut short Babalatchi's protestations by a contemptuous wave of the hand and reseated himself with dignity.

"I shall go," said Babalatchi, "and the white man will remain here, alone with the spirit of the dead and with her who has been the delight of his heart. He, being white, cannot hear the voice of those that died. . . . Tell me, Tuan," he went on, looking at Lingard with curiosity—"tell me, Tuan, do you white people ever hear the voices of the invisible ones?"

"We do not," answered Lingard, "because those that we cannot see do not speak."

"Never speak! And never complain with sounds that are not words?" exclaimed Babalatchi, doubtingly. "It may be so—or your ears are dull. We Malays hear many sounds near the places where men are buried. To-night I heard . . . Yes, even I have heard. . . . I do not want to hear any more," he added, nervously. "Perhaps I was wrong when I . . . There are things I regret. The trouble was heavy in his heart when he died. Sometimes I think I was wrong . . . but I do not want to hear the complaint of invisible lips. Therefore I go, Tuan. Let the unquiet spirit speak to his enemy the white man who knows not fear, or love, or mercy—knows nothing but contempt and violence. I have been wrong! I have! Haï! Haï!"

He stood for awhile with his elbow in the palm of his left hand, the fingers of the other over his lips as if to stifle the expression of inconvenient remorse; then, after glancing at the torch, burnt out nearly to its end, he moved towards the wall by the chest, fumbled about there and suddenly flung open a large shutter of attaps woven in a light framework of sticks. Lingard swung his legs quickly round the corner of his seat.

"Hallo!" he said, surprised.

The cloud of smoke stirred, and a slow wisp curled out through the new opening. The torch flickered, hissed, and went out, the glowing end falling on the mat, whence Babalatchi snatched it up and tossed it outside through the open square. It described a vanishing curve of red light, and lay below, shining feebly in the vast darkness. Babalatchi remained with his arm stretched out into the empty night.

"There," he said, "you can see the white man's courtyard, Tuan, and his house."

"I can see nothing," answered Lingard, putting his head through the shutter-hole. "It's too dark."

"Wait, Tuan," urged Babalatchi. "You have been looking long at the burning torch. You will soon see. Mind the gun, Tuan. It is loaded."

"There is no flint in it. You could not find a fire-stone for a hundred miles round this spot," said Lingard, testily. "Foolish thing to load that gun."

"I have a stone. I had it from a man wise and pious that lives in Menang Kabau. A very pious man—very good fire. He spoke words over that stone that make its sparks good. And the gun is good—carries straight and far. Would carry from here to the door of the white man's house, I believe, Tuan."

"Tida apa. Never mind your gun," muttered Lingard, peering into the formless darkness. "Is that the house—that black thing over there?" he asked.

"Yes," answered Babalatchi; "that is his house. He lives there by the will of Abdulla, and shall live there till . . . From where you stand, Tuan, you can look over the fence and across the courtyard straight at the door—at the door from which he comes out every morning, looking like a man that had seen Jehannum in his sleep."

Lingard drew his head in. Babalatchi touched his shoulder with a groping hand.

"Wait a little, Tuan. Sit still. The morning is not far off now—a morning without sun after a night without stars. But there will be light enough to see the man who said not many days ago that he alone has made you less than a child in Sambir."

He felt a slight tremor under his hand, but took it off directly and began feeling all over the lid of the chest, behind Lingard's back, for the gun.

"What are you at?" said Lingard, impatiently. "You do worry about that rotten gun. You had better get a light."

"A light! I tell you, Tuan, that the light of heaven is very near," said Babalatchi, who had now obtained possession of the object of his solicitude, and grasping

it strongly by its long barrel, grounded the stock at his
feet.

"Perhaps it is near," said Lingard, leaning both his
elbows on the lower cross-piece of the primitive window
and looking out. "It is very black outside yet," he
remarked carelessly.

Babalatchi fidgeted about.

"It is not good for you to sit where you may be seen,"
he muttered.

"Why not?" asked Lingard.

"The white man sleeps, it is true," explained Babalatchi, softly; "yet he may come out early, and he has
arms."

"Ah! he has arms?" said Lingard.

"Yes; a short gun that fires many times—like yours
here. Abdulla had to give it to him."

Lingard heard Babalatchi's words, but made no
movement. To the old adventurer the idea that firearms
could be dangerous in other hands than his own
did not occur readily, and certainly not in connection
with Willems. He was so busy with the thoughts about
what he considered his own sacred duty, that he could
not give any consideration to the probable actions of
the man of whom he thought—as one may think of an
executed criminal—with wondering indignation tem-
pered by scornful pity. While he sat staring into the
darkness, that every minute grew thinner before his
pensive eyes, like a dispersing mist, Willems appeared
to him as a figure belonging already wholly to the past
—a figure that could come in no way into his life again.
He had made up his mind, and the thing was as well as
done. In his weary thoughts he had closed this fatal,
inexplicable, and horrible episode in his life. The
worst had happened. The coming days would see the
retribution.

He had removed an enemy once or twice before, out of his path; he had paid off some very heavy scores a good many times. Captain Tom had been a good friend to many: but it was generally understood, from Honolulu round about to Diego Suarez,* that Captain Tom's enmity was rather more than any man single-handed could easily manage. He would not, as he said often, hurt a fly as long as the fly left him alone; yet a man does not live for years beyond the pale of civilized laws without evolving for himself some queer notions of justice. Nobody of those he knew had ever cared to point out to him the errors of his con-ceptions. It was not worth anybody's while to run counter to Lingard's ideas of the fitness of things—that fact was acquired to the floating wisdom of the South Seas, of the Eastern Archipelago, and was nowhere better understood than in out-of-the-way nooks of the world; in those nooks which he filled, unresisted and masterful, with the echoes of his noisy presence. There is not much use in arguing with a man who boasts of never having regretted a single action of his life, whose answer to a mild criticism is a good-natured shout—"You know nothing about it. I would do it again. Yes, sir!" His associates and his acquaintances accepted him, his opinions, his actions . like things preordained and unchangeable; looked upon his many-sided manifestations with passive wonder not unmixed with that admiration which is only the rightful due of a successful man. But nobody had ever seen him in the mood he was in now. Nobody had seen Lingard doubtful and giving way to doubt, unable to make up his mind and unwilling to act; Lingard timid and hesitating one minute, angry yet inactive the next; Lingard puzzled in a word, because confronted with a situation that discomposed him by its unprovoked malevolence, by its ghastly injustice, that to his rough but unsophisticated palate tasted distinctly of sulphurous fumes from the deepest hell.

The smooth darkness filling the shutter-hole grew paler and became blotchy with ill-defined shapes, as if a new universe was being evolved out of sombre chaos. Then outlines came out, defining forms without any details, indicating here a tree, there a bush; a black belt of forest far off; the straight lines of a house, the ridge of a high roof near by. Inside the hut, Babalatchi, who lately had been only a persuasive voice, became a human shape leaning its chin imprudently on the muzzle of a gun and rolling an uneasy eye over the reappearing world. The day came rapidly, dismal and oppressed by the fog of the river and by the heavy vapours of the sky—a day without colour and without sunshine: incomplete, disappointing, and sad.

Babalatchi twitched gently Lingard's sleeve, and when the old seaman had lifted up his head interrogatively, he stretched out an arm and a pointing forefinger towards Willems' house, now plainly visible to the right and beyond the big tree of the courtyard.

"Look, Tuan!" he said. "He lives there. That is the door—his door. Through it he will appear soon, with his hair in disorder and his mouth full of curses. That is so. He is a white man, and never satisfied. It is in my mind he is angry even in his sleep. A dangerous man. As Tuan may observe," he went on, obsequiously, "his door faces this opening, where you condescend to sit, which is concealed from all eyes. Faces it—straight—and not far. Observe, Tuan, not at all far."

"Yes, yes; I can see. I shall see him when he wakes."

"No doubt, Tuan. When he wakes. . . . If

you remain here he can not see you. I shall withdraw quickly and prepare my canoe myself. I am only a poor man, and must go to Sambir to greet Lakamba when he opens his eyes. I must bow before Abdulla, who has strength—even more strength than you. Now if you remain here, you shall easily behold the man who boasted to Abdulla that he had been your friend, even while he prepared to fight those who called you protector. Yes, he plotted with Abdulla for that cursed flag. Lakamba was blind then, and I was deceived. But you, Tuan! Remember, he deceived you more. Of that he boasted before all men."

He leaned the gun quietly against the wall close to the window, and said softly: "Shall I go now, Tuan? Be careful of the gun. I have put the fire-stone in. The fire-stone of the wise man, which never fails."

Lingard's eyes were fastened on the distant doorway. Across his line of sight, in the grey emptiness of the courtyard, a big fruit-pigeon flapped languidly towards the forests with a loud booming cry, like the note of a deep gong: a brilliant bird looking in the gloom of threatening day as black as a crow. A serried flock of white rice-birds rose above the trees with a faint scream, and hovered, swaying in a disordered mass that suddenly scattered in all directions, as if burst asunder by a silent explosion. Behind his back Lingard heard a shuffle of feet—women leaving the hut. In the other courtyard a voice was heard complaining of cold, and coming very feeble, but exceedingly distinct, out of the vast silence of the abandoned houses and clearings. Babalatchi coughed discreetly. From under the house the thumping of wooden pestles husking the rice started with unexpected abruptness. The weak but clear voice in the yard again urged, "Blow up the embers, O brother!" Another voice answered,

drawling in modulated, thin sing-song, "Do it yourself,
O shivering pig!" and the drawl of the last words stopped
short, as if the man had fallen into a deep hole. Babalatchi coughed again a little impatiently, and said in a
confidential tone—

"Do you think it is time for me to go, Tuan? Will
you take care of my gun, Tuan? I am a man that
knows how to obey; even obey Abdulla, who has deceived me. Nevertheless this gun carries far and true
—if you would want to know, Tuan. And I have put
in a double measure of powder, and three slugs. Yes,
Tuan. Now—perhaps—I go."

When Babalatchi commenced speaking, Lingard
turned slowly round and gazed upon him with the dull
and unwilling look of a sick man waking to another
day of suffering. As the astute statesman proceeded,
Lingard's eyebrows came close, his eyes became animated, and a big vein stood out on his forehead, ac-
centuating a lowering frown. When speaking his last
words Babalatchi faltered, then stopped, confused,
before the steady gaze of the old seaman.

Lingard rose. His face cleared, and he looked down
at the anxious Babalatchi with sudden benevolence.

"So! That's what you were after," he said, laying
a heavy hand on Babalatchi's yielding shoulder. "You
thought I came here to murder him. Hey? Speak!
You faithful dog of an Arab trader!"

"And what else, Tuan?" shrieked Babalatchi, exasperated into sincerity. "What else, Tuan! Remember what he has done; he poisoned our ears with his talk
about you. You are a man. If you did not come to
kill, Tuan, then either I am a fool or . . ." He
paused, struck his naked breast with his open palm, and
finished in a discouraged whisper—"or, Tuan, you are."

Lingard looked down at him with scornful serenity.

After his long and painful gropings amongst the obscure abominations of Willems' conduct, the logical if tortuous evolutions of Babalatchi's diplomatic mind were to him welcome as daylight. There was something at last he could understand—the clear effect of a simple cause. He felt indulgent towards the disappointed sage.

"So you are angry with your friend, O one-eyed one!" he said slowly, nodding his fierce countenance close to Babalatchi's discomfited face. "It seems to me that you must have had much to do with what happened in Sambir lately. Hey? You son of a burnt father."

"May I perish under your hand, O Rajah of the sea, if my words are not true!" said Babalatchi, with reckless excitement. "You are here in the midst of your enemies. He the greatest. Abdulla would do nothing without him, and I could do nothing without Abdulla. Strike me—so that you strike all!"

"Who are you," exclaimed Lingard contemptuously —"who are you to dare call yourself my enemy! Dirt! Nothing! Go out first," he went on severely. "Lekas! quick. March out!"

He pushed Babalatchi through the doorway and followed him down the short ladder into the courtyard. The boatmen squatting over the fire turned their slow eyes with apparent difficulty towards the two men; then, unconcerned, huddled close together again, stretching forlornly their hands over the embers. The women stopped in their work and with uplifted pestles flashed quick and curious glances from the gloom under the house.

"Is that the way?" asked Lingard with a nod towards the little wicket-gate of Willems' enclosure.

"If you seek death, that is surely the way," answered Babalatchi in a dispassionate voice, as if he had exhausted all the emotions. "He lives there: he who destroyed your friends; who hastened Omar's death; who plotted with Abdulla first against you, then against me. I have been like a child. O shame! . . . But go, Tuan. Go there."

"I go where I like," said Lingard, emphatically, "and you may go to the devil; I do not want you any more. The islands of these seas shall sink before I, Rajah Laut, serve the will of any of your people. Tau? But I tell you this: I do not care what you do with him after to-day. And I say that because I am merciful."

"Tida! I do nothing," said Babalatchi, shaking his head with bitter apathy. "I am in Abdulla's hand and care not, even as you do. No! no!" he added, turning away, "I have learned much wisdom this morning. There are no men anywhere. You whites are cruel to your friends and merciful to your enemies —which is the work of fools."

He went away towards the riverside, and, without once looking back, disappeared in the low bank of mist that lay over the water and the shore. Lingard followed him with his eyes thoughtfully. After awhile he roused himself and called out to his boatmen—

"Haï—ya there! After you have eaten rice, wait for me with your paddles in your hands. You hear?"

"Ada, Tuan!" answered Ali through the smoke of the morning fire that was spreading itself, low and gentle, over the courtyard—"we hear!"

Lingard opened slowly the little wicket-gate, made a few steps into the empty enclosure, and stopped. He had felt about his head the short breath of a puff of wind that passed him, made every leaf of the big tree shiver— and died out in a hardly perceptible tremor of branches

and twigs. Instinctively he glanced upwards with a
seaman's impulse. Above him, under the grey motionless waste of a stormy sky, drifted low black vapours,
in stretching bars, in shapeless patches, in sinuous wisps
and tormented spirals. Over the courtyard and the
house floated a round, sombre, and lingering cloud,
dragging behind a tail of tangled and filmy streamers
—like the dishevelled hair of a mourning woman.

CHAPTER THREE

"BEWARE!"

The tremulous effort and the broken, inadequate tone of the faint cry, surprised Lingard more than the unexpected suddenness of the warning conveyed, he did not know by whom and to whom. Besides himself there was no one in the courtyard as far as he could see. The cry was not renewed, and his watchful eyes, scanning warily the misty solitude of Willems' enclosure, were met everywhere only by the stolid impassiveness of inanimate things: the big sombre-looking tree, the shut-up, sightless house, the glistening bamboo fences, the damp and drooping bushes further off—all these things, that condemned to look for ever at the incomprehensible afflictions or joys of mankind, assert in their aspect of cold unconcern the high dignity of lifeless matter that surrounds, incurious and unmoved, the restless mysteries of the ever-changing, of the never-ending life.

Lingard, stepping aside, put the trunk of the tree between himself and the house, then, moving cautiously round one of the projecting buttresses, had to tread short in order to avoid scattering a small heap of black embers upon which he came unexpectedly on the other side. A thin, wizened, little old woman, who, standing behind the tree, had been looking at the house, turned towards him with a start, gazed with faded, expressionless eyes at the intruder, then made a limping attempt to get away. She seemed, however, to realize directly the hopelessness or the difficulty of the undertaking, stopped, hesitated, tottered back slowly; then, after blinking dully, fell suddenly on her knees amongst the white ashes, and, bending over the heap of smouldering coals, distended her sunken cheeks in a steady effort to blow up the hidden sparks into a useful blaze. Lingard looked down on her, but she seemed to have made up her mind that there was not enough life left in her lean body for anything else than the discharge of the simple domestic duty, and, apparently, she begrudged him the least moment of attention. After waiting for awhile, Lingard asked—

"Why did you call, O daughter?"

"I saw you enter," she croaked feebly, still grovelling with her face near the ashes and without looking up, "and I called—the cry of warning. It was her order. Her order," she repeated, with a moaning sigh.

"And did she hear?" pursued Lingard, with gentle composure.

Her projecting shoulder-blades moved uneasily under the thin stuff of the tight body jacket. She scrambled up with difficulty to her feet, and hobbled away, muttering peevishly to herself, towards a pile of dry brushwood heaped up against the fence.

Lingard, looking idly after her, heard the rattle of loose planks that led from the ground to the door of the house. He moved his head beyond the shelter of the tree and saw Aïssa coming down the inclined way into the courtyard. After making a few hurried paces towards the tree, she stopped with one foot advanced in an appearance of sudden terror, and her eyes glanced wildly right and left. Her head was uncovered. A blue cloth wrapped her from her head to foot in close slanting folds, with one end thrown over her shoulder. A tress of her black hair strayed across her bosom. Her bare arms pressed down close to her body, with hands open and outstretched fingers; her slightly elevated shoulders and the backward inclination of her torso gave her the aspect of one defiant yet shrinking from a coming blow. She had closed the door of the house behind her; and as she stood solitary in the unnatural and threatening twilight of the murky day, with everything unchanged around her, she appeared to Lingard as if she had been made there, on the spot, out of the black vapours of the sky and of the sinister gleams of feeble sunshine that struggled, through the thickening clouds, into the colourless desolation of the world.

After a short but attentive glance towards the shut-up house, Lingard stepped out from behind the tree and advanced slowly towards her. The sudden fixity of her—till then—restless eyes and a slight twitch of her hands were the only signs she gave at first of having seen him. She made a long stride forward, and putting herself right in his path, stretched her arms across; her black eyes opened wide, her lips parted as if in an uncertain attempt to speak—but no sound came out to break the significant silence of their meeting. Lingard stopped and looked at her with stern curiosity. After a while he said composedly—

"Let me pass. I came here to talk to a man. Does he hide? Has he sent you?"

She made a step nearer, her arms fell by her side, then she put them straight out nearly touching Lingard's breast.

"He knows not fear," she said, speaking low, with a forward throw of her head, in a voice trembling but distinct. "It is my own fear that has sent me here. He sleeps."

"He has slept long enough," said Lingard, in measured tones. "I am come—and now is the time of his

waking. Go and tell him this—or else my own voice
will call him up. A voice he knows well."

He put her hands down firmly and again made as if
to pass by her.

"Do not!" she exclaimed, and fell at his feet as if
she had been cut down by a scythe. The unexpected
suddenness of her movement startled Lingard, who
stepped back.

"What's this?" he exclaimed in a wondering whisper
—then added in a tone of sharp command: "Stand up!"

She rose at once and stood looking at him, timorous
and fearless; yet with a fire of recklessness burning in
her eyes that made clear her resolve to pursue her purpose—even to the death. Lingard went on in a severe
voice—

"Go out of my path. You are Omar's daughter,
and you ought to know that when men meet in daylight
women must be silent and abide their fate."

"Women!" she retorted, with subdued vehemence.
"Yes, I am a woman! Your eyes see that, O Rajah
Laut, but can you see my life? I also have heard—O
man of many fights—I also have heard the voice of firearms; I also have felt the rain of young twigs and of
leaves cut up by bullets fall down about my head; I also
know how to look in silence at angry faces and at strong
hands raised high grasping sharp steel. I also saw men
fall dead around me without a cry of fear and of mourning; and I have watched the sleep of weary fugitives,
and looked at night shadows full of menace and death
with eyes that knew nothing but watchfulness. And,"
she went on, with a mournful drop in her voice, "I have
faced the heartless sea, held on my lap the heads of
those who died raving from thirst, and from their cold
hands took the paddle and worked so that those with
me did not know that one man more was dead. I did

all this. What more have you done? That was my life. What has been yours?"

The matter and the manner of her speech held Lingard motionless, attentive and approving against his will. She ceased speaking, and from her staring black eyes with a narrow border of white above and below, a double ray of her very soul streamed out in a fierce desire to light up the most obscure designs of his heart. After a long silence, which served to emphasize the meaning of her words, she added in the whisper of bitter regret—

"And I have knelt at your feet! And I am afraid!"

"You," said Lingard deliberately, and returning her look with an interested gaze, "you are a woman whose heart, I believe, is great enough to fill a man's breast: but still you are a woman, and to you, I, Rajah Laut, have nothing to say."

She listened bending her head in a movement of forced attention; and his voice sounded to her unexpected, far off, with the distant and unearthly ring of voices that we hear in dreams, saying faintly things startling, cruel or absurd, to which there is no possible reply. To her he had nothing to say! She wrung her hands, glanced over the courtyard with that eager and distracted look that sees nothing, then looked up at the hopeless sky of livid grey and drifting black; at the unquiet mourning of the hot and brilliant heaven that had seen the beginning of her love, that had heard his entreaties and her answers, that had seen his desire and her fear; that had seen her joy, her surrender—and his defeat. Lingard moved a little, and this slight stir near her precipitated her disordered and shapeless thoughts into hurried words.

"Wait!" she exclaimed in a stifled voice, and went on disconnectedly and rapidly—"Stay. I have heard.

Men often spoke by the fires . . . men of my people. And they said of you—the first on the sea—they
said that to men's cries you were deaf in battle, but after
. . . No! even while you fought, your ears were
open to the voice of children and women. They said
. . . that. Now I, a woman, I . . ."

She broke off suddenly and stood before him with
dropped eyelids and parted lips, so still now that she
seemed to have been changed into a breathless, an
unhearing, an unseeing figure, without knowledge of
fear or hope, of anger or despair. In the astounding
repose that came on her face, nothing moved but the
delicate nostrils that expanded and collapsed quickly,
flutteringly, in interrupted beats, like the wings of a
snared bird.

"I am white," said Lingard, proudly, looking at her
with a steady gaze where simple curiosity was giving
way to a pitying annoyance, "and men you have
heard, spoke only what is true over the evening fires.
My ears are open to your prayer. But listen to me
before you speak. For yourself you need not be afraid.
You can come even now with me and you shall find
refuge in the household of Syed Abdulla—who is of your
own faith. And this also you must know: nothing that
you may say will change my purpose towards the man
who is sleeping—or hiding in that house."

Again she gave him the look that was like a stab,
not of anger but of desire; of the intense, overpowering
desire to see in, to see through, to understand everything: every thought, emotion, purpose; every impulse,
every hesitation inside that man; inside that white-clad
foreign being who looked at her, who spoke to her, who
breathed before her like any other man, but bigger, red-
faced, white-haired and mysterious. It was the future
clothed in flesh; the to-morrow; the day after; all the

days, all the years of her life standing there before her
alive and secret, with all their good or evil shut up within
the breast of that man; of that man who could be persuaded, cajoled, entreated, perhaps touched, worried;
frightened—who knows?—if only first he could be
understood! She had seen a long time ago whither
events were tending. She had noted the contemptuous
yet menacing coldness of Abdulla; she had heard—
alarmed yet unbelieving—Babalatchi's gloomy hints,
covert allusions and veiled suggestions to abandon the
useless white man whose fate would be the price of the
peace secured by the wise and good who had no need of
him any more. And he—himself! She clung to him.
There was nobody else. Nothing else. She would try
to cling to him always—all the life! And yet he was
far from her. Further every day. Every day he
seemed more distant, and she followed him patiently,
hopefully, blindly, but steadily, through all the devious
wanderings of his mind. She followed as well as she
could. Yet at times—very often lately—she had felt
lost like one strayed in the thickets of tangled undergrowth of a great forest. To her the ex-clerk of old
Hudig appeared as remote, as brilliant, as terrible, as
necessary, as the sun that gives life to these lands: the
sun of unclouded skies that dazzles and withers; the sun
beneficent and wicked—the giver of light, perfume,
and pestilence. She had watched him—watched him
close; fascinated by love, fascinated by danger. He
was alone now—but for her; and she saw—she thought
she saw—that he was like a man afraid of something.
Was it possible? He afraid? Of what? Was it of
that old white man who was coming—who had come?
Possibly. She had heard of that man ever since she
could remember. The bravest were afraid of him!
And now what was in the mind of this old, old man who

looked so strong? What was he going to do with the
light of her life? Put it out? Take it away? Take it
away for ever!—for ever!—and leave her in darkness:—
not in the stirring, whispering, expectant night in which
the hushed world awaits the return of sunshine; but in
the night without end, the night of the grave, where
nothing breathes, nothing moves, nothing thinks—
the last darkness of cold and silence without hope of
another sunrise.

She cried—"Your purpose! You know nothing. I
must . . ."

He interrupted—unreasonably excited, as if she had, by
her look, inoculated him with some of her own distress.

"I know enough."

She approached, and stood facing him at arm's
length, with both her hands on his shoulders; and he,
surprised by that audacity, closed and opened his
eyes two or three times, aware of some emotion arising
within him, from her words, her tone, her contact; an
emotion unknown, singular, penetrating and sad—at
the close sight of that strange woman, of that being
savage and tender, strong and delicate, fearful and
resolute, that had got entangled so fatally between their
two lives—his own and that other white man's, the
abominable scoundrel.

"How can you know?" she went on, in a persuasive
tone that seemed to flow out of her very heart—"how
can you know? I live with him all the days. All the
nights. I look at him; I see his every breath, every
glance of his eye, every movement of his lips. I see
nothing else! What else is there? And even I do not
understand. I do not understand him!—Him!—My
life! Him who to me is so great that his presence hides
the earth and the water from my sight!"

Lingard stood straight, with his hands deep in the

pockets of his jacket. His eyes winked quickly, because she spoke very close to his face. She disturbed him and he had a sense of the efforts he was making to get hold of her meaning, while all the time he could not help telling himself that all this was of no use.

She added after a pause—"There has been a time when I could understand him. When I knew what was in his mind better than he knew it himself. When I felt him. When I held him. . . . And now he has escaped."

"Escaped? What? Gone away!" shouted Lingard.

"Escaped from me," she said; "left me alone. Alone. And I am ever near him. Yet alone."

Her hands slipped slowly off Lingard's shoulders and her arms fell by her side, listless, discouraged, as if to her—to her, the savage, violent, and ignorant creature—had been revealed clearly in that moment the tremendous fact of our isolation, of the loneliness impenetrable and transparent, elusive and everlasting; of the indestructible loneliness that surrounds, envelopes, clothes every human soul from the cradle to the grave, and, perhaps, beyond.

"Aye! Very well! I understand. His face is turned away from you," said Lingard. "Now, what do you want?"

"I want . . . I have looked—for help . . . everywhere . . . against men. . . . All men . . . I do not know. First they came, the invisible whites, and dealt death from afar . . . then he came. He came to me who was alone and sad. He came; angry with his brothers; great amongst his own people; angry with those I have not seen: with the people where men have no mercy and women have no shame. He was of them, and great amongst them. For he was great?"

Lingard shook his head slightly. She frowned at him, and went on in disordered haste—

"Listen. I saw him. I have lived by the side of brave men . . . of chiefs. When he came I was the daughter of a beggar—of a blind man without strength and hope. He spoke to me as if I had been brighter than the sunshine—more delightful than the cool water of the brook by which we met—more . . ."

Her anxious eyes saw some shade of expression pass on her listener's face that made her hold her breath for a second, and then explode into pained fury so violent that it drove Lingard back a pace, like an unexpected blast of wind. He lifted both his hands, incongruously paternal in his venerable aspect, bewildered and soothing, while she stretched her neck forward and shouted at him.

"I tell you I was all that to him. I know it! I saw it! . . . There are times when even you white men speak the truth. I saw his eyes. I felt his eyes, I tell you! I saw him tremble when I came near—when I spoke—when I touched him. Look at me! You have been young. Look at me. Look, Rajah Laut!"

She stared at Lingard with provoking fixity, then, turning her head quickly, she sent over her shoulder a glance, full of humble fear, at the house that stood high behind her back—dark, closed, rickety and silent on its crooked posts.

Lingard's eyes followed her look, and remained gazing expectantly at the house. After a minute or so he muttered, glancing at her suspiciously—

"If he has not heard your voice now, then he must be far away—or dead."

"He is there," she whispered, a little calmed but still anxious—"he is there. For three days he waited. Waited for you night and day. And I waited with

him. I waited, watching his face, his eyes, his lips;
listening to his words.—To the words I could not
understand.—To the words he spoke in daylight; to
the words he spoke at night in his short sleep. I
listened. He spoke to himself walking up and down
here—by the river; by the bushes. And I followed.
I wanted to know—and I could not! He was tormented by things that made him speak in the words
of his own people. Speak to himself—not to me.
Not to me! What was he saying? What was he
going to do? Was he afraid of you?—Of death? What
was in his heart? . . . Fear? . . . Or anger?
. . . what desire? . . . what sadness? He
spoke; spoke; many words. All the time! And I could
not know! I wanted to speak to him. He was deaf
to me. I followed him everywhere, watching for
some word I could understand; but his mind was in
the land of his people—away from me. When I
touched him he was angry—so!"

She imitated the movement of some one shaking off
roughly an importunate hand, and looked at Lingard
with tearful and unsteady eyes.

After a short interval of laboured panting, as if she
had been out of breath with running or fighting, she
looked down and went on—

"Day after day, night after night, I lived watching
him—seeing nothing. And my heart was heavy—
heavy with the presence of death that dwelt amongst
us. I could not believe. I thought he was afraid.
Afraid of you! Then I, myself, knew fear. . . .
Tell me, Rajah Laut, do you know the fear without
voice—the fear of silence—the fear that comes when
there is no one near—when there is no battle, no cries,
no angry faces or armed hands anywhere? . . .
The fear from which there is no escape!"

She paused, fastened her eyes again on the puzzled Lingard, and hurried on in a tone of despair—

"And I knew then he would not fight you! Before —many days ago—I went away twice to make him obey my desire; to make him strike at his own people so that he could be mine—mine! O calamity! His hand was false as your white hearts. It struck forward, pushed by my desire—by his desire of me. . . . It struck that strong hand, and—O shame!—it killed nobody! Its fierce and lying blow woke up hate without any fear. Round me all was lies. His strength was a lie. My own people lied to me—and to him. And to meet you—you, the great!—he had no one but me? But me—with my rage, my pain, my weakness. Only me! And to me he would not even speak. The fool!"

She came up close to Lingard, with the wild and stealthy aspect of a lunatic longing to whisper out an insane secret—one of those misshapen, heart-rending, and ludicrous secrets; one of those thoughts that, like monsters—cruel, fantastic, and mournful, wander about terrible and unceasing in the night of madness. Lingard looked at her, astounded but unflinching. She spoke in his face, very low.

"He is all! Everything. He is my breath, my light, my heart. . . . Go away. . . . Forget him. . . . He has no courage and no wisdom any more . . . and I have lost my power. . . . Go away and forget. There are other enemies. . . . Leave him to me. He had been a man once. . . . You are too great. Nobody can withstand you. . . . I tried. . . . I know now. . . . I cry for mercy. Leave him to me and go away."

The fragments of her supplicating sentences were as if tossed on the crest of her sobs. Lingard, outwardly impassive, with his eyes fixed on the house, experienced that feeling of condemnation, deep-seated, persuasive, and masterful; that illogical impulse of disapproval which is half disgust, half vague fear, and that wakes up in our hearts in the presence of anything new or unusual, of anything that is not run into the mould of our own conscience; the accursed feeling made up of disdain, of anger, and of the sense of superior virtue that leaves us deaf, blind, contemptuous and stupid before anything which is not like ourselves.

He answered, not looking at her at first, but speaking towards the house that fascinated him—

"*I* go away! He wanted me to come—he himself did! . . . *You* must go away. You do not know what you are asking for. Listen. Go to your own people. Leave him. He is . . ."

He paused, looked down at her with his steady eyes; hesitated, as if seeking an adequate expression; then snapped his fingers, and said—

"Finish."

She stepped back, her eyes on the ground, and pressed her temples with both her hands, which she raised to her head in a slow and ample movement full of unconscious tragedy. The tone of her words was gentle and vibrating, like a loud meditation. She said—

"Tell the brook not to run to the river; tell the river not to run to the sea. Speak loud. Speak angrily. Maybe they will obey you. But it is in my mind that the brook will not care. The brook that springs out of the hillside and runs to the great river. He would not care for your words: he that cares not for the very mountain that gave him life; he that tears the earth from which he springs. Tears it, eats it, destroys it—to hurry faster to the river—to the river in which he is lost for ever. . . . O Rajah Laut! I do not care."

She drew close again to Lingard, approaching slowly, reluctantly, as if pushed by an invisible hand, and added in words that seemed to be torn out of her—

"I cared not for my own father. For him that died. I would have rather . . . You do not know what I have done . . . I . . . ."

"You shall have his life," said Lingard, hastily.

They stood together, crossing their glances; she suddenly appeased, and Lingard thoughtful and uneasy under a vague sense of defeat. And yet there was no defeat. He never intended to kill the fellow—not after the first moment of anger, a long time ago. The days of bitter wonder had killed anger; had left only a bitter indignation and a bitter wish for complete justice. He felt discontented and surprised. Unexpectedly he had come upon a human being—a woman at that—who had made him disclose his will before its time. She should have his life. But she must be told, she must know, that for such men as Willems there was no favour and no grace.

"Understand," he said slowly, "that I leave him his life not in mercy but in punishment."

She started, watched every word on his lips, and after he finished speaking she remained still and mute in astonished immobility. A single big drop of rain, a drop enormous, pellucid and heavy—like a superhuman tear coming straight and rapid from above, tearing its way through the sombre sky—struck loudly the dry ground between them in a starred splash. She wrung her hands in the bewilderment of the new and incomprehensible fear. The anguish of her whisper was more piercing than the shrillest cry.

"What punishment! Will you take him away then? Away from me? Listen to what I have done. . . . It is I who . . ."

"Ah!" exclaimed Lingard, who had been looking at the house.

"Don't you believe her, Captain Lingard," shouted Willems from the doorway, where he appeared with swollen eyelids and bared breast. He stood for a while, his hands grasping the lintels* on each side of the door, and writhed about, glaring wildly, as if he had been crucified there. Then he made a sudden rush head foremost down the plankway that responded with hollow, short noises to every footstep.

She heard him. A slight thrill passed on her face and the words that were on her lips fell back unspoken into her benighted heart; fell back amongst the mud, the stones—and the flowers, that are at the bottom of every heart.

CHAPTER FOUR

WHEN he felt the solid ground of the courtyard under his feet, Willems pulled himself up in his headlong rush and moved forward with a moderate gait. He paced stiffly, looking with extreme exactitude at Lingard's face; looking neither to the right nor to the left but at the face only, as if there was nothing in the world but those features familiar and dreaded; that white-haired, rough and severe head upon which he gazed in a fixed effort of his eyes, like a man trying to read small print at the full range of human vision. As soon as Willems' feet had left the planks, the silence which had been lifted up by the jerky rattle of his footsteps fell down again upon the courtyard; the silence of the cloudy sky and of the windless air, the sullen silence of the earth oppressed by the aspect of coming turmoil, the silence of the world collecting its faculties to withstand the storm.

Through this silence Willems pushed his way, and stopped about six feet from Lingard. He stopped simply because he could go no further. He had started from the door with the reckless purpose of clapping the old fellow on the shoulder. He had no idea that the man would turn out to be so tall, so big and so unapproachable. It seemed to him that he had never, never in his life, seen Lingard.

He tried to say—

"Do not believe . . ."

A fit of coughing checked his sentence in a faint splutter. Directly afterwards he swallowed—as it were—a couple of pebbles, throwing his chin up in the act; and Lingard, who looked at him narrowly, saw a bone, sharp and triangular like the head of a snake, dart up and down twice under the skin of his throat. Then that, too, did not move. Nothing moved.

"Well," said Lingard, and with that word he came unexpectedly to the end of his speech. His hand in his pocket closed firmly round the butt of his revolver bulging his jacket on the hip, and he thought how soon and how quickly he could terminate his quarrel with that man who had been so anxious to deliver himself into his hands—and how inadequate would be that ending! He could not bear the idea of that man escaping from him by going out of life; escaping from fear, from doubt, from remorse into the peaceful certitude of death. He held him now. And he was not going to let him go—to let him disappear for ever in the faint blue smoke of a pistol shot. His anger grew within him. He felt a touch as of a burning hand on his heart. Not on the flesh of his breast, but a touch on his heart itself, on the palpitating and untiring particle of matter that responds to every emotion of the soul; that leaps with joy, with terror, or with anger.

He drew a long breath. He could see before him the bare chest of the man expanding and collapsing under the wide-open jacket. He glanced aside, and saw the bosom of the woman near him rise and fall in quick respirations that moved slightly up and down her hand, which was pressed to her breast with all the fingers spread out and a little curved, as if grasping something too big for its span. And nearly a minute passed. One of those minutes when the voice is silenced, while the thoughts flutter in the head, like captive birds inside a cage, in rushes desperate, exhausting and vain.

During that minute of silence Lingard's anger kept rising, immense and towering, such as a crested wave running over the troubled shallows of the sands. Its roar filled his ears; a roar so powerful and distracting that, it seemed to him, his head must burst directly with the expanding volume of that sound. He looked at that man. That infamous figure upright on its feet, still, rigid, with stony eyes, as if its rotten soul had departed that moment and the carcass hadn't had the time yet to topple over. For the fraction of a second he had the illusion and the fear of the scoundrel having died there before the enraged glance of his eyes. Willems' eyelids fluttered, and the unconscious and passing tremor in that stiffly erect body exasperated Lingard like a fresh outrage. The fellow dared to stir! Dared to wink, to breathe, to exist; here, right before his eyes! His grip on the revolver relaxed gradually. As the transport of his rage increased, so also his contempt for the instruments that pierce or stab, that interpose themselves between the hand and the object of hate. He wanted another kind of satisfaction. Naked hands, by heaven! No firearms. Hands that could take him by the throat, beat down his defence, batter his face into shapeless flesh; hands that could feel all the desperation of his resistance and overpower it in the violent delight of a contact lingering and furious, intimate and brutal.

He let go the revolver altogether, stood hesitating, then throwing his hands out, strode forward—and everything passed from his sight. He could not see the man, the woman, the earth, the sky—saw nothing, as if in that one stride he had left the visible world behind to step into a black and deserted space. He heard screams round him in that obscurity, screams like the melancholy and pitiful cries of sea-birds that dwell on the lonely reefs of great oceans. Then suddenly a face appeared within a few inches of his own. His face. He felt something in his left hand. His throat . . . Ah! the thing like a snake's head that darts up and down . . . He squeezed hard. He was back in the world. He could see the quick beating of eyelids over a pair of eyes that were all whites, the grin of a drawn-up lip, a row of teeth gleaming through the drooping hair of a moustache . . . Strong white teeth. Knock them down his lying throat . . . He drew back his right hand, the fist up to the shoulder, knuckles out. From under his feet rose the screams of sea-birds. Thousands of them. Something held his legs . . . What the devil . . . He delivered his blow straight from the shoulder, felt the jar right up his arm, and realized suddenly that he was striking something passive and unresisting. His heart sank within him with disappointment, with rage, with mortification. He pushed with his left arm, opening the hand with haste, as if he had just perceived that he got hold by accident of something repulsive—and he watched with stupefied eyes Willems tottering backwards in groping strides, the white sleeve of his jacket across his face. He watched his distance from that man increase, while he remained motionless, without being able to account to himself for the fact that so much empty space had come in between them. It should have been the other way. They ought to have been very close, and . . . Ah! He wouldn't fight, he wouldn't resist, he wouldn't defend himself! A cur!* Evidently a cur! . . . He was amazed and aggrieved—profoundly—bitterly—with the immense and blank desolation of a small child robbed of a toy. He shouted—unbelieving:

"Will you be a cheat to the end?"

He waited for some answer. He waited anxiously
with an impatience that seemed to lift him off his feet.
He waited for some word, some sign; for some threatening stir. Nothing! Only two unwinking eyes glittered intently at him above the white sleeve. He saw
the raised arm detach itself from the face and sink along
the body. A white-clad arm, with a big stain on the
white sleeve. A red stain. There was a cut on the
cheek. It bled. The nose bled too. The blood ran
down, made one moustache look like a dark rag stuck
over the lip, and went on in a wet streak down the clip-
ped beard on one side of the chin. A drop of blood
hung on the end of some hairs that were glued together;
it hung for a while and took a leap down on the ground.
Many more followed, leaping one after another in close
file. One alighted on the breast and glided down instantly with devious vivacity, like a small insect running away; it left a narrow dark track on the white
skin. He looked at it, looked at the tiny and active
drops, looked at what he had done, with obscure satisfaction, with anger, with regret. This wasn't much
like an act of justice. He had a desire to go up nearer
to the man, to hear him speak, to hear him say something atrocious and wicked that would justify the violence of the blow. He made an attempt to move, and
became aware of a close embrace round both his legs,
just above the ankles. Instinctively, he kicked out
with his foot, broke through the close bond and felt at
once the clasp transferred to his other leg; the clasp
warm, desperate and soft, of human arms. He looked
down bewildered. He saw the body of the woman
stretched at length, flattened on the ground like a dark
blue rag. She trailed face downwards, clinging to his
leg with both arms in a tenacious hug. He saw the top
of her head, the long black hair streaming over his foot,

all over the beaten earth, around his boot. He couldn't
see his foot for it. He heard the short and repeated
moaning of her breath. He imagined the invisible face
close to his heel. With one kick into that face he could
free himself. He dared not stir, and shouted down—
"Let go! Let go! Let go!"

The only result of his shouting was a tightening of
the pressure of her arms. With a tremendous effort
he tried to bring his right foot up to his left, and succeeded partly. He heard distinctly the rub of her body
on the ground as he jerked her along. He tried to
disengage himself by drawing up his foot. He stamped.
He heard a voice saying sharply—

"Steady, Captain Lingard, steady!"

His eyes flew back to Willems at the sound of that
voice, and, in the quick awakening of sleeping memories,
Lingard stood suddenly still, appeased by the clear ring
of familiar words. Appeased as in days of old, when
they were trading together, when Willems was his
trusted and helpful companion in out-of-the-way and
dangerous places; when that fellow, who could keep his
temper so much better than he could himself, had spared
him many a difficulty, had saved him from many an act
of hasty violence by the timely and good-humoured
warning, whispered or shouted, "Steady, Captain Lingard, steady." A smart fellow. He had brought him
up. The smartest fellow in the islands. If he had
only stayed with him, then all this . . . He called
out to Willems—

"Tell her to let me go or . . ."

He heard Willems shouting something, waited for
awhile, then glanced vaguely down and saw the woman
still stretched out perfectly mute and unstirring, with
her head at his feet. He felt a nervous impatience
that, somehow, resembled fear.

"Tell her to let go, to go away, Willems, I tell you. I've had enough of this," he cried.

"All right, Captain Lingard," answered the calm voice of Willems, "she has let go. Take your foot off her hair; she can't get up."

Lingard leaped aside, clean away, and spun round quickly. He saw her sit up and cover her face with both hands, then he turned slowly on his heel and looked at the man. Willems held himself very straight, but was unsteady on his feet, and moved about nearly on the same spot, like a tipsy man attempting to preserve his balance. After gazing at him for a while, Lingard called, rancorous and irritable—

"What have you got to say for yourself?"

Willems began to walk towards him. He walked slowly, reeling a little before he took each step, and Lingard saw him put his hand to his face, then look at it holding it up to his eyes, as if he had there, concealed in the hollow of the palm, some small object which he wanted to examine secretly. Suddenly he drew it, with a brusque movement, down the front of his jacket and left a long smudge.

"That's a fine thing to do," said Willems.

He stood in front of Lingard, one of his eyes sunk deep in the increasing swelling of his cheek, still repeating mechanically the movement of feeling his damaged face; and every time he did this he pressed the palm to some clean spot on his jacket, covering the white cotton with bloody imprints as of some deformed and monstrous hand. Lingard said nothing, looking on. At last Willems left off staunching*the blood and stood, his arms hanging by his side, with his face stiff and distorted under the patches of coagulated blood; and he seemed as though he had been set up there for a warning: an incomprehensible figure marked all over with some awful and symbolic signs of deadly import. Speaking with difficulty, he repeated in a reproachful tone—

"That was a fine thing to do."

"After all," answered Lingard, bitterly, "I had too good an opinion of you."

"And I of you.   Don't you see that I could have had that fool over there killed and the whole thing burnt to the ground, swept off the face of the earth.   You wouldn't have found as much as a heap of ashes had I liked. I could have done all that.   And I wouldn't."

"You—could—not.   You dared not.   You scoundrel!" cried Lingard.

"What's the use of calling me names?"

"True," retorted Lingard—"there's no name bad enough for you."

There was a short interval of silence.   At the sound of their rapidly exchanged words, Aïssa had got up from the ground where she had been sitting, in a sorrowful and dejected pose, and approached the two men.   She stood on one side and looked on eagerly, in a desperate effort of her brain, with the quick and distracted eyes of a person trying for her life to penetrate the meaning of sentences uttered in a foreign tongue: the meaning portentous and fateful that lurks in the sounds of mysterious words; in the sounds surprising, unknown and strange.

Willems let the last speech of Lingard pass by; seemed by a slight movement of his hand to help it on its way to join the other shadows of the past.   Then he said—

"You have struck me; you have insulted me . . ."

"Insulted you!" interrupted Lingard, passionately. "Who—what can insult you . . . you . . ."

He choked, advanced a step.

"Steady! steady!" said Willems calmly. "I tell you I shan't fight. Is it clear enough to you that I shan't? I—shall—not—lift—a—finger."

As he spoke, slowly punctuating each word with a slight jerk of his head, he stared at Lingard, his right eye open and big, the left small and nearly closed by the swelling of one half of his face, that appeared all drawn out on one side like faces seen in a concave glass. And they stood exactly opposite each other: one tall, slight and disfigured; the other tall, heavy and severe.

Willems went on—

"If I had wanted to hurt you—if I had wanted to destroy you, it was easy. I stood in the doorway long enough to pull a trigger—and you know I shoot straight."

"You would have missed," said Lingard, with assurance. "There is, under heaven, such a thing as justice."

The sound of that word on his own lips made him pause, confused, like an unexpected and unanswerable rebuke. The anger of his outraged pride, the anger of his outraged heart, had gone out in the blow; and there remained nothing but the sense of some immense infamy—of something vague, disgusting and terrible, which seemed to surround him on all sides, hover about him with shadowy and stealthy movements, like a band of assassins in the darkness of vast and unsafe places. Was there, under heaven, such a thing as justice? He looked at the man before him with such an intensity of prolonged glance that he seemed to see right through him, that at last he saw but a floating and unsteady mist in human shape. Would it blow away before the first breath of the breeze and leave nothing behind?

The sound of Willems' voice made him start violently. Willems was saying—

"I have always led a virtuous life; you know I have. You always praised me for my steadiness; you know you have. You know also I never stole—if that's what you're thinking of. I borrowed. You know how much I repaid. It was an error of judgment. But then consider my position there. I had been a little unlucky in my private affairs, and had debts. Could I let myself go under before the eyes of all those men who envied me? But that's all over. It was an error of judgment. I've paid for it. An error of judgment."

Lingard, astounded into perfect stillness, looked down. He looked down at Willems' bare feet. Then, as the other had paused, he repeated in a blank tone—

"An error of judgment . . ."

"Yes," drawled out Willems, thoughtfully, and went on with increasing animation: "As I said, I have always led a virtuous life. More so than Hudig—than you. Yes, than you. I drank a little, I played cards a little. Who doesn't? But I had principles from a boy. Yes, principles. Business is business, and I never was an ass. I never respected fools. They had to suffer for their folly when they dealt with me. The evil was in them, not in me. But as to principles, it's another matter. I kept clear of women. It's forbidden—I had no time—and I despised them. Now I hate them!"

He put his tongue out a little; a tongue whose pink and moist end* ran here and there, like something independently alive, under his swollen and blackened lip; he touched with the tips of his fingers the cut on his cheek, felt all round it with precaution: and the unharmed side of his face appeared for a moment to be preoccupied and uneasy about the state of that other side which was so very sore and stiff.

He recommenced speaking, and his voice vibrated as though with repressed emotion of some kind.

"You ask my wife, when you see her in Macassar, whether I have no reason to hate her. She was nobody, and I made her Mrs. Willems. A half-caste girl! You ask her how she showed her gratitude to me. You ask . . . Never mind that. Well, you came and dumped me here like a load of rubbish; dumped me here and left me with nothing to do—nothing good to remember—and damn little to hope for. You left me here at the mercy of that fool, Almayer, who suspected me of something. Of what? Devil only knows. But he suspected and hated me from the first; I suppose because you befriended me. Oh! I could read him like a book. He isn't very deep, your Sambir partner, Captain Lingard, but he knows how to be disagreeable. Months passed. I thought I would die of sheer weariness, of my thoughts, of my regrets. And then . . ."

He made a quick step nearer to Lingard, and as if moved by the same thought, by the same instinct, by the impulse of his will, Aïssa also stepped nearer to them. They stood in a close group, and the two men could feel the calm air between their faces stirred by the light breath of the anxious woman who enveloped them both in the uncomprehending, in the despairing and wondering glances of her wild and mournful eyes.

CHAPTER FIVE

WILLEMS turned a little from her and spoke lower.

"Look at that," he said, with an almost imperceptible movement of his head towards the woman to whom he was presenting his shoulder. "Look at that! Don't believe her! What has she been saying to you? What? I have been asleep. Had to sleep at last. I've been waiting for you three days and nights. I had to sleep some time. Hadn't I? I told her to remain awake and watch for you, and call me at once. She did watch. You can't believe her. You can't believe any woman. Who can tell what's inside their heads? No one. You can know nothing. The only thing you can know is that it isn't anything like what comes through their lips. They live by the side of you. They seem to hate you, or they seem to love you; they caress or torment you; they throw you over or stick to you closer than your skin for some inscrutable and awful reason of their own—which you can never know! Look at her—and look at me. At me!—her infernal work. What has she been saying?"

His voice had sunk to a whisper. Lingard listened with great attention, holding his chin in his hand, which grasped a great handful of his white beard. His elbow was in the palm of his other hand, and his eyes were still fixed on the ground. He murmured, without looking up—

"She begged me for your life—if you want to know —as if the thing were worth giving or taking!"

"And for three days she begged me to take yours,"

said Willems quickly. "For three days she wouldn't give me any peace. She was never still. She planned ambushes. She has been looking for places all over here where I could hide and drop you with a safe shot as you walked up. It's true. I give you my word."

"Your word," muttered Lingard, contemptuously. Willems took no notice.

"Ah! She is a ferocious creature," he went on. "You don't know . . . I wanted to pass the time —to do something—to have something to think about —to forget my troubles till you came back. And . . . look at her . . . she took me as if I did not belong to myself. She did. I did not know there was something in me she could get hold of. She, a savage. I, a civilized European, and clever! She that knew no more than a wild animal! Well, she found out something in me. She found it out, and I was lost. I knew it. She tormented me. I was ready to do anything. I resisted—but I was ready. I knew that too. That frightened me more than anything; more than my own sufferings; and that was frightful enough, I assure you."

Lingard listened, fascinated and amazed like a child listening to a fairy tale, and, when Willems stopped for breath, he shuffled his feet a little.

"What does he say?" cried out Aïssa, suddenly.

The two men looked at her quickly, and then looked at one another.

Willems began again, speaking hurriedly—

"I tried to do something. Take her away from those people. I went to Almayer; the biggest blind fool that you ever . . . Then Abdulla came—and she went away. She took away with her something of me which I had to get back. I had to do it. As far as you are concerned, the change here had to happen sooner or later; you couldn't be master here for ever. It isn't what I have done that torments me. It is the why. It's the madness that drove me to it. It's that thing that came over me. That may come again, some day."

"It will do no harm to anybody then, I promise you," said Lingard, significantly.

Willems looked at him for a second with a blank stare, then went on—

"I fought against her. She goaded me to violence and to murder. Nobody knows why. She pushed me to it persistently, desperately, all the time. Fortunately Abdulla had sense. I don't know what I wouldn't have done. She held me then. Held me like a nightmare that is terrible and sweet. By and by it was another life. I woke up. I found myself beside an animal as full of harm as a wild cat. You don't know through what I have passed. Her father tried to kill me—and she very nearly killed him. I believe she would have stuck at nothing. I don't know which was more terrible! She would have stuck at nothing to defend her own. And when I think that it was me—me—Willems . . . I hate her. To-morrow she may want my life. How can I know what's in her? She may want to kill me next!"

He paused in great trepidation, then added in a scared tone—

"I don't want to die here."

"Don't you?" said Lingard, thoughtfully.

Willems turned towards Aïssa and pointed at her with a bony forefinger.

"Look at her! Always there. Always near. Always watching, watching . . . for something. Look at her eyes. Ain't they big? Don't they stare? You wouldn't think she can shut them like human beings do. I don't believe she ever does. I go to sleep, if I can, under their stare, and when I wake up I see them fixed on me and moving no more than the eyes of a corpse. While I am still they are still. By God—she can't move them till I stir, and then they follow me like a pair of jailers. They watch me; when I stop they seem to wait patient and glistening till I am off my guard —for to do something. To do something horrible. Look at them! You can see nothing in them. They are big, menacing—and empty. The eyes of a savage; of a damned mongrel, half-Arab, half-Malay. They hurt me! I am white! I swear to you I can't stand this! Take me away. I am white! All white!"

He shouted towards the sombre heaven, proclaiming desperately under the frown of thickening clouds the fact of his pure and superior descent.* He shouted, his head thrown up, his arms swinging about wildly; lean, ragged, disfigured; a tall madman making a great disturbance about something invisible; a being absurd, repulsive, pathetic, and droll. Lingard, who was looking down as if absorbed in deep thought, gave him a quick glance from under his eyebrows: Aïssa stood with clasped hands. At the other end of the courtyard the old woman, like a vague and decrepit apparition, rose noiselessly to look, then sank down again with a stealthy movement and crouched low over the small glow of the fire. Willems' voice filled the enclosure, rising louder with every word, and then, suddenly, at its very loudest, stopped short—like water stops running from an overturned vessel. As soon as it had ceased the thunder seemed to take up the burden in a low growl coming from the inland hills. The noise approached in confused mutterings which kept on increasing, swelling into a roar that came nearer, rushed down the river, passed close in a tearing crash—and instantly sounded faint, dying away in monotonous and dull repetitions amongst the endless sinuosities of the lower reaches. Over the great forests, over all the innumerable people of unstirring trees—over all that living people immense, motionless, and mute—the silence, that had rushed in on the track of the passing tumult, remained suspended as deep and complete as if it had never been disturbed from the beginning of remote ages.* Then, through it, after a time, came to Lingard's ears the voice of the running river: a voice low, discreet, and sad, like the persistent and gentle voices that speak of the past in the silence of dreams.

He felt a great emptiness in his heart. It seemed to him that there was within his breast a great space without any light, where his thoughts wandered forlornly, unable to escape, unable to rest, unable to die, to vanish—and to relieve him from the fearful oppression of their existence. Speech, action, anger, forgiveness, all appeared to him alike useless and vain, appeared to him unsatisfactory, not worth the effort of hand or brain that was needed to give them effect. He could not see why he should not remain standing there, without ever doing anything, to the end of time. He felt something, something like a heavy chain, that held him there. This wouldn't do. He backed away a little from Willems and Aïssa, leaving them close together, then stopped and looked at both. The man and the woman appeared to him much further than they really were. He had made only about three steps backward, but he believed for a moment that another step would take him out of earshot for ever. They appeared to him slightly under life size, and with a great cleanness of outlines, like figures carved with great precision of detail and highly finished by a skilful hand. He pulled himself together. The strong consciousness of his

own personality came back to him. He had a notion
of surveying them from a great and inaccessible height.

He said slowly: "You have been possessed of a devil."

"Yes," answered Willems gloomily, and looking at
Aïssa. "Isn't it pretty?"

"I've heard this kind of talk before," said Lingard,
in a scornful tone; then paused, and went on steadily
after a while: "I regret nothing. I picked you up by
the waterside, like a starving cat—by God. I regret
nothing; nothing that I have done. Abdulla—twenty
others—no doubt Hudig himself, were after me. That's
business—for them. But that you should . . .
Money belongs to him who picks it up and is strong
enough to keep it—but this thing was different. It was
part of my life. . . . I am an old fool."

He was. The breath of his words, of the very
words he spoke, fanned the spark of divine folly in his
breast, the spark that made him—the hard-headed,
heavy-handed adventurer—stand out from the crowd,
from the sordid, from the joyous, unscrupulous, and
noisy crowd of men that were so much like himself.

Willems said hurriedly: "It wasn't me. The evil
was not in me, Captain Lingard."

"And where else—confound you! Where else?"
interrupted Lingard, raising his voice. "Did you
ever see me cheat and lie and steal? Tell me that.
Did you? Hey? I wonder where in perdition you
came from when I found you under my feet. . . .
No matter. You will do no more harm."

Willems moved nearer, gazing upon him anxiously.
Lingard went on with distinct deliberation—

"What did you expect when you asked me to see
you? What? You know me. I am Lingard. You
lived with me. You've heard men speak. You knew
what you had done. Well! What did you expect?"

274 AN OUTCAST OF THE ISLANDS

"How can I know?" groaned Willems, wringing his hands; "I was alone in that infernal savage crowd. I was delivered into their hands.* After the thing was done, I felt so lost and weak that I would have called the devil himself to my aid if it had been any good—if he hadn't put in all his work already. In the whole world there was only one man that had ever cared for me. Only one white man. You! Hate is better than being alone! Death is better! I expected . . . anything. Something to expect. Something to take me out of this. Out of her sight!"

He laughed. His laugh seemed to be torn out from him against his will, seemed to be brought violently on the surface from under his bitterness, his self-contempt, from under his despairing wonder at his own nature.

"When I think that when I first knew her it seemed to me that my whole life wouldn't be enough to . . . And now when I look at her! She did it all. I must have been mad. I was mad. Every time I look at her I remember my madness. It frightens me. . . . And when I think that of all my life, of all my past, of all my future, of my intelligence, of my work, there is nothing left but she, the cause of my ruin, and you whom I have mortally offended . . ."

He hid his face for a moment in his hands, and when he took them away he had lost the appearance of comparative calm and gave way to a wild distress.

"Captain Lingard . . . anything . . . a deserted island . . . anywhere . . . I promise . . ."

"Shut up!" shouted Lingard, roughly.

He became dumb,* suddenly, completely.

The wan light of the clouded morning retired slowly from the courtyard, from the clearings, from the river, as if it had gone unwillingly to hide in the enigmatical solitudes of the gloomy and silent forests. The clouds over their heads thickened into a low vault of uniform blackness. The air was still and inexpressibly oppressive. Lingard unbuttoned his jacket, flung it wide open and, inclining his body sideways a little, wiped his forehead with his hand, which he jerked sharply afterwards. Then he looked at Willems and said—

"No promise of yours is any good to me. I am going to take your conduct into my own hands. Pay attention to what I am going to say. You are my prisoner."

Willems' head moved imperceptibly; then he became rigid and still. He seemed not to breathe.

"You shall stay here," continued Lingard, with sombre deliberation. "You are not fit to go amongst people. Who could suspect, who could guess, who could imagine what's in you? I couldn't! You are my mistake. I shall hide you here. If I let you out you would go amongst unsuspecting men, and lie, and steal, and cheat for a little money or for some woman. I don't care about shooting you. It would be the safest way though. But I won't. Do not expect me to forgive you. To forgive one must have been angry and become contemptuous, and there is nothing in me now—no anger, no contempt, no disappointment. To me you are not Willems, the man I befriended and helped through thick and thin, and thought much of . . . You are not a human being that may be destroyed or forgiven. You are a bitter thought, a something without a body and that must be hidden . . . You are my shame."

He ceased and looked slowly round. How dark it was! It seemed to him that the light was dying prematurely out of the world and that the air was already dead.

"Of course," he went on, "I shall see to it that you don't starve."

"You don't mean to say that I must live here, Captain Lingard?" said Willems, in a kind of mechanical voice without any inflections.

"Did you ever hear me say something I did not mean?" asked Lingard. "You said you didn't want to die here—well, you must live . . . Unless you change your mind," he added, as if in involuntary afterthought.

He looked at Willems narrowly, then shook his head.

"You are alone," he went on. "Nothing can help you. Nobody will. You are neither white nor brown. You have no colour as you have no heart. Your accomplices have abandoned you to me because I am still somebody to be reckoned with. You are alone but for that woman there. You say you did this for her. Well, you have her."

Willems mumbled something, and then suddenly caught his hair with both his hands and remained standing so. Aïssa, who had been looking at him, turned to Lingard.

"What did you say, Rajah Laut?" she cried.

There was a slight stir amongst the filmy threads of her disordered hair, the bushes by the river sides trembled, the big tree nodded precipitately over them with an abrupt rustle, as if waking with a start from a troubled sleep—and the breath of hot breeze passed, light, rapid, and scorching, under the clouds that whirled round, unbroken but undulating, like a restless phantom of a sombre sea.

Lingard looked at her pityingly before he said—

"I have told him that he must live here all his life . . . and with you."

The sun seemed to have gone out at last like a flickering light away up beyond the clouds, and in the stifling gloom of the courtyard the three figures stood colourless and shadowy, as if surrounded by a black and superheated mist. Aïssa looked at Willems, who remained still, as though he had been changed into stone in the very act of tearing his hair. Then she turned her head towards Lingard and shouted—

"You lie! You lie! . . . White man. Like you all do. You . . . whom Abdulla made small. You lie!"

Her words rang out shrill and venomous with her secret scorn, with her overpowering desire to wound regardless of consequences; in her woman's reckless desire to cause suffering at any cost, to cause it by the sound of her own voice—by her own voice, that would carry the poison of her thought into the hated heart.

Willems let his hands fall, and began to mumble again. Lingard turned his ear towards him instinctively, caught something that sounded like "Very well"—then some more mumbling—then a sigh.

"As far as the rest of the world is concerned," said Lingard, after waiting for awhile in an attentive attitude, "your life is finished. Nobody will be able to throw any of your villainies in my teeth; nobody will be able to point at you and say, 'Here goes a scoundrel of Lingard's up-bringing.' You are buried here."

"And you think that I will stay . . . that I will submit?" exclaimed Willems, as if he had suddenly recovered the power of speech.

"You needn't stay here—on this spot," said Lingard, drily. "There are the forests—and here is the river. You may swim. Fifteen miles up, or forty down. At one end you will meet Almayer, at the other the sea. Take your choice."

He burst into a short, joyless laugh, then added with severe gravity—

"There is also another way."

"If you want to drive my soul into damnation by trying to drive me to suicide you will not succeed," said Willems in wild excitement. "I will live. I shall repent. I may escape. . . . Take that woman away—she is sin."

A hooked dart of fire tore in two the darkness of the distant horizon and lit up the gloom of the earth with a dazzling and ghastly flame. Then the thunder was heard far away, like an incredibly enormous voice muttering menaces.

Lingard said—

"I don't care what happens, but I may tell you that without that woman your life is not worth much —not twopence. There is a fellow here who . . . and Abdulla himself wouldn't stand on any ceremony. Think of that! And then she won't go."

He began, even while he spoke, to walk slowly down towards the little gate. He didn't look, but he felt as sure that Willems was following him as if he had been leading him by a string. Directly he had passed through the wicket-gate into the big courtyard he heard a voice, behind his back, saying—

"I think she was right. I ought to have shot you. I couldn't have been worse off."

"Time yet," answered Lingard, without stopping or looking back. "But, you see, you can't. There is not even that in you."

"Don't provoke me, Captain Lingard," cried Willems.

Lingard turned round sharply. Willems and Aïssa stopped. Another forked flash of lightning split up the clouds overhead, and threw upon their faces a sudden burst of light—a blaze violent, sinister and fleeting; and in the same instant they were deafened by a near, single crash of thunder, which was followed by a rushing noise, like a frightened sigh of the startled earth.

"Provoke you!" said the old adventurer, as soon as he could make himself heard. "Provoke you! Hey! What's there in you to provoke? What do I care?"

"It is easy to speak like that when you know that in the whole world—in the whole world—I have no friend," said Willems.

"Whose fault?" said Lingard, sharply.

Their voices, after the deep and tremendous noise, sounded to them very unsatisfactory—thin and frail, like the voices of pigmies—and they became suddenly silent, as if on that account. From up the courtyard Lingard's boatmen came down and passed them, keeping step in a single file, their paddles on shoulder, and holding their heads straight with their eyes fixed on the river. Ali, who was walking last, stopped before Lingard, very stiff and upright. He said—

"That one-eyed Babalatchi is gone, with all his women. He took everything. All the pots and boxes. Big. Heavy. Three boxes."

He grinned as if the thing had been amusing, then added with an appearance of anxious concern, "Rain coming."

"We return," said Lingard. "Make ready."

"Aye, aye, sir!" ejaculated Ali with precision, and moved on. He had been quartermaster with Lingard before making up his mind to stay in Sambir as Almayer's head man.* He strutted towards the landing-place thinking proudly that he was not like those other ignorant boatmen, and knew how to answer properly the very greatest of white captains.

"You have misunderstood me from the first, Captain Lingard," said Willems.

"Have I? It's all right, as long as there is no mistake about my meaning," answered Lingard, strolling slowly to the landing-place. Willems followed him, and Aïssa followed Willems.

Two hands were extended to help Lingard in embarking. He stepped cautiously and heavily into the long and narrow canoe, and sat in the canvas folding-chair that had been placed in the middle. He leaned back and turned his head to the two figures that stood on the bank a little above him. Aïssa's eyes were fastened on his face in a visible impatience to see him gone. Willems' look went straight above the canoe, straight at the forest on the other side of the river.

"All right, Ali," said Lingard, in a low voice.

A slight stir animated the faces, and a faint murmur ran along the line of paddlers. The foremost man pushed with the point of his paddle, canted the fore end out of the dead water into the current; and the canoe fell rapidly off before the rush of brown water, the stern rubbing gently against the low bank.

"We shall meet again, Captain Lingard!" cried Willems, in an unsteady voice.

"Never!" said Lingard, turning half round in his chair to look at Willems. His fierce red eyes glittered remorselessly over the high back of his seat.

"Must cross the river. Water less quick over there," said Ali.

He pushed in his turn now with all his strength, throwing his body recklessly right out over the stern. Then he recovered himself just in time into the squatting attitude of a monkey perched on a high shelf, and shouted: "Dayong!"

The paddles struck the water together. The canoe

darted forward and went on steadily crossing the river with a sideways motion made up of its own speed and the downward drift of the current.

Lingard watched the shore astern. The woman shook her hand at him, and then squatted at the feet of the man who stood motionless. After a while she got up and stood beside him, reaching up to his head—and Lingard saw then that she had wetted some part of her covering and was trying to wash the dried blood off the man's immovable face, which did not seem to know anything about it. Lingard turned away and threw himself back in his chair, stretching his legs out with a sigh of fatigue. His head fell forward; and under his red face the white beard lay fan-like on his breast, the ends of fine long hairs all astir in the faint draught made by the rapid motion of the craft that carried him away from his prisoner—from the only thing in his life he wished to hide.

In its course across the river the canoe came into the line of Willems' sight and his eyes caught the image, followed it eagerly as it glided, small but distinct, on the dark background of the forest. He could see plainly the figure of the man sitting in the middle. All his life he had felt that man behind his back, a reassuring presence ready with help, with commendation, with advice; friendly in reproof, enthusiastic in approbation; a man inspiring confidence by his strength, by his fearlessness, by the very weakness of his simple heart. And now that man was going away. He must call him back.

He shouted, and his words, which he wanted to throw across the river, seemed to fall helplessly at his feet. Aïssa put her hand on his arm in a restraining attempt, but he shook it off. He wanted to call back his very life that was going away from him. He shouted again—and this time he did not even hear himself. No use. He would never return. And he stood in sullen silence looking at the white figure over there, lying back in the chair in the middle of the boat; a figure that struck him suddenly as very terrible, heartless and astonishing, with its unnatural appearance of running over the water in an attitude of languid repose.

For a time nothing on earth stirred, seemingly, but the canoe, which glided up-stream with a motion so even and smooth that it did not convey any sense of movement. Overhead, the massed clouds appeared solid and steady as if held there in a powerful grip, but on their uneven surface there was a continuous and trembling glimmer, a faint reflection of the distant lightning from the thunderstorm that had broken already on the coast and was working its way up the river with low and angry growls. Willems looked on, as motionless as everything round him and above him. Only his eyes seemed to live, as they followed the canoe on its course that carried it away from him, steadily, unhesitatingly, finally, as if it were going, not up the great river into the momentous excitement of Sambir, but straight into the past, into the past crowded yet empty, like an old cemetery full of neglected graves, where lie dead hopes that never return.

From time to time he felt on his face the passing, warm touch of an immense breath coming from beyond the forest, like the short panting of an oppressed world. Then the heavy air round him was pierced by a sharp gust of wind, bringing with it the fresh, damp feel of the falling rain; and all the innumerable tree-tops of the forests swayed to the left and sprang back again in a tumultuous balancing of nodding branches and shuddering leaves. A light frown ran over the river, the clouds stirred slowly, changing their aspect but not their place,

as if they had turned ponderously over; and when the
sudden movement had died out in a quickened tremor
of the slenderest twigs, there was a short period of for-
midable immobility above and below, during which the
voice of the thunder was heard, speaking in a sustained,
emphatic and vibrating roll, with violent louder bursts
of crashing sound, like a wrathful and threatening discourse of an angry god. For a moment it died out, and
then another gust of wind passed, driving before it a
white mist which filled the space with a cloud of water-
dust that hid suddenly from Willems the canoe, the
forests, the river itself; that woke him up from his
numbness in a forlorn shiver, that made him look round
despairingly to see nothing but the whirling drift of rain
spray before the freshening breeze, while through it
the heavy big drops fell about him with sonorous
and rapid beats upon the dry earth. He made a few
hurried steps up the courtyard and was arrested by an
immense sheet of water that fell all at once on him, fell
sudden and overwhelming from the clouds, cutting
his respiration, streaming over his head, clinging to him,
running down his body, off his arms, off his legs. He
stood gasping while the water beat him in a vertical
downpour, drove on him slanting in squalls, and he
felt the drops striking him from above, from everywhere; drops thick, pressed and dashing at him as if
flung from all sides by a mob of infuriated hands. From
under his feet a great vapour of broken water floated up,
he felt the ground become soft—melt under him—and
saw the water spring out from the dry earth to meet
the water that fell from the sombre heaven. An insane
dread took possession of him, the dread of all that water
around him, of the water that ran down the courtyard
towards him, of the water that pressed him on every
side, of the slanting water that drove across his face in

wavering sheets which gleamed pale red with the flicker
of lightning streaming through them, as if fire and water
were falling together, monstrously mixed, upon the
stunned earth.

He wanted to run away, but when he moved it was
to slide about painfully and slowly upon that earth
which had become mud so suddenly under his feet. He
fought his way up the courtyard like a man pushing
through a crowd, his head down, one shoulder forward,
stopping often, and sometimes carried back a pace or
two in the rush of water which his heart was not stout
enough to face. Aïssa followed him step by step,
stopping when he stopped, recoiling with him, moving
forward with him in his toilsome way up the slippery
declivity of the courtyard, of that courtyard, from which
everything seemed to have been swept away by the
first rush of the mighty downpour. They could see
nothing. The tree, the bushes, the house, and the
fences—all had disappeared in the thickness of the falling rain. Their hair stuck, streaming, to their heads;
their clothing clung to them, beaten close to their bodies;
water ran off them, off their heads over their shoulders.
They moved, patient, upright, slow and dark, in the
gleam clear or fiery of the falling drops, under the roll
of unceasing thunder, like two wandering ghosts of the
drowned that, condemned to haunt the water for ever,
had come up from the river to look at the world under a
deluge.

On the left the tree seemed to step out to meet
them, appearing vaguely, high, motionless and patient;
with a rustling plaint of its innumerable leaves through
which every drop of water tore its separate way with
cruel haste. And then, to the right, the house surged
up in the mist, very black, and clamorous with the
quick patter of rain on its high-pitched roof above the

steady splash of the water running off the eaves.
Down the plankway leading to the door flowed a
thin and pellucid stream, and when Willems began
his ascent it broke over his foot as if he were going
up a steep ravine in the bed of a rapid and shallow
torrent. Behind his heels two streaming smudges of
mud stained for an instant the purity of the rushing
water, and then he splashed his way up with a spurt
and stood on the bamboo platform before the open
door under the shelter of the overhanging eaves—
under shelter at last!

A low moan ending in a broken and plaintive mutter
arrested Willems on the threshold. He peered round
in the half-light under the roof and saw the old woman
crouching close to the wall in a shapeless heap, and
while he looked he felt a touch of two arms on his
shoulders. Aïssa! He had forgotten her. He turned,
and she clasped him round the neck instantly, pressing
close to him as if afraid of violence or escape. He
stiffened himself in repulsion, in horror, in the mysterious revolt of his heart; while she clung to him—clung
to him as if he were a refuge from misery, from storm,
from weariness, from fear, from despair; and it was on
the part of that being an embrace terrible, enraged and
mournful, in which all her strength went out to make
him captive, to hold him for ever.

He said nothing. He looked into her eyes while he
struggled with her fingers about the nape of his neck,
and suddenly he tore her hands apart, holding her arms
up in a strong grip of her wrists, and bending his swollen face close over hers, he said—

"It is all your doing. You . . ."

She did not understand him—not a word. He
spoke in the language of his people—of his people that
know no mercy and no shame. And he was angry.

Alas! he was always angry now, and always speaking words that she could not understand. She stood in silence, looking at him through her patient eyes, while he shook her arms a little and then flung them down.

"Don't follow me!" he shouted. "I want to be alone —I mean to be left alone!"*

He went in, leaving the door open.

She did not move. What need to understand the words when they are spoken in such a voice? In that voice which did not seem to be his voice—his voice when he spoke by the brook, when he was never angry and always smiling! Her eyes were fixed upon the dark doorway, but her hands strayed mechanically upwards; she took up all her hair, and, inclining her head slightly over her shoulder, wrung out the long black tresses, twisting them persistently, while she stood, sad and absorbed, like one listening to an inward voice— the voice of bitter, of unavailing regret. The thunder had ceased, the wind had died out, and the rain fell perpendicular and steady through a great pale clearness —the light of remote sun coming victorious from amongst the dissolving blackness of the clouds. She stood near the doorway. He was there—alone in the gloom of the dwelling. He was there. He spoke not. What was in his mind now? What fear? What desire? Not the desire of her as in the days when he used to smile . . . How could she know? . . .

A sigh coming from the bottom of her heart, flew out into the world through her parted lips. A sigh faint, profound, and broken; a sigh full of pain and fear, like the sigh of those who are about to face the unknown: to face it in loneliness, in doubt, and without hope. She let go her hair, that fell scattered over her shoulders like a funeral veil, and she sank down suddenly by the door. Her hands clasped her ankles; she rested her head on her drawn-up knees, and remained still, very still, under the streaming mourning of her hair. She was thinking of him; of the days by the brook; she was thinking of all that had been their love—and she sat in the abandoned posture of those who sit weeping by the dead, of those who watch and mourn over a corpse.

PART V

PART V

CHAPTER ONE

ALMAYER propped, alone on the verandah of his house, with both his elbows on the table, and holding his head between his hands, stared before him, away over the stretch of sprouting young grass in his courtyard, and over the short jetty with its cluster of small canoes, amongst which his big whale-boat floated high, like a white mother of all that dark and aquatic brood. He stared on the river, past the schooner anchored in mid-stream, past the forests of the left bank; he stared through and past the illusion of the material world.

The sun was sinking. Under the sky was stretched a network of white threads, a network fine and close-meshed, where here and there were caught thicker white vapours of globular shape; and to the eastward, above the ragged barrier of the forests, surged the summits of a chain of great clouds, growing bigger slowly, in imperceptible motion, as if careful not to disturb the glowing stillness of the earth and of the sky. Abreast of the house the river was empty but for the motionless schooner. Higher up, a solitary log came out from the bend above and went on drifting slowly down the straight reach: a dead and wandering tree going out to its grave in the sea, between two ranks of trees motionless and living.

And Almayer sat, his face in his hands, looking on and hating all this: the muddy river; the faded blue of the sky; the black log passing by on its first and last voyage; the green sea of leaves—the sea that glowed, shimmered, and stirred above the uniform and

291

impenetrable gloom of the forests—the joyous sea of
living green powdered with the brilliant dust of oblique
sun-rays. He hated all this; he begrudged every day
—every minute—of his life spent amongst all these
things; he begrudged it bitterly, angrily, with enraged
and immense regret, like a miser compelled to give up
some of his treasure to a near relation. And yet all
this was very precious to him. It was the present
sign of a splendid future.

He pushed the table away impatiently, got up,
made a few steps aimlessly, then stood by the balustrade and again looked at the river—at that river
which would have been the instrument for the making
of his fortune if . . . if . . . .

"What an abominable brute!" he said.

He was alone, but he spoke aloud, as one is apt to
do under the impulse of a strong, of an overmastering
thought.

"What a brute!" he muttered again.

The river was dark now, and the schooner lay on
it, a black, a lonely, and a graceful form, with the
slender masts darting upwards from it in two frail
and raking lines. The shadows of the evening crept
up the trees, crept up from bough to bough, till at
last the long sunbeams coursing from the western
horizon skimmed lightly over the topmost branches,
then flew upwards amongst the piled-up clouds, giving
them a sombre and fiery aspect in the last flush of
light. And suddenly the light disappeared*as if lost in
the immensity of the great, blue, and empty hollow
overhead. The sun had set: and the forests became
a straight wall of formless blackness. Above them, on
the edge of lingering clouds, a single star glimmered
fitfully, obscured now and then by the rapid flight of
high and invisible vapours.

Almayer fought with the uneasiness within his breast. He heard Ali, who moved behind him preparing his evening meal, and he listened with strange attention to the sounds the man made—to the short, dry bang of the plate put upon the table, to the clink of glass and the metallic rattle of knife and fork. The man went away. Now he was coming back. He would speak directly; and Almayer, notwithstanding the absorbing gravity of his thoughts, listened for the sound of expected words. He heard them, spoken in English* with painstaking distinctness.

"Ready, sir!"

"All right," said Almayer, curtly. He did not move. He remained pensive, with his back to the table upon which stood the lighted lamp brought by Ali. He was thinking: Where was Lingard now? Halfway down the river probably, in Abdulla's ship. He would be back in about three days—perhaps less. And then? Then the schooner would have to be got out of the river, and when that craft was gone they—he and Lingard— would remain here; alone with the constant thought of that other man, that other man living near them! What an extraordinary idea to keep him there for ever. For ever! What did that mean—for ever? Perhaps a year, perhaps ten years. Preposterous! Keep him there ten years—or may be twenty! The fellow was capable of living more than twenty years. And for all that time he would have to be watched, fed, looked after. There was nobody but Lingard to have such notions. Twenty years! Why, no! In less than ten years their fortune would be made and they would leave this place, first for Batavia—yes, Batavia—and then for Europe. England, no doubt. Lingard would want to go to England. And would they leave that man here? How would that fellow look in ten years?

Very old probably. Well, devil take him. Nina would be fifteen. She would be rich and very pretty and he himself would not be so old then. . . ."

Almayer smiled into the night.

. . . Yes, rich! Why! Of course! Captain Lingard was a resourceful man, and he had plenty of money even now. They were rich already; but not enough. Decidedly not enough. Money brings money. That gold business was good. Famous! Captain Lingard was a remarkable man. He said the gold was there—and it was there. Lingard knew what he was talking about. But he had queer ideas. For instance, about Willems. Now what did he want to keep him alive for? Why?

"That scoundrel," muttered Almayer again.

"Makan Tuan!" ejaculated Ali suddenly, very loud in a pressing tone.

Almayer walked to the table, sat down, and his anxious visage dropped from above into the light thrown down by the lamp-shade. He helped himself absently, and began to eat in great mouthfuls.

. . . Undoubtedly, Lingard was the man to stick to! The man undismayed, masterful and ready. How quickly he had planned a new future when Willems' treachery destroyed their established position in Sambir! And the position even now was not so bad. What an immense prestige that Lingard had with all those people—Arabs, Malays and all. Ah, it was good to be able to call a man like that father. Fine! Wonder how much money really the old fellow had. People talked—they exaggerated surely, but if he had only half of what they said . . .

He drank, throwing his head up, and fell to again.

. . . Now, if that Willems had known how to play his cards well, had he stuck to the old fellow he would

have been in his position, he would be now married
to Lingard's adopted daughter with his future assured
—splendid . . .

"The beast!" growled Almayer, between two mouthfuls.

Ali stood rigidly straight with an uninterested face,
his gaze lost in the night which pressed round the
small circle of light that shone on the table, on the
glass, on the bottle, and on Almayer's head as he
leaned over his plate moving his jaws.

. . . A famous man Lingard—yet you never knew
what he would do next. It was notorious that he had
shot a white man once for less than Willems had done.
For less? . . . Why, for nothing, so to speak! It
was not even his own quarrel. It was about some
Malay returning from pilgrimage with wife and children.
Kidnapped, or robbed, or something. A stupid story—
an old story. And now he goes to see that Willems
and—nothing. Comes back talking big about his
prisoner; but after all he said very little. What did
that Willems tell him? What passed between them?
The old fellow must have had something in his mind
when he let that scoundrel off. And Joanna! She
would get round the old fellow. Sure. Then he would
forgive perhaps. Impossible. But at any rate he
would waste a lot of money on them. The old man
was tenacious in his hates, but also in his affections.
He had known that beast Willems from a boy. They
would make it up in a year or so. Everything is
possible: why did he not rush off at first and kill the
brute? That would have been more like Lingard. . . .

Almayer laid down his spoon suddenly, and pushing
his plate away, threw himself back in the chair.

. . . Unsafe. Decidedly unsafe. He had no
mind to share Lingard's money with anybody. Lin-

gard's money was Nina's money in a sense. And if
Willems managed to become friendly with the old
man it would be dangerous for him—Almayer. Such
an unscrupulous scoundrel! He would oust him from his
position. He would lie and slander. Everything would
be lost. Lost. Poor Nina. What would become of her?
Poor child. For her sake he must remove that Willems. Must. But how? Lingard wanted to be obeyed.
Impossible to kill Willems. Lingard might be angry.
Incredible, but so it was. He might . . . .

A wave of heat passed through Almayer's body,
flushed his face, and broke out of him in copious
perspiration. He wriggled in his chair, and pressed
his hands together under the table. What an awful
prospect! He fancied he could see Lingard and
Willems reconciled and going away arm-in-arm, leaving
him alone in this God-forsaken hole—in Sambir—in
this deadly swamp! And all his sacrifices, the sacrifice
of his independence, of his best years, his surrender to
Lingard's fancies and caprices, would go for nothing!
Horrible! Then he thought of his little daughter—his
daughter!—and the ghastliness of his supposition overpowered him. He had a deep emotion, a sudden emotion that made him feel quite faint at the idea of that
young life spoiled before it had fairly begun. His dear
child's life! Lying back in his chair he covered his
face with both his hands.

Ali glanced down at him and said, unconcernedly—
"Master finish?"

Almayer was lost in the immensity of his com-
miseration for himself, for his daughter, who was—
perhaps—not going to be the richest woman in the
world—notwithstanding Lingard's promises. He did
not understand the other's question, and muttered
through his fingers in a doleful tone—

"What did you say? What? Finish what?"

"Clear up meza," explained Ali.

"Clear up!" burst out Almayer, with incomprehensible exasperation. "Devil take you and the table. Stupid! Chatterer! Chelakka! Get out!"

He leaned forward, glaring at his head man, then sank back in his seat with his arms hanging straight down on each side of the chair. And he sat motionless in a meditation so concentrated and so absorbing, with all his power of thought so deep within himself, that all expression disappeared from his face in an aspect of staring vacancy.

Ali was clearing the table. He dropped negligently the tumbler into the greasy dish, flung there the spoon and fork,* then slipped in the plate with a push amongst the remnants of food. He took up the dish, tucked up the bottle under his armpit, and went off.

"My hammock!" shouted Almayer after him.

"Ada! I come soon," answered Ali from the doorway in an offended tone, looking back over his shoulder. . . . How could he clear the table and hang the hammock at the same time. Ya—wa! Those white men were all alike. Wanted everything done at once. Like children . . .

The indistinct murmur of his criticism went away, faded and died out together with the soft footfall of his bare feet in the dark passage.

For some time Almayer did not move. His thoughts were busy at work shaping a momentous resolution, and in the perfect silence of the house he believed that he could hear the noise of the operation as if the work had been done with a hammer. He certainly felt a thumping of strokes, faint, profound, and startling, somewhere low down in his breast; and he was aware of a sound of dull knocking, abrupt and rapid, in his ears. Now and then he held his breath, unconsciously, too long, and had to relieve himself by a deep expiration that whistled dully through his pursed lips. The lamp standing on the far side of the table threw a section of a lighted circle on the floor, where his out-stretched legs stuck out from under the table with feet rigid and turned up like the feet of a corpse; and his set face with fixed eyes would have been also like the face of the dead, but for its vacant yet conscious aspect; the hard, the stupid, the stony aspect of one not dead, but only buried under the dust, ashes, and corruption of personal thoughts, of base fears, of selfish desires.

"I will do it!"

Not till he heard his own voice did he know that he had spoken. It startled him. He stood up. The knuckles of his hand, somewhat behind him, were resting on the edge of the table as he remained still with one foot advanced, his lips a little open, and thought: It would not do to fool about with Lingard. But I must risk it. It's the only way I can see. I must tell her. She has some little sense. I wish they were a thousand miles off already. A hundred thousand miles. I do. And if it fails. And she blabs out then to Lingard? She seemed a fool. No; probably they will get away. And if they did, would Lingard be-lieve me? Yes. I never lied to him. He would believe. I don't know . . . Perhaps he won't. . . . "I must do it. Must!" he argued aloud to himself.

For a long time he stood still, looking before him with an intense gaze, a gaze rapt and immobile, that seemed to watch the minute quivering of a delicate balance, coming to a rest.

To the left of him, in the whitewashed wall of the house that formed the back of the verandah, there

was a closed door. Black letters were painted on it
proclaiming the fact that behind that door there was
the office of Lingard & Co. The interior had been
furnished by Lingard when he had built the house
for his adopted daughter and her husband, and it had
been furnished with reckless prodigality. There was
an office desk, a revolving chair, bookshelves, a safe:
all to humour the weakness of Almayer, who thought
all those paraphernalia necessary to successful trading.
Lingard had laughed, but had taken immense trouble
to get the things. It pleased him to make his protégé,
his adopted son-in-law, happy. It had been the
sensation of Sambir some five years ago. While
the things were being landed, the whole settlement
literally lived on the river bank in front of the Rajah
Laut's house, to look, to wonder, to admire. . . .
What a big meza, with many boxes fitted all over it
and under it! What did the white man do with
such a table? And look, look, O Brothers! There
is a green square box, with a gold plate on it, a box
so heavy that those twenty men cannot drag it
up the bank. Let us go, brothers, and help pull
at the ropes, and perchance we may see what's inside.
Treasure, no doubt. Gold is heavy and hard to
hold, O Brothers! Let us go and earn a recompense from the fierce Rajah of the Sea who shouts over
there, with a red face. See! There is a man carrying
a pile of books from the boat! What a number of
books. What were they for? . . . And an old in-
valided jurumudi, who had travelled over many seas
and had heard holy men speak in far-off countries,
explained to a small knot of unsophisticated citizens
of Sambir that those books were books of magic—
of magic that guides the white men's ships over the
seas, that gives them their wicked wisdom and their

strength; of magic that makes them great, powerful, and irresistible while they live, and—praise be to Allah!—the victims of Satan, the slaves of Jehannum when they die.

And when he saw the room furnished, Almayer had felt proud. In his exultation of an empty-headed quill-driver, he thought himself, by the virtue of that furniture, at the head of a serious business. He had sold himself to Lingard for these things—married the Malay girl of his adoption for the reward of these things and of the great wealth that must necessarily follow upon conscientious book-keeping. He found out very soon that trade in Sambir meant something entirely different. He could not guide Patalolo, control the irrepressible old Sahamin, or restrain the youthful vagaries of the fierce Bahassoen with pen, ink, and paper. He found no successful magic in the blank pages of his ledgers; and gradually he lost his old point of view in the saner appreciation of his situation. The room known as the office became neglected then like a temple of an exploded superstition. At first, when his wife reverted to her original savagery, Almayer, now and again, had sought refuge from her there; but after their child began to speak, to know him, he became braver, for he found courage and consolation in his unreasoning and fierce affection for his daughter—in the impenetrable mantle of selfishness he wrapped round both their lives: round himself, and that young life that was also his.

When Lingard ordered him to receive Joanna into his house, he had a truckle bed put into the office— the only room he could spare. The big office desk was pushed on one side, and Joanna came with her little shabby trunk and with her child and took possession in her dreamy, slack, half-asleep way; took possession of the dust, dirt, and squalor, where she appeared naturally at home, where she dragged a melancholy and dull existence; an existence made up of sad remorse and frightened hope, amongst the hopeless disorder—the senseless and vain decay of all these emblems of civilized commerce. Bits of white stuff; rags yellow, pink, blue: rags limp, brilliant and soiled, trailed on the floor, lay on the desk amongst the sombre covers of books soiled, grimy, but stiff-backed, in virtue, perhaps, of their European origin. The biggest set of bookshelves was partly hidden by a petticoat, the waist-band of which was caught upon the back of a slender book pulled a little out of the row so as to make an improvised clothes-peg. The folding canvas bedstead stood nearly in the middle of the room, stood anyhow, parallel to no wall, as if it had been, in the process of transportation to some remote place, dropped casually there by tired bearers. And on the tumbled blankets that lay in a disordered heap on its edge, Joanna sat almost all day with her stockingless feet upon one of the bed pillows that were somehow always kicking about the floor. She sat there, vaguely tormented at times by the thought of her absent husband, but most of the time thinking tearfully of nothing at all, looking with swimming eyes at her little son—at the big-headed, pasty-faced, and sickly Louis Willems—who rolled a glass inkstand, solid with dried ink, about the floor, and tottered after it with the portentous gravity of demeanour and absolute absorption by the business in hand that characterize the pursuits of early child-hood. Through the half-open shutter a ray of sunlight, a ray merciless and crude, came into the room, beat in the early morning upon the safe in the far-off corner, then, travelling against the sun, cut at midday the big desk in two with its solid and clean-edged brilliance;

with its hot brilliance in which a swarm of flies hovered in dancing flight over some dirty plate forgotten there amongst yellow papers for many a day. And towards the evening the cynical ray seemed to cling to the ragged petticoat, lingered on it with wicked enjoyment of that misery it had exposed all day; lingered on the corner of the dusty bookshelf, in a red glow intense and mocking, till it was suddenly snatched by the setting sun out of the way of the coming night. And the night entered the room. The night abrupt, impenetrable and all-filling with its flood of darkness; the night cool and merciful; the blind night that saw nothing, but could hear the fretful whimpering of the child, the creak of the bedstead, Joanna's deep sighs as she turned over, sleepless, in the confused conviction of her wickedness, thinking of that man masterful, fair-headed, and strong—a man hard perhaps, but her husband; her clever and handsome husband to whom she had acted so cruelly on the advice of bad people, if her own people; and of her poor, dear, deceived mother.

To Almayer, Joanna's presence was a constant worry, a worry unobtrusive yet intolerable; a constant, but mostly mute, warning of possible danger. In view of the absurd softness of Lingard's heart, every one in whom Lingard manifested the slightest interest was to Almayer a natural enemy. He was quite alive to that feeling, and in the intimacy of the secret intercourse with his inner self had often congratulated himself upon his own wide-awake comprehension of his position. In that way, and impelled by that motive, Almayer had hated many and various persons at various times. But he never had hated and feared anybody so much as he did hate and fear Willems. Even after Willems' treachery, which seemed to remove him beyond the pale of all human sympathy,

Almayer mistrusted the situation and groaned in spirit every time he caught sight of Joanna.

He saw her very seldom in the daytime. But in the short and opal-tinted twilights, or in the azure dusk of starry evenings, he often saw, before he slept, the slender and tall figure trailing to and fro the ragged tail of its white gown over the dried mud of the riverside in front of the house. Once or twice when he sat late on the verandah, with his feet upon the deal table on a level with the lamp, reading the seven months' old copy of the *North China Herald*,* brought by Lingard, he heard the stairs creak, and, looking round the paper, he saw her frail and meagre form rise step by step and toil across the verandah, carrying with difficulty the big, fat child, whose head, lying on the mother's bony shoulder, seemed of the same size as Joanna's own. Several times she had assailed him with tearful clamour or mad entreaties: asking about her husband, wanting to know where he was, when he would be back; and ending every such outburst with despairing and incoherent self-reproaches that were absolutely incomprehensible to Almayer. On one or two occasions she had overwhelmed her host with vituperative abuse, making him responsible for her husband's absence. Those scenes, begun without any warning, ended abruptly in a sobbing flight and a bang of the door; stirred the house with a sudden, a fierce, and an evanescent disturbance; like those inexplicable whirlwinds that rise, run, and vanish without apparent cause upon the sun-scorched dead level of arid and lamentable plains.

But to-night the house was quiet, deadly quiet, while Almayer stood still, watching that delicate balance where he was weighing all his chances: Joanna's intelligence, Lingard's credulity, Willems' reckless

audacity, desire to escape, readiness to seize an unexpected opportunity. He weighed, anxious and attentive, his fears and his desires against the tremendous
risk of a quarrel with Lingard. . . . Yes. Lingard would be angry. Lingard might suspect him
of some connivance in his prisoner's escape—but
surely he would not quarrel with him—Almayer—
about those people once they were gone—gone to the
devil in their own way. And then he had hold of
Lingard through the little girl. Good. What an
annoyance! A prisoner! As if one could keep him
in there. He was bound to get away some time or
other. Of course. A situation like that can't last.
Anybody could see that. Lingard's eccentricity passed
all bounds. You may kill a man, but you mustn't
torture him. It was almost criminal. It caused
worry, trouble, and unpleasantness. . . . Almayer
for a moment felt very angry with Lingard. He made
him responsible for the anguish he suffered from, for
the anguish of doubt and fear; for compelling him—
the practical and innocent Almayer—to such painful
efforts of mind in order to find out some issue for absurd
situations created by the unreasonable sentimentality
of Lingard's unpractical impulses.

"Now if the fellow were dead it would be all right,"
said Almayer to the verandah.

He stirred a little, and scratching his nose thoughtfully, revelled in a short flight of fancy, showing him
his own image crouching in a big boat, that floated
arrested—say fifty yards off—abreast of Willems'
landing-place. In the bottom of the boat there was
a gun. A loaded gun. One of the boatmen would
shout, and Willems would answer—from the bushes.
The rascal would be suspicious. Of course. Then
the man would wave a piece of paper urging Willems

to come to the landing-place and receive an important message. "From the Rajah Laut" the man would yell as the boat edged in-shore, and that would fetch Willems out. Wouldn't it? Rather! And Almayer saw himself jumping up at the right moment, taking aim, pulling the trigger—and Willems tumbling over, his head in the water—the swine!

He seemed to hear the report of the shot. It made him thrill from head to foot where he stood. . . . How simple! . . . Unfortunate . . . Lingard . . . He sighed, shook his head. Pity. Couldn't be done. And couldn't leave him there either! Suppose the Arabs were to get hold of him again—for instance to lead an expedition up the river! Goodness only knows what harm would come of it. . . .

The balance was at rest now and inclining to the side of immediate action. Almayer walked to the door, walked up very close to it, knocked loudly, and turned his head away, looking frightened for a moment at what he had done. After waiting for a while he put his ear against the panel and listened. Nothing. He composed his features into an agreeable expression while he stood listening and thinking to himself: I hear her. Crying. Eh? I believe she has lost the little wits she had and is crying night and day since I began to prepare her for the news of her husband's death—as Lingard told me. I wonder what she thinks. It's just like father to make me invent all these stories for nothing at all. Out of kindness. Kindness! Damn! . . . She isn't deaf, surely.

He knocked again, then said in a friendly tone, grinning benevolently at the closed door—

"It's me, Mrs. Willems. I want to speak to you. I have . . . have . . . important news. . . ."

"What is it?"

"News," repeated Almayer, distinctly. "News about your husband. Your husband! . . . Damn him!" he added, under his breath.

He heard a stumbling rush inside. Things were overturned. Joanna's agitated voice cried—

"News! What? What? I am coming out."

"No," shouted Almayer. "Put on some clothes, Mrs. Willems, and let me in. It's . . . very confidential. You have a candle, haven't you?"

She was knocking herself about blindly amongst the furniture in that room. The candlestick was upset. Matches were struck ineffectually. The matchbox fell. He heard her drop on her knees and grope over the floor while she kept on moaning in maddened distraction.

"Oh, my God! News! Yes . . . yes. . . . Ah! where . . . where . . . candle. Oh, my God! . . . I can't find . . . Don't go away, for the love of Heaven . . ."

"I don't want to go away," said Almayer, impatiently, through the keyhole; "but look sharp. It's confi . . . it's pressing."

He stamped his foot lightly, waiting with his hand on the door-handle. He thought anxiously: The woman's a perfect idiot. Why should I go away? She will be off her head. She will never catch my meaning. She's too stupid.

She was moving now inside the room hurriedly and in silence. He waited. There was a moment of perfect stillness in there, and then she spoke in an exhausted voice, in words that were shaped out of an expiring sigh—out of a sigh light and profound, like words breathed out by a woman before going off into a dead faint—

"Come in."

He pushed the door. Ali, coming through the

passage with an armful of pillows and blankets pressed
to his breast high up under his chin, caught sight of
his master before the door closed behind him. He
was so astonished that he dropped his bundle and
stood staring at the door for a long time. He heard
the voice of his master talking. Talking to that
Sirani woman! Who was she? He had never thought
about that really. He speculated for a while hazily
upon things in general. She was a Sirani woman—
and ugly. He made a disdainful grimace, picked up
the bedding, and went about his work, slinging the
hammock between two uprights of the verandah. . . .
Those things did not concern him. She was ugly, and
brought here by the Rajah Laut, and his master spoke
to her in the night. Very well. He, Ali, had his work
to do. Sling the hammock—go round and see that
the watchmen were awake—take a look at the moorings
of the boats, at the padlock of the big storehouse—then
go to sleep. To sleep! He shivered pleasantly. He
leaned with both arms over his master's hammock and
fell into a light doze.

A scream, unexpected, piercing—a scream beginning at once in the highest pitch of a woman's voice
and then cut short, so short that it suggested the swift
work of death—caused Ali to jump on one side away
from the hammock, and the silence that succeeded
seemed to him as startling as the awful shriek. He
was thunderstruck with surprise. Almayer came out
of the office, leaving the door ajar, passed close to his
servant without taking any notice, and made straight
for the water-chatty hung on a nail in a draughty
place. He took it down and came back, missing the
petrified Ali by an inch. He moved with long strides,
yet, notwithstanding his haste, stopped short before
the door, and, throwing his head back, poured a thin

stream of water down his throat. While he came and went, while he stopped to drink, while he did all this, there came steadily from the dark room the sound of feeble and persistent crying, the crying of a sleepy and frightened child. After he had drunk, Almayer went in, closing the door carefully.

Ali did not budge. That Sirani woman shrieked! He felt an immense curiosity very unusual to his stolid disposition. He could not take his eyes off the door. Was she dead in there? How interesting and funny! He stood with open mouth till he heard again the rattle of the door-handle. Master coming out. He pivoted on his heels with great rapidity and made believe to be absorbed in the contemplation of the night outside. He heard Almayer moving about behind his back. Chairs were displaced. His master sat down.

"Ali," said Almayer.

His face was gloomy and thoughtful. He looked at his head man, who had approached the table, then he pulled out his watch. It was going. Whenever Lingard was in Sambir Almayer's watch was going. He would set it by the cabin clock, telling himself every time that he must really keep that watch going for the future. And every time, when Lingard went away, he would let it run down and would measure his weariness by sunrises and sunsets in an apathetic indifference to mere hours; to hours only; to hours that had no importance in Sambir life, in the tired stagnation of empty days; when nothing mattered to him but the quality of guttah and the size of rattans; where there were no small hopes to be watched for; where to him there was nothing interesting, nothing supportable, nothing desirable to expect; nothing bitter but the slowness of the passing days; nothing

sweet but the hope, the distant and glorious hope—
the hope wearying, aching and precious, of getting
away.

He looked at the watch. Half-past eight. Ali
waited stolidly.

"Go to the settlement," said Almayer, "and tell
Mahmat Banjer*to come and speak to me to-night."

Ali went off muttering. He did not like his errand.
Banjer and his two brothers were Bajow vagabonds
who had appeared lately in Sambir and had been allowed
to take possession of a tumbledown abandoned hut,
on three posts, belonging to Lingard & Co., and standing just outside their fence. Ali disapproved of the
favour shown to those strangers. Any kind of dwelling
was valuable in Sambir at that time, and if master did
not want that old rotten house he might have given it
to him, Ali, who was his servant, instead of bestowing it
upon those bad men. Everybody knew they were
bad. It was well known that they had stolen a boat
from Hinopari, who was very aged and feeble and had
no sons; and that afterwards, by the truculent recklessness of their demeanour, they had frightened the poor
old man into holding his tongue about it. Yet everybody knew of it. It was one of the tolerated scandals
of Sambir, disapproved and accepted, a manifestation
of that base acquiescence in success, of that inexpressed
and cowardly toleration of strength, that exists, infamous and irremediable, at the bottom of all hearts,
in all societies; whenever men congregate; in bigger
and more virtuous places than Sambir, and in Sambir
also, where, as in other places, one man could steal a
boat with impunity while another would have no right
to look at a paddle.

Almayer, leaning back in his chair, meditated. The
more he thought, the more ·he felt convinced that

Banjer and his brothers were exactly the men he wanted. Those fellows were sea gipsies,* and could disappear without attracting notice; and if they returned, nobody—and Lingard least of all—would dream of seeking information from them. Moreover, they had no personal interest of any kind in Sambir affairs—had taken no sides—would know nothing anyway.

He called in a strong voice: "Mrs. Willems!"

She came out quickly, almost startling him, so much did she appear as though she had surged up through the floor, on the other side of the table. The lamp was between them, and Almayer moved it aside, looking up at her from his chair. She was crying. She was crying gently, silently, in a ceaseless welling up of tears that did not fall in drops, but seemed to overflow in a clear sheet from under her eyelids— seemed to flow at once all over her face, her cheeks, and over her chin that glistened with moisture in the light. Her breast and her shoulders were shaken repeatedly by a convulsive and noiseless catching in her breath, and after every spasmodic sob her sorrowful little head, tied up in a red kerchief, trembled on her long neck, round which her bony hand gathered and clasped the disarranged dress.

"Compose yourself, Mrs. Willems," said Almayer.

She emitted an inarticulate sound that seemed to be a faint, a very far off, a hardly audible cry of mortal distress. Then the tears went on flowing in profound stillness.

"You must understand that I have told you all this because I am your friend—real friend," said Almayer, after looking at her for some time with visible dissatisfaction. "You, his wife, ought to know the danger he is in. Captain Lingard is a terrible man, you know."

She blubbered out, sniffing and sobbing together.

"Do you . . . you . . . speak . . . the . . . the truth now?"

"Upon my word of honour. On the head of my child," protested Almayer. "I had to deceive you till now because of Captain Lingard. But I couldn't bear it. Think only what a risk I run in telling you —if ever Lingard was to know! Why should I do it? Pure friendship. Dear Peter was my colleague in Macassar for years, you know."

"What shall I do . . . what shall I do!" she exclaimed, faintly, looking around on every side as if she could not make up her mind which way to rush off.

"You must help him to clear out, now Lingard is away. He offended Lingard, and that's no joke. Lingard said he would kill him. He will do it, too," said Almayer, earnestly.

She wrung her hands. "Oh! the wicked man. The wicked, wicked man!" she moaned, swaying her body from side to side.

"Yes. Yes! He is terrible," assented Almayer. "You must not lose any time. I say! Do you understand me, Mrs. Willems? Think of your husband. Of your poor husband. How happy he will be. You will bring him his life—actually his life. Think of him."

She ceased her swaying movement, and now, with her head sunk between her shoulders, she hugged herself with both her arms; and she stared at Almayer with wild eyes, while her teeth chattered, rattling violently and uninterruptedly, with a very loud sound, in the deep peace of the house.

"Oh! Mother of God!" she wailed. "I am a miserable woman. Will he forgive me? The poor, innocent man. Will he forgive me? Oh, Mr. Almayer,

he is so severe. Oh! help me. . . . I dare not.
. . . You don't know what I've done to him.
. . . I daren't! . . . I can't! . . . God
help me!"

The last words came in a despairing cry. Had she
been flayed alive she could not have sent to heaven a
more terrible, a more heart-rending and anguished plaint.

"Sh! Sh!" hissed Almayer, jumping up. "You
will wake up everybody with your shouting."

She kept on sobbing then without any noise, and
Almayer stared at her in boundless astonishment.
The idea that, maybe, he had done wrong by con-
fiding in her, upset him so much that for a moment
he could not find a connected thought in his head.

At last he said: "I swear to you that your husband
is in such a position that he would welcome the devil
. . . listen well to me . . . the devil himself
if the devil came to him in a canoe. Unless I am much
mistaken," he added, under his breath. Then again,
loudly: "If you have any little difference to make up
with him, I assure you—I swear to you—this is your
time!"

The ardently persuasive tone of his words—he
thought—would have carried irresistible conviction
to a graven image. He noticed with satisfaction that
Joanna seemed to have got some inkling of his meaning. He continued, speaking slowly—

"Look here, Mrs. Willems. I can't do anything.
Daren't. But I will tell you what I will do. There
will come here in about ten minutes a Bugis man—
you know the language; you are from Macassar. He
has a large canoe; he can take you there. To the
new Rajah's clearing, tell him. They are three brothers, ready for anything if you pay them . . . you
have some money. Haven't you?"

She stood—perhaps listening—but giving no sign of intelligence, and stared at the floor in sudden immobility, as if the horror of the situation, the overwhelming sense of her own wickedness and of her husband's great danger, had stunned her brain, her heart, her will—had left her no faculty but that of breathing and of keeping on her feet. Almayer swore to himself with much mental profanity that he had never seen a more useless, a more stupid being.

"D'ye hear me?" he said, raising his voice. "Do try to understand. Have you any money? Money. Dollars. Guilders. Money! What's the matter with you?"

Without raising her eyes she said, in a voice that sounded weak and undecided as if she had been making a desperate effort of memory—

"The house has been sold. Mr. Hudig was angry."

Almayer gripped the edge of the table with all his strength. He resisted manfully an almost uncontrollable impulse to fly at her and box her ears.

"It was sold for money, I suppose," he said with studied and incisive calmness. "Have you got it? Who has got it?"

She looked up at him, raising her swollen eyelids with a great effort, in a sorrowful expression of her drooping mouth, of her whole besmudged and tear-stained face. She whispered resignedly—

"Leonard had some. He wanted to get married. And uncle Antonio; he sat at the door and would not go away. And Aghostina—she is so poor . . . and so many, many children—little children. And Luiz the engineer. He never said a word against my husband. Also our cousin Maria. She came and shouted, and my head was so bad, and my heart was worse. Then cousin Salvator and old Daniel da Souza, who . . ."

Almayer had listened to her speechless with rage. He thought: I must give money now to that idiot. Must! Must get her out of the way now before Lingard is back. He made two attempts to speak before he managed to burst out—

"I don't want to know their blasted names! Tell me, did all those infernal people leave you anything? To you! That's what I want to know!"

"I have two hundred and fifteen dollars," said Joanna, in a frightened tone.

Almayer breathed freely. He spoke with great friendliness—

"That will do. It isn't much, but it will do. Now when the man comes I will be out of the way. You speak to him. Give him some money; only a little, mind! And promise more. Then when you get there you will be guided by your husband, of course. And don't forget to tell him that Captain Lingard is at the mouth of the river—the northern entrance. You will remember. Won't you? The northern branch. Lingard is—death."

Joanna shivered. Almayer went on rapidly—

"I would have given you money if you had wanted it. 'Pon my word! Tell your husband I've sent you to him. And tell him not to lose any time. And also say to him from me that we shall meet—some day. That I could not die happy unless I met him once more. Only once. I love him, you know. I prove it. Tremendous risk to me—this business is!"

Joanna snatched his hand and before he knew what she would be at, pressed it to her lips.

"Mrs. Willems! Don't. What are you . . ." cried the abashed Almayer, tearing his hand away.

"Oh, you are good!" she cried, with sudden exaltation. "You are noble . . . I shall pray every

day . . . to all the saints . . . I
shall . . ."

"Never mind . . . never mind!" stammered
out Almayer, confusedly, without knowing very well
what he was saying. "Only look out for Lingard.
. . . I am happy to be able . . . in your sad
situation . . . believe me. . . ."

They stood with the table between them, Joanna
looking down, and her face, in the half-light above
the lamp, appeared like a soiled carving of old ivory—
a carving, with accentuated anxious hollows, of old,
very old ivory. Almayer looked at her, mistrustful,
hopeful. He was saying to himself: How frail she
is! I could upset her by blowing at her. She seems
to have got some idea of what must be done, but will
she have the strength to carry it through? I must
trust to luck now!

Somewhere far in the back courtyard Ali's voice
rang suddenly in angry remonstrance—

"Why did you shut the gate, O father of all mis-
chief? You a watchman! You are only a wild man.
Did I not tell you I was coming back? You . . ."

"I am off, Mrs. Willems," exclaimed Almayer.
"That man is here—with my servant. Be calm. Try
to . . ."

He heard the footsteps of the two men in the passage, and without finishing his sentence ran rapidly
down the steps towards the riverside.

CHAPTER TWO

·FOR the next half-hour Almayer, who wanted to give
Joanna plenty of time, stumbled amongst the lumber
in distant parts of his enclosure, sneaked along the
fences, or held his breath, flattened against grass
walls behind various outhouses: all this to escape Ali's
inconveniently zealous search for his master. He
heard him talk with the head watchman—sometimes
quite close to him in the darkness—then moving off,
coming back, wondering, and, as the time passed,
growing uneasy.

"He did not fall into the river?—say, thou blind
watcher!" Ali was growling in a bullying tone, to the
other man. "He told me to fetch Mahmat, and when
I came back swiftly I found him not in the house.
There is that Sirani woman there, so that Mahmat
cannot steal anything, but it is in my mind, the night
will be half gone before I rest."

He shouted—

"Master! O master! O mast . . ."

"What are you making that noise for?" said Almayer,
with severity, stepping out close to them.

The two Malays leaped away from each other in
their surprise.

"You may go. I don't want you any more to-
night, Ali," went on Almayer. "Is Mahmat there?"

"Unless the ill-behaved savage got tired of waiting.
Those men know not politeness. They should not
be spoken to by white men," said Ali, resentfully.

Almayer went towards the house, leaving his servants to wonder where he had sprung from so unexpectedly. The watchman hinted obscurely at powers of invisibility possessed by the master, who often at night . . . Ali interrupted him with great scorn. Not every white man has the power. Now, the Rajah Laut could make himself invisible. Also, he could be in two places at once, as everybody knew; except he—the useless watchman—who knew no more about white men than a wild pig! Ya—wa!

And Ali strolled towards his hut, yawning loudly.

As Almayer ascended the steps he heard the noise of a door flung to, and when he entered the verandah he saw only Mahmat there, close to the doorway of the passage. Mahmat seemed to be caught in the very act of slinking away, and Almayer noticed that with satisfaction. Seeing the white man, the Malay gave up his attempt and leaned against the wall. He was a short, thick, broad-shouldered man with very dark skin and a wide, stained, bright red mouth that uncovered, when he spoke, a close row of black and glistening teeth. His eyes were big, prominent, dreamy and restless. He said sulkily, looking all over the place from under his eyebrows—

"White Tuan, you are great and strong—and I a poor man. Tell me what is your will, and let me go in the name of God. It is late."

Almayer examined the man thoughtfully. How could he find out whether . . . He had it! Lately he had employed that man and his two brothers as extra boatmen to carry stores, provisions, and new axes to a camp of rattan cutters some distance up the river. A three days' expedition. He would test him now in that way. He said negligently—

"I want you to start at once for the camp, with a surat for the Kavitan. One dollar a day."

The man appeared plunged in dull hesitation, but Almayer, who knew his Malays, felt pretty sure from his aspect that nothing would induce the fellow to go. He urged—

"It is important—and if you are swift I shall give two dollars for the last day."

"No, Tuan. We do not go," said the man, in a hoarse whisper.

"Why?"

"We start on another journey."

"Where?"

"To a place we know of," said Mahmat, a little louder, in a stubborn manner, and looking at the floor.

Almayer experienced a feeling of immense joy. He said, with affected annoyance—

"You men live in my house—and it is as if it were your own. I may want my house soon."

Mahmat looked up.

"We are men of the sea and care not for a roof when we have a canoe that will hold three, and a paddle apiece. The sea is our house. Peace be with you, Tuan."

He turned and went away rapidly, and Almayer heard him directly afterwards in the courtyard calling to the watchman to open the gate. Mahmat passed through the gate in silence, but before the bar had been put up behind him he had made up his mind that if the white man ever wanted to eject him from his hut, he would burn it and also as many of the white man's other buildings as he could safely get at. And he began to call his brothers before he was inside the dilapidated dwelling.

"All's well!" muttered Almayer to himself, taking some loose Java tobacco* from a drawer in the table.

"Now if anything comes out I am clear. I asked the man to go up the river. I urged him. He will say so himself. Good."

He began to charge the china bowl of his pipe, a pipe with a long cherry stem and a curved mouthpiece, pressing the tobacco down with his thumb and thinking: No. I shan't see her again. Don't want to. I will give her a good start, then go in chase—and send an express boat after father. Yes! that's it.

He approached the door of the office and said, holding his pipe away from his lips—

"Good luck to you, Mrs. Willems. Don't lose any time. You may get along by the bushes; the fence there is out of repair. Don't lose time. Don't forget that it is a matter of . . . life and death. And don't forget that I know nothing. I trust you."

He heard inside a noise as of a chest-lid falling down. She made a few steps. Then a sigh, profound and long, and some faint words which he did not catch. He moved away from the door on tiptoe, kicked off his slippers in a corner of the verandah, then entered the passage puffing at his pipe; entered cautiously in a gentle creaking of planks and turned into a curtained entrance to the left. There was a big room. On the floor a small binnacle lamp—that had found its way to the house years ago from the lumber-room of the *Flash*—did duty for a nightlight. It glimmered very small and dull in the great darkness. Almayer walked to it, and picking it up revived the flame by pulling the wick with his fingers, which he shook directly after with a grimace of pain. Sleeping shapes, covered—head and all—with white sheets, lay about on the mats on the floor. In the middle of the room a small cot, under a square white mosquito net, stood—the only piece of furniture between the four walls—looking like an altar of transparent marble in a gloomy temple. A woman, half-lying on the floor with her head dropped on her arms, which were crossed on the foot of the cot, woke up as Almayer strode over her outstretched legs. She sat up without a word, leaning forward, and, clasping her knees, stared down with sad eyes, full of sleep.

Almayer, the smoky light in one hand, his pipe in the other, stood before the curtained cot looking at his daughter—at his little Nina—at that part of himself, at that small and unconscious particle of humanity that seemed to him to contain all his soul. And it was as if he had been bathed in a bright and warm wave of tenderness, in a tenderness greater than the world, more precious than life; the only thing real, living, sweet, tangible, beautiful and safe amongst the elusive, the distorted and menacing shadows of existence. On his face, lit up indistinctly by the short yellow flame of the lamp, came a look of rapt attention while he looked into her future. And he could see things there! Things charming and splendid passing before him in a magic unrolling of resplendent pictures; pictures of events brilliant, happy, inexpressibly glorious, that would make up her life. He would do it! He would do it. He would! He would—for that child! And as he stood in the still night, lost in his enchanting and gorgeous dreams, while the ascending, thin thread of tobacco smoke spread into a faint bluish cloud above his head, he appeared strangely impressive and ecstatic: like a devout and mystic worshipper, adoring, transported and mute; burning incense before a shrine, a diaphanous shrine of a child-idol with closed eyes; before a pure and vaporous shrine of a small god—fragile, powerless, unconscious and sleeping.

When Ali, roused by loud and repeated shouting of his name, stumbled outside the door of his hut, he saw a narrow streak of trembling gold above the forests and a pale sky with faded stars overhead: signs of the coming day. His master stood before the door waving a piece of paper in his hand and shouting excitedly— "Quick, Ali! Quick!" When he saw his servant he rushed forward, and pressing the paper on him objurgated him, in tones which induced Ali to think that something awful had happened, to hurry up and get the whale-boat ready to go immediately—at once, at once—after Captain Lingard. Ali remonstrated, agitated also, having caught the infection of distracted haste.

"If must go quick, better canoe. Whale-boat no can catch, same as small canoe."

"No, no! Whale-boat! whale-boat! You dolt! you wretch!" howled Almayer, with all the appearance of having gone mad. "Call the men! Get along with it. Fly!"

And Ali rushed about the courtyard kicking the doors of huts open to put his head in and yell frightfully inside; and as he dashed from hovel to hovel, men shivering and sleepy were coming out, looking after him stupidly, while they scratched their ribs with bewildered apathy. It was hard work to put them in motion. They wanted time to stretch themselves and to shiver a little. Some wanted food. One said he was sick. Nobody knew where the rudder was. Ali darted here and there, ordering, abusing, pushing one, then another, and stopping in his exertions at times to wring his hands hastily and groan, because the whale-boat was much slower than the worst canoe and his master would not listen to his protestations.

Almayer saw the boat go off at last, pulled anyhow

by men that were cold, hungry, and sulky; and he remained on the jetty watching it down the reach. It was broad day then, and the sky was perfectly cloudless. Almayer went up to the house for a moment. His household was all astir and wondering at the strange disappearance of the Sirani woman, who had taken her child and had left her luggage. Almayer spoke to no one, got his revolver, and went down to the river again. He jumped into a small canoe and paddled himself towards the schooner. He worked very leisurely, but as soon as he was nearly alongside he began to hail the silent craft with the tone and appearance of a man in a tremendous hurry.

"Schooner ahoy! schooner ahoy!" he shouted.

A row of blank faces popped up above the bulwark. After a while a man with a woolly head of hair said—
"Sir!"

"The mate! the mate! Call him, steward!" said Almayer, excitedly, making a frantic grab at a rope thrown down to him by somebody.

In less than a minute the mate put his head over. He asked, surprised—

"What can I do for you, Mr. Almayer?"

"Let me have the gig at once, Mr. Swan—at once. I ask in Captain Lingard's name. I must have it. Matter of life and death."

The mate was impressed by Almayer's agitation.

"You shall have it, sir. . . . Man the gig there! Bear a hand, serang! . . . It's hanging astern, Mr. Almayer," he said, looking down again. "Get into it, sir. The men are coming down by the painter."

By the time Almayer had clambered over into the stern sheets, four calashes were in the boat and the oars were being passed over the taffrail. The mate was looking on. Suddenly he said—

"Is it dangerous work? Do you want any help? I would come . . ."

"Yes, yes!" cried Almayer. "Come along. Don't lose a moment. Go and get your revolver. Hurry up! hurry up!"

Yet, notwithstanding his feverish anxiety to be off, he lolled back very quiet and unconcerned till the mate got in and, passing over the thwarts, sat down by his side. Then he seemed to wake up, and called out—

"Let go—let go the painter!"

"Let go the painter—the painter!" yelled the bow-man, jerking at it.

People on board also shouted "Let go!" to one another, till it occurred at last to somebody to cast off the rope; and the boat drifted rapidly away from the schooner in the sudden silencing of all voices.

Almayer steered. The mate sat by his side, pushing the cartridges into the chambers of his revolver. When the weapon was loaded he asked—

"What is it? Are you after somebody?"

"Yes," said Almayer, curtly, with his eyes fixed ahead on the river. "We must catch a dangerous man."

"I like a bit of a chase myself," declared the mate, and then, discouraged by Almayer's aspect of severe thoughtfulness, said nothing more.

Nearly an hour passed. The calashes stretched forward head first and lay back with their faces to the sky, alternately, in a regular swing that sent the boat flying through the water; and the two sitters, very up-right in the stern sheets, swayed rhythmically a little at every stroke of the long oars plied vigorously.

The mate observed: "The tide is with us."

"The current always runs down in this river," said Almayer.

"Yes—I know," retorted the other; "but it runs faster on the ebb. Look by the land at the way we get over the ground! A five-knot current here, I should say."

"H'm!" growled Almayer. Then suddenly: "There is a passage between two islands that will save us four miles. But at low water*the two islands, in the dry season, are like one with only a mud ditch between them. Still, it's worth trying."

"Ticklish job that, on a falling tide," said the mate, coolly. "You know best whether there's time to get through."

"I will try," said Almayer, watching the shore intently. "Look out now!"

He tugged hard at the starboard yoke line.

"Lay in your oars!" shouted the mate.

The boat swept round and shot through the narrow opening of a creek that broadened out before the craft had time to lose its way.

"Out oars! . . . Just room enough," muttered the mate.

It was a sombre creek of black water speckled with the gold of scattered sunlight falling through the boughs that met overhead in a soaring, restless arc full of gentle whispers passing, tremulous, aloft amongst the thick leaves. The creepers climbed up the trunks of serried trees that leaned over, looking insecure and undermined by floods which had eaten away the earth from under their roots. And the pungent, acrid smell of rotting leaves, of flowers, of blossoms and plants dying in that poisonous and cruel gloom, where they pined for sunshine in vain, seemed to lay heavy, to press upon the shiny and stagnant water in its tortuous windings amongst the everlasting and invincible shadows.

Almayer looked anxious. He steered badly. Several times the blades of the oars got foul of the bushes on one side or the other, checking the way of the gig. During one of those occurrences, while they were getting clear, one of the calashes said something to the others in a rapid whisper. They looked down at the water. So did the mate.

"Hallo!" he exclaimed. "Eh, Mr. Almayer! Look! The water is running out. See there! We will be caught."

"Back! back! We must go back!" cried Almayer.

"Perhaps better go on."

"No; back! back!"

He pulled at the steering line, and ran the nose of the boat into the bank. Time was lost again in getting clear.

"Give way, men! give way!" urged the mate, anxiously.

The men pulled with set lips and dilated nostrils, breathing hard.

"Too late," said the mate, suddenly. "The oars touch the bottom already. We are done."

The boat stuck. The men laid in the oars, and sat, panting, with crossed arms.

"Yes, we are caught," said Almayer, composedly. "That is unlucky!"

The water was falling round the boat. The mate watched the patches of mud coming to the surface. Then in a moment he laughed, and pointing his finger at the creek—

"Look!" he said; "the blamed river is running away from us. Here's the last drop of water clearing out round that bend."

Almayer lifted his head. The water was gone, and he looked only at a curved track of mud—of mud soft and black, hiding fever, rottenness, and evil under its level and glazed surface.

"We are in for it till the evening," he said, with cheerful resignation. "I did my best. Couldn't help it."

"We must sleep the day away," said the mate. "There's nothing to eat," he added, gloomily.

Almayer stretched himself in the stern sheets. The Malays curled down between thwarts.

"Well, I'm jiggered!" said the mate, starting up after a long pause. "I was in a devil of a hurry to go and pass the day stuck in the mud. Here's a holiday for you! Well! well!"

They slept or sat unmoving and patient. As the sun mounted higher the breeze died out, and perfect stillness reigned in the empty creek. A troop of long-nosed monkeys appeared, and crowding on the outer boughs, contemplated the boat and the motionless men in it with grave and sorrowful intensity, disturbed now and then by irrational outbreaks of mad gesticulation. A little bird with sapphire breast balanced a slender twig across a slanting beam of light, and flashed in it to and fro like a gem dropped from the sky. His minute round eye stared at the strange and tranquil creatures in the boat. After a while he sent out a thin twitter that sounded impertinent and funny in the solemn silence of the great wilderness; in the great silence full of struggle and death.*

CHAPTER THREE

On Lingard's departure solitude and silence closed
round Willems; the cruel solitude of one abandoned
by men; the reproachful silence which surrounds an
outcast ejected by his kind, the silence unbroken by
the slightest whisper of hope; an immense and impenetrable silence that swallows up without echo the
murmur of regret and the cry of revolt. The bitter
peace of the abandoned clearings entered his heart, in
which nothing could live now but the memory and
hate of his past. Not remorse. In the breast of a
man possessed by the masterful consciousness of his
individuality with its desires and its rights; by the
immovable conviction of his own importance, of an
importance so indisputable and final that it clothes all
his wishes, endeavours, and mistakes with the dignity
of unavoidable fate, there could be no place for such a
feeling as that of remorse.

The days passed. They passed unnoticed, unseen,
in the rapid blaze of glaring sunrises, in the short
glow of tender sunsets, in the crushing oppression
of high noons without a cloud. How many days?
Two—three—or more? He did not know. To
him, since Lingard had gone, the time seemed to
roll on in profound darkness. All was night within
him. All was gone from his sight. He walked
about blindly in the deserted courtyards, amongst the
empty houses that, perched high on their posts, looked
down inimically on him, a white stranger, a man
from other lands; seemed to look hostile and mute

out of all the memories of native life that lingered between their decaying walls. His wandering feet stumbled against the blackened brands of extinct fires, kicking up a light black dust of cold ashes that flew in drifting clouds and settled to leeward on the fresh grass sprouting from the hard ground, between the shade trees. He moved on, and on; ceaseless, unresting, in widening circles, in zigzagging paths that led to no issue; he struggled on wearily with a set, distressed face behind which, in his tired brain, seethed his thoughts: restless, sombre, tangled, chilling, horrible and venomous,* like a nestful of snakes.

From afar, the bleared eyes of the old serving woman, the sombre gaze of Aïssa followed the gaunt and tottering figure in its unceasing prowl along the fences, between the houses, amongst the wild luxuriance of riverside thickets. Those three human beings abandoned* by all were like shipwrecked people left on an insecure and slippery ledge by the retiring tide of an angry sea— listening to its distant roar, living anguished between the menace of its return and the hopeless horror of their solitude—in the midst of a tempest of passion, of regret, of disgust, of despair. The breath of the storm had cast two of them there, robbed of everything— even of resignation. The third, the decrepit witness of their struggle and their torture, accepted her own dull conception of facts; of strength and youth gone; of her useless old age; of her last servitude; of being thrown away by her chief, by her nearest, to use up the last and worthless remnant of flickering life between those two incomprehensible and sombre outcasts: a shrivelled, an unmoved, a passive companion of their disaster.

To the river Willems turned his eyes like a captive that looks fixedly at the door of his cell. If there was any hope in the world it would come from the river, by the river. For hours together he would stand in sunlight while the sea breeze sweeping over the lonely reach fluttered his ragged garments; the keen salt breeze that made him shiver now and then under the flood of intense heat. He looked at the brown and sparkling solitude of the flowing water, of the water flowing ceaseless and free in a soft, cool murmur of ripples at his feet. The world seemed to end there. The forests of the other bank appeared unattainable, enigmatical, for ever beyond reach like the stars of heaven—and as indifferent. Above and below, the forests on his side of the river came down to the water in a serried multitude of tall, immense trees towering in a great spread of twisted boughs above the thick undergrowth; great, solid trees, looking sombre, severe, and malevolently stolid, like a giant crowd of pitiless enemies pressing round silently to witness his slow agony. He was alone, small, crushed. He thought of escape—of something to be done. What? A raft! He imagined himself working at it, feverishly, desperately; cutting down trees, fastening the logs together and then drifting down with the current, down to the sea into the straits. There were ships there—ships, help, white men. Men like himself. Good men who would rescue him, take him away, take him far away where there was trade, and houses, and other men that could understand him exactly, appreciate his capabilities; where there was proper food, and money; where there were beds, knives, forks, carriages, brass bands, cool drinks, churches with well-dressed people praying in them. He would pray also. The superior land of refined delights where he could sit on a chair, eat his tiffin off a white tablecloth, nod to fellows—good fellows; he would be popular; always was—where

he could be virtuous, correct, do business, draw a
salary, smoke cigars, buy things in shops—have boots
. . . be happy, free, become rich. O God! What
was wanted? Cut down a few trees. No! One would
do. They used to make canoes by burning out a tree
trunk, he had heard. Yes! One would do. One tree
to cut down . . . He rushed forward, and suddenly stood still as if rooted in the ground. He had a
pocket-knife.

And he would throw himself down on the ground
by the riverside. He was tired, exhausted; as if that
raft had been made, the voyage accomplished, the
fortune attained. A glaze came over his staring eyes,
over his eyes that gazed hopelessly at the rising river
where big logs and uprooted trees drifted in the shine
of mid-stream: a long procession of black and ragged
specks. He could swim out and drift away on one of
these trees. Anything to escape! Anything! Any
risk! He could fasten himself up between the dead
branches. He was torn by desire, by fear; his heart
was wrung by the faltering of his courage. He turned
over, face downwards, his head on his arms. He had
a terrible vision of shadowless horizons where the blue
sky and the blue sea met; or a circular and blazing
emptiness where a dead tree and a dead man drifted
together, endlessly, up and down, upon the brilliant
undulations of the straits. No ships there. Only
death. And the river led to it.

He sat up with a profound groan.

Yes, death. Why should he die? No! Better
solitude, better hopeless waiting, alone. Alone. No!
he was not alone, he saw death looking at him from
everywhere; from the bushes, from the clouds—he
heard her speaking to him in the murmur of the river,
filling the space, touching his heart, his brain with a

cold hand. He could see and think of nothing else. He saw it—the sure death—everywhere. He saw it so close that he was always on the point of throwing out his arms to keep it off. It poisoned all he saw, all he did; the miserable food he ate, the muddy water he drank; it gave a frightful aspect to sunrises and sunsets,* to the brightness of hot noon, to the cooling shadows of the evenings. He saw the horrible form among the big trees, in the network of creepers in the fantastic outlines of leaves, of the great indented leaves that seemed to be so many enormous hands with big broad palms, with stiff fingers outspread to lay hold of him; hands gently stirring, or hands arrested in a frightful immobility, with a stillness attentive and watching for the opportunity to take him, to enlace him, to strangle him, to hold him till he died; hands that would hold him dead, that would never let go, that would cling to his body for ever till it perished—disappeared in their frantic and tenacious grasp.

And yet the world was full of life. All the things, all the men he knew, existed, moved, breathed; and he saw them in a long perspective, far off, diminished, distinct, desirable, unattainable, precious . . . lost for ever. Round him, ceaselessly, there went on without a sound the mad turmoil of tropical life. After he had died all this would remain! He wanted to clasp, to embrace solid things; he had an immense craving for sensations; for touching, pressing, seeing, handling, holding on, to all these things. All this would remain—remain for years, for ages, for ever. After he had miserably died there, all this would remain, would live, would exist in joyous sunlight, would breathe in the coolness of serene nights. What for, then? He would be dead.* He would be stretched upon the warm moisture of the ground, feeling nothing, seeing nothing, knowing nothing; he would lie stiff, passive, rotting slowly; while over him, under him, through him—unopposed, busy, hurried—the endless and minute throngs of insects, little shining monsters of repulsive shapes, with horns, with claws, with pincers, would swarm in streams, in rushes, in eager struggle for his body; would swarm countless, persistent, ferocious and greedy—till there would remain nothing but the white gleam of bleaching bones in the long grass; in the long grass that would shoot its feathery heads between the bare and polished ribs.* There would be that only left of him; nobody would miss him; no one would remember him.

Nonsense! It could not be. There were ways out of this. Somebody would turn up. Some human beings would come. He would speak, entreat—use force to extort help from them. He felt strong; he was very strong. He would . . . The discouragement, the conviction of the futility of his hopes would return in an acute sensation of pain in his heart. He would begin again his aimless wanderings. He tramped till he was ready to drop, without being able to calm by bodily fatigue the trouble of his soul. There was no rest, no peace within the cleared grounds of his prison. There was no relief but in the black release of sleep, of sleep without memory and without dreams; in the sleep coming brutal and heavy, like the lead that kills. To forget in annihilating sleep; to tumble headlong, as if stunned, out of daylight into the night of oblivion, was for him the only, the rare respite from this existence which he lacked the courage to endure—or to end.

He lived, he struggled with the inarticulate delirium of his thoughts under the eyes of the silent Aïssa.

She shared his torment in the poignant wonder, in the
acute longing, in the despairing inability to understand the cause of his anger and of his repulsion; the
hate of his looks; the mystery of his silence; the menace of his rare words—of those words in the speech
of white people that were thrown at her with rage,
with contempt, with the evident desire to hurt her;
to hurt her who had given herself, her life—all she had
to give—to that white man; to hurt her who had wanted
to show him the way to true greatness, who had tried
to help him, in her woman's dream of everlasting, en-
during, unchangeable affection. From the short contact with the whites in the crashing collapse of her old
life, there remained with her the imposing idea of irresistible power and of ruthless strength. She had
found a man of their race—and with all their qualities.
All whites are alike. But this man's heart was full of
anger against his own people, full of anger existing there
by the side of his desire of her. And to her it had been
an intoxication of hope for great things born in the
proud and tender consciousness of her influence. She
had heard the passing whisper of wonder and fear in the
presence of his hesitation, of his resistance, of his com-
promises; and yet with a woman's belief in the durable
steadfastness of hearts, in the irresistible charm of her
own personality, she had pushed him forward, trusting
the future, blindly, hopefully; sure to attain by his side
the ardent desire of her life, if she could only push him
far beyond the possibility of retreat. She did not know,
and could not conceive, anything of his—so exalted—
ideals. She thought the man a warrior and a chief,
ready for battle, violence, and treachery to his own
people—for her. What more natural? Was he not a
great, strong man? Those two, surrounded each by
the impenetrable wall of their aspirations, were hope-

lessly alone,* out of sight, out of earshot of each other;
each the centre of dissimilar and distant horizons;
standing each on a different earth, under a different
sky. She remembered his words, his eyes, his trembling
lips, his outstretched hands; she remembered the great,
the immeasurable sweetness of her surrender, that
beginning of her power which was to last until death.
He remembered the quaysides and the warehouses;
the excitement of a life in a whirl of silver coins; the
glorious uncertainty of a money hunt; his numerous
successes, the lost possibilities of wealth and consequent
glory. She, a woman, was the victim of her heart,
of her woman's belief that there is nothing in the world
but love—the everlasting thing. He was the victim
of his strange principles, of his continence, of his blind
belief in himself, of his solemn veneration for the voice
of his boundless ignorance.

In a moment of his idleness, of suspense, of discouragement, she had come—that creature—and by
the touch of her hand had destroyed his future, his
dignity of a clever and civilized man; had awakened
in his breast the infamous thing which had driven him
to what he had done, and to end miserably in the
wilderness and be forgotten, or else remembered with
hate or contempt. He dared not look at her, because
now whenever he looked at her his thought seemed to
touch crime, like an outstretched hand. She could
only look at him—and at nothing else. What else
was there? She followed him with a timorous gaze,
with a gaze for ever expecting, patient, and entreating.
And in her eyes there was the wonder and desolation
of an animal that knows only suffering, of the incomplete soul that knows pain but knows not hope; that
can find no refuge from the facts of life in the illusory
conviction of its dignity, of an exalted destiny beyond;

in the heavenly consolation of a belief in the momentous origin of its hate.

For the first three days after Lingard went away he would not even speak to her. She preferred his silence to the sound of hated and incomprehensible words he had been lately addressing to her with a wild violence of manner, passing at once into complete apathy. And during these three days he hardly ever left the river, as if on that muddy bank he had felt himself nearer to his freedom. He would stay late; he would stay till sunset; he would look at the glow of gold passing away amongst sombre clouds in a bright red flush, like a splash of warm blood. It seemed to him ominous and ghastly with a foreboding of violent death that beckoned him from everywhere —even from the sky.

One evening he remained by the riverside long after sunset, regardless of the night mist that had closed round him, had wrapped him up and clung to him like a wet winding-sheet. A slight shiver recalled him to his senses, and he walked up the courtyard towards his house. Aïssa rose from before the fire, that glimmered red through its own smoke, which hung thickening under the boughs of the big tree. She approached him from the side as he neared the plankway of the house. He saw her stop to let him begin his ascent. In the darkness her figure was like the shadow of a woman with clasped hands put out beseechingly. He stopped—could not help glancing at her. In all the sombre gracefulness of the straight figure, her limbs, features—all was indistinct and vague but the gleam of her eyes in the faint starlight. He turned his head away and moved on. He could feel her footsteps behind him on the bending planks, but he walked up without turning his head. He knew what she

wanted. She wanted to come in there. He shuddered
at the thought of what might happen in the impenetrable darkness of that house if they were to find themselves alone—even for a moment. He stopped in the
doorway, and heard her say—

"Let me come in. Why this anger? Why this
silence? . . . Let me watch . . . by your side.
. . . Have I not watched faithfully? Did harm
ever come to you when you closed your eyes while I
was by? . . . I have waited . . . I have
waited for your smile, for your words . . . I can
wait no more. . . . Look at me . . . speak to
me. Is there a bad spirit in you? A bad spirit that
has eaten up your courage and your love? Let me
touch you. Forget all . . . All. Forget the
wicked hearts, the angry faces . . . and remember
only the day I came to you . . . to you! O my
heart! O my life!"

The pleading sadness of her appeal filled the space
with the tremor of her low tones, that carried tenderness
and tears into the great peace of the sleeping world.
All around them the forests, the clearings, the river,
covered by the silent veil of night, seemed to wake up
and listen to her words in attentive stillness. After
the sound of her voice had died out in a stifled sigh they
appeared to listen yet; and nothing stirred among the
shapeless shadows but the innumerable fireflies that
twinkled in changing clusters, in gliding pairs, in wandering and solitary points—like the glimmering drift
of scattered star-dust.

Willems turned round slowly, reluctantly, as if compelled by main force. Her face was hidden in her
hands, and he looked above her bent head, into the
sombre brilliance of the night. It was one of those
nights that give the impression of extreme vastness,

when the sky seems higher, when the passing puffs of
tepid breeze seem to bring with them faint whispers
from beyond the stars.* The air was full of sweet
scent, of the scent charming, penetrating, and violent
like the impulse of love. He looked into that great
dark place odorous with the breath of life, with the
mystery of existence, renewed, fecund, indestructible;
and he felt afraid of his solitude, of the solitude of his
body, of the loneliness of his soul in the presence of
this unconscious and ardent struggle, of this lofty
indifference, of this merciless and mysterious purpose,
perpetuating strife and death through the march of
ages. For the second time in his life he felt, in a
sudden sense of his significance, the need to send a
cry for help into the wilderness, and for the second
time he realized the hopelessness of its unconcern.
He could shout for help on every side—and nobody
would answer. He could stretch out his hands, he
could call for aid, for support, for sympathy, for relief
—and nobody would come.* Nobody. There was no
one there—but that woman.

His heart was moved, softened with pity at his own
abandonment. His anger against her, against her
who was the cause of all his misfortunes, vanished
before his extreme need for some kind of consolation.
Perhaps—if he must resign himself to his fate—she
might help him to forget. To forget! For a moment,
in an access of despair so profound that it seemed
like the beginning of peace, he planned the deliberate
descent from his pedestal, the throwing away of his
superiority, of all his hopes, of old ambitions, of the
ungrateful civilization. For a moment, forgetfulness
in her arms seemed possible; and lured by that possibility the semblance of renewed desire possessed
his breast in a burst of reckless contempt for every-

thing outside himself—in a savage disdain of Earth
and of Heaven. He said to himself that he would
not repent. The punishment for his only sin was too
heavy. There was no mercy under Heaven. He did
not want any. He thought, desperately, that if he
could find with her again the madness of the past,
the strange delirium that had changed him, that had
worked his undoing, he would be ready to pay for it
with an eternity of perdition. He was intoxicated
by the subtle perfumes of the night; he was carried
away by the suggestive stir of the warm breeze; he
was possessed by the exaltation of the solitude, of
the silence, of his memories, in the presence of that
figure offering herself in a submissive and patient devotion; coming to him in the name of the
past, in the name of those days when he could see
nothing, think of nothing, desire nothing—but her
embrace.

He took her suddenly in his arms, and she clasped
her hands round his neck with a low cry of joy and
surprise. He took her in his arms and waited for the
transport, for the madness, for the sensations remembered and lost; and while she sobbed gently on his
breast he held her and felt cold, sick, tired, exasperated
with his failure—and ended by cursing himself. She
clung to him trembling with the intensity of her happiness and her love. He heard her whispering—her
face hidden on his shoulder—of past sorrow, of coming
joy that would last for ever; of her unshaken belief
in his love. She had always believed. Always! Even
while his face was turned away from her in the dark
days while his mind was wandering in his own land,
amongst his own people. But it would never wander
away from her any more, now it had come back. He
would forget the cold faces and the hard hearts of the

cruel people. What was there to remember? Nothing?
Was it not so? . . .

He listened hopelessly to the faint murmur. He
stood still and rigid, pressing her mechanically to his
breast while he thought that there was nothing for
him in the world. He was robbed of everything;
robbed of his passion, of his liberty, of forgetfulness,
of consolation. She, wild with delight, whispered on
rapidly, of love, of light, of peace, of long years. . . .
He looked drearily above her head down into the
deeper gloom of the courtyard. And, all at once, it
seemed to him that he was peering into a sombre
hollow, into a deep black hole full of decay and of
whitened bones; into an immense and inevitable
grave full of corruption where sooner or later he must,
unavoidably, fall.*

In the morning he came out early, and stood for a
time in the doorway, listening to the light breathing
behind him—in the house. She slept. He had not
closed his eyes through all that night. He stood
swaying—then leaned against the lintel* of the door.
He was exhausted, done up; fancied himself hardly
alive. He had a disgusted horror of himself that, as
he looked at the level sea of mist at his feet, faded
quickly into dull indifference. It was like a sudden
and final decrepitude of his senses, of his body, of his
thoughts. Standing on the high platform, he looked
over the expanse of low night fog above which, here
and there, stood out the feathery heads of tall bamboo
clumps and the round tops of single trees, resembling
small islets emerging black and solid from a ghostly
and impalpable sea. Upon the faintly luminous background of the eastern sky, the sombre line of the great
forests bounded that smooth sea of white vapours with
an appearance of a fantastic and unattainable shore.

He looked without seeing anything—thinking of himself. Before his eyes the light of the rising sun burst above the forest with the suddenness of an explosion. He saw nothing. Then, after a time, he murmured with conviction—speaking half aloud to himself in the shock of the penetrating thought:

"I am a lost man."*

He shook his hand above his head in a gesture careless and tragic, then walked down into the mist that closed above him in shining undulations under the first breath of the morning breeze.

CHAPTER FOUR

Willems moved languidly towards the river, then retraced his steps to the tree and let himself fall on the seat under its shade. On the other side of the immense trunk he could hear the old woman moving about, sighing loudly, muttering to herself, snapping dry sticks, blowing up the fire. After a while a whiff of smoke drifted round to where he sat. It made him feel hungry, and that feeling was like a new indignity added to an intolerable load of humiliations. He felt inclined to cry. He felt very weak. He held up his arm before his eyes and watched for a little while the trembling of the lean limb. Skin and bone, by God! How thin he was! . . . He had suffered from fever a good deal, and now he thought with tearful dismay that Lingard, although he had sent him food—and what food, great Lord: a little rice and dried fish; quite unfit for a white man—had not sent him any medicine. Did the old savage think that he was like the wild beasts that are never ill? He wanted quinine.*

He leaned the back of his head against the tree and closed his eyes. He thought feebly that if he could get hold of Lingard he would like to flay him alive; but it was only a blurred, a short and a passing thought. His imagination, exhausted by the repeated delineations of his own fate, had not enough strength left to grip the idea of revenge. He was not indignant and rebellious. He was cowed. He was cowed by the immense cataclysm of his disaster. Like most men, he had carried solemnly within his breast the whole universe, and the approaching end of all things in the destruction of his own personality filled him with paralyzing awe. Everything was toppling over. He blinked his eyes quickly, and it seemed to him that the very sunshine of the morning disclosed in its brightness a suggestion of some hidden and sinister meaning. In his unreasoning fear he tried to hide within himself. He drew his feet up, his head sank between his shoulders, his arms hugged his sides. Under the high and enormous tree soaring superbly out of the mist in a vigorous spread of lofty boughs, with a restless and eager flutter of its innumerable leaves in the clear sunshine, he remained motionless, huddled up on his seat: terrified and still.

Willems' gaze roamed over the ground, and then he watched with idiotic fixity half a dozen black ants entering courageously a tuft of long grass which, to them, must have appeared a dark and a dangerous jungle. Suddenly he thought: There must be something dead in there. Some dead insect. Death everywhere! He closed his eyes again in an access of trembling pain. Death everywhere—wherever one looks. He did not want to see the ants. He did not want to see anybody or anything. He sat in the darkness of his own making, reflecting bitterly that there was no peace for him. He heard voices now. . . . Illusion! Misery! Torment! Who would come? Who would speak to him? What business had he to hear voices? . . . yet he heard them faintly, from the river. Faintly, as if shouted far off over there, came the words "We come back soon." . . . Delirium and mockery! Who would come back? Nobody ever comes back! Fever comes back. He had it on him this morning. That was it. . . . He heard unexpectedly the old woman muttering something near by. She had come round to his side of the tree. He opened his eyes and saw her bent back before him. She stood, with her hand shading her eyes, looking towards the landing-place. Then she glided away. She had seen —and now she was going back to her cooking; a woman incurious; expecting nothing; without fear and without hope.

She had gone back behind the tree, and now Willems could see a human figure on the path to the landing-place. It appeared to him to be a woman, in a red gown, holding some heavy bundle in her arms; it was an apparition unexpected, familiar and odd. He cursed through his teeth . . . It had wanted only this! See things like that in broad daylight! He was very bad—very bad. . . . He was horribly scared at this awful symptom of the desperate state of his health.

This scare lasted for the space of a flash of lightning, and in the next moment it was revealed to him that the woman was real; that she was coming towards him; that she was his wife! He put his feet down to the ground quickly, but made no other movement. His eyes opened wide. He was so amazed that for a time he absolutely forgot his own existence.' The only idea in his head was: Why on earth did she come here?

Joanna was coming up the courtyard with eager, hurried steps. She carried in her arms the child, wrapped up in one of Almayer's white blankets that she had snatched off the bed at the last moment, before leaving the house. She seemed to be dazed by the sun in her eyes; bewildered by her strange surroundings. She moved on, looking quickly right and left in impatient expectation of seeing her husband at any moment. Then, approaching the tree, she perceived suddenly a kind of a dried-up, yellow corpse, sitting very stiff on a bench in the shade and looking at her with big eyes that were alive. That was her husband.

She stopped dead short. They stared at one another in profound stillness, with astounded eyes, with eyes maddened by the memories of things far off that seemed lost in the lapse of time. Their looks crossed, passed each other, and appeared to dart at them through fantastic distances, to come straight from the Incredible.

Looking at him steadily she came nearer, and deposited the blanket with the child in it on the bench. Little Louis, after howling with terror in the darkness of the river most of the night, now slept soundly and did not wake. Willems' eyes followed his wife, his head turning slowly after her. He accepted her presence there with a tired acquiescence in its fabulous improbability. Anything might happen. What did she come for? She was part of the general scheme of his misfortune. He half expected that she would rush at him, pull his hair, and scratch his face. Why not? Anything might happen! In an exaggerated sense of his great bodily weakness he felt somewhat apprehensive of possible assault. At any rate, she would scream at him. He knew her of old. She could screech. He had thought that he was rid of her for ever. She came now probably to see the end. . . .

Suddenly she turned, and embracing him slid gently to the ground. This startled him. With her forehead on his knees she sobbed noiselessly. He looked down dismally at the top of her head. What was she up to? He had not the strength to move—to get away. He heard her whispering something, and bent over to listen. He caught the word "Forgive."

That was what she came for! All that way. Women are queer. Forgive. Not he! . . . All at once this thought darted through his brain: How did she come? In a boat. Boat! boat!

He shouted "Boat!" and jumped up, knocking her over. Before she had time to pick herself up he pounced upon her and was dragging her up by the shoulders. No sooner had she regained her feet than she clasped him tightly round the neck, covering his face, his eyes, his mouth, his nose with desperate kisses. He dodged his head about, shaking her arms, trying to keep her off, to speak, to ask her. . . . She came in a boat, boat, boat! . . . They struggled and swung round, tramping in a semicircle. He blurted out, "Leave off. Listen," while he tore at her hands. This meeting of lawful love and sincere joy resembled fight. Louis Willems slept peacefully under his blanket.

At last Willems managed to free himself, and held her off, pressing her arms down. He looked at her. He had half a suspicion that he was dreaming. Her lips trembled; her eyes wandered unsteadily, always coming back to his face. He saw her the same as ever, in his presence. She appeared startled, tremulous, ready to cry. She did not inspire him with confidence. He shouted—

"How did you come?"

She answered in hurried words, looking at him intently—

"In a big canoe with three men. I know everything. Lingard's away. I come to save you. I know. . . . Almayer told me."

"Canoe!—Almayer—Lies. Told you—You!" stammered Willems in a distracted manner. "Why you?— Told what?"

Words failed him. He stared at his wife, thinking with fear that she—stupid woman—had been made a tool in some plan of treachery . . . in some deadly plot.

She began to cry—

"Don't look at me like that, Peter. What have I done? I come to beg—to beg—forgiveness. . . . Save—Lingard—danger."

He trembled with impatience, with hope, with fear. She looked at him and sobbed out in a fresh outburst of grief—

"Oh! Peter. What's the matter?—Are you ill? . . . Oh! you look so ill . . ."

He shook her violently into a terrified and wondering silence.

"How dare you!—I am well—perfectly well. . . . Where's that boat? Will you tell me where that boat is—at last? The boat, I say . . . You! . . ."

"You hurt me," she moaned.

He let her go, and, mastering her terror, she stood quivering and looking at him with strange intensity. Then she made a movement forward, but he lifted his finger, and she restrained herself with a long sigh. He calmed down suddenly and surveyed her with cold criticism, with the same appearance as when, in the old days, he used to find fault with the household expenses. She found a kind of fearful delight in this abrupt return into the past, into her old subjection.

He stood outwardly collected now, and listened to her disconnected story. Her words seemed to fall round him with the distracting clatter of stunning hail. He caught the meaning here and there, and straightway would lose himself in a tremendous effort to shape out some intelligible theory of events. There was a boat. A boat. A big boat that could take him to sea if necessary. That much was clear. She brought it. Why did Almayer lie to her so? Was it a plan to decoy him into some ambush? Better that than hopeless solitude. She had money. The men were ready to go anywhere . . . she said.

He interrupted her—

"Where are they now?"

"They are coming directly," she answered, tearfully. "Directly. There are some fishing stakes near here —they said. They are coming directly."

Again she was talking and sobbing together. She wanted to be forgiven. Forgiven? What for? Ah! the scene in Macassar. As if he had time to think of that! What did he care what she had done months ago? He seemed to struggle in the toils of complicated dreams where everything was impossible, yet a matter of course, where the past took the aspects of the future and the present lay heavy on his heart— seemed to take him by the throat like the hand of an enemy. And while she begged, entreated, kissed his hands, wept on his shoulder, adjured him in the name of God, to forgive, to forget, to speak the word for which she longed, to look at his boy, to believe in her sorrow and in her devotion—his eyes, in the fascinated immobility of shining pupils, looked far away, far beyond her, beyond the river, beyond this land, through days, weeks, months; looked into liberty, into the future, into his triumph . . . into the great possibility of a startling revenge.

He felt a sudden desire to dance and shout. He shouted—

"After all, we shall meet again, Captain Lingard."

"Oh, no! No!" she cried, joining her hands.

He looked at her with surprise. He had forgotten she was there till the break of her cry in the monotonous tones of her prayer recalled him into that courtyard from the glorious turmoil of his dreams. It was very strange to see her there—near him. He

felt almost affectionate towards her. After all, she
came just in time. Then he thought: That other one.
I must get away without a scene. Who knows; she
may be dangerous! . . . And all at once he felt
he hated Aïssa with an immense hatred that seemed to
choke him. He said to his wife—

"Wait a moment."

She, obedient, seemed to gulp down some words
which wanted to come out. He muttered: "Stay here,"
and disappeared round the tree.

The water in the iron pan on the cooking fire boiled
furiously, belching out volumes of white steam that
mixed with the thin black thread of smoke. The old
woman appeared to him through this as if in a fog,
squatting on her heels, impassive and weird.

Willems came up near and asked, "Where is she?"

The woman did not even lift her head, but answered
at once, readily, as though she had expected the question for a long time.

"While you were asleep under the tree, before the
strange canoe came, she went out of the house. I saw
her look at you and pass on with a great light in her
eyes. A great light. And she went towards the place
where our master Lakamba had his fruit trees. When
we were many here. Many, many. Men with arms
by their side. Many . . . men. And talk . . .
and songs . . ."

She went on like that, raving gently to herself for
a long time after Willems had left her.

Willems went back to his wife. He came up close
to her and found he had nothing to say. Now all his
faculties were concentrated upon his wish to avoid
Aïssa. She might stay all the morning in that grove.
Why did those rascally boatmen go? He had a physical
repugnance to set eyes on her. And somewhere, at

the very bottom of his heart, there was a fear of her.
Why? What could she do? Nothing on earth could
stop him now. He felt strong, reckless, pitiless, and
superior to everything. He wanted to preserve before
his wife the lofty purity of his character. He thought:
She does not know. Almayer held his tongue about
Aïssa. But if she finds out, I am lost. If it hadn't
been for the boy I would . . . free of both of
them. . . . The idea darted through his head.
Not he! Married. . . . Swore solemnly. No
. . . sacred tie. . . . Looking on his wife, he
felt for the first time in his life something approaching
remorse. Remorse, arising from his conception of the
awful nature of an oath before the altar. . . . She
mustn't find out. . . . Oh, for that boat! He
must run in and get his revolver. Couldn't think of
trusting himself unarmed with those Bajow fellows.
Get it now while she is away. Oh, for that boat! . . .
He dared not go to the river and hail. He thought:
She might hear me. . . . I'll go and get . . .
cartridges . . . then will be all ready . . .
nothing else. No.

And while he stood meditating profoundly before
he could make up his mind to run to the house, Joanna
pleaded, holding to his arm—pleaded despairingly,
broken-hearted, hopeless whenever she glanced up at
his face, which to her seemed to wear the aspect of
unforgiving rectitude, of virtuous severity, of merciless
justice. And she pleaded humbly—abashed before
him, before the unmoved appearance of the man she
had wronged in defiance of human and divine laws.
He heard not a word of what she said till she raised her
voice in a final appeal—

". . . Don't you see I loved you always? They
told me horrible things about you. . . . My own

mother! They told me—you have been—you have been unfaithful to me, and I . . ."

"It's a damned lie!" shouted Willems, waking up for a moment into righteous indignation.

"I know! I know—Be generous.—Think of my misery since you went away—Oh! I could have torn my tongue out. . . . I will never believe anybody—Look at the boy—Be merciful—I could never rest till I found you. . . . Say—a word—one word. . ."

"What the devil do you want?" exclaimed Willems, looking towards the river. "Where's that damned boat? Why did you let them go away? You stupid!"

"Oh, Peter!—I know that in your heart you have forgiven me—You are so generous—I want to hear you say so. . . . Tell me—do you?"

"Yes! yes!" said Willems, impatiently. "I forgive you. Don't be a fool."

"Don't go away. Don't leave me alone here. Where is the danger? I am so frightened. . . . Are you alone here? Sure? . . . Let us go away!"

"That's sense," said Willems, still looking anxiously towards the river.

She sobbed gently, leaning on his arm.

"Let me go," he said.

He had seen above the steep bank the heads of three men glide along smoothly. Then, where the shore shelved down to the landing-place, appeared a big canoe which came slowly to land.

"Here they are," he went on, briskly. "I must get my revolver."

He made a few hurried paces towards the house, but seemed to catch sight of something, turned short round and came back to his wife. She stared at him, alarmed by the sudden change in his face. He ap-

peared much discomposed. He stammered a little as
he began to speak.

"Take the child. Walk down to the boat and tell
them to drop it out of sight, quick, behind the bushes.
Do you hear? Quick! I will come to you there
directly. Hurry up!"

"Peter! What is it? I won't leave you. There is
some danger in this horrible place."

"Will you do what I tell you?" said Willems, in an
irritable whisper.

"No! no! no! I won't leave you. I will not lose
you again. Tell me, what is it?"

From beyond the house came a faint voice singing.
Willems shook his wife by the shoulder.

"Do what I tell you! Run at once!"

She gripped his arm and clung to him desperately.
He looked up to heaven as if taking it to witness of
that woman's infernal folly. The song grew louder,
then ceased suddenly, and Aïssa appeared in sight,
walking slowly, her hands full of flowers.

She had turned the corner of the house, coming
out into the full sunshine, and the light seemed to
leap upon her in a stream brilliant, tender, and caress-
ing, as if attracted by the radiant happiness of her face.
She had dressed herself for a festive day, for the memor-
able day of his return to her, of his return to an affection that would last for ever. The rays of the morning
sun were caught by the oval clasp of the embroidered
belt that held the silk sarong round her waist. The
dazzling white stuff of her body jacket was crossed
by a bar of yellow and silver of her scarf, and in the
black hair twisted high on her small head shone the
round balls of gold pins amongst crimson blossoms and
white star-shaped flowers,* with which she had crowned
herself to charm his eyes; those eyes that were hence-

forth to see nothing in the world but her own resplendent image. And she moved slowly, bending her face over the mass of pure white champakas and jasmine pressed to her breast, in a dreamy intoxication of sweet scents and of sweeter hopes.

She did not seem to see anything, stopped for a moment at the foot of the plankway leading to the house, then, leaving her high-heeled wooden sandals there, ascended the planks in a light run; straight, graceful, flexible, and noiseless, as if she had soared up to the door on invisible wings. Willems pushed his wife roughly behind the tree, and made up his mind quickly for a rush to the house, to grab his revolver and . . . Thoughts, doubts, expedients seemed to boil in his brain. He had a flashing vision of delivering a stunning blow, of tying up that flower bedecked woman in the dark house—a vision of things done swiftly with enraged haste—to save his prestige, his superiority—something of immense importance. . . . He had not made two steps when Joanna bounded after him, caught the back of his ragged jacket, tore out a big piece, and instantly hooked herself with both hands to the collar, nearly dragging him down on his back. Although taken by surprise, he managed to keep his feet. From behind she panted into his ear—

"That woman! Who's that woman? Ah! that's what those boatmen were talking about. I heard them . . . heard them . . . heard . . . in the night. They spoke about some woman. I dared not understand. I would not ask . . . listen . . . believe! How could I? Then it's true. No. Say no. . . . Who's that woman?"

He swayed, tugging forward. She jerked at him till the button gave way, and then he slipped half out of his jacket and, turning round, remained strangely motionless. His heart seemed to beat in his throat. He choked—tried to speak—could not find any words. He thought with fury: I will kill both of them.

For a second nothing moved about the courtyard in the great vivid clearness of the day. Only down by the landing-place a waringan-tree, all in a blaze of clustering red berries, seemed alive with the stir of little birds that filled with the feverish flutter of their feathers the tangle of overloaded branches. Suddenly the variegated flock rose spinning in a soft whirr and dispersed, slashing the sunlit haze with the sharp outlines of stiffened wings. Mahmat and one of his brothers appeared coming up from the landing-place, their lances in their hands, to look for their passengers.

Aïssa coming now empty-handed out of the house, caught sight of the two armed men. In her surprise she emitted a faint cry, vanished back and in a flash reappeared in the doorway with Willems' revolver in her hand. To her the presence of any man there could only have an ominous meaning. There was nothing in the outer world but enemies. She and the man she loved were alone, with nothing round them but menacing dangers. She did not mind that, for if death came, no matter from what hand, they would die together.

Her resolute eyes took in the courtyard in a circular glance. She noticed that the two strangers had ceased to advance and now were standing close together leaning on the polished shafts of their weapons. The next moment she saw Willems, with his back towards her, apparently struggling under the tree with some one. She saw nothing distinctly, and, unhesitating, flew down the plankway calling out: "I come!"

He heard her cry, and with an unexpected rush

drove his wife backwards to the seat. She fell on it; he jerked himself altogether out of his jacket, and she covered her face with the soiled rags. He put his lips close to her, asking—

"For the last time, will you take the child and go?"

She groaned behind the unclean ruins of his upper garment. She mumbled something. He bent lower to hear. She was saying—

"I won't. Order that woman away. I can't look at her!"

"You fool!"

He seemed to spit the words at her, then, making up his mind, spun round to face Aïssa. She was coming towards them slowly now, with a look of unbounded amazement on her face. Then she stopped and stared at him—who stood there, stripped to the waist, bareheaded and sombre.

Some way off, Mahmat and his brother exchanged rapid words in calm undertones. . . . This was the strong daughter of the holy man who had died. The white man is very tall. There would be three women and the child to take in the boat, besides that white man who had the money. . . . The brother went away back to the boat, and Mahmat remained looking on. He stood like a sentinel, the leaf-shaped blade of his lance glinting above his head.

Willems spoke suddenly.

"Give me this," he said, stretching his hand towards the revolver.

Aïssa stepped back. Her lips trembled. She said very low: "Your people?"

He nodded slightly. She shook her head thoughtfully, and a few delicate petals of the flowers dying in her hair fell like big drops of crimson and white at her feet.

"Did you know?" she whispered.

"No!" said Willems.   "They sent for me."

"Tell them to depart.   They are accursed.   What is there between them and you—and you who carry my life in your heart!"

Willems said nothing.   He stood before her looking down on the ground and repeating to himself: I must get that revolver away from her, at once, at once. I can't think of trusting myself with those men without firearms.   I must have it.

She asked, after gazing in silence at Joanna, who was sobbing gently—

"Who is she?"

"My wife," answered Willems, without looking up. "My wife according to our white law, which comes from God!"

"Your law!   Your God!" murmured Aïssa, contemptuously.

"Give me this revolver," said Willems, in a peremptory tone.   He felt an unwillingness to close with her, to get it by force.

She took no notice and went on—

"Your law . . . or your lies?   What am I to believe?   I came—I ran to defend you when I saw the strange men.   You lied to me with your lips, with your eyes.   You crooked heart! . . . Ah!" she added, after an abrupt pause.   "She is the first!   Am I then to be a slave?"

"You may be what you like," said Willems, brutally. "I am going."

Her gaze was fastened on the blanket under which she had detected a slight movement.   She made a long stride towards it.   Willems turned half round.   His legs seemed to him to be made of lead.   He felt faint and so weak that, for a moment, the fear of dying there where he stood, before he could escape from sin and disaster, passed through his mind in a wave of despair.

She lifted up one corner of the blanket, and when she saw the sleeping child a sudden quick shudder shook her as though she had seen something inexpressibly horrible. She looked at Louis Willems with eyes fixed in an unbelieving and terrified stare. Then her fingers opened slowly, and a shadow seemed to settle on her face as if something obscure and fatal had come between her and the sunshine. She stood looking down, absorbed, as though she had watched at the bottom of a gloomy abyss the mournful procession of her thoughts.

Willems did not move. All his faculties were concentrated upon the idea of his release. And it was only then that the assurance of it came to him with such force that he seemed to hear a loud voice shouting in the heavens that all was over, that in another five, ten minutes, he would step into another existence; that all this, the woman, the madness, the sin, the regrets, all would go, rush into the past, disappear, become as dust, as smoke, as drifting clouds—as nothing! Yes! All would vanish in the unappeasable past which would swallow up all—even the very memory of his temptation and of his downfall. Nothing mattered. He cared for nothing. He had forgotten Aïssa, his wife, Lingard, Hudig—everybody, in the rapid vision of his hopeful future.

After a while he heard Aïssa saying—

"A child! A child! What have I done to be made to devour this sorrow and this grief? And while your man-child and the mother lived you told me there was nothing for you to remember in the land from which you came! And I thought you could be mine. I thought that I would . . ."

Her voice ceased in a broken murmur, and with it, in her heart, seemed to die the greater and most precious hope of her new life. She had hoped that in the future the frail arms of a child would bind their two lives together in a bond which nothing on earth could break, a bond of affection, of gratitude, of tender respect. She the first—the only one! But in the instant she saw the son of that other woman she felt herself removed into the cold, the darkness, the silence of a solitude impenetrable and immense—very far from him, beyond the possibility of any hope, into an infinity of wrongs without any redress.

She strode nearer to Joanna. She felt towards that woman anger, envy, jealousy. Before her she felt humiliated and enraged. She seized the hanging sleeve of the jacket in which Joanna was hiding her face and tore it out of her hands, exclaiming loudly—

"Let me see the face of her before whom I am only a servant and a slave. Ya—wa! I see you!"

Her unexpected shout seemed to fill the sunlit space of cleared grounds, rise high and run on far into the land over the unstirring tree-tops of the forests. She stood in sudden stillness, looking at Joanna with surprised contempt.

"A Sirani woman!" she said, slowly, in a tone of wonder.

Joanna rushed at Willems—clung to him, shrieking: "Defend me, Peter! Defend me from that woman!"

"Be quiet. There is no danger," muttered Willems, thickly.

Aïssa looked at them with scorn. "God is great! I sit in the dust at your feet," she exclaimed jeeringly, joining her hands above her head in a gesture of mock humility. "Before you I am as nothing." She turned to Willems fiercely, opening her arms wide. "What have you made of me?" she cried, "you lying child of an accursed mother! What have you made of me? The slave of a slave. Don't speak! Your words are worse than the poison of snakes. A Sirani woman. A woman of a people despised by all."

She pointed her finger at Joanna, stepped back, and began to laugh.

"Make her stop, Peter!" screamed Joanna. "That heathen woman. Heathen! Heathen! Beat her, Peter."

Willems caught sight of the revolver which Aïssa had laid on the seat near the child. He spoke in Dutch to his wife, without moving his head.

"Snatch the boy—and my revolver there. See. Run to the boat. I will keep her back. Now's the time."

Aïssa came nearer. She stared at Joanna, while between the short gusts of broken laughter she raved, fumbling distractedly at the buckle of her belt.

"To her! To her—the mother of him who will speak of your wisdom, of your courage. All to her. I have nothing. Nothing. Take, take."

She tore the belt off and threw it at Joanna's feet. She flung down with haste the armlets, the gold pins, the flowers; and the long hair, released, fell scattered over her shoulders, framing in its blackness the wild exaltation of her face.

"Drive her off, Peter. Drive off the heathen savage," persisted Joanna. She seemed to have lost her head altogether. She stamped, clinging to Willems' arm with both her hands.

"Look," cried Aïssa. "Look at the mother of your son! She is afraid. Why does she not go from before my face? Look at her. She is ugly."

Joanna seemed to understand the scornful tone of the words. As Aïssa stepped back again nearer to the tree she let go her husband's arm, rushed at her madly, slapped her face, then, swerving round, darted at the child who, unnoticed, had been wailing for some time, and, snatching him up, flew down to the waterside, sending shriek after shriek in an access of insane terror.

Willems made for the revolver. Aïssa passed swiftly, giving him an unexpected push that sent him staggering away from the tree. She caught up the weapon, put it behind her back, and cried—

"You shall not have it. Go after her. Go to meet danger. . . . Go to meet death. . . . Go unarmed. . . . Go with empty hands and sweet words . . . as you came to me. . . . Go helpless and lie to the forests, to the sea . . . to the death that waits for you. . . ."

She ceased as if strangled. She saw in the horror of the passing seconds the half-naked, wild-looking man before her; she heard the faint shrillness of Joanna's insane shrieks for help somewhere down by the riverside. The sunlight streamed on her, on him, on the mute land, on the murmuring river—the gentle brilliance of a serene morning that, to her, seemed traversed by ghastly flashes of uncertain darkness. Hate filled the world, filled the space between them —the hate of race, the hate of hopeless diversity, the hate of blood; the hate against the man born in the land of lies and of evil from which nothing but misfortune comes to those who are not white. And as she stood, maddened, she heard a whisper near her, the whisper of the dead Omar's voice saying in her ear: "Kill! Kill!"

She cried, seeing him move—

"Do not come near me . . . or you die now!
Go while I remember yet . . . remember. . . ."
Willems pulled himself together for a struggle. He
dared not go unarmed. He made a long stride, and
saw her raise the revolver. He noticed that she had
not cocked it, and said to himself that, even if she did
fire, she would surely miss. Go too high; it was a
stiff trigger. He made a step nearer—saw the long
barrel moving unsteadily at the end of her extended
arm. He thought: This is my time . . . He bent
his knees slightly, throwing his body forward, and took
off with a long bound for a tearing rush.

He saw a burst of red flame before his eyes, and
was deafened by a report that seemed to him louder
than a clap of thunder. Something stopped him
short, and he stood aspiring* in his nostrils the acrid
smell of the blue smoke that drifted from before his
eyes like an immense cloud. . . . Missed, by
Heaven! . . . Thought so! . . . And he saw
her very far off, throwing her arms up, while the revolver, very small, lay on the ground between them.
. . . Missed! . . . He would go and pick it
up now. Never before did he understand, as in that
second, the joy, the triumphant delight of sunshine and
of life. His mouth was full of something salt and warm.
He tried to cough; spat out. . . . Who shrieks:
In the name of God, he dies!—he dies!—Who dies?—
Must pick up—Night!—What? . . . Night already. . . .

* * * * *

Many years afterwards Almayer was telling the
story of the great revolution in Sambir to a chance
visitor from Europe. He was a Roumanian,* half

naturalist, half orchid-hunter for commercial purposes, who used to declare to everybody, in the first five minutes of acquaintance, his intention of writing a scientific book about tropical countries. On his way to the interior he had quartered himself upon Almayer. He was a man of some education, but he drank his gin neat, or only, at most, would squeeze the juice of half a small lime into the raw spirit. He said it was good for his health, and, with that medicine before him, he would describe to the surprised Almayer the wonders of European capitals; while Almayer, in exchange, bored him by expounding, with gusto, his unfavourable opinions of Sambir's social and political life. They talked far into the night, across the deal table on the verandah, while, between them, clearwinged, small, and flabby insects, dissatisfied with moonlight, streamed in and perished in thousands round the smoky light of the evil-smelling lamp.

Almayer, his face flushed, was saying—

"Of course, I did not see that. I told you I was stuck in the creek on account of father's—Captain Lingard's—susceptible temper. I am sure I did it all for the best in trying to facilitate the fellow's escape; but Captain Lingard was that kind of man—you know —one couldn't argue with. Just before sunset the water was high enough, and we got out of the creek. We got to Lakamba's clearing about dark. All very quiet; I thought they were gone, of course, and felt very glad. We walked up the courtyard—saw a big heap of something lying in the middle. Out of that she rose and rushed at us. By God. . . . You know those stories of faithful dogs watching their masters' corpses . . . don't let anybody approach . . . got to beat them off—and all that. . . . Well, 'pon my word we had to beat her off. Had to!

She was like a fury. Wouldn't let us touch him. Dead—of course. Should think so. Shot through the lung, on the left side, rather high up, and at pretty close quarters too, for the two holes were small. Bullet came out through the shoulder-blade. After we had overpowered her—you can't imagine how strong that woman was; it took three of us—we got the body into the boat and shoved off. We thought she had fainted then, but she got up and rushed into the water after us. Well, I let her clamber in. What could I do? The river's full of alligators. I will never forget that pull up-stream in the night as long as I live. She sat in the bottom of the boat, holding his head in her lap, and now and again wiping his face with her hair. There was a lot of blood dried about his mouth and chin. And for all the six hours of that journey she kept on whispering tenderly to that corpse! . . . I had the mate of the schooner with me. The man said afterwards that he wouldn't go through it again—not for a handful of diamonds. And I believed him—I did. It makes me shiver. Do you think he heard? No! I mean somebody—something—heard? . . ."

"I am a materialist," declared the man of science, tilting the bottle shakily over the emptied glass.

Almayer shook his head and went on—

"Nobody saw how it really happened but that man Mahmat. He always said that he was no further off from them than two lengths of his lance. It appears the two women rowed each other while that Willems stood between them. Then Mahmat says that when Joanna struck her and ran off, the other two seemed to become suddenly mad together. They rushed here and there. Mahmat says—those were his very words: 'I saw her standing holding the pistol that fires many times and pointing it all over the campong. I was

afraid—lest she might shoot me, and jumped on one
side. Then I saw the white man coming at her swiftly.
He came like our master the tiger when he rushes out
of the jungle at the spears held by men.* She did not
take aim. The barrel of her weapon went like this—
from side to side, but in her eyes I could see suddenly a
great fear. There was only one shot. She shrieked while
the white man stood blinking his eyes and very straight,
till you could count slowly one, two, three; then he
coughed and fell on his face. The daughter of Omar
shrieked without drawing breath, till he fell. I went
away then and left silence behind me. These things
did not concern me, and in my boat there was that
other woman who had promised me money. We left
directly, paying no attention to her cries. We are only
poor men—and had but a small reward for our trouble!'
That's what Mahmat said. Never varied. You ask
him yourself. He's the man you hired the boats from,
for your journey up the river."

"The most rapacious thief I ever met!" exclaimed
the traveller, thickly.

"Ah! He is a respectable man. His two brothers
got themselves speared—served them right. They
went in for robbing Dyak graves. Gold ornaments in
them you know. Serve them right. But he kept
respectable and got on. Aye! Everybody got on—
but I. And all through that scoundrel who brought the
Arabs here."

"De mortuis nil ni . . . num,'"* muttered Almayer's guest.

"I wish you would speak English instead of jab-
bering in your own language, which no one can understand," said Almayer, sulkily.

"Don't be angry," hiccoughed the other. "It's
Latin, and it's wisdom. It means: Don't waste your

breath in abusing shadows. No offence there. I like
you. You have a quarrel with Providence—so have
I. I was meant to be a professor, while—look."

His head nodded. He sat grasping the glass. Almayer walked up and down, then stopped suddenly.

"Yes, they all got on but I. Why? I am better
than any of them. Lakamba calls himself a Sultan,
and when I go to see him on business sends that one-
eyed fiend of his—Babalatchi—to tell me that the
ruler is asleep; and shall sleep for a long time. And
that Babalatchi! He is the Shahbandar of the State
—if you please. Oh Lord! Shahbandar! The pig!
A vagabond I wouldn't let come up these steps when
he first came here. . . . Look at Abdulla now.
He lives here because—he says—here he is away from
white men. But he has hundreds of thousands. Has
a house in Penang. Ships. What did he not have
when he stole my trade from me! He knocked everything here into a cocked hat; drove father to gold-
hunting—then to Europe, where he disappeared.
Fancy a man like Captain Lingard disappearing as
though he had been a common coolie. Friends of
mine wrote to London asking about him. Nobody
ever heard of him there! Fancy! Never heard of
Captain Lingard!"

The learned gatherer of orchids lifted his head.

"He was a sen—sentimen—tal old buc—buccaneer,"
he stammered out, "I like him. I'm sent—tal myself."

He winked slowly at Almayer, who laughed.

"Yes! I told you about that gravestone.* Yes!
Another hundred and twenty dollars thrown away.
Wish I had them now. He would do it. And the
inscription. Ha! ha! ha! 'Peter Willems, Delivered
by the Mercy of God from his Enemy.' What enemy
—unless Captain Lingard himself? And then it has

no sense. He was a great man—father was—but
strange in many ways. . . . You haven't seen the
grave? On the top of that hill, there, on the other
side of the river. I must show you. We will go
there."

"Not I!" said the other. "No interest—in the
sun—too tiring. . . . Unless you carry me there."

As a matter of fact he was carried there a few months
afterwards, and his was the second white man's grave
in Sambir; but at present he was alive if rather drunk.
He asked abruptly—

"And the woman?"

"Oh! Lingard, of course, kept her and her ugly
brat in Macassar. Sinful waste of money—that!
Devil only knows what became of them since father
went home. I had my daughter to look after. I shall
give you a word to Mrs. Vinck in Singapore*when you
go back. You shall see my Nina there. Lucky man.
She is beautiful, and I hear so accomplished, so . . ."

"I have heard already twenty . . . a hundred times
about your daughter. What ab—about—that—that
other one, Aï—ssa?"

"She! Oh! we kept her here. She was mad for
a long time in a quiet sort of way. Father thought a
lot of her. He gave her a house to live' in, in my
campong. She wandered about, speaking to nobody
unless she caught sight of Abdulla, when she would
have a fit of fury, and shriek and curse like anything.
Very often she would disappear—and then we all had
to turn out and hunt for her, because father would
worry till she was brought back. Found her in all
kinds of places. Once in the abandoned campong of
Lakamba. Sometimes simply wandering in the bush.
She had one favourite spot we always made for at first.
It was ten to one on finding her there—a kind of a

grassy glade on the banks of a small brook. Why she preferred that place, I can't imagine! And such a job to get her away from there. Had to drag her away by main force. Then, as the time passed, she became quieter and more settled, like. Still, all my people feared her greatly. It was my Nina that tamed her. You see the child was naturally fearless and used to have her own way, so she would go to her and pull at her sarong, and order her about, as she did everybody. Finally she, I verily believe, came to love the child. Nothing could resist that little one— you know. She made a capital nurse. Once when the little devil ran away from me and fell into the river off the end of the jetty, she jumped in and pulled her out in no time. I very nearly died of fright. Now of course she lives with my serving girls, but does what she likes. As long as I have a handful of rice or a piece of cotton in the store she shan't want for anything. You have seen her. She brought in the dinner with Ali."

"What! That doubled-up crone?"

"Ah!" said Almayer. "They age quickly here. And long foggy nights spent in the bush will soon break the strongest backs—as you will find out yourself soon."

"Dis . . . disgusting," growled the traveller.

He dozed off. Almayer stood by the balustrade looking out at the bluish sheen of the moonlit night. The forests, unchanged and sombre, seemed to hang over the water, listening to the unceasing whisper of the great river; and above their dark wall the hill on which Lingard had buried the body of his late prisoner rose in a black, rounded mass, upon the silver paleness of the sky. Almayer looked for a long time at the clean-cut outline of the summit, as if trying to make out through darkness and distance the shape of that expensive tombstone. When he turned round at last he saw his guest sleeping, his arms on the table, his head on his arms.

"Now, look here!" he shouted, slapping the table with the palm of his hand.

The naturalist woke up, and sat all in a heap, staring owlishly.

"Here!" went on Almayer, speaking very loud and thumping the table, "I want to know. You, who say you have read all the books, just tell me . . . why such infernal things are ever allowed. Here I am! Done harm to nobody, lived an honest life . . . and a scoundrel like that is born in Rotterdam or some such place at the other end of the world somewhere, travels out here, robs his employer, runs away from his wife, and ruins me and my Nina—he ruined me, I tell you—and gets himself shot at last by a poor miserable savage, that knows nothing at all about him really. Where's the sense of all this? Where's your Providence? Where's the good for anybody in all this? The world's a swindle! A swindle! Why should I suffer? What have I done to be treated so?"

He howled out his string of questions, and suddenly became silent. The man who ought to have been a professor made a tremendous effort to articulate distinctly—

"My dear fellow, don't—don't you see that the ba— bare fac—the fact of your éxistence is off—offensive. . . . I—I like you—like . . ."

He fell forward on the table, and ended his remarks by an unexpected and prolonged snore.

Almayer shrugged his shoulders and walked back to the balustrade. He drank his own trade gin very seldom, but, when he did, a ridiculously small quantity of the stuff could induce him to assume a rebellious attitude towards the scheme of the universe. And now, throwing his body over the rail, he shouted impudently into the night, turning his face towards that far-off and invisible slab of imported granite upon which Lingard had thought fit to record God's mercy and Willems' escape.

"Father was wrong—wrong!" he yelled. "I want you to smart for it. You must smart for it! Where are you, Willems? Hey? . . . Hey? . . . Where there is no mercy for you—I hope!"

"Hope," repeated in a whispering echo[*] the startled forests, the river and the hills; and Almayer, who stood waiting, with a smile of tipsy attention on his lips, heard no other answer.

THE END

EXPLANATORY NOTES

The following notes reflect the findings of a number of Conrad scholars, but two books deserve special grateful mention, Norman Sherry's *Conrad's Eastern World* (1966) and Zdzisław Najder's *Joseph Conrad: A Chronicle* (1983). For foreign words, nautical expressions, and other terms possibly requiring elucidation, see the Glossary. South-East Asian geographical names can be found on the map (see pp. xxxvi–xxxvii).

An Outcast of the Islands (written 1894–5 and originally intended to be called 'Two Vagabonds') is the centre-piece of a trilogy-in-reverse, of which *Almayer's Folly* (Conrad's first book, written 1889–94) and *The Rescue* (written 1896–1919) are the other volumes. The cast of *An Outcast* thus comprises many names of what have been called 'transtextual characters', known to readers of *Almayer's Folly*: Syed Abdulla bin Selim, Ali, Almayer (husband Kaspar, nameless wife, daughter Nina), Babalatchi, Bulangi, Captain Ford, Hudig, Jim-Eng, Lakamba, Tom Lingard, Mahmat Banjer, Mr and Mrs Vinck. Willems plays no role in Conrad's first novel, having been killed before its story unfolds (as, by the way, have Mahmat Banjer's two brothers).

The chronology of the three volumes moves backwards, hence the trilogy-in-reverse. The texts suggest that *Almayer's Folly* is set about 1887, *An Outcast* around 1872, and *The Rescue* in the 1850s. Conrad visited what the novels call 'Sambir' four times between September and December 1887. In that period he met with or was told about several people who have contributed to his fictional characters. Other names and background details (even minor ones, such as fruit-pigeons and Mataram-made guns) can be traced to Conrad's reading: books on nineteenth-century South-East Asian history (for instance, on the life of Sir James Brooke, the white rajah of Sarawak), and *The Malay Archipelago* by the naturalist Alfred Russel Wallace (first published 1869;

abbreviated in the notes as 'Wallace', with page-references to the seventh edition of 1880). Many of Conrad's Islamic terms and his references to Moslem beliefs and customs can be traced to Richard Francis Burton, *Personal Narrative of a Pilgrimage to El Medinah and Meccah* (first published 1855–6; the second edition of 1857 is referred to in the notes as 'Burton').

Echoes of Conrad's reading of the works of the great nineteenth-century French novelists, notably Flaubert, Maupassant, and Pierre Loti, are treated exhaustively in Yves Hervouet, *The French Face of Joseph Conrad* (1990; referred to in the notes as 'Hervouet').

xxxviii *Epigraph*: from Pedro Calderón de la Barca's play with a Polish setting *La vida es sueño* (Life Is a Dream; 1635): 'For the greatest crime of man is that he was born.' Conrad may have found the lines in *The World as Will and Idea* (1883), a translation of the major work of the German philosopher Arthur Schopenhauer. Conrad, whose knowledge of Spanish was slender, never corrected his spelling error *nacito*. The reference to Calderón recurs in *Last Essays* and in a letter of 21 November 1922 from Conrad to Christopher Sandeman.

xli *Dedication*: Edward Lancelot Sanderson (1867–1939), schoolmaster and civil servant, was one of Conrad's earliest English friends. He was a passenger in the *Torrens* from Adelaide to London, on Conrad's last long voyage as a ship's officer (1893).

xliii *for print*: *Almayer's Folly* was published on 29 April 1895, by which date over half of *An Outcast of the Islands* had actually been written.

Garnett's: Edward William Garnett (1868–1937), publisher's reader and unsuccessful playwright, has been described as 'a discoverer of literary talent and a sensitive critic of literature'.

xliv *before I slept*: see 'Introduction', pp. ix–x.

xlv *'exotic writer'*: An anonymous reviewer in the London *Bookman* compared *An Outcast* to the works of the French novelist Pierre Loti, which he labelled as exotic.

xlvi *Arabs into the river*: the *Vidar*, the steamer in which Conrad made his voyages to north-east Borneo, was owned by the Arab merchant in Singapore who had found out the secret of negotiating the river.

Almayer: the Java-born Kaspar Almayer is to a large extent based on the Java-born Dutch Eurasian William Charles Olmeijer (1848–1900). In *A Personal Record* Conrad wrote of Olmeijer (the pronunciation of his surname is virtually identical with that of his fictional counterpart) 'if I had not got to know Almayer pretty well it is almost certain there would never have been a line of mine in print': *The Mirror of the Sea and A Personal Record* (World's Classics Edition, 1988), 87.

Sambir: the area is actually called Berau, which name has, apparently inadvertently, survived in *Almayer's Folly* in a single mention as Brow. Somewhat larger in area than Wales or Massachusetts, Berau was divided into two sultanates (Gunung Tabur in the north and Sambaliung in the south) with not more than five thousand inhabitants each. The main settlement was and is called Tanjung Redeb.

xlvii *protagonist*: Conrad may have had the term 'prototype' in mind for one of his novels' protagonists.

4 *Hudig*: the name of a Dutch banker (with Netherlands East Indies connections) Conrad had met in early 1887 in Amsterdam.

calico: plain cotton cloth, originally from Calicut (now Kozhikoda) on the Malabar coast in south-west India.

Portuguese conquerors: in South-East Asia Portuguese surnames do not necessarily indicate European descent, since slaves were often given the names of their Portuguese masters at baptism. In Conrad's days there were literally dozens of persons called De Souza in what is now Malaysia. For 'a Malacca Portuguese who had been clerk in some commercial house in the Dutch colonies', see *Lord Jim* (World's Classics Edition, 1983), 220.

5 *Willems*: the identity of the man behind Peter Willems (from Rotterdam) remains somewhat unclear, although in the 'Author's Note' Conrad claimed to have met him in Berau.

Kwang-tung: also Kwangtung (nowadays Guandong): south-eastern province of China (capital: Canton) with the foreign-held coastal territories of Hong Kong and Macao.

Sunda Hotel: the same Macassar hotel is mentioned in *Almayer's Folly*.

7 *Chinaman*: until well after the turn of the century the now-offensive designation had a more neutral connotation.

8 *the trip to Lombok for ponies*: mentioned by Wallace (pp. 172, 176).

hen-coop: Conrad apparently read a newspaper report that the sultan of Sulu owned a coach used precisely for this purpose (*Straits Times*, 12 Jan. 1884, as discovered by Norman Sherry).

9 *she did not rebel*: Lawrence Thornton has pointed out in his 1973 doctoral dissertation that this paragraph owes much to the beginning of Gustave Flaubert's *Madame Bovary* (1857).

Sunday card-parties of the Governor: Conrad had found a mention of these parties in Macassar in Wallace (p. 227).

10 *There's Willems*: there are (in relative terms) more than five times as many contractions in reported speech in this novel as in *Almayer's Folly*: Conrad was still reconnoitring the conventions of his newly adopted language.

12 *French mind ... Egyptian muscle*: the French engineer

Ferdinand de Lesseps was the promoter of the Suez Canal, opened in 1869.

13 *Tom Lingard*: Lingard owes much to a man Conrad never met, but heard much about, a trader named William Lingard (1829–88). The 'Tom' may derive from a Lingard entry in the *Dictionary of National Biography*.

Flash: this 'little brig' (also mentioned in *Almayer's Folly*) is called *Lightning* in the printed text of *The Rescue*, although the early part of the manuscript still uses the former name.

14 *yacht . . . down Carimata way*: this reference is the nucleus of the story told in *The Rescue*.

King of the Sea: the Malay title 'Rajah Laut' was actually bestowed upon the historical Captain Lingard by the sultan of Gunung Tabur (in Berau) in 1862, perhaps as reward for assistance rendered in a fight with the praus of the neighbouring sultan of Bulungan. When Lingard bought a formerly Norwegian barque in 1879 he renamed her *Rajah Laut*.

Kosmopoliet IV: there were Rotterdam ships of this name, and Conrad may have read that the *Kosmopoliet III*, which did call at Samarang, was broken up around 1887.

under weigh: properly 'under way'—this form comes from a false derivation from the term 'to weigh anchor'.

15 *to Sourabaya*: in 1887 Conrad had to leave the ship in which he served as first mate for a stay in hospital in Singapore. This was in the Samarang roads, with the ship, the *Highland Forest*, continuing 'a little way' to Sourabaya (Surabaya).

16 *his place*: the quarters for the ordinary sailors were in the bows, before the mast.

17 *Long-headed*: clever, smart.

18 *india-rubber*: see Glossary under 'guttah'.

19 *Bun-Hin*: the name recurs in 'Typhoon', not at a Macassar location, but again connected with the counting of money. A Chinese of that name owned the steamer *Fair Penang*, as Conrad will have read in the *Straits Times* of 30 January 1888, reporting on an accident she had had the preceding July. This Bun Hin was the most important Chinese shipowner in Singapore in the 1880s.

mail-boat for Ternate: cf. 'the Dutch mail steamer for Amboyna and Ternate' (Wallace, p. 240 and cf. p. 99).

Caroline: between 1873 and 1884 the historical Lingard owned a small schooner-rigged wooden steamer, which he named *Johanna Carolina* after his wife, Johanna Carolina Olmeijer.

26 *Strait-Settlements*: correctly Straits Settlements, between 1867 and 1900 consisting of the British colonies Penang, the Dindings, Malacca (all three in what is now West Malaysia), and Singapore.

28 *whites*: in the Netherlands East Indies colony no legal distinctions were made between white and Eurasian inhabitants, all classified as Europeans from 1854.

35 *curaçoa*: orange-flavoured liqueur (variant of 'curaçao', from the Caribbean island).

42 *Life is very long*: these words are taken over by T. S. Eliot in 'The Hollow Men' (1925), the poem that also has a Conradian epigraph from 'Heart of Darkness' (Vilis Sarang, in *Notes and Queries* for February 1968).

43 *guttah and rattans*: the main forest products exported from 'Sambir', together with damar-gum (for all three, see Glossary), in quantities of respectively 120, 250, and 300 tons per year, according to the *Eastern Archipelago Pilot* (1893).

45 *Dutch Excellency*: the governor-general of the Netherlands East Indies, residing in Batavia, the colonial name of Jakarta, capital of present-day Indonesia.

46 *Babalatchi*: Conrad's source for this name is a bill of lading (now at Yale), showing that goods were shipped by one Babalatchie in Donggala on the west coast of Celebes (Sulawesi).

  the Merciful: for Moslems one of Allah's ninety-nine attributes or names, several of which are later mentioned in the text. See John Lester, *Conrad and Religion* (1988).

47 *white teeth*: because she does not chew betel (see Glossary).

  Baghdadi: from Bagdad.

48 *our ... refuge is with*: an Islamic expression that Conrad found in Burton (i. 71, 72; ii. 190–2, 381).

50 *fourteen miles*: for the rounded-off fifteen miles, see p. 277. In *Almayer's Folly* the distance is given as seven miles (Dent's Collected Edition, p. 24).

52 *country ships*: ships registered locally, not in the United Kingdom.

  Bombay: important trading city on the west coast of India. Conrad stayed there for some six weeks in 1884 before sailing in the *Narcissus*. Bombay is also the location of the inquiry in *Lord Jim*.

  Mascati Sultan: the sultan of Muscat in what is now Oman.

  Sacred Stone: the Kaaba in the Great Mosque at Mecca.

54 *Æneas*: Trojan prince and founder of the Roman people in Virgil's *Æneid*. After fleeing the sack of Troy he made a long and troubled sea-voyage before landing in Italy.

56 *Pantai*: maps show that the rivers Segah (or Makam) and Kelai have their confluence at 'Sambir', from where the stream continues seawards as the Berau (or Kuran) River. Its name in Conrad's novels comes from Muara Pantai, the southernmost mouth of the estuary with its 'twenty outlets' (p. 112).

stranger in the land: see Exodus 2: 22: 'I have been a stranger in a strange land'.

57 *the Ruler down in Batavia*: see note to p. 45.

63 *dry season*: see Glossary under 'monsoon'.

64 *Malay girl*: the real Mrs Olmeijer was the Eurasian daughter of a Dutch soldier, not an adopted Indonesian girl like Mrs Almayer. Conrad will have seen the Olmeijer children, all still quite young (whereas Almayer's only daughter is a young adult in *Almayer's Folly*).

66 *run away yelling*: as reported by Wallace (pp. 65, 223, 584).

68 *bamboo vessels full of water*: also reported by Wallace (pp. 65, 80, 196).

74 *flight of white rice-birds*: Hervouet (p. 29) has pointed out that the description of the flight of white birds may derive from Guy de Maupassant's novel *Une Vie* (1883), but Conrad specifies the name of the birds—even his borrowings are used as well-considered strands in the pattern of his fabric.

76 *spikes of . . . orchids*: see Wallace (p. 81).

77 *looked seriously at him*: according to Hervouet (p. 24) the description in this paragraph closely follows a similar passage in Gustave Flaubert's *Madame Bovary* (1857).

90 *Do you think I am mad?*: the passage with this question and what follows has been identified (Hervouet, p. 24) as a close parallel to the relationship described in Guy de Maupassant's story 'Fou?' (Mad?) in the collection *Mademoiselle Fifi* (1883).

92 *cent*: since Almayer and Willems are both Dutch, the reference is probably to Dutch colonial coinage (see Glossary under 'guilder').

96 *checkered pattern*: cf. 'the checkered pattern in common use' and 'gay checked colours' (Wallace, pp. 222, 212).

97 *ejaculated*: Burton often uses the verb in this sense.

102 *Syed*: descendant of Mohammed through his daughter
     Fatima; also spelled Said, Say(y)id, Seid, Sidi.

103 *the stoned*: a symbolical lapidation that forms part of
     the Islamic pilgrimage ritual in Mecca involves the
     throwing of pebble-sized stones to drive the devil away
     (Burton, ii. 226–8, 244–5).

104 *time of prayer*: Conrad may have observed the Islamic
     sunset prayer while serving in the *Vidar*; it is also
     described by Wallace (p. 408).

106 *eater of swine*: pork is forbidden to Moslems.

109 *Calcutta*: Calcutta, the capital of Bengal, close to the
     mouth of the Ganges, is an important trading centre in
     north-east India. Conrad spent almost two months
     there in 1885–6 while serving in the *Tilkhurst*.

110 *his hand*: to keep it from being kissed.

113 *Daoud Sahamin and Hamet Bahassoen*: a bill of lading for
     Conrad's second voyage to 'Sambir' at Yale shows that
     Abdulla Bahasoean of Singapore shipped goods to
     Sahamin of Berau. The name Daoud may derive from
     Conrad's reading (Wallace, pp. 155, 162).

     dragged its slow length: allusion to Alexander Pope, *An
     Essay on Criticism* (1711), line 359 of the Twickenham
     edition; the same expression occurs in a letter from
     Conrad to Edward Garnett of 13 November 1899.

120 *take refuge with*: see note to p. 48.

122 *playing ... with live embers*: perhaps another borrowing
     from Burton (ii. 234).

124 *Tse!*: Tut!

128 *veiling herself*: Willems experiences Aïssa's adherence to
     Islamic custom as distancing and alienating.

131 *face-veil*: Moslem custom demands that a woman's
     skin should not be touched by a strange man (Burton,
     i. 286).

135 *are back*: this abrupt change in tense from past to
     present Conrad described as 'the new style' in a letter

of 8 March 1895 to Garnett. His friend's reaction will not have been encouraging: after the next break Conrad returned to the earlier tense.

136 *Lord of the Isles*: Conrad may have remembered the ship's name from his first stay in Singapore (1883).

Tanjong Mirrah: a cape of this name is near the mouth of a Bornean river further north, not that of the 'Pantai' (see map).

145 *woke*: here a variant of 'woken'.

147 *on all fours*: in 'Heart of Darkness' (World's Classics Edition, 1990), 142 ff. another man, also to die soon, crawls on all fours at night, while fires are burning.

150 *into stone*: in Greek mythology whoever looked at Medusa with her serpent-covered head was changed into stone.

154 *human hearts*: this paragraph owes much to Guy de Maupassant's *Bel-Ami* (1885) (Hervouet, pp. 26–7).

161 *Formosa Straits*: between Taiwan and the Chinese mainland.

166 *six-pounders*: guns firing six-pound shells.

168 *nigger*: Almayer apparently applies the now pejorative term to Babalatchi because of his brown skin.

174 *in the well*: in *A Personal Record* (*The Mirror of the Sea, and A Personal Record*, World's Classics Edition, 1988), p. 84 Conrad explains that Almayer stored the guttah he had collected in an 'eight-foot-deep well' near his house.

179 *the Great White Ruler in Batavia*: see note to p. 45.

Dutch flag: note the irony that Willems hoists his country's tricolour after his fellow-countryman Almayer had run up the Union Jack (pp. 176, 181) in Dutch colonial territory.

181 *Jim-Eng*: a bill of lading among Conrad's papers at Yale mentions a Sing Jimmung of Singapore.

182 *Englishman*: the implication is that Jim-Eng was a

natural-born British subject from the Straits Settlements.

185 *under the protection of the Netherlands*: actually recognized by Great Britain as being part of the Dutch colony. The last border problems were later solved in an Anglo-Dutch treaty of 1891.

Eighty-three hundredweight!: Conrad will have had long hundredweights in mind, 83 of which amount to nearly 930 lb. or over 420 kg.

186 *opium*: in the final chapter of *Almayer's Folly* both Jim-Eng and Almayer are addicted to opium.

187 *young Ford*: Captain Ford in *Almayer's Folly* was modelled on Captain James Craig (1846–1929) of the *Vidar*, the steamer Conrad served in.

188 *second capital*: apparently Macassar, which never had such a status.

189 *Craig in Palembang*: apparently not the Craig mentioned in the note to p. 187, but Captain Thomas Morgan Craig, 'an old crony' of the historical Lingard. The passage is reminiscent of Marlow's efforts on behalf of Jim in *Lord Jim*.

191 *clothes-line*: an allusion to the way sailors had to pass the night after they had spent the wages received at their discharge, lying on mattresses slung across a rope that was cut in the morning to wake them up.

red curtain: the colour of the curtain is mentioned five times in *Almayer's Folly*, evidently a detail Conrad vividly remembered.

192 *sleeveless robe*: perhaps the gallicism 'robe' for a woman's dress.

193 *alluvial gold*: G. J. Resink has shown that the historical prototype of Almayer actually petitioned the governor-general of the Netherlands East Indies for permission to prospect for gold in north-east Borneo in 1890 (in the Indonesian periodical *Medan Ilmu Pengetahuan*, 1960).

194 *Company*: Conrad's friend G. F. W. Hope (to whom, with his wife, he dedicated *Lord Jim*) formed several unsuccessful companies and involved himself in the South African gold boom of 1895.

195 *California ... Victoria*: references to the discovery of gold in America (1849) and Australia (1851), when the fictional Lingard earned enough to buy his first ship.

196 *bath-chair*: hooded, wheeled chair for invalids.

197 *grave*: the first of several passages in which echoes of words, ideas, and themes encountered in Pierre Loti's *Le Roman d'un spahi* (1881) can be detected (Hervouet, p. 30).

198 *Falmouth Bay*: Conrad spent eight months in Falmouth (in Cornwall) when his ship was under repair in 1882. The 'Mission to Fishermen and Seamen' may have been among the 'precious pictures of his youthful days that lingered in his memory'. He may also have come across such a mission when he first set foot on the soil of England in Lowestoft, in June 1878.

200 *entrances to that river*: the historical Lingard had discovered how seagoing ships could reach 'Sambir' via the southernmost entrance in the estuary. Lingard's Beacon, indicating where ships had to cross from the left to the right bank, was still standing at the time of the Second World War. There is a description of precisely such a river beacon in the manuscript of *The Rescue* (omitted from the printed text), as consisting of whitewashed trees and a triangle of bamboo poles with a basket on top.

Arcadia: picturesque mountain district in ancient Greece, inhabited by simple, pastoral people; figuratively a rustic region or scene of simple pleasure and quiet.

201 *gambols*: Wallace (p. 133) uses the same word when describing monkeys.

203 *a green silk wrapper*: cf. 'enclosed in silk envelopes', p. 111. Letters from Malay rulers were usually conveyed in yellow silk envelopes (see Wallace, p. 214). Conrad will consciously have changed the royal yellow into Moslem green (see also Burton, ii. 233).

208 *bundles*: of rattan.

218 *I am not hungry*: Lingard may have been on his guard against being poisoned.

220 *Mataram make*: Wallace explains in detail how guns were manufactured in Mataram on Lombok (pp. 168–70).

223 *verdict*: apparently a confusion of verdict and sentence.

225 *feel not*: perhaps a faint echo of the Sermon on the Mount, 'they [the fowls of the air] sow not, neither do they reap ... Consider the lilies of the field, how they grow; they toil not, neither do they spin' (Matthew 6: 26, 28).

226 *black tiger*: tigers are not indigenous to Borneo, but Conrad may have meant a tiger-cat like the black panther (see Wallace, p. 33).

227 *his name*: the name of Omar has not been mentioned by Babalatchi.

228 *a white sheet*: according to Islamic custom the dead are buried without a coffin, wrapped in a white shroud (see also p. 230; *The Rescue* (Dent's Collected Edition, p. 74), and Wallace, pp. 479, 508).

235 *Diego Suarez*: a port city in northern Madagascar.

256 *lintels*: other examples occur in Conrad's works (some corrected by his publishers) suggesting he believed that not only the horizontal top beams of door-frames, but also the upright posts are called lintels in English.

260 *cur*: cowardly fellow. In *Lord Jim* (pp. 70, 73) Jim believes that the word 'cur', meant for a low-bred yellow dog, had been applied to him.

261   *clinging to his leg*: Hervouet (p. 30) identifies a parallel of the situation in Pierre Loti's *Le Roman d'un spahi* (1881).

263   *staunching*: variant of 'stanching', checking the flow of.

266   *pink and moist end*: Hervouet (pp. 24–5) has shown that a tongue is described in the very same terms in the story 'Fou?' in Guy de Maupassant's collection *Mademoiselle Fifi* (1883).

271   *superior descent*: according to Hervouet (pp. 29–30) a similar claim to superiority occurs in Pierre Loti's *Le Roman d'un spahi* (1881).

272   *remote ages*: not the only description of forests and rivers as primeval and silent by Conrad; see 'Heart of Darkness', 182–3, 191.

274   *delivered into their hands*: see Luke 9: 44, 'the Son of man shall be delivered into the hands of men.'

      became dumb: according to Hervouet (p. 25), Conrad drew inspiration for this exchange from Guy de Maupassant's *Bel-Ami* (1885).

277   *finished*: further circumstantial evidence that Conrad relied on Pierre Loti's *Le Roman d'un spahi*, according to Hervouet (p. 29).

      forty down: the precise distance is 34 miles according to the *Eastern Archipelago Pilot* (1893). Cf. *A Personal Record* (p. 74): 'a . . . wharf forty miles up, more or less, a Bornean river.'

279   *quartermaster . . . head man*: Ali appears as Lingard's quartermaster in *The Rescue* and Wallace (pp. 407, 490) mentions an Ali as his own headman.

281   *shook her hand*: Lingard's departure in a canoe while he watches Aïssa and Willems on the shore is paralleled in 'Heart of Darkness' by Marlow's departure in a steamer with Kurtz, with the latter's African mistress on shore stretching out her arms. See World's Classics Edition, 135–6, 146.

      going away: another parallel with *Le Roman d'un spahi* (Hervouet, p. 29).

286 *left alone*: this expression and the passage it concludes provide further parallels with Loti's novel (see previous note).

292 *the light disappeared*: on and near the equator the transition from day to night is not gradual, but quick.

293 *in English*: Conrad stresses in *Almayer's Folly* (p. 202) that Ali could understand English.

297 *spoon and fork*: Conrad may have noticed that Olmeijer followed the prevalent custom of eating with these two utensils (but cf. 'knife and fork' on p. 293).

303 *North China Herald*: the full name of this English-language newspaper, published in Shanghai since 1850, was *The North-China Herald and Supreme Court & Consular Gazette*.

309 *Mahmet Banjer*: the bill of lading mentioned in the note to p. 113 adds Orang Banjar to the name Sahamin, but these two words merely indicate his origin from south-east Borneo (Kalimantan). There was a Mahamat on board the *Vidar* while Conrad served in her.

310 *sea gipsies*: see Glossary under 'Bajow'.

318 *Java tobacco*: commercial tobacco culture was introduced in central and eastern Java in the 1830s.

324 *low water*: 'in flood the river rises 9 feet' according to the *Eastern Archipelago Pilot* (1893).

326 *struggle and death*: this paragraph is perhaps the most convincing of Hervouet's examples (pp. 30–1) of the influence of Pierre Loti's *Le Roman d'un spahi* on Conrad's text, but the specification of the monkeys as long-nosed comes from Wallace (p. 53). Conrad's borrowings are closely interlaced.

328 *venomous*: Conrad has often been chided for the abundance of paired or tripled adjectives in his early works, often placed after the noun they qualify. This six-some is perhaps Conrad at his most prolix.

abandoned: as pointed out by Hervouet (p. 30), the opening of the sentence closely follows a description in Pierre Loti's *Le Roman d'un spahi* (1881).

331   *sunrises and sunsets*: Paul Kirschner in his *Conrad: The
       Psychologist as Artist* (1968) first pointed out that the
       sensation of impending death in the first sentences of
       this paragraph is closely patterned upon a passage in
       Guy de Maupassant's *Bel-Ami* (1885).

       He would be dead: most of this paragraph parallels a
       passage in Guy de Maupassant's *Yvette* (1885), as
       Hervouet (p. 28) has found.

332   *polished ribs*: possibly a recollection of what Conrad
       had seen on the bank of the Congo (Zaïre), first put on
       paper here; cf. 'Heart of Darkness': 'the grass growing
       through his ribs was tall enough to hide his bones.
       They were all there.' (p. 144).

334   *hopelessly alone*: the beginning of this sentence is the
       first of a series of parallels with passages in Guy de
       Maupassant's *Bel-Ami* (1885), according to Hervouet
       (pp. 26–8).

337   *beyond the stars*: the second parallel to *Bel-Ami*.

       nobody would come: the third parallel to *Bel-Ami*.

339   *unavoidably, fall*: the fourth parallel to *Bel-Ami*.

       lintel: see note to p. 256.

340   *lost man*: the fifth parallel to *Bel-Ami*.

341   *quinine*: medication against malarial fever made from
       cinchona bark. The cinchona tree was introduced into
       Indonesia in 1852 and into India in 1859. Wallace was
       an early user of the medicine during his travels in the
       Netherlands East Indies, 1854–6 (pp. 29, 214).

351   *crimson blossoms and . . . star-shaped flowers*: cf. 'star-like
       crimson flowers' (Wallace, p. 82).

360   *stood aspiring*: according to Hervouet (p. 30), perhaps
       from Pierre Loti's *Le Roman d'un spahi*, which would
       explain the gallicism 'aspiring' for breathing, respir-
       ing.

       Roumanian: Conrad may have heard about a Hungar-
       ian, Franz (or Ferenc) Witti, who died in the forests of
       Borneo in 1882, as does the Roumanian (p. 365).

363   *spears held by men*: Wallace describes precisely this way
      of killing a tiger on Java (p. 108), but the animal is not
      indigenous to Borneo (Kalimantan).

      De mortuis nil ni ... num: in full 'De mortuis nil nisi
      bonum', Latin saying meaning 'of the dead [say]
      nothing but good'.

364   *gravestone*: Conrad apparently saw the gravestones of
      Olmeijer's children and the first European trader in
      'Sambir'.

365   *Mrs. Vinck in Singapore*: she had apparently moved
      from Macassar (p. 10) to Singapore, the city where,
      according to *Almayer's Folly* (pp. 29–31), she cared for
      Nina.

368   *"Hope," repeated in a whispering echo*: Andrzej Busza
      points out in a private communication that this is a
      practically literal translation of words occurring in
      Part III of *Konrad Wallenrod* (1827), a romantic tale in
      verse by Adam Mickiewicz, one of Poland's national
      poets ('Polonism I have taken into my works from
      Mickiewicz', as Conrad confessed in 1914).

GLOSSARY

This glossary attempts to explain all nautical terms (with asterisks indicating cross-references) and all words of Malay origin. Other foreign and English terms are included only if they (or their specific meanings) are not to be found in *The Concise Oxford Dictionary*. These latter terms are glossed in the Explanatory Notes if they occur only once in the novel's text. The present-day spelling of Malay words follows the *Kamus besar Bahasa Indonesia*, published in Jakarta for the Ministry of Education (1st edn. 1988; 2nd edn. 1989). The codes (B) and (W) at the end of entries indicate that Conrad may have borrowed the term from, respectively, Richard Francis Burton, *Personal Narrative of a Pilgrimage to El Medinah and Meccah* (first published 1855–6) and Alfred Russel Wallace, *The Malay Archipelago* (first published 1869).

ada (Malay): to be, to be present.

aft: behind, towards the stern* of a vessel.

ague: malarial fever, with cold, hot, and sweating stages (W).

aloft: upward.

anak (Malay): child.

apa (Malay): what, which.

areca: genus of palm (esp. *Areca cathecu*) with slender ringed trunk and orange-coloured nut-like fruit used in chewing (*see* betel and siri) (W).

astern: in the direction of the stern*.

athwart: sideways; across at right angles to the fore-and-aft* line of a vessel.

attap (Malay: *atap*): thatching, often of leaves of the nipa* palm.

awnings: canvas roof-like construction erected above the deck* of a vessel as protection from the sun.

ay—wa: corruption of *ay'w'Allah*, Arabic for 'yes by Allah' (B).

Badavi: Bedouin, an Arab of the desert (B).

Bajow (Malay: *Bajau*): maritime Malays (also known as sea nomads and sea gypsies) inhabiting the coastal regions of Borneo (Kalimantan), Celebes (Sulawesi), and the southern Philippines; 'people, who have no country', according to Conrad's story 'Karain' (W).

bamboo (Malay: *bambu*): giant woody grasses with hollow stems used for utensils or for building furniture.

barque (variant of 'bark'): a three-masted vessel with fore-* and mainmasts* square-rigged* and mizzen-* or rear mast fore-and-aft* rigged.

berth: mooring-place.

besar (Malay): great, big, large.

betel: drupe (nut-like seed) of areca* palm, used in chewing with the pungent betel-leaf (of *Piper betle*) (*see* siri) (W).

betul (Malay): right, correct, true, sure.

bezique (French): card-game for two or four, played with a pack of sixty-four cards.

binnacle: case or stand holding the ship's compass and lamp.

Blanda (Malay: *Belanda*): Dutch(man).

blocks: pulleys* and their casings.

bluebottle fly: larger than house fly, esp. blowfly (*Calliphora erythrocephala*) with steel-blue abdomen and hairy thorax (W).

boatswain (pronounced 'bo'sn'): petty officer in charge of sails, rigging*, etc., and summoning crew to duty with whistle.

boom: long spar used to extend the foot of a sail or to facilitate handling of cargo and mooring.

bow(s): forward part of vessel, where it begins to curve to the stern*.

bowman: rower nearest to the bow*.

braces: long ropes by means of which the yards* are turned.

brig: two-masted square-rigged* vessel.

Bugis: people of south-west Celebes (Sulawesi) or their descendants. 'The men of that race are intelligent, enterprising, revengeful, but with a more frank courage than the other Malays, and restless under oppression' (*Lord Jim*, p. 256).

bulwarks: raised woodwork along the sides of a vessel, protecting the deck*.

calashes (Malay: *kelasi*): Malay sailors.

campong (Malay: *kampung*): village or quarter, sometimes fortified with palisades.

cant: tilt, swing (round).

cent: *see* dollar and guilder.

chain-cable: cable of the fastening for shrouds*.

champaka (Malay: *cempaka*): tree and shrub with large white, red, or yellow fragrant flowers, like frangipani and jasmine varieties.

chatty (Anglo-Indian, from Tamil): porous earthen pot for cooling water, etc.

chelakka (Malay: *celaka*): bad luck, damn it.

cheroot (Malay: *cerutu*): cigar.

chronometer: very accurate seagoing clock unaffected by motion of the vessel.

coaster: vessel engaged in taking on and off cargo at many ports of call along a coast.

coir: fibre of coconut husk, used for cordage and matting (W).

compound: *see* campong.

coolie (Malay: *kuli*): labourer, often Chinese.

coxswain: steersman of rowing-boat.

cutwater: knee at head of vessel, dividing the water before it reaches the bow*.

damar-gum (Malay: *damar*): inflammable resin obtained from various coniferous trees (W).

dayong (Malay: *dayung*): row, paddle.

deal: (piece of sawn) fir or pine wood.

deck: plank platform extending from side to side of a vessel.

dollar: silver coin, divided into 100 cents, introduced as Straits Settlements currency in 1867; until the 1930s worth 2*s*. 4*d*. sterling or US $0.56.

dredge: move a vessel's position by using a dropped anchor to guide or control course downstream.

dug-out: canoe made from a hollowed-out log or tree trunk.

Dyaks (Malay: *Dayak*): people from (esp. central) Borneo (Kalimantan) (W).

fall off: run away from the wind.

fore-and-aft (of sails): set lengthwise, not to yards*.

forebrace: rope used to change settings of a foresail*.

forecastle (pronounced 'fok'sl'): enclosed area at foremost end of a vessel; a deck* is above it and the crew's quarters may be located within it.

foremast: the forward, or lower, mast of a vessel.

foresail: the principal, lowest sail on the foremast*.

frigate: fast three-masted, full-rigged* warship, particularly for cruising or scouting.

fruit-pigeons: large groups of pigeons noted for their beautiful colours, such as the *Ptilonopus roseicollis* (with green plumage and rosy pink head and neck) and *Carpophaga* varieties (W).

full-rigged: said of a vessel with three (or more) masts*, each with its full complement of square sails (*see* square-rigged).

gaff: spar* to which head of a fore-and-aft* sail can be attached.

gale: wind of between 7 and 8 on the Beaufort scale (35–8 miles per hour).

gambier (Malay: *gambir*): yellowish astringent substance derived from climbing shrub, used for chewing with betel-nut (*see* betel and siri).

gangway: passage on a vessel, esp. the platform connecting the quarter-deck* and forecastle*; opening in bulwarks* by which a vessel is entered or left; bridge laid across this to the shore.

genii (variant of *djinns* and *jinns*, singular also 'genie' and 'jinnee'): spirits or goblins of Arabian tales, lower than angels, but with supernatural powers.

gharry (Anglo-Indian, from Hindi): box-like carriage drawn by horse or pony and plying for hire.

gig: narrow, light ship's boat propelled by oars or sails; captain's boat.

godown (Malay: *gudang*): storehouse, warehouse.

gong (Malay): metal disc with turned rim giving resonant note when struck on outer side.

guard-rail: hand or other rail to prevent falling, etc.

guilder: silver Netherlands East Indies coin, since 1858 divided into 100 cents and until the 1930s worth 1*s*. 8*d*. sterling or US $0.40.

gunwale (pronounced 'gun'nal'): upper rails or edges of a boat's sides.

guttah (Malay: *getah*): leathery material obtained from latex or gum of various trees, also called gutta-percha (Malay: *getah perca*), tree gum, and india-rubber.

haï (Malay: *hai*): ho, there!

haï—ya (Malay: *hai ya*): there, will you.

halyards (variant of 'halliards'): rope or tackle* for raising or lowering sails and yards*.

haul: pull (upon).

head-yards: yards* on the foremast*.

heel (have the heels of): out-run.

helm: steering apparatus (tiller* or wheel) by which the rudder* is controlled, esp. helmsman's wheel.

hooker: mildly derogatory term for an old-fashioned or clumsy vessel.

houri: nymph of Islamic paradise.

hove (nautical past tense and past participle of to heave): haul up by rope.

hull: body or frame of a vessel.

ikat (Malay): bind, fasten, tie.

india-rubber: *see* guttah.

jammed: fixed in awkward position, blocked.

Jehannum: Islamic term for hell (B).

jurumudi (Malay): helmsman.

kapal (Malay): ship, boat.

kassi (Malay: *kasih*): give.

kavitan (possible misprint for *kapitan*; Malay: *kapten*): captain.

keel: lowest longitudinal timber of a vessel, on which the framework of the whole is built up.

knot (as in five-knot): unit of speed, 1 nautical mile (6,080 feet or 1.85 km) per hour.

kriss (variant of *creese*; Malay: *keris*): dagger with scalloped or wavy edges.

landlubbers: landsmen ignorant of ships and maritime ways.

laut (Malay): sea.

layer (Malay: *layar*): sail.

lee: sheltered against wind.

leeward: towards sheltered side (*see* lee), downwind; opposite of windward*.

lekas (Malay): quick.

lighter: open boat used for loading and unloading vessels.

log: float attached to a line wound on reel for gauging speed of vessel.

log-line: line to which the log* is attached.

lumberingly: in clumsy, blundering, noisy manner.

made fast: with sail-ropes secured.

maindeck: uppermost deck* between poop* and forecastle*.

mainmast: second mast* from the front.

makan (Malay): eat.

Malay (Malay: *Melayu*): adjective and noun denoting persons, country, and language. In correct usage the English adjective Malayan refers only to Malaya, the western, mainland part of what is now Malaysia.

man-of-war: armed ship in a country's navy.

mangroves: evergreen trees and shrubs forming dense thickets on coasts and muddy ground.

mast: long pole of timber set up on ship's keel* to support sails.

mast-head: top of mast*.

mem (Anglo-Indian; Malay): Mrs, (European) mistress, lady.

meza (Malay: *meja*): table.

mirrah (Malay: *merah*): red.

mizzen-mast: rear mast* in a two- or three-masted vessel.

monsoon (Malay: *musim*, from Arabic): season, seasonal wind (in 'Sambir', north of the equator, from north-east, dry and hot, esp. from August through October, and from south-west, wet and less hot, esp. from December through March).

mynah (variant of *mina*): eastern passerine bird.

nakhoda (Malay: *nakhoda, nakoda*): (Asian) ship's captain, leading trader.

nipa (Malay: *nipah*): palm (*Nypa fruticans*) with pinnate leaves used for thatching and making mats.

orang (Malay): person, human being.

painter: rope in bow* of boat for securing or towing her.

palm: metallic disc attached to strap and worn on hand-palm, used to push needle through canvas in sewing sails.

pantai (Malay): river, beach, sea-shore.

peak: upper aftermost corner of fore-and-aft* sail.

poop: raised deck* in vessel's stern*, containing accommodation for ship's officers.

port(side): left-hand side of a vessel as one faces forward.

prau (variant of *proa*; Malay: *perahu*): native boat (usually undecked), dug-out*, or plank-built craft that is rowed, paddled, or sailed.

pulley: sheave or small wheel with grooved rim with a cord or rope passing through, used for increasing speed or power.

pumelo (variant of *pomelo*): orange-like shaddock (*Citrus grandis*) or grapefruit (*Citrus paradisi*).

punkah (Anglo-Indian, from Hindi): large fan, often in the form of a flap, raised and lowered manually by means of a cord and a pulley.

putih (Malay): white.

quarter-deck: rear part of maindeck* between mainmast* and poop*, used by the ship's officers.

quartermaster: petty officer responsible for the operation of the ship's helm*, binnacle*, and log-line* under the master or navigator.

quay: harbour structure of timber or stone equipped for loading and unloading ships.

quill-driver: clerk (pejorative).

rajah (Malay): prince, ruler.

raking: deviation of vessel's masts* from the perpendicular to the keel*.

rattan (Malay: *rotan*): climbing palm (genus *Calamus*) whose long, thin stems are used for wickerwork, canes, matting, ropes, screens, etc.

rib: curved frame-timber extending from ship's keel* to top of hull* to which the planking is nailed.

rice-bird: Java sparrow (*Munia oryzivora*), the white variety of which is mostly encountered in captivity.

ridge pole: horizontal pole along the ridge of roof.

riding light: white light hanging in rigging* near the bow* when a vessel is riding at anchor at night.

rigging: collective for a vessel's ropes and chains that set or trim* sails and raise or lower masts* and spars*.

roadstead: sheltered expanse of water near the shore (esp. a bay) where ships may ride safely at anchor.

rudder: broad flat wooden piece for steering attached to vessel's stern*-post.

sagueir (variant of *sagwire*; Malay: *saguer, saguir*): toddy or palm-wine from sap of feather palm (*Saguerus pinnatus*) or *Arenga sacchifera* (W).

sail-twine: a strong string of two or more strands twisted together and used in sewing sails.

salaam (Malay: *salam*): greet(ing), peace.

sarong (Malay: *sarung*): sort of skirt, made by wrapping single length of cloth around the body.

savee (pidgin English): know, understand.

schooner: a fore-and-aft* rigged vessel with two (later also more) masts*, with the smaller sail on the foremast* and mainmast* stepped nearly amidships. Lingard's ship was a two-master.

seacannie (variant of '-canny'): person knowledgeable in nautical affairs.

serang (Malay): native quartermaster* or boatswain*.

shahbandar (Malay: *syahbandar, sahbandar*): harbour-master.

sheer: upward curvature of ship's deck*.

sheets: ropes used to control sails.

shrouds: ropes (usually in pairs or threes) stretching from the mast-heads* to the vessel's sides to support masts* against lateral strain.

Sirani (Malay: *Serani*): 'Nazarene', i.e. Christian (W).

siri (Malay: *sirih*): quid consisting of areca*-nut, betel*-leaf, gambier*, and lime that colours saliva and lips red and teeth black.

spars: general term for stout poles used as a vessel's masts*, yards*, etc.

square-rigged: with rectangular sails on yards* slung athwart*.

starboard: right-hand side of a vessel as one faces forward.

stern: rear of a vessel.

stern sheets: area of a boat between the stern* and the nearest rowing bench.

stunsail (shortened form of 'studding-sail'; pronounced 'stun'sl'): light auxiliary sail set outboard on a spar* to either side of a square sail (*see* square-rigged).

sultan (Malay): ruler.

surat (Malay): letter, epistle.

Syed (variant of *Said*, *Sayid*, *Seid*; Malay: *Sayid*, *Said*): Moslem claiming descent from Mohammed through his daughter Fatima.

tack: to change direction to take advantage of the wind; here (p. 191) a course of action.

tackle: mechanism esp. of ropes, pulley-blocks (*see* blocks), hooks, etc. for managing sails, spars*, etc.

taffrail: rear rail of a vessel, following the curve of the stern*.

tanjong (Malay: *tanjung*): cape, headland.

tau (Malay: *tahu*, *tau*): know.

thwarts: planks which extend crosswise in a boat and may be used as seats.

tida (Malay: *tidak*): no, not.

tiffin (Anglo-Indian): light midday meal, lunch.

tiller: horizontal bar for steering fitted to the head of the rudder*.

topmast: second mast* from the deck*, in a brig* the higher of the two, in a schooner* the lower one; here (p. 199) the stunsail* on that mast.

trim: arrange the yards* and sails to suit the wind.

trima (Malay: *terima*): thank(s).

truckle bed: folding canvas bedstead.

trusses: heavy iron fittings securing the lower yards* to the mast*.

tuan (Malay): sir, master, gentleman.

wah (Malay): why, well, you don't say.

waringan (Malay: *beringin*, *waringin*): kind of fig-tree (*Ficus benjamina*) with aerial roots, resembling the banian-tree (W).

warp: rope used for hauling* or drawing a vessel.

water-logged: so filled with water as to be barely able to float.

whale-boat: long, narrow boat, often steered with an oar, like those used in whaling.

windlass: rotating cylinder used for raising or lowering the anchor.

windward: side against which the wind blows; opposite of leeward*.

ya (Malay): yes, that is so.

ya—wa (Malay): strong affirmative, yes.

yards: spars* that cross a mast* horizontally and from which a sail can be suspended.

yawl: two-masted sailing vessel, rigged fore-and-aft*, with large mainmast* and small mizzen-mast*.

yoke line(s): line(s) with which the rudder* is worked; also steering line.

THE WORLD'S CLASSICS

A Select List

SERGEI AKSAKOV: A Russian Gentleman
Translated by J. D. Duff
Edited by Edward Crankshaw

HANS ANDERSEN: Fairy Tales
Translated by L. W. Kingsland
Introduction by Naomi Lewis
Illustrated by Vilhelm Pedersen and Lorenz Frølich

JANE AUSTEN: Emma
Edited by James Kinsley and David Lodge

Mansfield Park
Edited by James Kinsley and John Lucas

ROBERT BAGE: Hermsprong
Edited by Peter Faulkner

WILLIAM BECKFORD: Vathek
Edited by Roger Lonsdale

CHARLOTTE BRONTË: Jane Eyre
Edited by Margaret Smith

THOMAS CARLYLE: The French Revolution
Edited by K. J. Fielding and David Sorensen

LEWIS CARROLL: Alice's Adventures in Wonderland
and Through the Looking Glass
Edited by Roger Lancelyn Green
Illustrated by John Tenniel

GEOFFREY CHAUCER: The Canterbury Tales
Translated by David Wright

ANTON CHEKHOV: The Russian Master and Other Stories
Translated by Ronald Hingley

JOSEPH CONRAD: Victory
Edited by John Batchelor
Introduction by Tony Tanner

CHARLES DICKENS: Christmas Books
Edited by Ruth Glancy

ANTHONY TROLLOPE: The American Senator
Edited by John Halperin

Dr. Wortle's School
Edited by John Halperin

Orley Farm
Edited by David Skilton

VILLIERS DE L'ISLE-ADAM: Cruel Tales
Translated by Robert Baldick
Edited by A. W. Raitt

VIRGIL: The Aeneid
Translated by C. Day Lewis
Edited by Jasper Griffin

HORACE WALPOLE: The Castle of Otranto
Edited by W. S. Lewis

IZAAK WALTON and CHARLES COTTON:
The Compleat Angler
Edited by John Buxton
Introduction by John Buchan

OSCAR WILDE: Complete Shorter Fiction
Edited by Isobel Murray

The Picture of Dorian Gray
Edited by Isobel Murray

ÉMILE ZOLA:
The Attack on the Mill and other stories
Translated by Douglas Parmeé

A complete list of Oxford Paperbacks, including The World's Classics, OPUS, Past Masters, Oxford Authors, Oxford Shakespeare, and Oxford Paperback Reference, is available in the UK from the Arts and Reference Publicity Department (RS), Oxford University Press, Walton Street, Oxford OX2 6DP.

In the USA, complete lists are available from the Paperbacks Marketing Manager, Oxford University Press, 200 Madison Avenue, New York, NY 10016.

Oxford Paperbacks are available from all good bookshops. In case of difficulty, customers in the UK can order direct from Oxford University Press Bookshop, Freepost, 116 High Street, Oxford, OX1 4BR, enclosing full payment. Please add 10 per cent of published price for postage and packing.